STILL I STAND
THE SEMIDEUS CHRONICLES

T.M. Ford

"When realms collide and shadows rise, only a spark of hope can ignite the light."

For my Nana, Kendell, and Ezekiel

To my Nana, who sang sweet songs that still echo in my heart. Every hummingbird reminds me of the love and warmth you gave, and though you're no longer here, I miss you every day.

If I were a bird I would fly to the store.

To Kendell, my love, and Ezekiel, my joy—you've encouraged me through every step, and I love you both to the moon and back. This book exists because of you.

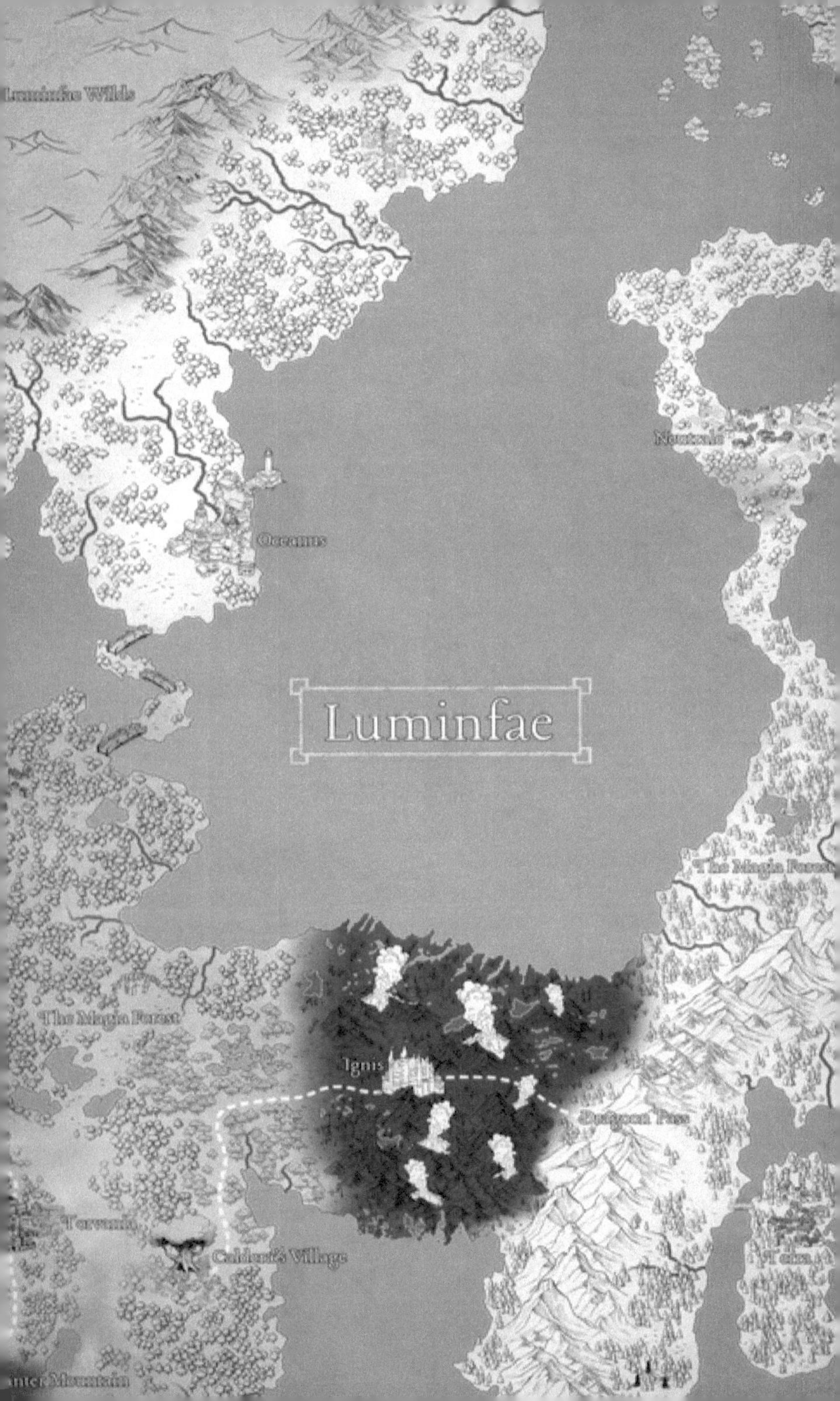

Luminfae Wilds
Oceanus
Noratula
Luminfae
The Magic Forest
The Magic Forest
Ignis
Dragon Pass
Tarvania
Caldera's Village
Winter Mountain

Contents

Chapter 1

Derek

To bridge the gap, unite the world's divide,
    With courage, he'll mend what's torn inside.
The realms tremble as the battle draws near.
In his hands, the fate of all appears.

"BRRRIIINNNGGG BRRRIIINNNNGGG,"

Derek's eyes flew open, heart pounding, as the piercing sound of his alarm jolted him awake. He lurched upright, tangled in the sheets, his chest heaving as the last remnants of sleep were ripped away. The room was still dark, the only light coming from the harsh glow of the clock's red digits. He blinked, disoriented, as he tried to silence the relentless ringing that had yanked him from his dream.

He hated the alarm clock his dad had bought him. It was old and outdated, but it was the noisiest they could find. He needed the loudest possible alarm to jolt him out of bed. After all, most nights, he barely fell asleep before three.

His mom and dad blamed his insomnia on cell phone addiction, but in reality, he used his phone and TV to keep the room from being too quiet. If it was too quiet, his mind would stir and the anxiety of what waited for him in his sleep would send him into a panic attack. They were already getting worse, so he tried anything that would keep his thoughts at bay. Ever since he was a little boy, he had the same recurring dream.

Feeling grass tickle the back of his neck, Derek opened his eyes to a fiery sunset streaking across the horizon, bathing the honey colored field in soft, warm light. Gentle hills rose and fell like waves in the distance, and the sweet scent of blooming flowers filled the air.

Warily, he stood and appraised his surroundings. Within moments, a vicious heat licked at Derek's skin as the scene around him changed. The once comforting warmth of the sky melted into a burning crimson. His skin continued to heat, but he felt no pain. Derek watched as fires raged through the fields surrounding him. The flames moved closer . . . closer . . . closer, until they were underneath his feet. But still no pain.

Sweat slicked Derek's skin. Was it the heat from the flames? Was it the adrenaline running through his veins? He tried to scream for help, but no sound came out. He tasted salt on his lips, whether from his sweat or tears, he wasn't sure, and then he heard it.

An unnerving voice rang out from the skies above him.
"To bridge the gap, unite the world's divide,
With courage, he'll mend what's torn inside.
The realms tremble as the battle nears.
In his hands, the fate of all appears."

Even now, he smelled the acrid, charred aroma of the burning fields. Last night was no different. As usual, he scrolled through his phone, fighting the urge to fall asleep. When his eyes could no longer stay open, the same dream crept into his mind. His ear-shattering alarm would inevitably wake him up, and he'd be shaky, covered in sweat, and just as exhausted as when he'd gone to bed. He'd debated telling his friends, or even a shrink, about the dreams for years. Despite desperately wanting to share this burden, his fear of them dismissively saying, "That's crazy!" or "It's only a dream!" kept his mouth firmly shut. He did his best to shake off the lingering remnants of the dream and jumped out of bed.

Despite another restless night, he was determined to make today a good day. It was Derek's first day of his senior year at Riverrun High School, the home of the Mustangs. He always thought the mascot was a bit cliche, but being the starting pitcher for the baseball team, he still took pride in his school.

Derek was a fairly popular young man, and for an eighteen-year-old, that's usually all that matters. Unfortunately, Derek didn't see what everyone else did. He would never share it, but the weight of his loneliness could be crushing, even though he knew he was surrounded by people that loved him.

To keep the morning moving, he walked into the bathroom, turned on the faucet, and splashed his face. The scratchy texture of his thick stubble was coarse beneath his hands as he let the frigid water chase away the fragments of his dream. He was wide awake now. He glanced in the mirror and chuckled humorlessly, thinking, "Another day in paradise."

Sure, he knew the 'popular jock' image he projected. Standing at six foot three, with his ice-blue eyes, sun-kissed skin, and 'a smile that could light up a room,' as his mother often cooed, he wasn't a bad-looking guy. The thing was, he never felt like that guy. In Derek's eighteen years, he had never been able to shake the impression that something was wrong with him. He felt out of place in this world, like he was meant for something else, meant to look like someone else, meant to *feel* like something else.

He pushed the thoughts away with a deep breath, seeking the familiar comfort of his practiced confidence and easy humor.

After showering, Derek put on the first outfit he saw in his closet; a red T-shirt with a dark blue jacket over the top and a pair of faded blue jeans. Once he was dressed, he slid his boots on and headed towards the kitchen to grab breakfast and tell his parents he was off to school. Walking into the empty kitchen, he found a note on the table instead.

"Dad and I had to get an early start this morning. There is money on the counter to get breakfast, and there should be enough left over to

get lunch, as well. We are both so proud of you, dear, and hope you have an amazing last, first day of high school!
Love Mom and Dad"

He smiled. looks like he was meeting up with his friends at the local gas station for breakfast. Derek grabbed his keys and rushed out the door, ready to tackle the day. As he got into his truck, he rolled down the windows, turned up the radio, and took a deep breath of the fresh countryside air. Singing along to his favorite song, he couldn't help the slow grin and lightness that overtook him. Today was going to be a good day; he just sensed it.

The wind whipped through Derek's hair as he relaxed into autopilot, following the familiar curves of the back roads, when a bright, azure light zipped out of nowhere and shot past him like a comet. He slammed on the brakes and skidded to a stop, his heart pounding as he searched the horizon for the source of the mysterious blue haze. He fumbled through his pockets in search of his phone, but by the time he got the camera open, all that remained were wispy traces of powdery, cerulean smoke slowly fading away.

Derek's knuckles whitened on the steering wheel as his mind raced. Had he imagined it? Was he still dreaming? He pinched himself hard and winced from the pain, confirming he was awake. Maybe it was just the sun reflecting off the clouds? Despite telling himself there had to be a logical explanation, he couldn't shake the irrational suspicion that it was connected to him. Like he was meant to see it. The blur of movement had been far too fast for a plane streaking past him like a bolt of lightning.

Easing his truck over to the side of the road, he noticed the two long tire marks behind him, like tar-colored scars on the asphalt. His hands slipped from the steering wheel as he came to a stop, and he wiped his sweaty palms off on his jeans. A headache pulsed while he tried to unravel what he had just witnessed. Before he had the chance, Derek's neck pricked with awareness, like he was being watched. Hesitantly, his eyes moved towards the rearview mirror, muscles he didn't know he had tensed up, his mind hyper fixated on the tire tracks behind him. To his horror, he watched them melt away into a viscous ooze of darkness and shadow. The burnt rubber formed into one long finger, then two, then three, until a grotesque hand of tar erupted from the ground. Dripping with burnt rubber, the hand inched closer and closer to his truck. As it did, a sharp, acrid scent filled the cab of his truck.

Derek shut his eyes tightly and rubbed them with his still damp hands. Bracing himself, he peered into the rearview mirror again. He instinctively held his breath and squinted until he could clearly make out the familiar sight of the streaks through the glass——they had returned to normal.

His chest tightened and brow furrowed as he looked around for any signs of the nightmare he'd just witnessed. Derek took a shaky breath and told himself it was just a trick of the light. He *really* needed to get a good night's sleep. Letting out a light, if not forced, chuckle at his imagination, he reminded himself that he would miss his chance to hang out with his friends if he didn't get moving. With one last shake of his head, Derek dismissed his suspicions as a symptom of nerves for starting his senior year at high school and drove off down the road.

Derek pulled into the little hometown gas station, quickly spotting his four closest friends hanging out at their favorite picnic table. Now, in a town this small, everyone was basically your friend. Of course, there were people you didn't always hang out with, or even like, for that matter, but growing up here meant it was important to get along . . . most of the time. No one seemed to understand how big the world around them was; this was all most of them had ever, or would ever, know. This group of friends, though? They were a family.

As Derek parked his truck, he noticed Johnathan striding towards him. A genuine smile stretched his lips, dispelling Derek's lingering worry, as he thought back to how much this man had been there for him through the years——the good times and the bad.

He watched as Johnathan took off his dusty old ball cap and scratched his head of short brown hair. Derek had met John when they were little, and although their lives were on two very different paths, they had always stuck side-by-side.

John strode up to Derek's small truck, an aging two-door that his dad had given him when he turned sixteen.

"Still driving the ole shitbox, huh?" he said with a smirk.

"Hey! Be nice to White Lightning here. She's got me through the worst of times."

"Oh come on buddy, ya know I love her," John grinned. "Just gotta shovel on ya every now and again."

"Well, she may be a shitbox, but at least I ain't covered in shit."

Derek chuckled at the sight of John's exaggerated angry expression, mocking his friend's feigned fury.

John shook his head in faux annoyance as he thought about all the times his family had asked him to clean the horse stalls on their farm. He had actually just finished doing that this morning before he made his way to the gas station.

The sun peeked through the cloudy sky just long enough for the symbol on John's neck to shimmer in the light. Derek looked at the strange mark, a swirl of blue just barely visible above his collar line.

He had asked John about the mark at least a dozen times, and John had always just laughed it off. But after the morning he was having, Derek found it harder to ignore his intricate swirl of bluish skin. John was adamant it was just a birthmark, but it was unlike any blemish he had ever seen.

Outside of the "birthmark," John was pretty much the average country boy. His boots were faded, his clothes well worn, and he was overdue for a shave.

Johnathan placed his hand on the bed of Derek's truck, breaking Derek's focus on the mark.

"Here, let me leave some manure on her for ya," Johnathan said with a hearty chuckle.

John put his hat back on, momentarily thinking back on the day Derek gave it to him. It was three years ago, right after Derek made the high school baseball team. John always wanted to play baseball and even tried out with Derek. When it was all said and done, Derek had made the team and he hadn't.

John had asked the coach if he could still maybe be the waterboy, bat boy, anything to be a part of the team. That's when Derek came up behind him and put the hat on his head. His words were forever etched into John's brain.

"I ain't playing on any team that you ain't a part of."

The coach smiled and told John he was always welcome to hang out in the dugout, and that he should try out again next year. Instead of trying out again, he took on the role of student manager.

He cherished that hat, a true gift from a friend. Derek may have been the one in the limelight, but John would always be right there beside him. The memory put a big smile on his face, and he tapped the truck bed.

"Come on now. Everyone is over at the picnic table."

Waving for Derek to follow, made his way over to the table. As he sat down, he noticed Derek was taking his sweet time to get over to them.

Derek stood still, staring at his friends around the table. Normally, he would just go sit down with everyone, but his mind was still on the blue streak. Trey motioned for him to come on over.

Trey was . . . different. He usually didn't want to hang out with anyone, one-on-one. He preferred when the whole group was around, and honestly, the group preferred it, too. Trey was the kind of guy that would drop everything he was doing to come help a friend, but you had to watch what you said around him, because the smallest things would get him upset. They had once seen him lose his temper just because he forgot his favorite pencil at home. In a fit of rage, he left a noticeable dent in his own car over something as trivial as a *pencil*. The group knew he had troubles at home, even if would never tell them exactly what those troubles were. They hoped that after school, he would get into a decent college and be able to shed the chip on his shoulder.

Derek gave a nod to Trey and started again towards his friends. As he got closer, he noticed the blue in Trey's eyes bore a striking resemblance to the blue streak he had seen on his way to the store. Derek had always thought something was *off* about Trey's eyes. Trey had always told his friends he had heterochromia, but Derek still couldn't understand it. One of Trey's eyes was hunter green, while the other had a split iris of light blue and dark red. After the blue streak he saw earlier, he found it harder than usual to ignore. As fate would have it, Derek could've sworn he saw puffs of the same blue haze emanating from behind Trey.

Derek felt a chill run through him as he watched the blue haze drift by. He glanced at his friends to see if anyone else noticed, but they were all busy discussing their plans now that they were finally seniors. Not wanting to seem crazy, he forced himself to break away and sat down in one of the chairs around the table, pretending to be distracted by his phone.

After a few moments of awkward silence, he heard his friend Trey call out to him, "You okay, man?"

Derek snapped his head up and saw his friends looking at him with concerned expressions. He tried to shrug it off with a casual "I'm alright," but they weren't convinced.

Barry, the loudest member of the group, scooted his chair closer and put a hand on Derek's shoulder.

"You better be, boy! We are finally seniors!" he cheered, shaking Derek's shoulder.

The group laughed together, and for just a moment, Derek was able to forget about the blue haze and focus on the joy of being surrounded by his friends.

Barry towered over his friends, standing at an intimidating six foot seven inches. Between his broad, muscular shoulders, short, black hair, and cleanly shaven jaw, Barry was the perfect image of a high school wide receiver. His golden-brown eyes, only a few shades lighter than his skin, scanned the parking lot as he talked with his friends. He fooled most people into thinking he was all brawn and no brains, but his eyes always gave it away. In reality, he was incredibly sharp and protective of his people. He was also a giant nerd who would rather stay up late playing video games than attending parties or hanging out with other jocks.

To keep his friends from asking if he was alright again, Derek decided to ask Barry how he thought the upcoming football season was going to go.

Barry's face lit up as he said, "If only a certain someone was our quarterback instead of playing baseball for Riverrun's second-rate team, we'd be going undefeated this year!"

Derek gave a small smile and retorted, "I'd rather stick to non-contact sports, Barry."

John chuckled, "What's the matter, buddy? You afraid you're gunna get trucked?"

Isabella, who had apparently heard enough sports talk, nearly bounced out of her seat as she excitedly announced that she had some news to share with everyone.

She had been the object of almost all the group's affection when they were younger. But now, she was much more than a middle grade crush–she was family. The guys all took up more of a 'big brother' mantle.

Izzy had the kind of energy that made you feel warm just being around her, reflected in the way her smile seemed to be lit from within. It was, however, her eyes, a blue that rivaled the depths of the Caribbean Ocean, that held court above all. Even though she only came up to around five and a half feet, she always made sure the guys knew that she could take care of herself if push ever came to shove.

Isabella burst out animatedly, "I had the best weekend!" She was overcome with giddiness. "I met someone, and he is perfect! He's hot, tall . . . freaking tall . . . and *so* dang sweet. He took me on the most magical date and even gave me a sweet little kiss goodnight!" Her eyes lit up, her voice taking on a faraway tone as she continued to go on about her 'perfect' guy. "He said he can't wait until this week——"

Afraid Izzy would never stop gushing about this 'perfect' fella, Barry cut in, "Alright, alright Izzy. What's this new dude's name? Who the heck is he?"

She grinned from ear to ear before replying, "His name is Ivan! And get this, he is transferring from Courtsville High to Riverrun . . . today!"

For a moment, Izzy felt a heat on her neck, the prickling sensation you get when someone is staring at you. She turned to look towards Trey, and sure enough, his eyes were narrowed into a fierce glare.

Derek caught the interaction between the two. At first, he rationalized Trey's anger as being the 'over protective brother,' but all sense of logic flew out the window when he saw the blue haze once again. His mouth went agape and his hands started to sweat. Derek blinked his eyes rapidly to clear his vision, but when he stopped, the haze was still there. It danced violently through the air, the color seeming to shift from a calming blue to a menacing red mist.

Derek leaped from his seat and stumbled a couple steps backwards. All his friends were now staring directly at him, but Trey seemed to be really studying him. Derek tried his best to pull himself together, still hoping not to sound crazy,

"Ahh. Damn spiders get worse every year." He swatted at his arm, pretending to knock a spider off of it.

Trey quickly tried to change the subject, his voice cracking like he was trying to force the words out.

"So guys, are you ready for our last, first day of high school?"

Barry chuckled while he lightly shoved Johnathan. "Maybe not John if his grades are as bad as last year."

The whole group, except for Derek, laughed. He balled his hands into fists and roughly rubbed his eyes. When he removed his hands from his face, the red mist had disappeared.

Trey, who was still looking at Derek with confusion, asked, "Hey man, are you okay? Did that spider bite you or something?"

Derek smiled as convincingly as possible and replied, "Yeah, I'm good, man. It just scared me. I can't stand them damn things."

Derek's mind was in turmoil as he looked around, trying to figure out what had happened. He knew he needed to keep his cool, but on the inside, he was panicking. Questions raced through his head. How is no one else seeing this? Why is there so much of the 'haze' around Trey? What on earth is causing all of this?

As his brain struggled to come up with a logical answer, John jabbed him in the arm, jolting him out of his trance.

John, his stomach echoing like a bear in a cave, "C'mon buddy, let's get us a biscuit before they run out of chicken. I'm freaking starvin!"

Derek forced a smile onto his face and silently followed John into the store, Trey close behind. Despite all his confusion, Derek made sure to keep a slight smile on his face, hoping his friends would stop asking if he was okay.

John darted off into the store, ahead of the other two, with the desperation of a man starved. The door slammed shut behind him, making Derek laugh a little as he reached out for the handle. As Derek grabbed the door, a tall figure in a long, tattered overcoat burst through the door, sending it crashing into Derek's head and causing him to stumble to the ground with a cry of pain. Through the shock, he could've sworn he saw another puff of the red mist behind the man. Trey hurried to help Derek stand, who was now clutching his throbbing temple.

Through the ringing in his ears, he heard a gruff voice say, "We need to show him."

Another voice, this one smoother than the last, replied, "No! Now is not the time!"

His hand still on his head, Derek looked for the peculiar man that knocked him down. Once he realized he was nowhere to be seen, he asked Trey,

"Where did that jackass go and what did he say to me?"

A flicker of surprise crossed Trey's face before his eye glowed an unnatural shade of red. Derek's eyes widened as a low rumble emanated from Trey's throat before he could quell it, the tension in the air growing thick.

"What on earth are you talking about? You slipped and face planted the door, you big dummy. The only thing you might have heard was John laughing like a donkey at you," Trey barked as he tried his best to cut the tension, running his hand across his dirty blonde hair and acting like everything was completely normal.

At that moment, John came barreling out of the gas station door, doubled over in laughter. Grease stains smudged down his shirt where remnants of his chicken biscuit clung and he could hardly draw breath between cackles.

"Buddy, I may smell like shit after working on the farm, but you just ate it!" he bellowed.

Derek was nearing his breaking point. He wanted to beg his friends to tell him he wasn't losing his mind, but something inside him refused to give in. Things had already been crazy this morning and the school day hadn't even started yet! How could Trey not see that man? Even more disturbing, if he did see him, why did he lie about it?

Derek had never experienced anything like this before; between the twirling blue haze, menacing red mist, and weird trench coat guy that *apparently* only he could see, he was losing it. He couldn't tell if it was real or if his countless sleepless nights were finally taking their toll on him.

Pale faced and brows furrowed, Derek's legs slightly trembled beneath him as his friend's laughter died out.

Johnathan squinted at him with concern. "Woah, you ain't looking so hot. You wanna ride with me to school? I can swing you by the nurse when we get there if you want."

Derek shook his head and rubbed at the back of it as if trying to ease a headache. "Nah, I just . . . I think I got my bell rung is all."

Trey put an arm around Derek's shoulders in sympathy and offered to get them breakfast from inside. "Come on, let's grab a biscuit. We will meet the others back at the table in a minute."

Derek cautiously followed his friend into the gas station and was immediately greeted by the familiar scents of grease and cigarette smoke. The place was dingy and full of broken items, but it certainly had a sense of comfort; it had been a constant since Derek was a young boy. He started to approach the counter when he again noticed the red mist radiating from the back of another man.

Derek pointed it out to his friend, but Trey just raised one eyebrow and answered with, "All I see is our principal man."

Trey was right. It was their principal, Mr. Prudence, but there was once again something weird going on. Derek, determined to prove what he was seeing, quickly pulled out his phone, positioned himself behind the principal to get a clear shot, and snapped a picture. He then thrust the phone in Trey's face, only to reveal that the only thing visible on the screen was the back of Mr. Prudence's head.

Derek stood in confused frustration for a few moments. Eventually, he shakily whispered,

"You know what? I'm not really all that hungry anymore. John might've been right about me seeing the school nurse."

Trey smiled and almost too eagerly promised to help him out if needed. With that, Derek turned and made his way out of the gas station. Trey lingered behind, taking time to grab a couple of biscuits——one for himself and one for Derek.

When Derek returned to the picnic table, only Barry and John were still there. Derek was about to ask where Izzy had gone when he heard her cheerful voice fill the air.

"See you boys at school!"

The roar of the lifted red truck she was riding shotgun in echoed far off into the distance.

Derek asked the other two who she was leaving with, but the answer came from Trey as he made his way back to the picnic table.

"Ivan."

Derek spun around to find Trey standing a few feet away, his eyebrows low and deep-set, mouth pressed into a thin line. He stared the truck down with burning intensity, one that seemed to be commonplace this morning.

Derek asked, "How do you know?"

Trey stumbled over his words as he handed a biscuit to Derek. "I . . . uh . . . I mean, who else could it be?

Barry finally chimed in, "Yea, that was her new dude. He is kinda strange; he wouldn't even get out of the truck. Izzy just walked over there and hopped in."

His face softened into one of concern.

"Yo Derek, John said you face planted the door over there, you good?"

Derek forced a smile, more brittle than the last, and told Barry, "Yea, man, I'm fine. I think I am going to go see the school nurse, though."

John clapped Derek on the shoulder and asked, "You gunna ride with me to school then, buddy?"

Derek gave him a quick nod and went to lock his own truck up. As he approached the driver's side, he looked back and saw John and Trey deep in conversation. To his amazement, the air around them seemed to shimmer and the small birthmark on Johnathan's neck glowed faintly. Derek's stomach knotted. He knew something was wrong, something beyond a concussion. Swaying on his feet, Derek shot his arm out to brace on the truck as an overwhelming wave of dizziness came over him. His vision blurred. Hard metal slammed into his shoulder as he crashed into the side of his truck, slumping to the ground.

Seconds later, John, Trey, and Barry rushed to his side to check on their friend.

Barry knelt down beside him, while Trey and Barry searched the bed of his truck for a bottle of water or anything they could get him to drink.

Derek slowly started to come to, looking around in confusion.

"What just happened?" he asked softly.

Trey nervously cleared his throat. "I think you fainted, man. You hit your head again, too."

"I think we oughta get you to the school nurse, bud," John added.

Barry helped Derek to his feet and served as a makeshift crutch for him as they slowly made their way towards John's pickup truck.

With Barry's help, Derek clambered into the passenger seat of the vehicle. To his dismay, he spotted the blue haze all over the inside of John's truck. Too exhausted to express his thoughts, he gulped and kept quiet. John got in the driver's side, cranked the motor over, and after several sputtering noises, it started.

Relieved at the normalcy, Derek looked at John with a half-hearted smile. "Do I need to let you drive my *shitbox* instead?"

Chuckling, some of the tension seeped out of John's shoulders as he replied, "Well, now there's the Diamond I know. See, you're feelin' better already!"

Derek thought that was the goofiest nickname, but Johnathan loved to use it. Barry had actually started it when Derek decided to play baseball instead of joining him on the football team.

"Okay, Diamond. Have fun in your sandbox." Unfortunately for Derek, it stuck.

With a smile, Barry shut the door as he headed off to his car.

Derek looked out the window and asked, "Where'd Trey go?"

"He went on to school. He's gunna find Izzy and let'er know what happened."

John pulled the truck out of the parking lot and they set off towards the highschool. Derek's head was pounding. He couldn't tell if it was from the double whammy he just took, or if it was from everything that had happened that morning. He watched as the blue haze seemed to dance around the truck, drawing him in as if it were taunting him.

Everything he had seen and was seeing must be hallucinations. Could he *actually* be losing his mind? "No," he thought to himself, "This is all real, right? Would I even know if it wasn't?"

He racked his brain. He just couldn't understand why no one else was reacting to the things he saw. His mind had been his own for eighteen years, but now it was like someone else had taken control and refused to let go.

Derek rolled down the window of John's truck, letting cool morning air fill the cab. He inhaled deeply, closing his eyes as he savored the scent of freshly mowed grass and wildflowers from the rolling hills surrounding them. Creeping through the brief moment of calm, Derek felt a chill as he sensed the blue haze descend over him. His skin began to tingle and spark, like electricity coursing through his veins. A wave of invigoration swept over him, washing away the fog of his mind.

After a few miles, Derek turned to John with a faint smile.

"I think I'm feeling better. Let's just meet up with the group, then I'll go see the nurse after orientation."

John glanced at him with hesitation. "You sure? We can do whatever you want, buddy. I just wanna make sure you're okay."

Derek laughed, "I think I'm gunna be just fine."

His morning was anything but ordinary, and he had more questions than answers, but at least he was clear-headed for the first time all day. "Here's hoping it'll last," he mumbled.

Chapter 2

Riverrun

The sound of water rippled along the bank of the river, a sound every 'Mustang' student knew all too well, signaling Derek and John's arrival to school. Riverrun High School earned its name thanks to the long river that split the campus in half. When the school was built, one building was enough to hold all the students, but as the years passed and the population grew, the need for a second building on the other side of the river arose. An elegant walking bridge was constructed to allow students easy access to the separate buildings, arches gracefully over the serene waterway, its sleek, minimalist design harmonizing with the surrounding landscape.

As Derek and John pulled into the parking lot, Derek looked around at all the familiar faces of his classmates of the last twelve years. They were mingling in the parking area, chit-chat and gossip all flying with just a few minutes until their last first day officially started. Like every school, there were, of course, *cliques*.

In the grass along the school building, there was a group of guys throwing a football. A picnic table was full of kids studying and going over their schedules. An intense hacky sack session was going down on the edge of the parking lot, and a few circles of students were filling each other in on the summer gossip.

Unlike most other schools, these student lines were only divided for a short time before they all blended together. With a graduating class of only about one hundred each year, it was fairly easy to be friends——or at least acquaintances——with everyone.

As John parked his truck, Derek noticed the blue haze that was covering the interior had all but disappeared. Only a small amount was still lingering, and even though he tried to brush it away, it clung to his arm. Not wanting to cause another scene, he got out of the truck and walked towards his group of friends waiting by the walking bridge. That's when he spotted *her*.

She stood in front of her bright pink convertible, her long, straight brunette hair cascading down her back in a waterfall of pink highlights as the sun shone on her golden skin. Her lips bore a playful, light pink lipstick, and her shirt——a bright pink tank top that complimented her figure perfectly——completed her outfit. Although he'd never dare say it out loud, Derek thought he could get lost in her eyes, reminiscent of a lush forest bathed in sunlight. Her name was Mia, and every student at Riverrun took notice of her when she transferred last year. The girls were full of envy, and the boys, well, they were full of whatever teenage boys are full of. She was sweet, caring, and just enough of a rebel to have an awesome, blue sunburst tattoo on her inner wrist.

Derek had tried to talk to her in the past, but had always chickened out. After the morning he was having, he decided today would be the day. What more could go wrong, right? As he was building up the courage to go and say hello to her, John came 'hootin and hollerin' from around his truck and jumped on Derek's back, nearly knocking him over in the process.

"Can you believe it, Diamond? We are so close to being done with school!"

Derek, slightly frustrated, just shook it off.

"Naw man, I can't. It's hard to believe this chapter of our lives is almost over."

As John got down from Derek's back, he noticed Derek's gaze locked on Mia, who was still getting things from her car. Eyes widening in disbelief, a shit-eating grin spread across John's face.

"Wait, wait, wait." John choked out between laughs. "Dang man, you were *actually* about to shoot your shot, huh?" he laughed harder, lightly shoving Derek.

Rolling his eyes, Derek replied, "Shut up, dude! I was just gunna see if she needed some help, but it looks like she has it handled now."

John, being his typical, unapologetic self, continued to poke fun at Derek, wagging his eyebrows with a lopsided smile. "Uh-oh, you better watch out, cause here she comes!"

Mia had gathered all her things and was strolling right towards the two boys. Mesmerized, Derek watched as she walked by, her perfume filling the air around them, an intoxicating lavender that could soothe the heart of a racehorse, even if it sent his own racing.

Derek swallowed the lump in his throat and attempted to say hello, but the only thing that came out of his mouth was, "Lavender!"

Mia turned around as Derek's face turned beet red. She saw how embarrassed he was and tried to ease his nerves with a slight smile.

"Thank you for noticing."

Derek, still too embarrassed to open his mouth again, curled his lips into a forced smile and rapidly walked towards his friends by the bridge. Johnathan tried his best not to laugh while Mia remained in earshot, but as they made their way to their friends, he couldn't contain himself any longer. Johnathan barely held back tears of laughter while he explained to the group what had just happened.

The gang of friends were doubled over in hysterics, at Derek's expense, of course, when a bell chimed, signaling five minutes until the start of classes. They raced across the walking bridge and into the school, dodging throngs of fellow students. Derek, Trey, Izzy, John and Barry all paused to look up at the colorful flyers hung around the hallways with messages proclaiming the start of the new year.

"Students! Please attend your first period class and then join us in the gymnasium for the orientation pep rally!"

They read it together before scattering in three different directions. Trey and Izzy went off towards their chemistry class, while

John and Barry made their way to calculus, John already thinking about how much time he'd need to set aside to tutor Barry this semester. Derek was left alone in his own corridor, starting his slow walk to English IV.

On his way to class, Derek spotted the one student who always made his day a living hell. For the past twelve years, this guy had always picked on him, and in such a small town, pretty much everyone knew about it. Even at a rural school, there was bound to be at least one bully, and for Derek, that was Hillmiens.

Matthew Hillmiens was a pompous jerk in every sense of the word. Towering over most, at a menacing six foot five and weighing north of three hundred pounds, he was a force to be reckoned with and a valuable member of the Riverrun High football team. Even though Barry looked out for Derek, he struggled to reign in his fellow teammate.

Today felt different, though. Derek's thoughts drifted to how the rest of his morning went. The confusing yet calming blue haze, the terrifying red mist, the strange man at the gas station, and the embarrassing encounter with Mia. It was like he had lived a lifetime in just a few short hours. While his mind raced, he attempted to keep his head down and walk past Hillmiens without incident, but *of course*, that would not be possible.

Hillmiens planted his palm on Derek's chest, stopping his escape and shouting,

"Hey there buddy! I want to introduce you to my new best friend, Ivan. He just transferred from one of them big city schools up in Courtsville."

From behind a row of lockers, Ivan stepped out. Matching the height of Hillmiens, the man's bulging muscles were intimidating, to say the least. His jet-black hair hung down to his shoulders, and his eyes held a strange mix of colors——one iris deep scarlet and the other a soft honey brown. His eyes reminded Derek of Trey's odd, red heterochromia, just another reason to make today even crazier. Ivan looked like he regularly bench pressed three times his own weight, and Derek wondered if that was from hours spent in the gym or if he was just blessed with good genetics.

Ivan smirked, quickly blinking his eyes until they were a matching brown.

"You must be one of the *boys* Izzy has been telling me about." His cool, open tone gave away nothing of how he felt, but the steely glint in his eyes had Derek on guard.

He extended his hand to shake Derek's. The same red mist he had seen earlier leaked from Ivan's sleeve. Startled, Derek took a step back.

With a smug tilt of his head, Ivan whispered, "Pretty cool trick, huh?"

Before Derek could respond, Hillmiens laughed tauntingly, "What's the matter? Scared the new kid is going to beat you up?"

Fortunately, Derek was, a little too literally, saved by the bell, this time signaling the start of class, and everyone scurried off. As Derek walked away, he glanced back at Ivan, who was staring menacingly back at him. Derek spun back around and headed towards his English class, a little faster than his pride wanted to admit.

The confusion and dread that filled Derek's mind was overwhelming. The world around him had suddenly become a strange and unfamiliar place. Was he starting to go mad? Or was he actually seeing these strange things? Every thought made his head spin faster, as he tried to decipher if what Ivan said was in reference to the red mist emanating from his sleeve. Derek wished he could go back to before he had woken up and everything had gotten all messed up. He was tumbling down a never-ending rabbit hole he didn't choose to jump into. Yet, part of him was desperate to find out the truth.

As Derek walked into his first period class, he found an open desk towards the rear of the room. He took a seat and removed his notebook from his backpack, listing all that had transpired up until this point.

Derek scribbled furiously, the lead of the mechanical pencil breaking when the voices of his classmates would distract him. He paused momentarily to take a breath when the familiar sound of the dismissal bell pierced through the hum of the classroom. The noise jolted him out of his own thoughts as he quickly put down his pencil and grabbed his notebook, ready to make an escape before anyone noticed his lack of attention. What seemed to be par for the course that day, he had no such luck. Just then, he felt a presence looming over him.

"Mr. Stratum?" his teacher questioned, her voice stern and exacting.

Derek, flustered, frantically attempted to stuff his notebook into his backpack, fumbling and missing as he did so.

"Derek Stratum?" she asked once more, her patience ebbing away in the silence of the room.

He glanced up at her. "Yes . . . yes, Ms . . . uh. Yes ma'am, that's me."

"Ms. Goltz." Her brows furrowed. "I see you were a little preoccupied today?"

Derek scrambled for an explanation. "Yes ma'am. I'm sorry; it won't happen again."

Her gaze softened slightly as some of the tension melted away. "I would hope not," she said, slightly warmer, "your teachers from last year spoke very highly of you. Now get down to the orientation and make tomorrow a better day."

"Yes ma'am, Ms. Goltz." Derek obediently replied.

As Derek dashed out the door, he took solace in just being a high school kid. He was scolded for not paying attention, and so far that was the most grounding thing that happened all day.

Meandering down the hallway, Derek was lost in his thoughts, murmuring *"blue haze, red mist, strange man, lavender . . ."* when he heard Isabella's cheerful call for him to come over and meet Ivan. Derek's back stiffened, racking up his already frayed nerves. Following closely behind the couple were Barry, John, and Trey. Isabella was in a full sprint, or at least as fast as she could move while tugging at Ivan's hand behind her.

Derek and Ivan locked eyes in a battle of wills until Derek finally broke away with an apologetic glance after Izzy gave him a slight nudge. He turned to her and his other friends, hoping they hadn't noticed the tension between them.

"We already met earlier," Derek said with forced calmness. Trying for as natural of a smile as he could with his clenched jaw, he pushed a bit of enthusiasm into his voice for Izzy's sake as he continued,

"He seems like a decent guy . . ." Derek's voice trailed off as he sensed the waves of fury radiating off Trey." Before Derek had the chance to take another breath, Trey lunged forward and slammed his fist into the locker beside him, causing Derek to flinch. A violent swirl of red and blue emanated from the dent in the metal.

Derek's eyes darted between the group as he took a step backwards. To his surprise, none of his friends were reacting to the red and blue dust, only looking at Trey with embarrassment and slight annoyance. Derek raised his hand, finger pointed at the locker, but before he could speak, Izzy swatted a hand at Trey's back, her temper quickly rising to meet Trey's unexpected outburst, but he had already walked far enough away that she missed. The missed slap only infuriated her more, her face growing beet red, and her voice crackling as it echoed down the hallway while she chased after Trey.

Ivan, seemingly *amused*, smirked at Derek one last time before walking outside and vanishing within a cloud of red mist.

Derek's head was spinning, an endless stream of 'What the actual hell?' going off in his mind. Ivan's disappearance was somehow the most shocking of it all. He felt like it was probably time to go see the nurse, or maybe a psychiatrist, but before he could make up his mind to do either, he heard an oddly familiar voice say,

"We can't wait any longer!"

With increasing confusion, Derek looked around but couldn't locate the source of the voice. Convinced he was losing his mind, he frantically searched the area, finally turning his pleading eyes towards his closest friend.

"Please . . . please, John, before I actually lose my freaking mind, please tell me you heard that?" he asked through the cracks in his voice.

To Derek's dismay, Johnathan looked to Barry, who shrugged his shoulders, and then slowly shook his head no, but the look in his eyes suggested he wanted to say more. Derek knew his best friend well enough to know that he was hiding something. With each passing moment, Derek was becoming more convinced that what he was seeing was not from hitting his head.

When Derek pressed him on it, he was disappointingly unsurprised when John answered,

"You hit your head pretty hard earlier buddy, twice. Why don't we get ya up to see the nurse?"

"You do look awfully pale, dude," Barry chimed in.

Stubbornly, Derek shook his head. "I'm fine!" he snapped out. "I just want to go to the orientation and be done with today." Everyone might want him to believe he just hit his head too hard, but he was done playing along.

Reluctantly, John agreed, and Derek, John, and Barry set off to find Trey and Izzy, a tense silence filling the air.

Chapter 3

Echoes of Power

Izzy cornered Trey by the gymnasium, determined to figure out why he was acting like a colossal jerk.

"What the hell is your problem?" she asked.

"Dammit Izzy, Ivan . . . Ivan is bad news." Trey gritted out.

Huffing a breath, Izzy stared irreverently at Trey. "And you would know that because . . ."

"I know because . . ." His eyes darted away, looking for anyone else that may be around before groaning, "Ugh! Never freaking mind."

Izzy crossed her arms and cocked her hip, firing back, "No, Trey Antonio Stafford, you tell me right now! Is this about what happened last month?"

"What the hell, Izzy? No! Of course not!" A hint of vulnerability crept into Trey's voice. "You promised we wouldn't talk about that."

Looking over Trey's shoulder, she noticed the other guys had found them and were listening in on their conversation. Her cheeks turned a bright shade of crimson, and she quickly turned her head towards the wall, whispering, "I'm sorry."

Derek, John, and Barry approached the other two and Derek, who just wanted one real answer today, blurted out, "What happened last month?"

Trey's eyes cut daggers at Izzy. "Thanks for that!" he thundered.

Neither would give Derek an answer.

Tired of seeing his friends mad at each other and knowing they were going to be late for orientation, Derek said,

"Well, alrighty folks, whatcha say we all head to the gym and just forget this little moment?"

John, never knowing when to keep his mouth shut, spit out, "Dagnabbit! I was just about to go find us some popcorn. This was getting good!"

Trey and Izzy's glares shifted towards John, as if in sync.

Derek tried to defuse the situation, putting his arm around Trey. "Come, on man, I bet if we get in there now, we can find some good seats for the pep rally."

Trey took a deep breath, shaking off Derek's arm as he stormed away towards the gym. Barry and Izzy followed closely behind, with Derek and John bringing up the rear.

The group made their way into the gymnasium with the last bit of stragglers. The deafening roar of all four grades jammed into the tiny space echoed in their ears. Derek paused for a moment, taking in the atmosphere and letting his mind forget, or at least try to forget, the craziness of the morning. Most of their classmates were already seated in the bleachers, each grade occupying a different section.

The group walked towards the senior section, scanning for any available seats. Trey found a spot near the top of the bleachers and sprinted up the stairs, motioning for his friends to follow. Barry and Izzy went right up behind him, but before Derek started up the bleachers, John tapped him on the shoulder. With a twinkling glint in his eye, John leaned towards Derek.

"Buddy, I'm sorry about all that with Mia earlier, but guess what?"

Derek opened his mouth, but before he could guess, John shouted, "Shoot your shot!" and playfully pushed Derek into the seat next to Mia.

If looks could kill, John would have dropped dead from the stare Derek was giving him. "Today of all freaking days?" he thought to himself, "My whole world is crashing around me, and John expects me to talk to Mia?"

Looking down at the ground to hide his bright red face, Derek tried to stand up, but Mia reached for his shoulder, letting him feel the warmth of her touch through his shirt.

With her hand on his shoulder, Derek's mind calmed, just as suddenly as it had in John's truck earlier that morning. He closed his eyes for a moment, letting the peace wash over him. His shoulders, tense from the day's chaotic events, slowly dropped.

Mia playfully giggled, "Well, hey there, Mr. Lavender!"

Derek's brain was finally still. He wasn't capable of responding, even if he wanted to. All he knew was that he didn't want this peace to go away. But it did. As soon as Mia's hand left his shoulder, his mind became clouded with the events of the morning again. Scrambling to find the right words to say, he opened his mouth, and all that came out was an awkward chuckle.

Mia's glistening green eyes, crinkling at the corners, seemed to sparkle with an unspoken humor as she said, "Oh boy, you're a nervous one, huh?"

Every fiber of his being was trying to find words to say. His palms grew damp, and he could hear the resounding "thump-thump, thump-thump" of his heart beating faster and faster in his chest.

"I really like Lavender" he blurted out, his face immediately returning to a bright crimson.

A soft smile formed across Mia's face, and she let out another playful giggle. Derek rested his elbows on his knees, burying his face in his hands as he contemplated whether it was possible to die from humiliation.

Before his foot could get any further in his mouth, the gym lights dimmed and music started playing as the principal stepped forward to address the students.

"Good morning, Riverrun High!" the stocky man shouted.

"It is my pleasure to have you all here today. I am thrilled to see what this year will bring, not only for each of you, but also for our lovely little school and community." He wiped the sweat off his brow and began pacing slowly around the gym floor.

"I will provide a quick overview of what we expect from all of you, and then we will dismiss the underclassmen and proceed with senior orientation."

Mr. Prudence's brow was permanently furrowed, deep lines etched across his forehead. His eyes, always narrowed, glinted with an intensity that made people uneasy. The corners of his mouth turned down slightly, as if weighed down by some invisible burden. He rarely smiled, and when he did, it was more a grimace than a grin, his jaw clenched tight as if he were biting back harsh words.

But today, he seemed oddly happy. He smiled through his entire speech. It was almost unsettling.

As the principal finished addressing the underclassmen, they began to file out of the gym.

Derek took a deep breath in an attempt to calm his nerves and turned to Mia.

Hands balmy and heart pounding, he asked, "How . . . how was your summer?"

Mia's face lit up in pleasant surprise as she responded, "Oh, it was amazing! I traveled to some really unbelievable places. It was truly wonderful, magical even!"

She spoke with genuine enthusiasm, and Derek couldn't believe how happy she looked while talking to him. Mr Prudence resumed speaking, preventing Derek from responding.

"Seniors, this is your last, first day of high school. Our sports teams are prepared to bring home state championships, our band will triumph in their state tournament, and our academic achievements will soar! None of this would be possible without the leadership of our upperclassmen, and for that, I am immensely proud of each and every one of you."

While Mr. Prudence continued his speech, Mia placed her hand on Derek's knee. His eyes darted to her hand and his heart squeezed tightly before taking off at a gallop. The girl he had a massive crush on was not only talking to him like she actually wanted to, she was touching his knee.

Why was she touching his knee? It didn't matter, he wasn't going to question his luck. She inched closer to him until their legs were touching. His heart couldn't possibly beat any faster. He could feel his body temperature rising, his face hot. Mia's grip got tighter, no longer just resting her hand, but squeezing his knee.

He didn't budge. He didn't want to ruin the moment, but then he felt the pain of her nails digging into his leg. Derek looked at Mia and saw her forest green eyes blinking rapidly, as if trying to clear the terror from her vision. Her gaze darted around the room, searching for an escape. She couldn't hide the tremor in her hand or the dread coursing through her.

Derek turned his gaze back out to the gym floor, seeing what Mia must have been seeing. Swirling tendrils of red mist surrounding Mr. Prudence. The mist spun around the principal, yet he carried on speaking as if nothing unusual was happening.

"I expect all of you to strive for excellence this year. Even if the odds are against you, never stop pushing, never give up on your dreams. Now go and make this senior year one you won't soon forget!"

As the lights came back on, the mist dissipated and the music started to play again. Everyone rose to leave as if nothing out of the ordinary had occurred. Derek turned to Mia to ask if she had seen the same thing as him, but before he could form the words, she leaped from her seat and rushed out of the gym.

A breath later, Derek darted off after her.

John watched as Derek stormed out of the gymnasium and motioned for their other friends to follow him as he sprinted down the bleachers. Frantically searching through the crowd of students, he realized Derek was already long gone.

"Alright, we should split up and find him. He seemed worried and has been acting strange all morning." John ran a hand through his hair "I reckon I'll go check the nurse's office in case he finally decided to go up there."

Barry chimed in, "I'll go check the field house. Maybe he needed to blow off some steam on the weight bench?"

"Uh, guys? I know we're looking for Derek, but where is Trey?" Izzy asked.

John looked around, but of course, Trey was also nowhere to be found. "Dadgummit. Alright Izzy, you go find Trey. Barry and I will find Derek."

Derek dashed through the hallways, searching for Mia, his heart racing with a sense of foreboding. With a deep certainty, he was now convinced that what he had witnessed all morning was indeed real. Mia *must* have seen the red mist around Mr. Prudence. Why else would she react the way she did? As Derek turned the final corner of the school's hallway, he anticipated finding Mia.

Instead, he skidded to a shocked stop, recognizing Trey's faux-hawked hair as he straddled Ivan's prone form. Just as Derek was processing the crunching sound of Trey's fist connecting with Ivan's jaw, the latter gained the upper hand with a sound right hook, flinging Trey off with surprising strength.

Trey sprang back to his feet and rushed towards his opponent, his fist striking Ivan in the center of the stomach. A shove with uncanny force sent Ivan into the cement wall behind him.

Ivan recovered quickly, his face twisted in an angry grimace. He surged forward, grappling with Trey, their feet scuffling against the tiled floor, each trying to gain the upper hand. Ivan hooked his leg behind Trey's, using the momentum to send them both crashing to the ground.

Pinned beneath Ivan, Trey twisted and turned, his fists flailing as he tried to escape. Ivan rained down punches, his knuckles reddening with each blow that connected. Trey, gritting his teeth against the pain, managed to buck Ivan off, rolling away and scrambling to his feet. They both stood panting, eyes blazing, ready for the next round.

The air was thick with the scent of sweat and the metallic tang of blood from Ivan's split lip.

Derek finally summoned the courage to intervene in the fight, but just as he went to step in, Trey caught him out of the corner of his eye and flung his arm out wildly as he bellowed,

"NO!"

His voice echoed through the hallways, and a blue haze erupted from his hands. Derek felt the air rush past him as he hurtled backward with astonishing force. Pain exploded along his spine and through the back of his head as he collided with the unyielding cement of the wall behind him.

Slumping against the wall, Derek struggled to focus on the fight past the ringing in his ears and doubling vision. Through the mental fog, he could hardly see the two——or was it four——individuals. The fight raged on, and with every punch Ivan threw, a red mist formed around his movements. Trey's own strikes also released the red mist, but the blue haze that had sent Derek flying into the wall seemed to form a protective aura around Trey.

Ivan's punches could not penetrate the blue aura. Seizing the opportunity, Trey drew his arm back for a powerful blow. The blue haze around him formed a sleeve, starting at his fist and extending all the way up his arm. Trey's fist connected with Ivan's chest with a thunderous boom, slamming him back into the wall. Ivan slid down to the floor, grasping at his shirt and gasping for air.

As Trey turned to help Derek, Mia came running around the corner. She ground to a halt, eyes widening and her mouth falling agape in what looked like a silent "oh." She stood in shock at the sight of Ivan bloodied on the ground, Trey bruised, and the red and blue mist floating in the air.

Pushing through the pounding pain in his skull——for the third time today——Derek tried to get up and go to her, but his movement broke her out of her frozen stance. Darting her eyes towards him, she bolted away once again. His own jaw dropping at the inhuman speed in which she rushed out the doors towards the parking lot.

Ivan staggered back to his feet, infuriated that Trey was getting the better of him. He twisted his fingers backward unnaturally and spoke in a dark, harsh tone, with clipped syllables that seemed ancient and echoing.

"Inpulsa fluctus!"

Derek didn't understand what Ivan said, but somehow, he instinctively knew what would happen next. He pulled his legs into his chest as a red shockwave surged from Ivan's hands. The powerful wave propelled Trey through the air, crashing his unconscious body against the far wall. Derek was thrown down the main hall, his back scraping painfully against the floor.

Ivan let out a disturbing laugh. "That ought to shut you up." He looked down at Trey, and almost as if he was toying with him, said, "Now, where is that girlfriend of *mine*?"

Derek watched helplessly as Ivan sauntered towards the parking lot to look for Izzy. Just as Ivan reached the door, his menacing eyes cut to Derek, and then he vanished in another cloud of red mist.

Derek tried to crawl towards Trey to check on him, attempting to pull himself along the cold tile, but his body refused to cooperate, his head throbbing relentlessly.

Through the fog, a distantly familiar voice resurfaced. "It's time to reveal ourselves. We can't wait any longer!"

Derek painstakingly spun himself around, trying to find the source of the voice. His vision was still blurred, but he was able to make out two shadowy figures that disappeared as soon as he reached out for them.

He closed his eyes for a few seconds. When they opened again, there was another figure. With each slow blink, they would get closer . . . closer, until he could faintly make out bright, glowing blue eyes. As he struggled to keep his eyes open, Derek was able to make out the fuzzy edges of the dusty old ball cap they were wearing.

"Johnathan?" He choked out. "What's wrong with your eyes?"

As Derek's consciousness waned, Johnathan's arms positioned themselves underneath Derek's limp body. The last thing Derek processed was a sensation of moving upward and the comforting sound of Johnathan's voice saying,

"Don't worry, buddy. Everything is gunna be okay."

Chapter 4

Torvania

Torvania, home of the fae. The same morning.

The wind whispered over Lake Talisade, carrying with it the soft song of birds that danced through the dawn-lit sky. Honey-colored grass swayed gently, catching the first rays of the rising sun, which cast a warm, golden hue across the heavens. Among the fields, purple flowers bloomed like scattered jewels, their fragrance mingling with the crisp morning air.

In the near distance, the majestic city of Torvania stood tall, a haven for the fae, its spires shimmering in the early light. By the lake's edge, Tah'quhal lingered quietly, lost in thought, as the world around him stirred to life with the promise of a new day.

Tah'quhal knelt down and gazed at his reflection in the lake. He ran his hand through his long, sleek, jet-black hair, stopping to trace the new *stigmata* on his pointed ears. The faint blue glow of the tattoo marked his mastering of conjuration without the use of incantations, a feat most fae don't achieve before their two hundredth birthday. Admiring the mark, he couldn't help but notice how weary his reflection appeared, despite his neatly kept beard and warrior's visage.

Splashing water from the lake onto his face, he rose to his feet. Standing at six-foot-five, Tah'quhal was among the tallest in Torvania. He was well admired in the village, and he loved every bit of it. His popularity was bolstered by his lineage as a direct descendant of Torviid, the village's namesake and the legendary fae who saved Torvania from Malum during the Battle of Laresque. Malum, an evil fae, sought to bend others to his will, but Torviid's heroism ensured the village's safety.

A soothing and friendly voice rang out from behind, breaking Tah'quhal out of his reflection.

"Tah'quhal! What are you doing down here? We are supposed to be meeting Komipea in ten minutes."

He turned to see two of his favorite fae, Sarika and Tarik. The former ran up to him, gracing him with a quick kiss on the cheek and a loving embrace. Her flowing blue hair brushed against him and the corner of his mouth quirked in a rare smile.

His smile quickly faded back to his usual stern expression.

"Sarika, your brother is right behind you."

Sarika's vibrant purple eyes met his steely stare. "Hush Tah'quhal. You know he knows about us."

Tarik sauntered towards the other fae, twisting the ends of his mustache to make sure the curls stayed perfectly shaped.

"Dearest sister, I don't think he is truly worried about me," he said with a chuckle. "If I dared to guess, I would imagine he is using me as an excuse to distance himself from you. I mean, you did say you two had agreed to break off your . . . *relationship* until after the Atunkmae Ritual, correct?"

Tah'quhal shifted from foot to foot. The conversation had only just begun, but already he was feeling uncomfortable. He turned his gaze to the amber colored sky, focusing instead on everything that had led to this day.

The three of them had trained together since they were young, each specializing in different sets of magic. Of course, every fae had to learn some of the basics, but truly disciplined ones dedicated their time to master a specific set. Sarika and Tarik were twins, but they couldn't have been more opposite.

Sarika was born with natural beauty, and she wasn't afraid to use it to her advantage. Much to her brother's dismay, she usually wore the most provocative outfits the toolers would make. She enjoyed the attention it garnished, and frequently used her looks and wits to get her way.

Tarik, on the other hand, was the trickster of the group. He loved to have a little fun, even if it was at the expense of others. His pranks and light-heartedness brought perfect balance to his twin ——the jokester to her cerebral.

Their whole lives had led up to this day, the Atunkmae Ritual, a tradition started after Torviid defeated Malum. Following Malum's defeat, a single rock was found where Torviid's body should have been. This rock was dubbed The Seer Stone. The Chieftain of the time discovered that, when the stone was placed through a portal to Earth, it would reveal a human's name and image. Convinced it was a sign from Torviid, the Chieftain initiated the ritual to recruit humans in case Malum ever resurfaced, as neither Torviid nor Malum's bodies were ever found.

A select few fae would travel to Earth every forty years via the Anchor, a portal at the base of a giant statue of Torviid, and find a human to bring back to their realm and teach magic. They called these humans *companions*.

After the companions were attuned to magic, they were asked to vow to help Torvania if they were ever in need. Humans were exceptional at learning magic once introduced, but of course, they were *only* humans. The fae knew they would want to share what they learned, so they always kept a few *forgoniums* on them when they visited Earth. This flower had a unique effect on humans, causing them to forget about magic altogether.

"The sky looks so dull today, a shame for such a momentous event." Tarik's gravelly voice rang out.

Tah'quhal snapped his attention back to his friend with a tight-lipped expression.

"Hush Tarik. Tah'quhal has anticipated this day his entire life." Sarika chastised.

Tah'quhal's brow furrowed. "I should be excited for today, yet I feel as if something is wrong."

"Oh, not this again." Tarik mocked. "Are you still hung up on these stupid rumors?"

Turning his back to his friends, Tah'quhal looked towards the lake. The subtle scent of damp loam and exotic blossoms filled his nostrils. He took a deep breath, savoring the crisp, clean aroma that carried a hint of silver pine from the surrounding trees. It was a scent that brought back memories of summer afternoons spent by the water, training and watching luminescent spiroflies dance above the surface.

"It is not the rumors that bother me." Tah'quhal graveled. "I am sure there will always be those who hide in the shadows, planting seeds of doubt, and hoping for Malum's return. That is why we train. Chieftain's Komipea refusal to speak on the rumors is what bothers me."

Sarika walked up behind him, placing her hand on the middle of his back. "I am sure the Chieftain has his reasons, Tah'quhal."

Tah'quhal eased away from her touch. "You are right. I should not let my mind wander so easily. We should head to the ritual." He spun on his heel and started towards the center of town, the siblings following closely behind.

Tarik tried one last time to reassure Tah'quhal, "My friend, *if* Komipea is hiding anything, it would be sweet rolls in his pocket. The old man is an open book."

As the three fae approached the massive statue of Torviid, Sarika grabbed Tarik's arm, urging him to slow down just a tad.

"Are we sure about doing this, brother?" She asked.

A slow grin, lacking any warmth, spread across Tarik's face, and his eyes gleamed with a mischievous glint. "There is no going back now, sister."

They watched as their friend continued to make his way towards the statue. Sarika blinked rapidly, trying to clear the stinging sensation from her eyes. Her throat tightened, and she swallowed hard, refusing to let any tears fall. Taking a deep breath, she steadied herself, her gaze fixed on the path ahead. Her hands trembled for a moment before she clenched them into fists, ready to face the ritual.

Tah'quhal arrived at the back of the crowd surrounding the statue of his ancestor, Sarika and Tarik a few steps behind him. They could hear the booming voice of the Chieftain over the excited noise of the crowd.

"Welcome everyone! Welcome to the Atunkmae Ritual!"

His announcement was met with cheers from the hundreds of fae and humans attending.

"Today, we shall use the Seer Stone to guide three of our finest young fae to find their companions!" The Chieftain proclaimed. "If I am not mistaken, I believe I see them in the back. Everyone, please make room for them to join me."

As the Chieftain spoke, the crowd parted almost in perfect unison and turned to look at the three fae. Tah'quhal led the way, sauntering through the spectators with his chest puffed out and chin upturned. He could hear their whispers.

"Look, it's Tah'quhal! I would give up magic to spend a day with him," one voice rang out.

Another one chiming in, "No. He's with Sarika. She will end you in a heartbeat."

"No silly, they broke up! Didn't you hear?" The first voice retorted.

Tah'quhal's lips tilted up ever so slightly; he rather enjoyed the gossip being centered on him. Then he heard the ramblings of an old fae.

"Save Luminfae and realms beyond compare."

He came to an abrupt halt and turned to face his elder. "What did you just say?" he demanded, but the old fae crept into anonymity among the crowd.

As Sarika and Tarik caught up to him, Tarik gave him a light shove. "Come on now, don't get nervous."

Tah'quhal snapped his head back around to face the Anchor, and he proceeded through the crowd. Standing at the base of the statue, he took one more deep, calming breath.

The Chieftain proclaimed, "Tah'quhal. Sarika. Tarik. Today is a momentous day! Not only for you three, but for Torvania as a whole. Today is the day that Torviid's own descendant travels to Earth for the first time."

Tah'quhal let out a slight grin. Once again, all the attention was on him.

"Tah'quhal, seeing as you are the one I speak of, I think it is only fitting you get the honor of going first!" Komipea exclaimed.

Bowing his head respectfully to the Chieftain, Tah'quhal turned to face the Anchor. His heart raced, and he fought the urge to rub his sweat slick palms along his robes. Willing his hands steady to keep his nervousness hidden from the crowd, he steeled his features and presented his open hand to the Chieftain.

Chieftain Komipea gracefully handed him the Seer Stone. Tah'quhal gazed at the statue of Torviid. Beneath the towering statue lay the Anchor, the gateway to Earth. Vivid blues and purples intertwined in a mesmerizing dance, swirling in hypnotic movements. The colors merged and separated like liquid silk, casting an ethereal glow that flickered and pulsed with a life of its own. The very air around it hummed with a soft, resonant energy, as if the portal were whispering, beckoning with the promise of distant realms and untold adventures.

His heart pounded in a rhythm that echoed the years of longing and anticipation. The moment was finally here. Eyes closed, he felt the weight of every past struggle and dream settle into his shoulders. Slowly, deliberately, he drew in a breath, the cool air filling his lungs and grounding him in the present. As he exhaled, the tension slipped away, replaced by a calm determination.

Tah'quhal reached forward and slid the hand holding the Seer Stone into the dancing colors of the Anchor. The portal greeted him with a deep, penetrating cold——nothing more, just a chill that seeped into his bones. Then, after a few heartbeats, a subtle tingling spread through his body, a gentle hum under his skin, signaling that the ritual was complete. As he pulled his arm back, he angled the stone to better catch the sun's light. The stone revealed the inscription of a name and an image of who the name belonged to: Derek Stratum.

His breath hitched as he murmured the name, moved by the magnitude and sanctity of the moment. He turned to face the crowd with his eyes full of pride. Tah'quhal held the stone up in the air, speaking the same words as the fae that had taken part in the ritual before him.

"Derek Stratum. I shall seek out this human and unveil to him the hidden magics that weave through his path. By his word, he shall pledge to guard Torvania, or let the memory of our meeting be lost to the shadows of time."

The crowd stood in awed quiet. Many of them had seen the ritual numerous times, but it was always a sanctimonious moment. A quick giggle shattered the reverent silence.

The eyes of nearly everyone in attendance cut to Tarik. His lips were upturned in a playful grin. "Oh, come on now. We hear this at every ritual; someone should *spice* it up a tad."

Chieftain Komipea snapped his head towards Tarik with a glare.

"Since you find our longest and most important ritual amusing, Tarik, you shall go last."

The Chieftain turned to Tah'quhal. "Now then, pass the Seer Stone to Sarika."

Tah'quhal nodded his head and did as he was told. Looking toward Tarik, Tah'quhal's eyes narrowed, and his jaw tightened. The muscles in his face went rigid, a storm brewing just beneath the surface. This was meant to be *his* big day. Damn all the rumors and whispers, but why did his friend have to make a mockery of it, too?

Sarika took the stone from Tah'quhal, her hand lingering on his for a brief second. She bit her lower lip, her eyes flickering with a hint of regret. Lifting her gaze, her lips curved into a tentative smile.

"I do apologize for my brother. He only knows how to make jokes, even in the worst of times."

Tah'quhal jerked his hand away from hers. "His antics, today of all days, are not appreciated."

She understood why he was upset, why he pulled away his hand. He wanted to focus on the ritual and have zero distractions. He was generally a cold and blunt fae, but she knew a softer side of him was in there; she had seen it countless times. She wished he would show it now——for her.

Sarika looked towards her brother, his mouth in a half-cocked smile, and watched him as he nodded his head in approval. Sarika approached the Anchor, pushing the stone through the portal. Just as her arm breached the barrier, a loud clap of thunder erupted through the sky, causing Sarika to yank her arm back. Her hand trembled as she dropped the stone, once again glancing at Tarik, his expression unchanged. Kneeling down to pick up the stone, her brow furrowed in apprehension. It bore the same name and image that Tah'quhal had just revealed.

Sarika fumbled the stone, trying to pick it up, and the Chieftain bent over to assist. Seeing the stone unchanged, Chieftain Komipea whispered,

"It must not have been in the Anchor long enough. Try again, my dear."

Hoping the Chieftain was right, Sarika approached the portal again, placing the stone through once more.

Again, thunder echoed through the air; however, this time she'd braced for it, managing not to embarrass herself a second time. After a few moments, she felt the tingle in her skin, and she pulled her arm back, only to find the same name and image as before.

Sarika showed the Seer Stone to Chieftain Komipea again, and with a nod of his head, he said,

"It is fate. Proceed with the ritual."

Sarika looked towards her brother one last time. She watched as his smile faded, his lips pressed into a thin, unyielding line. She raised the stone into the air and repeated the same words as Tah'quhal, her voice almost undetectably quivering.

"D . . . Derek Stratum. I shall seek out this human and unveil to him the hidden magics that weave through his path. By his word, he shall pledge to guard Torvania, or let the memory of our meeting be lost to the shadows of time."

Chapter 5

Ceremony

Tah'quhal's breath caught in his chest as the weight of the words crashed over him. His eyes widened in shock, frozen in place as the world around him blurred. Each slow blink felt like a desperate attempt to grasp a reality that was slipping through his fingers. When he found his voice, it was a barely audible whisper.

"What did you just say?"

He had been eagerly waiting for this moment, expecting his companion to be his own. How could the Seer Stone reveal the same human to two different fae?

Murmurs broke out amongst the crowd, many casting suspicious looks towards Tarik

Chieftain Komipea reassured Tah'quhal, making him a promise:

"Son, this *is* quite strange. We shall talk about it privately after the ceremony."

Still reeling from the disappointment, Tah'quhal silently nodded and crossed his arms, attempting to hide his disbelief out of a sense of pride. He watched as Sarika handed the Seer Stone over to Tarik, noticing a strange glint in the latter's eye.

Tarik gazed deeply into the portal and, with the Seer Stone in hand, whispered, *"Nunc percutite."*

Thunder erupted from the sky once more, louder than ever before. As if time itself had slowed, Tarik fell backwards, thrown back by the clap of thunder. Tah'quhal watched as the Seer Stone flew from his friend's hand and crashed to the ground.

A crimson lightning bolt shot from the clouds, thunder crashing as it tore through the sky. The crowd scattered in panic. The bolt struck the Seer Stone with a blinding flash, splitting it in two and leaving only a faint red glow.

Through the chaos and screams around him, Tah'quhal's eyes desperately scanned for his friends, landing on Tarik, who had rolled over onto his stomach and locked eyes with his sister.

Tah'quhal turned to check on Sarika. Her arms were drawn tightly around herself. She couldn't pull her stunned expression away from her twin.

Tarik's voice rang out sarcastically. "I told you, this whole thing needed a little spice."

Tah'quhal watched in horror as Tarik leapt towards the shining stone. As soon as his hand touched it, a bloom of red mist engulfed him.

Coughing as the red mist invaded her lungs, Sarika's desperate voice cut through the screaming throng around her as she called out for her brother.

"Tarik," Sarika choked out. "Where are you?"

The only response she received was a chilling, twisted laugh she couldn't reconcile as her brother's.

Tah'quhal, running on warrior's instinct, plunged into the cloud to find Tarik, to find his friend, but what he discovered rooted him in place.

Tarik's once blue stigmata had turned a haunting shade of red, his skin a sickly shade of pale. His once-vibrant, purple eyes had transformed into a deep, burgundy hue. Before Tah'quhal could utter a word or attempt to restrain him, a slow, wicked grin slid across Tarik's face. Tah'quhal's stomach turned as he watched Tarik disappear. He vanished as if he were made of the red mist surrounding them, leaving Tah'quhal bereft, grasping for a friend that was simply gone.

The red mist dissipated as quickly as Tarik, leaving Tah'quhal standing with nothing but half of the Seer Stone laying in front of him.

Sarika rushed to his side, clutching her chest as if trying to steady her racing heart. Her eyes darted wildly, her breath coming in rapid, shallow bursts.

"Where is my brother?"

Tah'quhal, frozen in shock and feeling lost within his inability to make sense of what transpired, was unable to form any kind of response he thought might've sufficed. As frustration took hold, Sarika's confusion turned to anger, her eyes sharpening.

"Where is Tarik!" she demanded.

Gravely, Chieftain Komipea approached the two fae and whispered one bone chilling word:

"Corrupted."

Sarika's face drained of color, leaving her pale as she clutched her stomach. Tah'quhal couldhear a faint ringing in his ears that grew louder with each passing second until it completely drowned out the screams of the panicking crowd. The spectators devolved into pure chaos as the gathered fae trampled each other in an urge to flee or rush the Anchor, seeking refuge and answers from the Chieftain.

Komipea motioned for the city guard to come and help calm everyone down and get them home, and then turned to Tah'quhal and Sarika, ushering them to move.

"We must retreat to my villa. We can talk about all that has happened there."

Sarika nodded her head in agreement, but Tah'quhal stood still, his ears still ringing. He could see his Chieftain trying to talk to him, but could not hear his words. Sarika approached him, placing her hand on the small of his back, and the ringing finally started to quiet down, replaced by the panicking crowd once more.

Komipea commanded, "Tah'quhal, now. Let's get to my home."

As they entered the villa, Tah'quhal bringing up the rear, he slammed the door shut behind him.

"What the hell is happening?" He shouted.

Sarika, with a touch of panic, "And where the hell did my brother go?"

The Chieftain calmly walked over to his bookshelf and pulled out an old tome.

"Tah'quhal, I understand that everything we have just witnessed seems inconceivable." He turned to Sarika, "I know you want answers about your brother." Komipea took a long, deep breath, and his eyes became imploring. "But you two must find this Derek Stratum. It cannot be a coincidence that the Seer Stone revealed him to you both, just as this darkness has returned."

"But Chieftain Komipea!" Embarrassed at the petulant tone his voice had taken. Tah'quhal cleared his throat before continuing with an air of sensitivity, "Sarika will be consumed with worry for her brother. Perhaps it would be best if I venture alone."

Wise to his motivations, Sarika interjected, her voice filled with determination and not a small amount of indignation.

"Do not dare presume to speak for me, Tah'quhal! I can and will accompany you to find *our* companion. Your ego is far less important than the fact that finding Derek Stratum could shed some light on what has happened to Tarik!"

Somewhat chastised, Tah'quhal took a step away from Sarika and the heat of the anger he could feel emanating from her. Chieftain

Komipea, ignoring both of them, continued to thumb through his tome, as if he was frantically searching for something.

Tah'quhal knew Sarika was right. His mind filled with worry for his friend and he began to rub his index finger and thumb on his right hand together. A trick he used to calm his mind.

Hesitantly, Tah'quhal looked to Komipea, "Chieftain, when Tarik disappeared, you spoke the word 'corrupted.' What did you mean?"

The Chieftain quickly closed the book in his hands and sat it back on the bookshelf, shrinking with a burden that seemed to age him by centuries.

"I'm sure both of you have heard the whispers of Malum's return and maybe even rumors of his supporters hiding in our city?"

Tah'quhal and Sarika both nodded their heads in agreement.

"Corrupted was a term that the old fae of Torvania used to describe followers of Malum."

Sarika let out an audible gasp, her eyes taking on a sheen of grief and disbelief. Tah'quhal's shoulders slumped, his voice wavering slightly as he asked,

"So it is true then? Malum has returned?"

The Chieftain paused, "I'm . . . not sure." He said slowly, sounding as if he were only hoping that it was not true. "Find Derek Stratum. Bring him back here. I will research all that I can, and will hopefully have answers for you upon your return."

Tah'quhal's eyes scanned down to the floor, and a deep furrow etched itself across his forehead as he looked towards the window.

"The red mist that took Tarik. It was similar to the *essence* that forms when we use our magic, just red instead of blue. What does that mean?"

The Chieftain walked over to him, placing a hand on his shoulder.

"There are many forms of magic. I do not know all the answers, but I do know that essence is all around us. It is in the air we breathe." He paused and took a long breath. "*Bonum* magic is what we here in Torvania have always practiced." His eyes squinted and his nose scrunched in displeasure. "*Odium* magic is a twisted form that Malum discovered. The way different forms of magic access the essence can change the colors that present when casting spells."

"So you do believe Tarik has truly been 'corrupted' by Malum?" Tah'quhal asked.

"I understand you are worried. I am as well. All I know for sure is that his essence was changed. I promise you, bring Derek Stratum here, and I will research and do my best to explain everything I know. For now, take solace in knowing Tarik lives."

Tah'quhal bowed his head in agreement, but Sarika was not content. Her gaze shifted to the bookcase where the Chieftain had been standing, and in an uncharacteristic outburst, Sarika erupted.

"That's not good enough! You must have more answers . . . you're the *Chieftain* of Torvania! There is no way you are this clueless!"

The Chieftain's lips were pressed tightly together, as if holding back a flood of words.

"I do not have them now, but I promise you both I will find answers." He said as calmly as possible.

Sarika huffed as she stormed towards the cooking area of Komipea's home.

"Where are you going?" The Chieftain asked.

Sarika shot back, "To get a glass of *nuktar* before we leave. And to see if there is anything else we may need for our journey." The morning had been rough, and she figured a strong drink would help calm her nerves.

"Yes. Yes, of course, my dear. Tah'quhal, would you like one as well?"

Tah'quhal responded with a nod and watched as the Chieftain and Sarika disappeared into the cooking area. He glanced towards the bookshelf, his eyes landing on the tome that Chieftain Komipea was reading. Seizing the opportunity, he rushed to the shelf and began searching through the book.

He listened for the sound of nuktar being poured while he swiftly scanned through the tome. His gaze fell on a worn page near the middle of the book. Tah'quhal read the last paragraph, trying to cement it in his mind.

"To save Luminfae and realms beyond compare,
He'll face the trials, his destiny to bear.

With magic yet awakened and a brotherhood born, mend the pages from the tome once torn."

Closing the tome as quietly as he could, Tah'quhal reached towards the bookshelf just as Sarika rounded the corner, catching him red-handed as he put the book back on the shelf. Subtly, she slipped in front of their Chieftain, blocking his entrance to the study. She captured his attention as she expressed her gratitude for the beverage. Tah'quhal internally thanked her for the few extra seconds to slide the book home and appear to be nonchalantly gazing out the window.

Komipea moved into the room. "Upon entering the Anchor, you two will arrive at the Monton Farm. Find Johnathan Monton, Torvania's Keeper."

Tah'quhal's eyes widened. "I finally get to meet the great Keeper of Torvania?"

"Of course. Who else would help you find Derek Stratum?" The Chieftain asked. "Johnathan Monton and his family have protected the Anchor on the Earth side for many generations. They may even know Derek Stratum personally."

With one last attempt, Tah'quhal asked, "Is there anything else you can tell us before we leave?"

Komipea only shook his head in response. Tah'quhal could tell the Chieftain would not loosen his lips any further, so he nodded his head and walked towards the door. Sarika met him by the exit, the two fae giving thanks to Komipea before taking their leave.

On the way back to the Anchor, Sarika beseechingly asked, "That tome, did you find anything useful?"

Tah'quhal repeated the phrase he read inside Komipea's book but admitted, with great reluctance, that he had no idea what it could mean.

Sarika murmured under her breath, "With magic yet awakened, and a brotherhood born."

Confused as to what she was mumbling, Tah'quhal asked what she said, but Sarika only looked up with wide-eyed innocence.

"Oh, sorry! Just talking to myself."

Tah'quhal stared at her for a moment and then he shook his head, choosing to let it go. As he pushed ahead towards the Anchor, Sarika followed behind him, her lips tilted in a self-satisfied smile.

The once crowded streets of Torvania lay eerily empty. Despite looking like a graveyard, one name could be heard in the wind, whispered from the windows of fae homes:

"Malum."

The two fae stood in front of the Anchor, staring into each other's eyes. Although neither had ever imagined sharing this moment with another, they took comfort knowing they wouldn't have to face it alone. Even with his struggle to once again see her as nothing more than a friend, Tah'quhal would not have chosen another to do this alongside.

Just below the comfort, the confusion, there was a burning resentment inside Tah'quhal. This was meant to be his moment.

He crossed his arms and raised a smug eyebrow when Sarika asked,

"Are you ready for this, old friend?"

Without hesitation, Tah'quhal replied, "I was born ready, Sarika."

Sarika reached out for his hand, but Tah'quhal remained still, trying to prove to himself that he was worthy of this, even in the shared spotlight. She let her hand drop.

Tah'quhal took the first step towards the Anchor, a knot growing in his stomach. He looked back at Sarika and the grand towers of Torvania looming behind them. A fierce resolve settled between them as they inhaled deeply, relishing the sweet Torvanian air, and stepped forward into the depths of the Anchor.

Chapter 6

Worlds Converge

The air was crisp and fresh, carrying a scent of grass like none they had known in Torvania. They stood before the portal that had brought them here, its archway made of simple stones without any elaborate engravings or statues to guard it, like the one back home. The colors were mesmerizing, a blend of reds and oranges that seemed to pulse with life.

The fae pair now stood in a realm they had only heard tales of. As much as they wanted to explore, or at least take a moment to bask in this new experience, they knew their priority was to locate Johnathan Monton, who would hopefully lead them to Derek.

Sarika gripped Tah'quhal's arm and spoke, *"Invisibilium integumento."*

A shimmering blue haze formed around them, rendering them undetectable to the human eyes, even for those attuned to magic.

Following Chieftain Komipea's instructions, they proceeded towards the house nestled at the heart of the Monton farm. As they walked across the farm and to the Monton family home, Tah'quhal glanced at Sarika, struck by how much had changed in such a short time. Both in their world and between them. Uncomfortable with the silence, he attempted small talk,

"Sarika, the air here . . . it feels strange, does it not?"

She nodded absentmindedly in agreement. Tah'quhal thought it quite odd. Normally Sarika would jump at the chance of conversation with him, even after . . . everything. As the silence of the walk stretched on, he took the opportunity to admire Sarika's stigmata with envy. The skin artist that designed hers had claimed to have visited Earth many times. The artist had even mentioned the intricate designs were inspired by a human invention known as *lace*. Unfortunately, before anyone else could receive a stigmata from that artist, they vanished through the Anchor.

They approached the wooden manor, alarmed by the sight in front of them. There were clear signs that some kind of turmoil had recently happened. The windows were shattered and pieces of wood were scattered throughout the yard. There was no noise coming from the inside of the home, but the wind howling around them was nerve-wracking. Almost like a siren call. Bone chilling, yet the sense of adventure and danger felt inviting.

Sarika and Tah'quhal crept up the wooden steps of the home, their eyes alert and scanning the area, their ears twitching with every creak of the steps. As they reached the door, Sarika extended her arm out, gently pushing against it. The already ajar door squeaked as it opened, and the two fae stepped inside. The floorboards popped and cracked beneath their feet as they surveyed the carnage inside. Furniture was overturned, carpets and rugs singed by flame, and a deep red and blue dust had seeped into every corner of the house. Sarika forced the knot in her throat down as she realized that a fierce battle must have taken place here not long before they arrived.

Kneeling down and running her hand through the colored dust, she said, "This essence is everywhere. The red is similar to what consumed Tarik."

The two fae proceeded further into the living room, where fading light streamed in through the windows. Still seeing no sign of life, Tah'quhal cupped his hands around his mouth and shouted,

"Johnathan Monton? Is anyone here?" His voice rang off the wooden walls and burnt floors. He tried again, "Hello? Is there anyone home? Johnathan Monton?" But the only response was his own echo.

As they further explored the home, Tah'quhal peered inside a bedroom that sat just to the side of the living room, spotting a family portrait sitting atop the dresser. He grabbed the photo and went to find Sarika, who was standing in the kitchen holding a note in front of the broken table.

"John Jr., do not be scared. I have trained you for this day. I need to find some friends, and then I will meet you back here and together we will visit Komipea. This isn't how I imagined your first trip into the fourth dimension going, but it is the cards we have been dealt."

Tah'quhal held up the picture and asked, "Is this boy John Jr., perhaps?"

Sarika's eyes studied the photo for a moment before she replied, "Perhaps, and judging by this letter, he may have claimed the title of Keeper from his father."

"What could have happened here to frighten a Keeper, and what could it mean that Johnathan Monton is ready to turn to Komipea?" Tah'quhal asked.

Sarika stiffened, her gaze turning uncharacteristically icy. "Focus." she snapped, her voice as cold as her stare. "The only thing that matters right *now* is finding Derek Stratum!"

Tah'quhal stared at his friend, but did not utter a word. His mind rationalized why she was acting so out of character. After all, her brother had just vanished right before them. She's entitled to feel a little on edge. He finally nodded his head in agreement and motioned towards the door.

The pair of fae stepped outside the home, their eyes sweeping over the rolling green hills and patchwork of fields that stretched endlessly before them. A distant, lowing sound carried on the breeze, a curious, deep bellow that echoed through the farmland.

Sarika pointed to the north side of the farm, saying, "I think the school is that way."

Again, Tah'quhal locked his stare on her. "Sarika, how do you know that?"

She was saved from answering by a trail of red mist zooming through the sky.

Tah'quhal started to run towards the trail, but Sarika put her hand into his chest, saying, "This will be faster."

She raised her hand, speaking a quick incantation, and in a flash of light, essence surrounded them. The incantation propelled them from the ground, toward Riverrun High, while a comet-like tail of blue followed behind them.

The sudden screech of tires on asphalt snapped Tah'quhal's attention to the road below. A truck had come to an abrupt halt, and through the windshield, he saw a young man gripping the steering wheel, eyes scanning the scene. Tah'quhal squinted, heart pounding——he recognized this human. It was Derek Stratum!

Tah'quhal signaled to Sarika, pointing out the stopped vehicle. The two descended behind a row of trees, their training making them cautious, despite their invisibility.

Sarika squinted her eyes. "Is that Derek Stratum driving the wheeled machine?"

"I believe so," Tah'quhal replied as he watched Derek gawk in shock.

Tah'quhal placed his hand on Sarika's shoulder. "Do you believe he saw us?"

Sarika bit her lip, her heartbeat steadying as Tah'quhal's touch sent a ripple of calm through her. Words of apology hovered on the tip of her tongue, but she swallowed them. His earlier insistence on pausing their relationship during the ritual echoed in her mind. If he wanted to create distance, then she would match his resolve.

"There is no way he saw us." She answered, while pulling her shoulder away from him.

Derek started driving again, and the two fae followed after him.

Sarika soared into the sky once more, with Tah'quhal close behind. They kept a careful distance, ensuring Derek couldn't see the essence propelling them forward.

They followed him to a marketplace and landed on the far side of the parking lot. Sarika shot her arm out, stopping Tah'quhal from approaching Derek.

"Easy, there are too many humans around."

As Derek said hello to his friends, Sarika pointed to one of them. "That boy with the stigmata on the back of his neck, is that the John Jr. from the photo?"

When Tah'quhal did not answer, she nudged his shoulder to get his attention.

"Sorry, I was focused on that other one. Look at his eye. It is two different colors and essence dances around him. I've never seen these humans in Torvania before," he replied.

Before they could continue their discussion, Tah'quhal felt a chill run through him. He turned to look at the entrance to the market and caught a glimpse of red mist seeping from the doors. His instincts screamed that this was connected to the destruction at the Monton family home and, without warning, he grabbed Sarika's arm and charged into the store. He had expected to confront something sinister, but what he saw was far worse than what his imagination could conjure.

Tah'quhal stood frozen in shock, watching in horror as a fog-shrouded Tarik swirled around an elderly man. He could hear his friend's voice hissing to the human,

"Ahhh, Mr. Prudence, today marks your first day as principal. Just imagine how many young minds we can shape to accomplish our ambition."

Sarika stared at her brother, the grief in her eyes evident. The person before her was a disfigured version of her brother, nothing like the one she had loved her whole life.

As Tarik's corrupted form continued circling the human, Tah'quhal warned, "Sarika, I fear that is no longer your brother."

"What do you mean? I can see him right there! Evil magic may have changed him, but that is still my brother!" She bit out.

They silently stared at each other, communicating everything and nothing. Sarika broke eye contact first, swiping a single tear from her cheek. She couldn't admit that Tah'quhal may be right, and he wasn't willing to let whatever had become of Tarik put a stop to his ritual.

Tah'quhal gave a nod to Sarika. Despite the ache of reluctance in her heart, she returned it with a reassuring nod of her own.

He approached Tarik and called out his name. Tarik's neck whipped around at a nearly unnatural angle, eyes narrowed into slits, before launching himself at Tah'quhal. Tarik's arms began shimmering with a thin mist that quickly thickened and solidified into dark red, oily tendrils. The grotesque points lashed out at Tah'quhal's face with razor-sharp tips, leaving a deep gouge in its wake. Tah'quhal stumbled back, his hand clutching at the fresh wound on his cheek. His skin throbbed with every heartbeat, each pulse sending another wave of discomfort through his body.

Watching her friend and brother fight, Sarika finally came to her senses. Her reflexes kicked in and her eyes began to glow a brilliant shade of purple. The icy blue hue of her hair intensified as she spoke a single, authoritative word:

"Enough."

With a flick of her wrist, an intense gust of wind burst forth from her palms, the force of which sent Tarik flying out of the market and onto the pavement outside.

Tah'quhal carefully wiped the blood from his face and stared at Sarika in awe. No incantation was said, yet she performed that magic perfectly. She had no stigmata representing elemental magic. Not even a week ago, she was his mate. He should have known if she was capable of this.

The customers in the store looked around and chalked the door swinging open to another windy day. All except one who watched the quick dispute from behind one of the store aisles. John Jr. quickly took a picture of Tah'quhal and Sarika on his phone before running up to the counter and buying a biscuit as the two fae walked towards the door.

Before Tah'quhal could question Sarika about her exceptional use of magic, their attention zeroed in on Derek's prostrate form. He must have been knocked to the ground when Tarik flew out of the door.

Tah'quhal shifted his gaze to Tarik, who was standing over Derek. He sprinted forward, arms outstretched to try to grab his *friend*, but by the time he reached him, only a faint trace of red essence remained.

Tah'quhal's eyes narrowed, fiery intensity flickering within them. His gaze shifted sharply from Derek to Sarika.

"We need to show him!" he growled, his voice edged with impatience.

Sarika, more worried about her brother at the moment, said, "No, now is not the time."

Tah'quhal turned to look at Derek, but instead, his eyes met the gaze of the one he believed was named Trey. For a split second, he felt as though Trey truly saw him. Sarika acted quickly, grabbing his arm with one hand and speaking an incantation as she gestured with the other.

The two fae were ushered up into the sky again. They could see a trail of the ominous red essence levitating in front of them. Knowing it had to be from Tarik, they took off in pursuit, heading towards Riverrun High.

Chapter 7

Full Circle

Tah'quhal and Sarika soared through the skies, their hearts heavy with what they had witnessed. They had to catch up to Tarik——a brother to one, a lifelong friend to the other. But now, they weren't sure who he had become. Was he still the Tarik they knew and loved, or had something darker irrevocably taken hold of him?

The trail of red essence grew thicker and thicker until they spotted Tarik flying in front of them. Tah'quhal's hand crackled with raw energy, a burgeoning fireball hovering just above his palm. His eyes never left Tarik's silhouette, but his heart wavered with every beat.

The fireball flickered, mirroring his hesitation. His breath hitched, and he clenched his jaw, feeling the weight of what he was about to do. Memories of shared laughter and unbreakable bonds flashed through his mind, each one a sharp pang against his resolve.

As they raced through the skies, the wind howled around him, a cacophony of doubt and duty. Tah'quhal's fist closed, the heat of the fireball intensifying in his palm.

His lips parted, but the words caught in his throat.

"*Ignis Gratis*," he whispered, the incantation leaden in his mouth.

The fireball erupted from his hand, flying straight for Tarik.

In a panic, Sarika whispered her own incantation, "*Ventorum Erinnys*," summoning a fierce gust of wind that not only extinguished the flames, but sent Tarik spiraling towards the Earth.

Tarik's body hit the ground with a loud thud, creating a cloud of red mist upon impact. The other two fae landed in front of him, but it was Sarika who stepped towards Tarik first, swirling her arms around in a graceful yet powerful manner.

Tarik rose to his feet, running his hands over his robes, knocking the dust and debris off. He raised his head just slightly, one corner of his mouth curling up.

"Nice try, *sister*. Maybe next time you will actually finish me off."

Sarika raised her arms in front of her face, her stigmata beginning to glow and her palms facing forward.

"Tarik! What exactly are you trying to achieve?"

No answer came from him, only a twisted smile that seemed to echo his corrupted nature.

Tah'quhal once again shouted his spell and flames flew towards Tarik. Just as before, Sarika stifled his flames with a spell of her own. With a laugh edged with darkness, Tarik turned his gaze to Riverrun High. With a swift clap of his hands, he disappeared into a burst of deep burgundy mist. A haunting whisper could be heard as he vanished.

"See you soon, *sister*."

Tah'quhal's voice boomed with anger in the open field, "What the hell was that, Sarika? My flames would have put an end to this madness!"

Sarika stood her ground, her eyes blazing. "You may have decided he is *your* enemy, but he is still *my* brother, you fool!" she hissed.

The tension crackled between them. Locked in an intense stare down, Tah'quhal shuttered. No longer able to maintain his composure, he lashed out as flames sprung forth from hands. Sarika quickly and elegantly danced around the incoming fire and sent gusts of wind flying towards him. Once again, the two fae stared each other down.

"If you are so concerned with helping Tarik, then why did you not try to reason with him . . . or capture him?" Tah'quhal demanded.

Sarika whispered, "He is and always will be my brother. I do not wish to see him harmed."

"Dammit! Then why not try to stop him before he does whatever he is here to do? We could have taken him home and let Komipea help us figure out how to reverse this corruption." Tah'quhal begged.

Sarika offered no response. She only turned away from him and faced the direction of Riverrun High.

Tah'quhal realized his anger was getting him nowhere. He took a long breath and put his hands down to his side. "Sari, please . . . tell me what is going on?"

Her eyes watered, and she bit her bottom lip to keep from making a sound. She thought back to the first time he had ever called her that—— the first night they spent together. The gentle way his voice whispered it just now almost cracked her resolve, but she was determined to not let him in. Steeling her nerves, she crossed her arms and continued to stare towards the school.

Tah'quhal reached his hand to touch her shoulder, but seeing her cross her arms, he let it fall back down to his side.

With a sigh, he said, "Fine. Do not provide an answer. Let us find Derek Stratum, and then we will deal with whatever this is." His attempt at a firm voice fell short, tinged with pain from the walls she was building.

Tah'quhal's instincts were screaming at him all day, warning him that something was terribly wrong with Sarika. Something more than her brother. The tense way she held herself, her eyes full of barely contained rage——it was like a gathering storm.

"We have to find Derek Stratum." He whispered under his breath.

He had to remind himself of the one reason they had come to Earth. Pushing aside his worries, he motioned towards the looming school building and watched as Sarika moved towards it silently. Even still, he couldn't shake the feeling that their partnership . . . their relationship . . . their friendship was falling apart. He had no choice but to stick by her side for now, even as the tension between them threatened to crack into a dangerous rift.

As they approached Riverrun High, Sarika's stigmata glowed. She glanced down at her hands to be sure her invisibility incantation was still active, and after seeing that it was, continued inside the school building.

They scoured the school for Derek, but they only found faint traces of red essence littered around the halls. After an hour of searching, they heard a loud bang. Glancing quickly at each other, they took off after it. They turned a corner to find Derek and his friends. Trey was pulling his fist away from a dented locker and they were astonished that both blue and red essence emanated from his knuckles.

"Did you see that?" asked Tah'quhal.

Sarika placed a single finger over her lips, reminding him to stay quiet.

His target so close in front of him, Tah'quhal could not hold his tongue. "We can not delay any longer!"

But Sarika, with her usual level-headedness, countered him calmly.

"We must wait. There are too many people around and too many questions without answers. We need to find a moment when he's alone."

Despite his frustrations with her, Tah'quhal had to admit that Sarika was right. They decided to wait in the hallway, keeping an eye out for a chance to intercept Derek when he was on his own. Tah'quhal was aware that Sarika always had a plan in motion, but as they stood together in the hallways, he couldn't help but wonder about her true motives. The thought lingered in his mind, distracting him from their current situation.

Guilt settled into his stomach from the doubts creeping into his mind. Their bond had been forged through years of training together, deepened still by the nights he spent alone with Sarika. Memories of breaking rules set by their Chieftain flooded back. He would tag along for some of Tarik's mischief, like using magic to light animal feces on fire before making it hover onto an unsuspecting fae's doorstep. No matter what, Sarika was always there to bail them out, and when he and Sarika would sneak out to the creek after long days of training to be alone, Tarik would always cover for them.

Even so, as they waited for their chance to approach Derek, Tah'quhal could not shake the feeling that something was off. Sarika was cold and distant, ready to snap at a moment's notice. Tarik . . . he couldn't even comprehend what was going on with Tarik.

To add fuel to the fire, Earth was nothing like he expected, or like the stories he was told. There was not supposed to be magic in abundance here; his entire belief system was being challenged. In Torvania, magic was plentiful. Not every fae used it, but they had access. Earth was supposed to be different. Only a few humans should have access, but they had witnessed essence swarming numerous people since arriving. Was the foundation of what he thought he knew a lie?

Knowing he would get no answers now, he exhaled slowly and deliberately, clearing his mind and honing in on the task ahead. Everyone back home was counting on him. He had trained his whole life to come to Earth. He was a direct descendant of the great Torviid. Failure was *not* an option for him.

From the safety of the shadows, Tah'quhal watched with keen eyes as both teachers and students bustled by, oblivious to the two fae standing among them. The illusion spell was performing flawlessly, keeping their true identities hidden from prying eyes. As they waited, they observed the steady stream of students all making their way towards the gymnasium, like tiny ants following a predetermined path. They quickly devised a plan. If all the humans were going to the gym, then at some point they all must come out. Their target, Derek, would soon leave the gymnasium and walk directly towards them.

Anticipation coiled in their stomachs as they positioned themselves at the end of the hallway, ready for a clear view of their mark. The boy that turned the corner, however, was not Derek.

Ivan strutted down the hallway, oozing confidence until he was abruptly halted by an enraged Trey waiting across the corridor. With lightning speed, Trey lunged at Ivan and slammed him into the wall.

"What the hell are you doing here, Ivan?" Trey demanded.

"Oh, ya know, just coming to see my favorite little brother and my lovely new girlfriend," Ivan retorted.

Trey gripped Ivan's shirt tighter, slamming him into the wall. "We may be brothers, but you are going to leave Izzy alone!"

"Awe, is little Trey upset?" Ivan joked.

"Shut up!" Trey shouted. "Shut up, shut up, shut up! You're not supposed to be here!"

Ivan mocked Trey with a smirk. "Doesn't your mommy always tell us to play nice?"

At that, Trey snapped, unleashing a brutal attack on Ivan that the latter was all too eager to return.

As the two brothers clashed, Tah'quhal and Sarika noticed Derek sprinting through the connecting hallway they had anticipated him coming down. Sarika began revealing herself to keep Derek from getting entangled in the brawl.

However, Tah'quhal's tactical training had kicked in. The possible intel was too valuable for Sarika to reveal herself now.

"Let us see how this plays out," he said.

"You have been wanting to reveal ourselves to Derek Stratum every time we are close to him, but now you want to stop me?" Sarika hushedly asked.

"Our mission is changing every step of the way, Sarika. There should not be this many attuned humans. I want to see what happens before we——"

Derek crashed into the wall next to them. The two fae gasped and, once again, Sarika attempted to intervene, but another student came darting down the hallway. Tah'quhal noticed the stigmata on

her wrist and knew it meant she was attuned. Although he did not recognize this human, he called out,

"Young lady! Help him!"

Mia, upon seeing the spectral image of Tah'quhal, grew startled and fled towards the parking lot, her blurred figure slipping through the doorway.

In response, Ivan let out a primal roar that echoed off the walls and sent a shockwave of crimson mist billowing outwards like a stormy cloud. The air pulsed with power and tension, as if the very fabric of reality was being shaken by the force of his anger.

Sarika made one last attempt to reach Derek, who had curled into a ball on the ground.

"We can't hide any longer. It's time to reveal ourselves," she urged.

But just as she spoke, another student burst into the hall-way——John Jr., the only one they still needed to find. Before they could dispel their concealment incantation, John knelt down next to Derek and muttered a few words, causing them to both vanish in a bright purple mist.

Tah'quhal kicked the locker closest to him. "Dammit!"

"We will find them again," Sarika said with confidence.

Tah'quhal turned to Sarika with a sense of urgency in his voice, "What's our next move?"

Trey staggered back onto his feet, his eyes glaring at them like daggers.

"Sarika, I think he can see us."

Trey stormed towards them, his voice laced with anger and disdain.

"I can see you both perfectly fine," he spat, "and I know exactly why you're here. What I don't understand is why you didn't lift a finger to help Derek when he needed it."

Tah'quhal opened his mouth to speak, but Trey wouldn't let him.

"It doesn't matter now. We're running out of time. Find Derek, find Johnathan, and save my friends before it's too late!" His eyes burned with urgency as he pleaded with them. "Go. Get them to safety!"

To Tah'quhal and Sarika's astonishment, Trey pointed his two trembling ring fingers at the ground, vanishing into a haze of blue and red essence. What kind of power did this human possess? But there was no time to ponder, for Trey had warned them that time was running out. With their hearts racing, they made haste to leave the school and find Johnathan and Derek. Clearly, there was more going on here on Earth than anyone in Torvania knew about.

As they emerged from the brick walls of the school, Tah'quhal's footsteps stuttered. He pointed to the skies, trying to show Sarika the drastic change. The once vivid blue was now tinged with a dullness that seemed to press down against their spirits. Even the fluffy cumulus clouds overhead bore a reddish hue, casting an eerie glow over the landscape below. Sarika thrust her hand towards the distant Monton Family Farm, uttering ancient incantations under her breath. In an instant, the two were soaring through the air, propelled by their magic and heading back to where they began.

Chapter 8

Explanations

Johnathan sat on the unforgiving wooden floor, his legs stretched out before him as he leaned against the bedroom wall. The chill of the floor crept through his clothes, and his grip tightened around the crumpled note, his father's words of warning etched deep into his mind. His eyes drifted to Derek, who lay sprawled on the bed, motionless except for the steady rise and fall of his chest. Then, something caught his eye——a brief flicker, a glint of light on Derek's wrist. Johnathan squinted, tilting his head slightly, his breath hitching as he thought, *what on Earth was that?*

He leaned forward, trying to get a better look at the light, before cautiously crawling towards the bed. He watched in awe as the light danced around Derek's arm. A small but bright white orb spun faster and faster around his friend's limb. And then it stopped. The light shifted to a brilliant blue, then a dark red, before settling into a solid white band around his wrist.

John touched his own neck, running his rough hand over his stigmata. His head spun. Derek wasn't attuned and knew nothing of magic, but after the day they were having, anything was possible. His thoughts jumped to the destruction of his home. He wiped the back of his hand across his eyes, leaving them wet with tears he didn't realize he had shed.

"It sure would be nice if dad was here right now," he thought to himself as he glanced back down at the note.

John's eyes remained fixed on the letter, his mind racing as he desperately searched for any answers that could be hidden in the chicken scratch. An unknown sound pierced through the stillness of his home, interrupting his train of thought. The noise seemed to come from the sky above, adding another layer of confusion and unease to John's already troubled mind.

He rushed to the closest window, scanning for any potential threat. His eyes landed on two fae beings descending from above. A familiar, blue haze surrounded their feet, and for a fleeting moment, he thought he saw it change to red——just like the band that had appeared on Derek's arm. It shifted back to blue too quickly for him to be sure. John's heart raced as he hurried to his closet and retrieved his Keeper staff, a powerful object that enhanced one's magical abilities.

As Johnathan rushed to his front door, staff in hand, he heard someone shout out a commanding phrase.

"Scutum Bulla!"

An almost transparent bubble formed around the house. John's heart stuttered, his hands slick with sweat. He recognized the incantation and knew it would prevent him from magically whisking Derek and himself away again. Little did he know, the two fae had only summoned the magical barrier to prevent Derek and himself from leaving without speaking to them first. Johnathan, fueled by his desire to protect his home and his best friend, assumed the strangers had malicious intent. He burst through the door, gripping his staff tightly, despite the shake in his arms. He confronted the two fae with a stout warning,

"This is my home, and it is my duty to protect it. I advise ya'll to leave before I'm forced to do something I'd *really* rather not!"

Sarika, sensing the tension, cautiously started to approach to introduce herself, but Johnathan interrupted her, his tone laced with suspicion.

"Don't take another step, damn it! I'm warning ya'll."

Growing increasingly impatient, Tah'quhal pushed past Sarika, growling, "Look here——"

"*Aqua, ventus et glacies!*" Johnathan shouted, a torrent of water surging from his staff.

The wave crashed into Tah'quhal, knocking him to the ground and freezing around him, effectively restraining him. Wind intensified around Sarika, sucking the oxygen from the air.

Water spewed from his mouth as Tah'quhal pleaded with Johnathan, "We mean no harm! Please release the spell!"

Johnathan, still wary, retorted, "Who the hell are ya'll, and what do you want?"

Sarika tried to speak, but nothing would come out. She clawed at her throat as the gusts around her sucked the air out of her lungs. She fell to her knees, turning her head back to Tah'quhal, her eyes begging for help.

Spitting out the last bit of water, Tah'quhal shouted with desperation, "Derek Stratum is our companion."

Upon hearing this, Johnathan swiftly lowered his staff, but his grip tightened around the handle. He felt a lump in his stomach, almost like it was trying to fight its way up his throat. He was well versed in magic, but had never had to use it offensively before. It was a feeling he was sure he did not enjoy.

The ice surrounding Tah'quhal melted away, and the wind gradually subsided to a gentle breeze. Cautiously and with a forced swallow to push the lump in his throat back down, Johnathan approached the fae, asking them to lower the barrier to prove their intent. Tah'quhal complied, gradually reducing the size of the shield. He and Sarika then introduced themselves and briefed Johnathan on the events surrounding the Atunkmae Ritual.

Relieved and more understanding, John agreed to allow them to come inside. Tah'quhal joked about having already been inside, but Johnathan cut him a glare, finding little humor given the state his home was in.

Johnathan ushered the two fae into the house and led them to the living room as Sarika asked, "Where is Derek Stratum?"

With a nod of his head, Johnathan directed her towards the bedroom. "He's still unconscious from the fight at school between Ivan and . . . Trey." A hint of worry tinged his voice as he realized he had left Trey lying in the hallway.

Hearing the pain in Johnathan's voice, Sarika asked, "This human Trey, did you know of his ties to magic?"

John just looked down at the ground, unsure of how to respond. He was supposed to be the next great Keeper of the Anchor. How could he not know Trey was attuned? Even after all these years of training, he had been oblivious to one of his closest friends' knowledge of magic. His understanding of the magical world seemed to be less comprehensive than he had believed. Looking back up, but keeping his eyes from meeting Sarika's, he could only offer a single word as a response.

"No."

The noise of the voices around him gradually pulled Derek from the recesses of unconsciousness. He could hear a conversation coming from the other side of the door. Johnathan's voice wasn't a surprise, but the other two were also oddly familiar. Trying to open his eyes, he was reminded of the throbbing pain in his head from the shockwave at school. Groaning, he gritted his teeth through the pain and stood up, feeling weak and grabbing the bed to steady himself.

He strained to focus on the voices swirling around him. One was soft and elegant, like a gentle breeze rustling through silk curtains. The other was low and rough, reminding him of a military commander. And then there was Johnathan's voice, familiar yet, after the events of the day, not exactly comforting. Memories flooded back of the disembodied voices he had heard all day, the ones that made him question his sanity, the ones Johnathan claimed not to hear. But now, those same voices were having a conversation with Johnathan right on the other side of the door.

As he stumbled towards the door, his mind and body fought against each other. His head throbbed with pain and the strange blue haze from before danced around him, reminding him just how completely his world had spun out of control. He fought between the urge to lay back down out of fear and exhaustion and the curiosity that urged him to see what lay beyond that door.

Curiosity winning out in the end, he cautiously approached the door and pressed his ear against it. Derek could make out bits of the conversation, as one of the unfamiliar voices said,

"There was a girl before you arrived. She ran away quickly when she saw us. She had a stigmata on her wrist, so we knew she was attuned, but we don't recognize her from Torvania."

Johnathan asked, "Do y'all recognize all humans who go to Torvania?"

The deep voice responded, "Not necessarily, and if today has shown us anything, it's that there is much we may not know or recognize."

After a brief pause, Johnathan asked, "Did the girl have brown hair witha' bit of pink mixed in?"

The smooth voice replied, "Yes!"

When Derek heard this, he pushed open the door and blurted, "Mia!"

As the door swung open, his brain felt like it was short circuiting at the sight before him. There was Johnathan, holding a long stick with an intricately carved dragon head at the top, looking awkward and out of place.

Derek's gaze shifted to the two other beings in the room. He rubbed his eyes, struggling to comprehend the sight before him. The tallest of the two loomed over everyone, a black beard and long hair framing a face that exuded a menacing aura. Beside him stood a woman with a stunning silhouette and eyes that radiated calmness, a stark contrast to the other.

Both figures bore intricate blue tattoos that seemed to pulse with an otherworldly glow. But it was their pointed ears that truly caught Derek's breath. He blinked, his mind racing. If not for the ink and ears, they might have passed as taller than average humans.

Derek's legs buckled and caught himself on the doorframe, his heart pounding like a war drum. A strange heat surged through his body, intensifying with every heartbeat. His vision blurred as the room around him was bathed in a brilliant white light. Johnathan and the two fae stood frozen, their eyes wide with awe and confusion.

Derek's forearms tingled, the sensation growing with the burning heat. He looked down at his arms. Glowing white bands appeared on his skin, their light pulsating in rhythm with his racing heart. The room seemed to hum with energy, the air thick with an otherworldly presence.

The sight of the glowing bands on his arms filled Derek with a mix of panic and amazement. He could feel power coursing through him, but had no idea what it was.

Johnathan couldn't take his eyes off the incredible scene in front of him. Despite encountering various forms of magic in his short life, nothing had ever been as breathtaking as this. Sarika's piercing stare was fixed on Derek, almost as if she were expecting something else to happen. Tah'quhal slowly approached Derek, reaching a hand out to steady him. Derek was still too stunned to react, but as soon as Tah'quhal's hand made contact with Derek's skin, his blue markings began to glow with the same brilliant white light.

For a moment, all of Tah'quhal's fear, arrogance, and confusion faded. He felt . . . at peace, a feeling he hadn't experienced in a very long time. As Derek finally realized the glowing light was coming from his own arms, he panicked and jerked away from Tah'quhal, falling to the ground. The light slowly dimmed, before completely disappearing from his arms, Tah'quhal's stigmata returning to their usual blue hue.

Startled at the sensation touching Derek's arm gave him, Tah'quhal shouted, "What was that magic Derek Stratum? What did you just do?"

"Who the hell . . . *what* the hell are you?" Derek replied.

As Derek's fight-or-flight response kicked in, he desperately tried to scramble towards the front door of Johnathan's house. Sarika and

John quickly blocked his path, leaving him feeling trapped like a dog in a kennel.

Johnathan knelt down beside him. "Please buddy, listen to what they have to say."

Fear and confusion pulsed through Derek's body, but beneath that was anger——anger with his friend for the lies. Anger that overshadowed his fear, causing him to nod his head yes, so he could *finally* get some answers. He locked eyes with John, silently demanding an explanation.

Johnathan sighed and stood up, offering his hand to Derek.

"Come on, follow me. I reckon it's time we talk." Casting a pointed glance at the two fae, "Y'all give us a minute and just stay put, would ya?"

As they made their way towards the Anchor, Johnathan unraveled the mysteries of the fae world.

"I hate that I had to keep a secret like this," Johnathan whispered.

"Like what, John?" Derek questioned.

John sighed and dropped his shoulders as they walked. "Magic is all around us, buddy. Earth is a pretty cool place, but it ain't nothing like all them other dimensions out there." John paused and patted Derek on the back as he grinned. "Well, I mean, I ain't ever been to any, but I know all about 'em!"

Derek stopped walking, his eyes studying his best friend's face, half waiting for his other friends to jump out of the trees and explain the prank to him. When no one came out laughing, he asked, "What do you mean *magic* and *dimensions*?"

John continued, "Magic, Diamond! Here, watch this."

John spun his staff with a swift, practiced motion, pointing its tip toward the ground. Instantly, the grass swayed as if caught in a gentle breeze, and rocks lifted from the earth, defying gravity. A blue haze seeped from the ground, swirling and dancing in the air, tracing the movements of John's staff with grace.

With every swipe of his staff, John could feel that knot in his stomach tighten. While he showed off, he couldn't make eye contact with Derek, afraid that his best friend would be furious with him for keeping all of this a secret for so long.

Derek stood frozen, his chest squeezing. It felt like a panic attack trying to rear its ugly head, but this was different, it was almost good. He watched the magic escape from John's staff. Derek wanted to be angry. He wanted to shout at his friend, his best friend, for never showing him any of this before. Instead, he felt his knees get weak. He wasn't mad; he was *relieved*, excited even. At last,things actually made sense. His lip quivered, eyes welling with tears. A quiet sniffle escaped him as he took a tentative step toward John.

"You mean I'm not going crazy?" he whispered, his voice trembling with a mix of hope and disbelief.

Johnathan lowered his staff and slowly turned around, seeing the tears in his friend's eyes. "Ya . . . ya ain't mad?"

"Mad? John, how could I be mad? I thought I was a few hours away from a padded wall vacation!"

John ran to him and wrapped his arms around Derek, "Naw buddy! You just didn't know."

After a moment, Derek stepped back from his friend's hug. "Okay, what was the white light coming from my arms?" He looked down to see the white bands, although not glowing, were still present on his skin. "And why does it look like I visited a tattoo parlor while unconscious?"

John laughed, relieved things were good enough between them that he was cracking jokes. "Well now . . . I ain't quite sure why you have it, but it's sorta like the mark on my neck. It's called a stigmata."

"A Stigwhata?" Derek asked.

"It's a magical mark. Ya normally get one when ya master a set of magic, and it's normally applied by another master of magic or a tattoo artist. Yours just sorta appeared, and that *is* weird."

Derek twisted his arms back and forth, taking note that there was one band on each arm, just about where a watch would sit, that wrapped all the way around. Still staring at his arms, he said, "Of course it's weird. It's me we are talking about here. What else can you tell me?"

"How about I show ya," John replied as he pointed towards the stone archway in front of them.

Derek looked up to see the intricately set stones. In the middle of the archway there were vivid reds and oranges swirling in fluid movements. Again he stood in amazement, asking, "What is that?"

John answered, "That is the Anchor. It is a gateway to Torvania in the fourth dimension."

"See, you keep mentioning that. What the hell do you mean by other dimensions?" Derek asked.

John's smile grew ear to ear, "Well ya got, the Start, Mythos, Torvania, and countless others, all of 'em waiting to be explored! I could tell you all the stories I have heard, but we'd be here for weeks. I know it's a lot to take in, but just give it some time. You're gunna love it!"

Derek's eyes were fixed on the Anchor, his mind telling him to step towards it, but he resisted as he asked, "How do you know all of this, John?"

"Oh, now that's a good question. Ya see, this property has been in my family for ages. When they moved in and found this arch, they saw a fae Chieftain come out of it."

"Hold up. What is a fae?" Derek asked.

"That's who was in my house. Hello, pointed ears? Well, not the same one my ancestor's saw, but the same kinda creature. Anyway, that Chieftain gave my great, great, however many greats, grandpa this very staff."

Derek looked at the staff as John held it up. John twirled it a couple of times and then continued on, "The fae told 'em of this really bad guy named Malum, and how they thought it was important to prepare other dimensions for threats like him. They came up with a plan for my family to forever protect the Anchor from the Earth's side and in exchange, they would teach them how to wield magic."

Derek took a couple steps towards the Anchor, finally giving in to what his mind was telling him.

"So I can go through this, and I will be in a land of magic?" He asked as he reached his hand for the portal.

Johnathan cautioned Derek, "Woah! Easy there, buddy. You might've gotten those fancy white bands earlier, but you ain't prepared for a journey like that just yet. Hell, I ain't even been."

Derek put his arms down to his side and took a step back. His mind swirled with the overwhelming amount of information, but at the same time, he felt comfort in his friend's words. The dream he had every night jumped to the front of his mind, and he blurted out,

"To bridge the gap, unite the world's divide. With courage, he'll mend what's torn inside."

John looked at him with one eyebrow raised. "What did you just say?"

Derek hesitated. He did not want to mention his dream, but he figured now was as good a time as any. "John. I have had a recurring dream for as long as I can remember. At the end of it, I hear those words and get surrounded by fire. Then I wake up covered in sweat. Do you think that could have any relation to this magic stuff?"

"I feel like I've heard those words before, but I can't quite place them. Maybe the fae can help?"

Derek nodded his head in uneasy agreement. He was willing to talk with the fae, even if he still wasn't quite sure what exactly they were. He took a step towards his friend's home, but Johnathan stopped him.

"One more thing, buddy. What happened at school earlier, with Trey and Ivan . . . I ain't sure if it connects to you, but I've never seen magic practiced so openly, or white magic like what happened to your arms. But I *will* help you figure all of this out, alright?"

Derek smiled softly at his friend's words, at the reassurance that he was just as confused. The two made their way back to the Monton home, filled with a longing for explanations, eager for new possibilities, and fearful of what the outcome may be.

Chapter 9

Remorse

Derek and John walked into the house to find two very impatient fae. Still slightly surprised by their otherworldly appearance, Derek cautiously extended his hand towards Tah'quhal. The imposing fae gave his hand a firm shake, causing Derek's arms to emit a bright white light once again. However, this time it was different——he was fully aware of what was happening and could sense Tah'quhal's emotions through the physical connection.

Derek shuttered at the overwhelming aura of fear and uncertainty emanating from the fae.

He met Tah'quhal's gaze and asked, "What are you scared of?"

Confused, Tah'quhal dropped Derek's hand. Derek then held out his hand to Sarika, but she brushed past it and wrapped her arms around him in an embrace. As her warmth enveloped him, a sense of relief came over him, but it soon became clear that she had put up walls, walls he had no idea how to see behind. His magic was still too new for him to understand how to use it. At that moment, he caught the faint scent of lavender in the air.

Stepping away from him, Sarika looked into Derek's eyes. They were returning to their normal blue color after being a bright white just moments before.

She could see the confusion in his expression. "What's wrong, Derek?"

His response was hesitant as he said, "I can smell lavender . . . I smelled it earlier on——"

The house shook violently, causing everyone to grab onto anything stable for support. The walls creaked and objects fell from shelves as a deafening boom echoed through the house.

"Could this dadgum day get any worse?" Johnathan yelled over the persistent thunder.

Everything stopped, leaving behind an eerie stillness. Johnathan rushed to the back windows, pressing his face against the glass to survey the outside. Tah'quhal darted out the front door to investigate. Sarika and Derek hurried to peer out Johnathan's bedroom windows.

Derek tried to peek out his window, but he couldn't take his eyes off Sarika as she stared out of hers. Something about her was captivating——he wasn't sure if it was her otherworldly presence or her impossible beauty, with her unnaturally soothing voice, flawless skin, and hypnotic purple eyes. An awkward smile grew on his face as he thought to himself, *"Her eyes are basically the color of lavender. Mia would get a kick out of that."*

He could faintly remember her showing up in the hallway when Trey and Ivan were fighting. Guilt twinged in his gut for admiring Sarika. Even though there was nothing going on between him and Mia, he really wanted there to be something.

He asked Sarika, "I heard you and Taco . . . Tahque . . . uh, Tah'quhal talking about Mia earlier. Where is she? Is she okay?"

Sarika turned to face Derek. Her gentle voice became even more soothing as she explained everything they had witnessed at the school. Even the air around them seemed to regain its freshness as she finished her story,

"And then Johnathan Monton Jr. came running to your——"

Another ear-splitting roar shook the house. Johnathan's panicked voice rang out,

"Get down y'all!"

Sarika turned back to her window, her muscles tensing as she saw the sky transform into a menacing shade of blood red. There was a deafening crash as Tah'quhal burst through the living room wall with an earth-shattering force. Wooden shards flew through the air like deadly missiles as he landed on his back amidst the rubble. Derek, Johnathan, and Sarika frantically rushed to his side, their eyes alternating between scanning him for injuries and trying to peer through the gaping hole in the home.

After the debris settled, Sarika squinted through the dim light to see a daunting silhouette standing in the yard in front of the house.

She took a step forward and demanded, "Who are you?"

A sinister cackle filled the air before a cold voice replied, "How sad that you can't even recognize your own twin, dear sister."

A thick cloud of dust swirled around the figure ahead, dissipating to reveal none other than Tarik. In his grip were chains attached to two familiar figures——Mia and Izzy! A piece of bent metal covered each of their mouths.

Derek's blood boiled at the sight, his body trembling with fury. Before he could second guess himself, he charged towards the twisted fae. Feeling emboldened by his new magic, he flung both arms forward——honestly unsure of what exactly to do. Brilliant white light crackled from his outstretched arms, but Tarik only chuckled in response. With a swift motion of his free hand, he sent Derek hurtling through the air, crashing onto the ground with a deafening thud. Tah'quhal leaped to his companion's aid, ready to defend him against an old friend turned fiend.

"Let the girls go!" Johnathan's voice boomed.

Tarik only smirked in response and pulled on the chain, forcing the girls to their knees, their muffled cries ringing in Derek's ears.

Undeterred, Johnathan raised his keeper staff, "Release them, ya creep!"

But Tarik showed no signs of giving in. Instead, he opened his other hand, conjuring bright red flames that danced on his fingertips and engulfed his arm. Hurrying to defend the girls, Johnathan cast powerful spells at Tarik with his staff.

"*Furia et flamma!*"

The spells struck their target, unleashing a barrage of black smoke into the air. However, as the smoke cleared, Tarik remained standing, seemingly unfazed by Johnathan's attacks.

Tarik stayed quiet but lifted his hand, pointing the flames towards the girls. Fear washed over Derek. He scrambled back to his feet and tried to rush towards this new foe, but he was still weak from being thrown. With a firm grip, Tah'quhal helped Derek stay on his feet, letting him lean against his own frame as he found his footing.

Tarik chanted a spell, his hand still pointed at the restrained girls. Pushing himself off of Tah'quhal, Derek managed to stand on his own,.

"What the hell do you want?"

Tarik locked his gaze onto Derek's and replied in a low voice, "You."

The sound of thunder boomed once more, sending a shiver down Derek's spine.

"What do you mean . . . me?" He croaked.

Tarik's baleful stare was the only response.

He looked to his best friend in hopes he would tell him what to do, help him understand, but once again, he was met with more silence. Pushing down his panic, he turned back to face Tarik. Derek had no clue what the right call was, but he did know that if he did nothing, he was putting his friends at risk.

Inhaling sharply, he shouted, "If I agree to go with you, will you release my friends?"

Tarik nodded in agreement, and with his heart in his throat, Derek took hesitant steps towards him.

Sarika came running from the front of the house, and Tah'quhal reached out for Derek's arm.

"Derek Stratum, do not go with him. Sarika's brother can not be trusted!" Tah'quhal begged.

Sarika slid to a halt next to Tah'quhal. "Please listen to us. My brother was a fun and light-hearted fae. The *thing* that stands there is not him."

Derek stopped in his tracks, turning back to face them once more. "Then what do you suggest I do?" he asked, flinging his arms out wildly. "My entire life, I've been searching for a purpose, a reason for feeling so lost. Today, I finally found it." He forced the lump in his throat down with a hard swallow. "And now, if I don't go with this creep, two people I care about may lose their lives." The ending came across loud but trembling. With resolve in his eyes, he continued towards Tarik.

Sarika had no response, but Tah'quhal had his own plan.

"Purus gratis," he breathed out.

The following moments seemed to stretch out in slow motion.

Sarika, who was the only one who heard the incantation, turned to Tah'quhal and cried out,

"Stop!"

But her warning came too late. Sarika's face was overcome with horror as a swirling blue haze materialized into a sharp spear in Tah'quhal's grasp. Derek, alerted by the commotion, swiftly turned around to witness the unfolding spectacle as the spear hurtled from Tah'quhal's hand.

The spear was meant for Tarik, but it was heading straight for Derek. He dodged out of the way just in time as the weapon sailed past him. Meanwhile, Sarika raced towards her brother, arms stretched out as if she could reach the spear in time. As the deadly projectile closed in on Tarik, a crimson mist materialized in front of him. The spear tore through the mist with a sickening thud and a piercing cry of pain.

Sarika fell to the ground, crying out in despair,

"Tah'quhal! What have you done?" She seethed, eyes blazing with barely leashed venom.

The only response was a heavy and eerie silence. Derek regained his footing and charged towards the thick mist where Mia and Izzy were trapped. He didn't waste his time searching for Tarik's body within the crimson haze, the dark mist making it impossible, even if he had wanted to.

Jonathan darted into the mist behind Derek, anxiously searching for their friend. As the two made their way through the fog, Derek called out for Johnathan's assistance and together they searched through the haze, stumbling across Mia first.

Derek reached for the chains binding her, and as he pulled on them, his arms faintly glowed with white light. The restraints snapped free and the metal covering her mouth fell to the ground. She leapt to her feet, throwing her arms around Derek, clinging tightly to his flannel shirt.

Intense relief rushed through her body, but the terror of the situation still lingered as she burst into tears. Pulling away, she whispered a heartfelt,

"Thank you."

Caught up in the moment, she leaned in and gently kissed him, pouring all of her gratitude and relief into that brief touch.

The scent of lavender filled him, and in the midst of all this chaos, Derek felt completely calm and powerful. Mia slowly pulled away from his lips. Izzy's muffled screams cut through their moment, grounding Derek in the present.

"You're safe now, but I have to find Izzy." Derek squeezed her arm in reassurance before he heard John shout,

"Here she is. Give me a hand, man!"

Mia and Derek scrambled over to John. Once he was there, Derek took over for Johnathan, using the glow of his arms to snap Izzy's bindings. He helped her to her feet.

"I think we need to get out of here."

The four of them ran out of the cloud and back towards the house. Izzy looked back at the horror they were escaping and skidded to a stop. Noticing that she was no longer running beside him, Derek turned back to see Izzy staring into the now dissipating mist.

Sarika tried to push herself forward to find her brother's body, but the grief was just too much. Every inch she moved seemed like a mile. She watched as John and Mia ran past her back towards the house.

Once the mist cleared, they could see a body lying on the ground, a body that was not Tarik's. Tah'quhal sprinted to Sarika's side and kept his gaze fixed on Tarik, who towered over a lifeless human on the frigid soil.

Derek looked in horror at the spear protruding out of Ivan's body. Somehow Ivan had used magic to teleport himself to where Tarik was but had unfortunately appeared just before the spear had met its true target.

Thunder rumbled, shaking the ground as the sky turned an even darker shade of red. Tarik's eyes were savage, ready to attack. Izzy's scream pierced through the chaos. Her tear-filled eyes were wide in horror at Ivan's lifeless body lying before her. She sprinted towards him, but Derek lunged after her, shouting desperately for her to stop.

"No, Izzy! It's too dangerous!"

His voice was drowned out by another deafening clap of thunder. Johnathan spun back to see Izzy running towards Tarik. His lips parted slightly, frozen mid-breath as he realized Ivan was the one on the ground..

Sarika knew the imminent danger of Tarik's rising anger and rushed over to help Derek.

Tarik pointed an accusing finger at Derek and shouted, "You brought this upon yourself, you foolish human! One life must be given in return!"

Sarika pleaded with her brother, "Please, Tarik, I know the real you is still in there! You have to fight this, brother!"

Tarik hesitated for a moment, his arm lowering slightly. "Fight? Fight against this gift? Now, why would I want to do that" he mocked.

Sarika couldn't hide her shaky smile as she tried to speak. "Tarik, our parents trained us for a moment just like this. Mother and father would never want us to be on opposing sides."

She watched as he shook his head and pounded his hand into his forehead. For a moment, it seemed like she was getting through to him. Once again, she pleaded with her brother,

"Tar . . . Tarik, think of the first time we traveled to the outskirts of town with our uncle and father. Remember how they told us we would always have to stick together?"

Sarika saw him struggling against the corruption as the red bands on his face turned blue. For a brief moment, Tarik broke through and managed to yell out one word before losing control once again.

"MALUM!"

Horror spread across everyone's face, except for Derek and Izzy, who had no clue who or what "Malum" was.

As Tarik's corruption set back in, he let out a blood curdling laugh and said, "Well, the secret is out."

A massive red lightning bolt slammed the ground in front of them, and a shadowy figure appeared for a fleeting moment before dissipating into the air.

Once again, time seemed to all but stop.

Tarik shouted, "*Mortem incarnatam!*"

Red essence swirled around him. Sarika's voice pierced through the chaos, urging Derek and Izzy to take cover. Johnathan quickly dragged Mia behind the safety of the house walls. Tah'quhal sprinted toward Sarika, tackling her to the ground and shielding her with his body.

Derek's grip tightened around Izzy's arm. With a swift motion, he turned her towards him, intending to pull her to safety. Yet, within a heartbeat, his world crumbled into his arms.

Izzy's once-vibrant blue eyes turned hollow, void of life, as if the light within her had been extinguished with the ease of a flickering flame. A sinister crimson mist poured from her parted, still rosy lips. Her 'five and a half foot' frame had never appeared so fragile as her limp body collapsed into the warmth of his embrace.

For a panicked moment, he feared Tarik had stolen his oxygen too, as he gasped hopelessly for air that would not come. He felt the warmth Izzy always radiated fade from her skin as the ground shifted beneath his feet. He barely registered the sharp pain of his knees driving into the ground. For a second, as he tucked strands of loose hair back into her braid, he convinced himself that his head injury earlier had trapped him in a coma, because there was no possible way a dimension without her bright joy could exist. His stomach twisted, and he had to hold back vomit thinking about the joy he'd experienced at discovering magic just an hour before. He would have lived the rest of his life, ignorant, out-of-place, feeling broken, if it would have brought her back.

The weight of sorrow crushed his spirit, robbing him of any sense of stability. His trembling limbs failed to support him, even on his knees, and he twisted his body, pulling Izzy into his lap. In that haunting moment, he faced the unfathomable reality of losing a cherished friend. Everything had just become all too real. He cradled Izzy to his chest and wept.

Sarika's eyes mirrored his horror, her mind grappling to understand the unforgivable act her brother had committed.

Tarik's cruel words echoed in the air. In a flash of blinding red mist, he vanished, leaving behind only sorrow and anguish. Johnathan and Mia rushed to Derek's side. Falling to the ground next to him, Johnathan frantically held Izzy's lifeless body to him, begging her to wake up. But there was no response, no breath left for her to take. Derek watched as John pointlessly tried to wake Izzy. He knew the agony his best friend was feeling. He wanted to comfort him, but his body wouldn't move. Derek could only let him take her body, crying out in grief as Mia tried to console him.

Tah'quhal's heart ached at the act his oldest friend had just committed. It solidified in his mind that the creature that was here was no longer Tarik.

"Hopefully," Tah'quhal whispered, his voice trembling, "her essence finds its way to the Eternal Dimension."

Derek looked at him with tear-filled eyes and choked out, "L . . . like Heaven?"

The fae forced a smile, nodding sadly as he noticed the tears falling from Derek's face shined with the same brilliant white light that once illuminated his arms. Without hesitation, he reached into his satchel and pulled out a small glass vial, offering it to Mia, who instinctively caught the falling tears. She gently wiped Derek's face dry and placed the glowing vial in his hand, squeezing it tightly. It was a symbol of their love and loss, forever etched into their souls.

Chapter 10

Into the Unkown

"What do we tell her parents?"

Derek's voice quivered, desperatcly seeking guidance in the abyss of despair.

His body was numb and his mind blank. The blue sky returning after Tarik vanished felt like a mockery to the impossible question he just asked.

"Damn it, Derek! How in the ever-living hell are we supposed to explain all this to them?" Johnathan lashed out as he looked up from Izzy's lifeless body for the first time. His usually calm brown eyes darkened, a storm brewing in their depths. He refused to let go of her, holding onto hope that she would take another breath.

"John . . . I . . . I'm sorry." Derek managed to choke out.

In that bleak moment, Mia recognized the burden consuming Derek's spirit, and she reached out, taking his trembling hand into her own. Using her free hand to anxiously rub her left elbow.

Johnathan wiped a tear from his face as he looked back at Izzy. "I know it ain't your fault. I know you couldnt'a stopped it. But this hurts, Derek. It freaking hurts."

Tah'quhal gazed up at the sky, searching for answers to questions he didn't even know how to ask. Without looking down, he gave a veiled attempt at being considerate. "We must find Tarik and Malum before they can cause any more harm."

Sarika stood, stoic and cold, not giving any hint of emotion away as she retorted, "And just what do you propose we do against someone as powerful as Malum?"

Tah'quhal studied his fae friend's face, searching for any hints of her true emotions. Something had changed after the ritual in Torvania; she was not acting like herself. The humans watched as the two fae argued, with Sarika growing increasingly irritable at every suggestion Tah'quhal made. Sarika tried to mask it as concern for Derek, his friends, and the one they lost, but it was clear that anger was bubbling beneath the surface.

Derek and Johnathan couldn't bring themselves to care about the fae's argument. Nothing else seemed important. Derek sat on the ground, and even with Mia sitting down next to him, his heart ached. Within a few fleeting hours, his world had been shattered, and the fragments lay scattered before him. Just as he began to find answers to his sense of displacement, Izzy was killed, and he was more lost than ever.

Finally, Tah'quhal suggested something that Sarika grudgingly agreed with,

"Fine! At the very least, we should take Derek Stratum to Komipea. Perhaps he can help us unravel the mysteries of the magic within him."

Derek met Mia's gaze, his expression filled with concern. She spoke in a steady voice, "Do you know *anything* about it?"

Derek shook his head solemnly. "I have no idea, but we can't leave Izzy's family clueless. They need to know what happened."

Sarika, visibly on edge, pulled out a purple flower from her bag. Approaching Derek, she huffed, "By Torviid's beard, we do not have time for this!"

Tah'quhal reacted quickly, knocking the flower out of her hand, and Mia raised her hand and commanded,

"*Ardeat!*"

A burst of flames consumed the flower, reducing it to ash.

Tah'quhal grabbed ahold of her arm, exclaiming, "Sarika, what are you doing?"

Brushing him off, she reached into her satchel again. "Removing the obstacle. If they only wish to delay us, I can make it seem like none of this occurred."

Tah'quhal countered incredulously, "And what about the Keeper of the Anchor? We can not simply erase his memories, can we?"

Derek's confusion quickly turned to anger, his words spoken with lethal precision. "What do you mean by wiping our memories?"

Johnathan whispered, "The forgonium . . . a flower," he pointed to Sarika and Tah'quhal, "that they use to wipe the memories of magic from humans."

Derek's vision was tinged with red. "What the hell is wrong with you?" He whipped. "You came here to find me, and now that I have lost one of my closest friends, at the hands of *your* brother no less, you want to *wipe* my mind?"

Derek could feel his hands shaking with leashed tension. He took a deep breath, trying to calm himself, but it was no use. "I have gone my entire life feeling like I do not belong! My friends are the only thing that kept me sane, and look!" He pointed to Izzy's lifeless body. "Izzy is *dead*."

His arms began glowing again. "Bring that flower near me. I dare you." He seethed, his narrowed eyes staring directly into Sarika's as she slowly pulled her hand out of her satchel.

Tah'quhal attempted to intervene, speaking cautiously, like one would to a wild animal, "Derek Stratum. Please understand, while I do not agree with Sarika, she is just attempting to do what she believes is best."

The brightness increased. Derek lashed out at Tah'quhal with a deep growl, "You're the reason Izzy is dead! Your careless throw of that damned spear got her killed!"

The warrior fae's voice took on a hard edge. "Watch it, Derek Stratum. You know very little of what you speak."

"I may not know much, but I know what I saw. You were impulsive. You were so eager to kill Tarik that you got an innocent girl murdered instead!"

"I did no such thing! Continue this path, and I will show you what a warrior from Torvania can do," Tah'quhal snarled as his stigmata glowed.

Derek raised his arms, ready to fight. "Well, why don't you tell me when one shows up!"

Just as it seemed they may come to blows, the sky rumbled with a deafening fury once more.

Derek's cry of frustration pierced through the darkening sky. "What now?!"

The thunder continued to rumble with unrelenting fury as the sky enveloped everything in a suffocating darkness once more. Johnathan, clutching his Keeper staff tightly, rose from beside Izzy's lifeless, wiping tears from his eyes and looked to the heavens. He was not willing to let anyone else get hurt. He had already failed enough.

Mia stood steadfastly by Derek's side, her stigmata glowing an intense blue. Tah'quhal and Sarika moved in perfect synchronization, creating a protective barrier of ethereal blue essence around the group. They instinctively drew closer together, finding comfort and strength in their unity. The forcefield contracted tightly around them, leaving Izzy's body outside of its grasp, concealed within the impenetrable veil of haze.

Ready to rage at the unfairness of it all, Derek charged towards the edge of the shield, unleashing a flurry of strikes that created blinding flashes of white light. He begged Tah'quhal and Sarika to lower the shield with each hit, his heart heavy with grief for Izzy.

Tah'quhal whispered, "I'm sorry, Derek Stratum. Saving her is not something we can do. She is already gone."

However, Sarika stopped moving and watched Derek with a mix of empathy and curiosity as he continued to strike at the shield. She couldn't help but be drawn to the radiant light coming from his arms. Slowly approaching him, she extended her hand to touch his face. As her fingers brushed his skin, her stigmata once again glowed with the bright white light emanating from his arms. For a brief moment, Derek felt a sense of calmness wash over him, sagging as his fight and anger abandoned him. This time, it was clear that Sarika was experiencing intense emotions as she tried to project a calming aura. But beneath the surface, he could sense great turmoil within her.

He tried to hone in on the emotions that Sarika seemed to be suppressing, but her soothing voice kept him distracted. Like a calm stream flowing through a forest, her influence weaved through his veins and calmed his raging heart. Gradually, the force field around them dissipated, revealing an empty patch of grass where Izzy's had been. Derek pulled away from Sarika, only to be hit with the piercing ache of losing his friend once again.. Above them, dark clouds similar to those from before were quickly moving in the direction of Riverrun High.

Derek walked to where Izzy had laid. He sat down next to the still indented grass and crossed his legs. Mia stood behind him, placing a hand on his shoulder.

"Are you okay?"

Derek's arms let off a faint flicker of light. "No. But I will be. I want to figure all of this out, and then I will be okay."

Johnathan walked towards his best friend. "Those clouds, they were heading towards the school. They might not be going there, but Barry and Trey are still there. I don't wanna lose anyone else."

Tah'quhal and Sarika approached the friend group. The former once again suggested going to Torvania to seek help from Komipea, emphasizing that he may be the only one who could shed light on the situation. Sarika agreed, but also knew that the humans would want to check on Riverrun. She proposed that she and Tah'quhal go with Derek to Torvania, while Johnathan and Mia make their way to the school and rendezvous with them in Torvania once they have uncovered the reason behind the disturbance.

Mia's grip on Derek's hand tightened, her eyes showing clear concern. His mind was still trying to process the rollercoaster of a day he was having.

"No," He said, "I won't go without Mia."

Sarika's tense jaw and flared nostril showed her disapproval, but luckily Johnathan chimed in,

"I reckon I can go to Riverrun by myself." He looked at his staff. "I probably got the best chance to escape if things get hairy, and maybe I'll find dad, too."

Johnathan walked over to his best friend and linked forearms, saying "We'll figure this out, buddy. You know I ain't lying."

Derek looked at him gratefully. Then, with a flick of his staff, Johnathan disappeared into a brilliant burst of blue light.

The remaining four members of their group headed towards the Anchor.

Sarika pointed to the glowing portal and explained, "Once we step through this, we'll be in Torvania."

Tah'quhal added that after the crazy events they had experienced that day, it might be best to go through in pairs.

Derek asked, "So, me and Mia first?"

Sarika sighed. "It would be better for each of you to travel with one of us, and I will be able to calm you if your anger rises, you should go through with me. It will only be a matter of seconds, Derek Stratum. We will all be together on the other side in no time."

Mia looked at Derek for his response, and after a moment of hesitation, he reluctantly agreed.

Mia tenderly caressed Derek's face, their eyes locked in a powerful gaze. She pulled her face closer to his and softly kissed him one last time. With a sly grin, she teased, "See you soon, lavender!"

Even amidst his grief, as Derek looked into her eyes, with the warmth of her lips still on his skin, a real smile ghosted his lips. As Mia turned to walk towards the Anchor's portal with her eyes still fixed on Derek, Tah'quhal interjected teasingly,

"Alright, you two lovebirds, that's enough! Come on, Mia, you'll only have to miss him for a minute."

Mia laughed and joined Tah'quhal by the portal.

As they stepped through, Derek called out with a silly smile on his face, "I'll be right there."

The phrase hung in the air as Mia and Tah'quhal disappeared into the glowing portal.

Sarika locked eyes with Derek as the other two vanished through the portal and spoke in an authoritative tone,

"Derek, as we step into the Anchor, focus your thoughts on Torvania. We will walk through and emerge beneath the statue of Torviid on the other side."

Derek nodded his understanding and together, they approached the shimmering portal. Just before they crossed its threshold, Sarika touched one of the engravings on the side of the stone arch. A small dust of red mist was left behind when her hand left the marking.

As they entered the portal, an unexpected tremor shook the Anchor, and a blinding white light enveloped them both.

In Torvania, Tah'quhal and Mia emerged from the portal, finding themselves in a relatively calm and serene environment, a stark contrast to the chaotic events they left behind on Earth. Mia's anxiety grew as she turned, hoping to see Derek stepping through the portal behind them, her gaze fixed on the entrance. Time seemed to stretch as a few moments passed in suspense. Echoing in her mind, she heard Derek's voice whisper,

"I'll be right there."

A warm smile spread across her face, filled with anticipation.

From the portal, a deafening roar, like thunder amplified a thousand times, erupted in an explosion of sound and energy that ripped through the peaceful air. The ground shook violently beneath their feet as the shockwave sent them stumbling backwards, their hearts racing with fear and adrenaline. Mia scrambled back to her feet and stared into the portal, eagerly awaiting Derek to emerge. The once serene moment was now shattered, throwing them back into the chaos once more.

Chapter 11

Wrong Turn

Derek and Sarika tumbled through a blinding white light, weightless and disoriented, in an endless sea of pure white. They tried to orient themselves, but the brightness was overwhelming and there was no sense of direction. Panic set in. They were falling for what seemed like forever. Derek reached out for something to grab onto, but he only flailed around in the void. Sarika attempted to shout, but even sound seemed nonexistent in this strange place.

In an instant, the blinding white vanished, plunging Derek into complete darkness. He crashed onto the hard, cold ground with a resounding thud. Sarika's body slammed into him shortly after, knocking the wind from his lungs. The air was thick and oppressive, reeking of sulfur and rotting vegetation. Strange, echoing noises filled the sky, disorienting him with their eerie, untraceable source. Derek squinted his eyes and called out a hesitant,

"Mia?"

Sarika wearily chuckled and replied, "Nope, just me," as she used her magic to swiftly lift herself back onto her feet.

Derek stood up, looking for the massive statue they were supposed to be under. Sarika solemnly shook her head in response to his unspoken question. Sarika looked toward the horizon and pointed at the dark purple hue in the sky, whispering,

"This is Mythos."

As if in response to her hushed words, a brilliant blue orb materialized in the sky ahead of them.

A voice neither recognized boomed through the air, "LEAVE!"

Shocked, Derek stumbled backwards and asked Sarika where they were.

She grinned mischievously, "I already told you, Derek Stratum. We're in Mythos, the second dimension."

"Okay, why do you keep calling me by my full name?" Derek questioned.

Sarika raised one eyebrow. "What do you mean? Your name is Derek Stratum, so that is what I call you."

Derek couldn't help but to laugh at the clear disconnect. "Stratum is my *last* name. Just Derek is fine."

"Why do you have two names if you do not wish to be called by both of them?"

"Well, actually I have thre . . . nevermind. You can just call me Derek." He shook his head and tried to conceal a laugh.

"Okay," she said slowly, "Derek it is for now. But I will need further explanation after we make our way out of here."

The orb streaked across the sky and came to a sudden halt at the edge of a massive river and waterfall. Sarika pointed to it.

"Looks like our next destination is the Fallen River. Ready for a hike?"

"Why would we follow that thing?" Derek asked, his face contorted.

"Supposedly, the only way out of Mythos is the Fallen River. That orb is hovering over a river, so I am thinking it is showing us how to get out of here."

Derek's gaze lingered on her, trying to make sense of why she didn't appear to be more distressed to have ended up in this place. As she met his eyes, he swore her usually bright purple irises took on a piercing crimson hue. Shaking it off as a trick of the environment, he gestured towards the river, eager to get out of this place.

As they made their way towards the Fallen River, Sarika stretched out her hand to conjure a light to guide their path. But instead of her usual ball of light, an uncontrollable surge of energy coursed through her body, creating a surprisingly large ring of light around her.

Confused, Derek mumbled, "That is a strange reaction for someone that is used to magic."

"This place," Sarika paused for a moment, "Mythos, it amplifies my magic. Normally I would need to speak an incantation for a spell I have not mastered, but here, the magic courses through me."

She then stopped and knelt down on the ground, pulling out glass vials from her satchel and filling them with soil.

"You never know when this might come in handy," she said with a smile.

Derek's confusion only deepened. Using their journey to seek answers, he peppered Sarika with questions about the use of magic. Back on Earth, he had heard the fae speak incantations before casting spells, but other times they seemed to use it with just a thought. Sarika explained that certain creatures are born with an innate ability to use magic without needing to channel it first. However, most beings with magical abilities need to use incantations for more complex spells, and some even train for years to master specific ones, earning stigmata as they train. Derek wondered if he fell into the first category, but Sarika reminded him that discovering the truth about his abilities was one of their main goals in Torvania.

They were nearly halfway to the river when a bone-chilling screech cut off Derek's next question. A shiver ran down his spine, his arms glowing with a blinding white light.

Sarika grinned. "Exactly what we were hoping for."

As Derek turned to ask her what she meant, he saw a blurred figure crash into Sarika, violently throwing her to the ground.

Derek rushed over to her and extended a hand to help her up. He turned his gaze towards the sky and a strong force surrounding him, causing his magic to pulse brighter. Just then, the unsettling screech reverberated once more, followed by a forceful gust of wind and the heavy thuds of clawed feet hitting the rocky ground.

Through the light cast by Derek's arms and Sarika's ring, they were able to make out the female figure before them——tall, slender, and winged. Derek couldn't move his eyes away and asked if it was an angel.

Sarika scoffed, "Harpy."

The harpy swiveled her head and cried out, "You are not welcome here! The power of Mythos shall not be taken!"

The harpy pounced towards Derek with astonishing speed. He tried to dodge her attack, but her wing grazed his cheek, leaving a trail of blood.

"Derek, run for the river!" Sarika cried out.

He took her advice and sprinted as fast as he could. Sarika swiftly retrieved another container from her bag and scooped up the blood coated soil before hurrying after him.

As the harpy dove towards her, Sarika twisted away, launching a fiery blast at it. The creature screeched and pulled back, giving her time to catch up to Derek.

He thought to himself, "*This is insane. I'm supposed to be at school, not running from a winged beast!*"

They hadn't gone too far before another piercing cry echoed through the sky as the harpy snatched Sarika into the air with its talons. Despite her cries for help, Derek lost sight of her in the darkness. He frantically scanned the skies, his chest heaving with every breath he took.

Derek shut his eyes and concentrated, trying to tune out all other sounds. He strained to pick up any clues of Sarika's whereabouts or the harpy's movements. The light radiating from his arms grew stronger. And then he heard it——the unmistakable sound of the harpy's powerful wings flapping directly above him. Without hesitation, he thrust one arm upwards towards the sky, the bright light revealing the terrifying creature in all its glory. Its large red wings were ragged and torn, like the rags that barely covered its body. Its feet were like something from a nightmare, with sharp claws digging into Sarika's shoulders as she dangled helplessly below.

Derek demanded that the harpy set Sarika free. Its laughter, dark and menacing, filled the air as it addressed him with a mocking "Your Eminency."

Derek's confusion only deepened, but he didn't have time to react before the harpy attacked Sarika, striking her on the head and knocking her unconscious. The harpy let her go, allowing her to plummet towards the ground.

Feet flying like never before, Derek raced towards Sarika's falling figure, his heart hammering in his chest as he realized he wouldn't reach her before she hit the ground. Driven by instinct, he leapt forward with outstretched arms, the radiant light shooting forward, cushioning Sarika's impact.

As the light faded and Sarika landed safely on the ground, Derek couldn't believe what he had just accomplished. But he quickly shifted his focus back to the harpy, determined to protect himself and Sarika from any further harm.

Closing his eyes, Derek felt the surge of magic within him. He could feel it pulse and flow beneath his skin, filling him with a sense of strength and invincibility.

Opening his eyes once more, he let out a deep exhale and shouted, "Enough!"

With Mythos amplifying his abilities, he unleashed a powerful blast of white lightning from his fingertips towards the harpy.

As Sarika slowly came to, her head aching intensely, she could sense Derek's energy around her. She blinked her eyes open to see him battling the flying creature with an impressive show of strength. The radiant glow emanating from his arms was both frightening and captivating.

Still shaking off her disorientation, Sarika found herself mesmerized by the display before her. Derek seemed like a completely different man than the one she had met only a few hours ago. As he unleashed his newfound magic, guarding her against The Harpy, she couldn't help but be moved by the strength and bravery he pulled forth for them——for her.

Sarika watched intently as Derek battled the harpy, slowly struggling to pull herself to her feet. With every move the harpy made, he made sure to launch another barrage of lightning at it. Sarika felt something inside her, something she had not anticipated. As the bright white light shined on Derek's arms, her heart raced for reasons not entirely related to their present danger. Her stomach fluttered, and as white light danced around him like a shield of righteousness, she couldn't help but feel a powerful draw to him, to his power. The intensity of the battle, the fierce determination in Derek's eyes, and the connection she felt with his awakening magic stirred something deep within her.

Pushing away her lingering dizziness, she focused her thoughts, running to Derek's side.

"We need to finish this."

The harpy cackled in response. In that moment, Derek's eyes glowed white as he charged towards the vile creature. He leapt into the air, channeling all of his energy into one powerful bolt of lightning that tore through the harpy's left wing with a blinding flash.

As the creature flapped its wings wildly, a pained howl escaped its throat. It desperately attempted to put out the fire consuming its wing, but it was already too late. With a final shriek, it flew high into the sky in retreat, leaving behind a chilling warning:

"I am just the beginning."

Derek watched until he was certain the harpy was gone, the glow from his arms sputtering and dimming with each passing second. He staggered, his strength waning, until his knees buckled and he crumpled to the ground, utterly spent. Sarika gently pulled his head into her lap in comfort, running her hand through his hair. As he drifted away from consciousness, he could barely make out her soft voice whispering,

"Extraordinary."

Chapter 12

Before the Turn

Mia's gaze fixated on the pulsing portal in front of her. The hypnotizing swirls of blue and purple seemed to draw her in, causing her to lose herself in its depths. Tah'quhal stood behind her with a calm demeanor, waiting for Derek and Sarika to appear.

"They should be arriving any moment now," Tah'quhal assured her.

Shortly after, Chieftain Komipea and a small group of guards came running up to the Anchor. Komipea looked to Tah'quhal.

"Who exactly have you brought back from Earth?"

Tah'quhal recounted everything in detail, but Komipea seemed more interested in Mia, studying her intently.

After Tah'quhal had finished speaking, the Chieftain inclined his head towards Mia. "Who attuned you?"

Mia didn't speak a word. She only looked at the ground.

Tah'quhal spoke again, "She is waiting for Derek Stratum. He and Sarika should have come through by now."

"Very well. We can talk more later. For now, we shall wait." The Chieftain offered.

But as seconds turned into minutes, and minutes into hours, their friends were still nowhere in sight. The townspeople of Torvania gathered around the two, watching as they stared anxiously at the Anchor with no sign of their companions.

As time passed, Mia's optimism dwindled and her heart grew heavy. Chieftain Komipea cautiously approached her, recommending that she and Tah'quhal spend the night at his home and resume their watch in the morning. Despite her stubbornness about staying, the Chieftain convinced her by reminding her that she was a foreigner in his city.

"Standing here all night will do you no good," he paused for a deep, contemplating breath. "I have met every attuned human that has ever walked through the Anchor for the past eight hundred years, and I do not recognize you. Please come with me. We can talk more in my home and I will leave the guard here to notify us if anything changes."

Mia nodded, but waited for Komipea to head towards his house before walking next to Tah'quhal.

"Derek is going to come through, right?" She asked.

Tah'quhal gently patted her back. "Of course."

Once settled at the Chieftain's residence, Tah'quhal immediately demanded, "Okay Chieftain, tell me what you know."

"Easy son, we have a guest. Allow me to introduce myself to her, and then you and I can have a conversation."

"No! You promised me answers. Now Sarika and Derek Stratum have not shown up, and I want to know everything you know." He pointed toward the book on the shelf he had thumbed through before he and Sarika had left. "To save Luminfae and realms beyond compare, He'll face the trials, his destiny to bear. With magic yet awakened and a heart so true, He'll make the promise come to life anew."

Komipea's eyes widened as he looked at the bookshelf. "You read something you were not meant to see."

Mia looked at him with a puzzled expression. "Why wouldn't he know about the prophecy?"

Tah'quhal was taken aback by her knowledge of it. No one in Torvania had ever mentioned it before. He had only found those words while snooping through the Chieftain's books. His eyebrows furrowed in hurt, masked as anger, as he confronted Komipea.

"I knew you were keeping something from us when we left to find Derek!"

Tah'quhal's outburst was met with a stare that signaled now is not the time. Komipea turned to Mia and asked the same question once again.

"Who attuned you?"

Mia hesitated before answering, but the Chieftain said, "It was not a fae from Torvania, was it, child?"

Tah'quhal's jaw clenched, his eyes hot with anger. His mind was swirling with countless questions that he couldn't seem to voice.

Komipea stood and sighed. "Come now, both of you. I believe it is time for an explanation."

The Chieftain led them to the rear of his home, where he pushed aside a table and snapped his fingers. A secret door appeared and opened to reveal a long spiral staircase. As they descended, recognition lit Tah'quhal's eyes as he noticed that the walls bore a striking resemblance to those of the Cressida Library in Torvania.

Komipea nodded knowingly. "You're observant, my boy. This is the entrance to the Chieftain's private section of the library. And soon, you will understand why the people of Torvania have remained isolated from the rest of the realm for all these years."

Tah'quhal's anger still smoldered brightly within him, but it was overshadowed by curiosity. No matter how furious he was with his Chieftain, he needed to know the secrets that were being kept from him. After they reached the end of the hallway, Komipea gestured towards a large table for them to take a seat.

Komipea walked over to a shelf and pulled out a hefty book labeled "Collection of Keepers." He set it down on the table and grabbed a bucket filled with scrolls. From there, he carefully unrolled a map of the city of Torvania and its surrounding fields.

Komipea waved his hand over the map. "This probably looks familiar so far, Tah'quhal. Do you see anything missing?"

Tah'quhal studied the map. "The dark mountain at the end of the fields is not on here."

Komipea's lips quirked slightly as he waved his hand again. The drawings began to move, and the words "Canter Mountain" materialized next to a towering volcanic peak.

Tah'quhal leaned into Mia and whispered, "In the sunlight, you can see the tower from the edge of town, but most Torvanians won't go near it. Rumor has it that Malum lived there, and it carries his curse." At least, that was what Tah'quhal had always been told.

Komipea explained, "Canter Mountain is a place to be feared, and it is true that Malum's origin is rumored to have come from there. There is even said to be a castle hidden within the rocks."

The Chieftain brought his hands together, and the map rustled once more, revealing a vast landscape with the word "Luminfae" written at the top. Tah'quhal turned to Komipea, expecting answers, but Komipea simply nodded towards Mia to continue. Mia nervously looked at the two fae, now understanding that those who live in Torvania truly believe they are the sole inhabitants of Luminfae.

She stuttered, "Tah'quhal, Luminfae *is* the fourth dimension. The map hasn't revealed it yet, but there are many other cities and villages scattered around. This city is not the only one." She paused for a moment as her brows raised incredulously. "What is the story you were told about Malum?"

Tah'quhal, trying to maintain his composure, inhaled deeply and began."It was five thousand years ago. Torvania was named Laresque, and it was a peaceful village nestled at the base of Canter Mountain." Trying to expel some of his building tension, he paced around the library, running his hand along ancient tomes.

"There was no Chieftain at the time, but my ancestor Torviid was seen as the leader." He paused for a moment and glanced back at the map Komipea had shown him. "One fateful evening, a star fell from the sky and crashed into the mountain. From its depths emerged the evil fae named Malum, bringing with him a powerful and insidious type of magic, along with an army of elves."

Mia crossed her arms, clenching her fists tightly. Her anger was evident, but she stayed silent to allow Tah'quhal to finish.

Tah'quhal continued, "When Malum approached the village, it was Torviid who stood against him. Malum demanded that Torviid bow down and join his quest to conquer all dimensions, but Torviid refused. A mighty battle ensued, nearly destroying Laresque in the process."

A sardonic snort escaped from Mia. She could feel her face turning red at the story she was hearing.

Tah'quhal looked at her tight expression and could tell everything he was saying must be wrong, but he continued on, "In the aftermath, Torviid was ready to surrender, knowing he could not defeat Malum and his forces. As a last resort, he attempted a powerful spell, warning anyone still alive that it would only buy time before Malum returned. His spell made both fae disappear. Malum's army scattered into the hills, while the remaining survivors rebuilt their town and renamed it Torvania."

The corner of his lips turned up. "Naming the city after the mighty Torviid himself."

Mia's eyes cut daggers at Komipea, hissing, "How dare you let that be the story your citizens believe!"

"Young lady, please. Allow me to reveal the rest of the map for Tah'quhal, and then we can tell him the truth."

Mia felt the urge to scold him more, but she knew that showing Tah'quhal the map would be more helpful. Komipea waved his hand over the map and with a rustle, it revealed all the locations in Luminfae.

"Tah'quhal, there are truths that will shatter the very foundation of what you believe.

"Neutrale, a village here on the far edge of the map, is a haven for fae who strive for equilibrium in their magic. A place of grace nestled between the ocean's vastness and a sprawling lake." Komipea watched as Tah'quhal studied every inch of the map.

"Their magic, though primarily protective, can unleash unspeakable forces when threatened. Neutrale's gates have always been open to outsiders——whether from distant fortresses or even from the human realm. They are led by a powerful fae named Nidalle."

Tah'quhal's eyes widened, his breath catching as the weight of his Chieftain's revelation crashed over him. Everything he thought he knew about his world began to unravel.

Chieftain Komipea placed his hand on Tah'quhal's shoulder, but Tah'quhal pulled away, saying, "Don't stop now. Tell me about the rest."

Next, he told him of Terra. It was the very first city to welcome a human from Earth. This city was nestled behind the Dragoon pass and built around a wellspring that was connected to the Fallen River in Mythos.

Tah'quhal pointed to a darkened area of the map nestled between Torvania and Terra. "What is this?"

Komipea continued explaining, "That would be Ignis. It is home to the supernatural descendants of fae and an unknown entity."

"What exactly does that mean?" Tah'quhal asked.

"These creatures call themselves the succubus. They wield fire magic with ease and require no incantations or actions to command it." The Chieftain paused and looked at his pupil. "They are also supernatural masters of seduction, so if you cannot avoid going there, you must do everything in your power to keep your wits."

For the first time since the map was revealed to him, Tah'quhal barked a short laugh.

Komipea pointed to the center of Ignis on the map. "There is a fiery portal in the middle of the city. It connects Ignis to Earth and burns endlessly, thanks to leaves stolen from the surrounding Magia Forest."

"What is so special about the Forest?" Tah'quhal asked.

"The Magia Forest consists of all the wooded areas on this map. It is home to numerous types of creatures, fae, orcs, pixies, and many more."

Tah'quhal interrupted, "I thought orcs were just a scary story told to keep young fae in line!"

Komipea let out a hearty chuckle, "Well, those stories aren't all wrong. They are formidable opponents. Luckily, they are mostly friendly."

As his eyes focused back on the map, Tah'quhal asked his Chieftain about the last location, "Oceanus. That one is pretty far away."

The Chieftain looked at Mia. "Perhaps you would like to give some insight on the great Oceanus, young lady?"

Mia's eyes widened slightly as she rubbed her arm up and down. "Uh, no, you go ahead."

"Very well," Komipea replied. "Oceanus is considered by many to be the most stunning city in Luminfae. It is home to the natare, a strong species of fae with a natural affinity for water."

"Oh great, now there are mermaids too?" Tah'quhal half joked.

Another grin grew on Komipea's face. "Not quite. They are very similar to the fae, like you and me, but they have an innate mastery of Bonum magic, and rarely need to use incantations to cast spells."

Komipea moved his hand around the map. "Even though this map shows many areas, it is far from complete. This is just the most updated one I have received. The Luminfae unmapped wilds lay west of Oceanus, and who knows what other small settlements have popped up. There could be friend or foe lurking in every corner of Luminfae."

Tah'quhal ran his hand along the map. "If all of this is out there, why can't we see it?"

Komipea's shoulder slumped. "A magical shield surrounds our city. It casts the illusion that this is all there is. The other cities around Luminfae agreed to allow Torvania to stay isolated after the First Fae Wars."

Komipea grabbed a book from a nearby shelf. As he handed it to Mia, he said, "This is the Book of Keepers. Every major city in Luminfae has one, but only a Keeper can open it. Maybe you should try?"

Before Mia could respond or try to open it, Tah'quhal said, "I thought Johnathan Monton was the only Keeper?"

"Sir!" A guard burst through the door. "Come quick, someone else has just come through the Anchor!"

"Derek." Mia exhaled. The book was left discarded on the floor as she bolted for the exit.

Chapter 13

Turning Around

As Derek's eyes fluttered open, he realized he was lying on rough terrain, cradled in Sarika's embrace.

Disoriented, he asked, "What's going on?"

She grinned at him and assisted him to his feet, teasingly remarking, "You slept like a newborn babe. You must have been tired, huh? Taking on a harpy all by yourself. Impressive, Derek, very impressive."

He blushed from the combination of pride and awkwardness. "I. . . I didn't even know I was capable of that. It just sort of happened," he replied bashfully, downplaying his actions.

Sarika's laughter tinkled through the air, her eyes sparkling with mischief. "Maybe you should let things 'just happen' more often," she suggested playfully. "I have a feeling there's more to you than meets the eye, lavender."

Derek furrowed his brow. His stomach knotted up hearing her call him that. Only Mia understood what it meant, and right now, he was missing her. He was supposed to be in Torvania with her, not stuck in Mythos.

"What do you mean?"

Sarika's grin grew wider, seemingly enlivened by their conversation. "Oh, nothing much. Just that you might have some hidden talents waiting to be discovered," she said with a wink.

Derek's cheeks turned red as he was suddenly acutely aware of their location and isolation. Thoughts of Mia flooded his mind, and a deep guilt wracked his brain. He gazed towards the distant horizon and suggested they resume their trek.

As they made their way towards the Fallen River, Derek couldn't help but notice Sarika's playful and daring nature. He thought that she had been focused . . . cold even, but he liked this other side of her. Her teasing comments and clever wit added a spark to the otherwise dreary environment, and he found himself relaxing in her presence, enjoying their time together. Every time she accidentally brushed against him, his stomach fluttered, but he would quickly dismiss it, telling himself that he was just hungry. There was no denying Sarika was beautiful, but he didn't know her, not like Mia. At least, he *felt* like he knew Mia. Truthfully, he hadn't even gotten the nerve to talk to her until this morning. *"Has it really only been a day?"* he thought incredulously.

Sarika braced herself against him as she climbed over a fallen tree. Nervously, Derek swallowed, causing him to realize how parched he was. It had been hours since he had anything to drink. He let out a dry cough and tried to clear his throat.

Sarika asked, "Is everything okay?"

"I'm just a little thirsty." He replied.

Sarika began searching through her satchel, pulling out a flat leather pouch.

"Uh, that looks empty." Derek teased.

Sarika narrowed her eyes, her lips curling into a knowing smirk. "Yes, I know. Just hold on."

She held the pouch out in front of her with one hand and hovered the other above it. She touched each finger of her free hand to her thumb, and just as she was about to speak an incantation, the leather began leaking with water. Her eyes lit up at the remembrance that she could simply will her magic to her command here.

Derek eagerly grabbed the flask, gulping down most of its contents. "So much better. Thank you, Sarika." He said, while wiping the excess water from his mouth.

Eyes twinkling, she gave him a polite smile and nod as she turned to continue towards the river.

The further Derek and Sarika delved into the depths of Mythos, the more the weight of the atmosphere seemed to increase, a sense of looming danger hanging over them. They made their way through a tangled maze of gnarled trees and shadows, their muscles tensing further with every snapped twig. Each step became cautious, both of them on high alert.

A rustle from some bushes nearby sent Derek leaping in the air. "Ahh! What the hell is that?"

A small, fuzzy creature rolled out of the foliage, its little beady eyes staring up at him. "Oh, well, would you look at that? Something cute in this horrible place," he said as he reached his hand out to pet it.

Sarika quickly swatted at Derek's hand and shooed the creature away. As it scurried off, she turned back to Derek. "It may appear cute, but if it lives in Mythos . . . it is dangerous."

Derek watched as Sarika continued towards the fallen river, following behind her, and whispering under his breath, "There is no way *that* little thing was dangerous."

Sarika's vibrant demeanor shifted as they turned a corner, their hearts skipping a beat at the sound of a menacing growl echoing through the air. Eyes wide, Sarika motioned silently for Derek to retreat. In the distance, the silhouette of a massive figure loomed, casting a terrifying shadow over them.

The creature turned around, not spotting them just yet, but giving Derek a clear view of the beast. The creature stood at least eight feet tall, its muscular frame that of a man honed by years of brutal combat, but with the fierce head of a bull. One horn was broken, a jagged remnant from a long-forgotten battle. Its scarred skin bore the marks of countless hard-fought victories. Fierce eyes burned with the memory of endless skirmishes. A tattered cloth draped loosely over its broad chest, more a relic of past battles than protection. In its massive hands, it gripped a battle ax, the blade chipped and stained from relentless use..

Sarika's voice trembled as she whispered, "Derek, that's a minotaur. They're the guardians of Mythos, and this one looks like it's been through many battles. We need to be cautious."

Despite his exhaustion, Derek stood tall, ready to face the beast. His heart raced in his chest as his arms began to emit a bright white light.

His voice sounded more confident than he was. "I'll do whatever it takes," but his arms started to flicker and fade. It was evident that he was still weakened from his encounter with the harpy.

Sarika turned to him and spoke in a low voice, "I've got this one. We may not be able to avoid a confrontation, but I know how to outsmart it. These creatures are known for their ferocity and territorial nature, but they do have vulnerabilities. And besides, I'll try to stay awake for this fight."

As the minotaur prowled closer, it let out a menacing growl that sent chills down Sarika's spine. She raised her hand, conjuring a ball of blue fire that illuminated the dark surroundings. Derek stood slightly behind her, his arms gradually returning to their normal state. The creature charged ferociously, its hooves pounding against the ground.

Without hesitation, Sarika hurled the fireball towards it, causing an explosion of light before plunging the entire area into darkness. They couldn't even see their hands in front of their faces, but they were met with a sweet smell in the air.

"Was that all it took?" Derek whispered in disbelief.

The answer came in the form of a deep rumble, a blast of hot air and mucus hitting Derek's face. Trembling, he lifted his faintly glowing hand, revealing the massive minotaur towering over him. It snarled with bloodshot eyes, its fur singed from Sarika's attack.

Sarika's voice rang out in a panicked shout, "Run!"

Derek was paralyzed with fear, but Sarika's loud yell caught the attention of the minotaur. It turned towards her and charged again. Sarika twirled her arms in a circular motion, conjuring up a blue mist from the ground that caused the beast to slip and fall. She hurled a barrage of blue fireballs at the horned creature, who let out a pained cry as each one found its mark.

With a momentary pause, Sarika conjured a sword made of the blue essence surrounding her. As the minotaur stood up again, she charged forward with her glowing sword. Every strike emitted a brilliant flash of blue light, and any attempt by the minotaur to advance was met with a powerful blast of wind from Sarika's hands.

As Sarika's wind blew through Derek's hair, admired how fearless she looked, standing face-to-face with the minotaur, undaunted by his size and strength. Eyes tracking the surety in which she grabbed her blade, he was mesmerized as he watched her battle, heart jumping into his throat as her nimble steps barely avoided a swipe to her shoulder. Her movements were graceful yet powerful, and each of her attacks hit their mark with precision.

The minotaur's desperation was evident as it lunged towards Sarika. She attempted to evade the attack, but the creature managed to grab hold of her with its massive hand. Thrown to the ground, she had a moment of panic as he snarled over her. At her cry of fear, adrenaline coursed through Derek's veins, filling him with small pulses of power. His muscles tightened as he charged the beast, his arms flickering with white light.

He shouted out, "Hey you, big angry cow! Over here!"

The minotaur was unbothered. It lifted its massive hand and prepared to bring it down on Sarika with lethal force. Acting swiftly, she conjured up a larger cloud of essence to shield herself from the brute's strike. Meanwhile, Derek, seizing the opportunity, attempted to summon bolts of lightning onto the minotaur, as he had done with the harpy earlier. To his dismay, nothing happened. As the minotaur's hand went to connect with Sarika's shield, Derek let out a primal roar that strained his vocal cords. Ripping through him with force, a burst of pure white light shot forth from arms and pierced straight through the Minotaur's hand.

Derek's light dimmed and his stomach turned as he realized he hadn't just pierced the hand but cleaved it clean off. With one final scream of pain, the minotaur turned and fled into the darkness

Sarika grunted, "That was amazing!"

Derek smiled. "Couldn't have done it without you. You were incredible!"

"Well, that is true. I did do most of the work anyway" she let out a soft but tired laugh, "Thank you."

Derek held his hand out to help her up. As she grabbed his hand, her stigmata once again lit up with white light. Derek could still sense the walls she was putting up, but there was something different this time. It was almost like the walls were falling over. She was opening up to him.

They exchanged a quick look before Sarika pulled away.

"Come on, we need to get to the river." She said, turning to hide her blush.

Derek's eyes squinted towards the distant waterfall, the blue orb still hovering above it. "You're right. Let's go."

The rest of their journey to the waterfall went smoothly, almost . . . pleasantly. Sarika seemed to have a natural way of putting Derek's mind at ease, speaking soothingly of the beauties of her world to distract him and playfully teasing him when he got too in his head. He had just learned of magic a few short hours ago, and he should be freaking out about fighting harpies and minotaurs in some godforsaken dimension. Instead, he found himself smiling as she danced ahead, revealing in her exploration of this other dimension, and blushing when she threw a wink over her shoulder after catching one of his increasingly frequent, lingering stares.

As they approached the river, the air grew thick and oppressive. With each step, the stench intensified. Finally reaching the shoreline and hearing the rush of water, Derek came to a halt. A pang of sorrow filled his chest as thoughts of Earth flooded his mind. What has Johnathan discovered at school? Has anyone realized he's missing? Has anyone learned about Izzy yet? And Mia . . . he'd barely gotten the chance to really know her, yet already, he missed her with a fierce ache.

Derek's gaze shifted to the river, letting the familiar sound wash through his mind and remind him of what he had to get back home to. The two of them made their way to the edge, peering down to see a massive whirlpool churning at the bottom. Derek couldn't look away from the violent water.

Sarika noticed Derek's posture change and asked, "Are you alright, Derek?"

He paused, struggling to find the right words to express his emotions. "I'm worried about everyone back home." His throat tightened as guilt set in. "Traveling through here with you, I almost forgot about Izzy." Derek slid his foot across the ground and wiped away a stray tear with his flannel sleeve. "She was kinda the glue that held me and the guys together." He took a long, deep breath. "And . . . I miss Mia," he confessed with a hint of caution, not wanting to hurt Sarika's feelings. "I thought we would be on this wild journey together. I can't wait to get to her, but I gotta admit, I'm also enjoying our time together. Even with the stank and darkness around us."

Sarika's lips curved into a gentle smile, recognizing the inner turmoil that consumed Derek. "I'll overlook that comment because I understand your true intention," she said soothingly. "It's natural to have conflicting emotions, Derek. You must not harbor guilt. Not about Mia, and not about," she walked over behind him, placing a hand on his back, "and not about what happened with Izzy. Neither of these things are under your control."

Derek shared a look of understanding with Sarika. No words came to him, but she could tell by the conviction in his eyes, her words hit home with him. He took a few minutes to stare into the water below.

"What do we do now?" he asked, overwhelmed and unsure of their next move.

Sarika took hold of his hand, excitement lighting up her face as she stepped closer to the edge.

Derek turned to meet her stare in confusion before he had a sinking realization of what exactly she intended. Nervously, he teased,

"This is no ordinary water slide."

Sarika playfully spun him around so that he was facing away from the cascading waterfall.

"Derek, do you trust me?"

He nodded slowly, but before he could speak, she cupped his face in her hands and pulled his lips to hers. Guilt coursed through his body. Guilt that this wasn't Mia——Mia who had kissed him sweetly, who he'd had a crush on forever, who was waiting for him to come back. Mia, who seemed like she might want to explore the connection they had. But there was another guilt. Because he *liked* the kiss.

The fact was, Sarika had been here for him in a way he never expected. Sarika was the one helping him through all of this. She was also showing an interest in him, and selfishly, he enjoyed it. The guilt faded as he melted into her. His heart pounded and his mind cleared of everything but this moment. Her lips were like the whisper of a breeze on a warm summer's evening.

Just as he wrapped his arms around her waist, Derek felt Sarika's smile curl into a mischievous grin, and then they were falling.

They fell for minutes with Sarika still holding tight to Derek, who was lost in his confusion about the kiss and the weightlessness of their tumble towards the whirlpool.

As they crashed into the water below, a blinding white void consumed them once again. Derek's heart sank as he realized he could no longer feel Sarika's comforting arms around him. Alone in this vast emptiness, he fell. Or was it more like floating? Memories began to flood his mind.

His mother's sweet voice echoed in his head, wishing him a good day on his first day of freshman year. He thrashed around, trying to find any way to steady himself.

He could see his friends waiting for him on some random day at school. Izzy, smiling, laughing, talking in an endless stream, the way only she could do. In the way he'd never hear again. He swung his arms around, hoping he could swim to her.

The pride in his father's face when he told him he made the baseball team. He stretched all of his limbs out, throwing his head back, screaming to see them all.

Soon enough, a chorus of voices surrounded Derek, a mix of familiar friends and new faces, creating a surreal symphony of chatter.

One last flash. He could see a dark, unrecognizable figure, cloaked in shadows and malice.

A shout escaped Derek's lips, and then there was a peculiar sensation beneath him. "*Is that grass?*" he wondered to himself. Slowly, he opened his eyes and took in the unfamiliar hue of the sky above. The air smelled fresher than anything he had ever experienced before. He wasn't in Mythos anymore.

Chapter 14

Almost Reunited

Mia ran towards the Anchor, her heart racing with hope for Derek's safe arrival. But instead of him, she found herself facing the familiar but exhausted faces of Johnathan, Barry, and Trey.

Mia's voice was shaky as she asked, "Where have you guys been?"

The trio exchanged looks, but before they could answer, Komipea appeared and used his powerful magic to lift Barry and Trey off the ground.

Komipea knew Johnathan by name, having heard about him from his father. The other two, however, were unfamiliar faces to him. John attempted to provide an explanation, but Trey interrupted and demanded to be released. When Komipea refused, Trey summoned a dangerous weapon made of red and blue essence, hurling it towards the Chieftain. Tah'quhal, even though still upset about the lies he had been told for so long, reacted swiftly and used his own magical abilities to dispel the deadly dagger.

Johnathan slammed down his keeper staff. A resounding boom echoed from the base of the Anchor, and the portal inside sealed shut.

"Enough!" Johnathan shouted.

Startled, Komipea lost concentration on his magic, freeing Trey and Barry. The Chieftain stared at Johnathan in shock.

"Oh my dear boy, what have you done?"

As Mia's eyes landed on the closed portal, she was overwhelmed with emotion. That was the only way she could find Derek. Tears cascaded down her cheeks as she launched herself at Johnathan, beating her fists uselessly against his chest, demanding that he re-open the portal. His arms wrapped tightly around her, soothingly murmuring reassurances to her like she was a skittish farm horse. Eventually, she calmed down enough to tell him what happened. She urgently explained that Derek and Sarika never made it through the Anchor and were now missing.

Johnathan drew a long deep breath.

"Mia, I promise I will explain about the portal, but there is something ya'll need to hear first."

Mia crossed her arms, jaw tight, but she listened.

John began to explain, "Trey here is not only attuned to magic, he is half fae. Can ya believe that?" He scanned the faces in front of him. "And Mia, get this, Ivan," his eyes darted to Tah'quhal as he pointed his finger towards him, "the boy *he* killed, was Trey's half brother."

Komipea glared at Tah'quhal in disappointment.

John continued, "Unfortunately, Trey won't say who the hell their daddy is, but there is more important information."

Barry coughed to remind John of his presence.

"Oh yea! First off, Chieftain Komipea, it is great to meet you. This here is one of mine and Derek's closest friends, Barry."

Komipea grew a cheerful smile and shook Barry's hand. "Well, a friend of the Keeper is a friend of mine. Great to meet you, Barry!"

"It actually might be easier if I show y'all all of this," John said as he pointed his Keeper staff toward the ground and touched two fingers to his temple. Essence poured from the tip, and it revealed an almost cinematic like scene in the haze.

Back at Riverrun High, the sight that greeted them was beyond comprehension. The school was engulfed in flames, with red clouds looming overhead and strange ripples appearing in the sky. Students and faculty were herded onto the football field by Tarik and other fae. It was clear that the evil fae were using mind control spells to manipulate the humans. Johnathan heard Trey's cries for help and quickly located him and Barry, who were being chased by Tarik. Thinking fast, Johnathan used his keeper staff to transport them all back to his farm.

Once they were back at the farm, he grilled Trey about his family and explained to Barry what all was happening. Just after John explained what had happened with Izzy, Tarik showed up with an army of elves and a shadowy figure beside him. The boys made a run for the Anchor, bringing them to Torvania.

John told the group that Tarik was slowly walking towards the Anchor when he stepped through. He sealed it, hoping that would prevent him from following them to Torvania. He admitted that he was unsure if he could reopen it, but if it can be sealed, it can be opened, right?

Mia looked up from the haze and noticed someone had gone missing. "Wait, where is Trey?"

The group frantically looked around, but he seemed to have vanished into thin air. Tah'quhal became enraged; the only person who may have knowledge about their situation was now gone without a trace.

"He must know something!" Tah'quhal yelled.

Komipea quickly signaled for his guards and sent them out to search for Trey. The others decided to split up and comb the city for any clues of his whereabouts, agreeing to reconvene at the Chieftain's house at nightfall.

As the sun sank below the horizon and shadows stretched across Torvania, the group sought refuge within the walls of Komipea's grand estate. Yet, their minds were restless. Tah'quhal relentlessly searched for Trey, his desperation driving him through the night. Mia couldn't stop thinking about Derek's absence, a deep ache that only worsened with time. Johnathan was torn with worry for Trey's well-being in Tah'quhal's grasp, while Barry struggled to make sense of this unfamiliar world he had been thrust into.

In the midst of this chaotic emotional storm, Komipea's unexpected warmth towards Barry came as a surprise. The Chieftain welcomed him with open arms, extending a fragile truce in the midst of brewing conflict. Komipea had never hosted a human that was not attuned before. He was eager to learn about the human world from someone with no access to magic. An unskewed opinion amidst so many biases. Not only was Barry recognized as a visitor, but also as a part of their realm——the first human to find shelter in the heart of Torvania without an invitation. This newfound sense of belonging brought confusion and comfort to Barry's mind.

The next morning, Tah'quhal brashy came through the door of the Chieftains home.

"I have searched all night, and there is still no sign of Trey!"

He looked around the main room, noticing Mia still sleeping on the sofa, and Barry and Johnathan seemingly having a competition of who could snore the loudest, on the ground in front of her.

A hearty chuckle echoed from the cooking area. "Oh my boy, looks like neither of us slept. You were out searching, and I was trying to find a spell to make their rumbles quieter."

Tah'quhal cut his eyes at the Chieftain as the latter walked through the archway separating the two rooms.

"You still have plenty to explain. I will wake the humans," Tah'quhal said.

"Do wake them. But Tah'quhal, allow me the day to get everything together. I know I promised answers, and I will provide them. Send Barry to meet me at the library when he is ready. I wish to ask him some questions of my own." Komipea's eyes softened. "Then, as the moon begins to rise, have everyone else meet us at the burning pit."

Before Tah'quhal could answer, the Chieftain walked out of the room. His fist clenched for a moment, but he took a deep breath to center himself. He turned to look back at the humans, seeing Barry stretching his arms and letting out a yawn.

"You," he pointed at Barry, "Wake the others and then meet the Chieftain at the Library."

"For why?" Barry asked, still half asleep.

Tah'quhal snapped, "Because he asked for you to. I will meet the rest of you at the burning pit tonight."

As Tah'quhal stormed out of the house, Barry threw his hand up in a mock salute, whispering, "Well, aye aye, Captain."

Barry nudged Johnathan and Mia to wake them up. "I guess you two are supposed to meet us tonight at some burning pit. I'm going to meet the Chieftain."

"Huh? Why are ya doing that?" Johnathan asked as he rubbed his eyes.

Barry made his way to the door, looking over his shoulder. "I dunno. Taj Mahal told me to, so I guess I gotta do it."

Mia chuckled, "So close, Barry, so close."

The rest of the day passed without any concern. Mia and Johnathan chose to stay in Komipea's home, Tah'quhal searched the city and surrounding area for Trey, and Barry answered the Chieftain's seemingly unimportant questions. As the sun began to set in Torvania, Mia and Johnathan were the first to arrive at the pit. Shortly after, Tah'quhal made his way down.

The Chieftain came from the Library, Barry in tow, carrying a tray full of cups. As the Komipea got to the pit, his stigmata shimmered with blue essence. Snapping his fingers, the pit erupted in flames.

The group settled in around the campfire that Komipea had made. He had brought out several cups of nectar for the story ahead. Seeing the drinks, Mia reached for a cup, but Komipea stopped her.

"No dear, I'll be needing all of these."

He downed the first cup while everyone found their spots. John sat on a log in front of the blaze, while Barry and Mia sat on either side of him. Tah'quhal stood behind them, arms crossed and shoulders tense.

"The truth about Torviid and Malum is a long one, but I will do my best to make it easy to understand," said Komipea as he reached for another cup of nectar. "The battle that is taught here in Torvania did take place, but it was hardly the first."

Tah'quhal grunted. He knew this story was coming but still wasn't ready to believe the Chieftain had lied to him all his life.

After another sip of his drink, Komipea continued, "Torviid and Malum were both raised in Laresque, what you all now know as Torvania, and they were very close as younglings."

Barry grinned, trying to lighten the mood as he joked, "Waaaiiit, *Malum* is the bad guy, right?"

A light thump to the back of the head from Tah'quhal reminded him that now was not the time to crack jokes.

Suppressing a smile, the Chieftain got back on track. "As they grew older, Malum became increasingly obsessed with manipulating the essence that grants us magic. After many years, he had successfully created a form known as *Odium*. It could twist other beings . . . corrupt them. Giving him full control over their body and mind."

"What about their souls?" Tah'quhal asked softly.

After a beat, Komipea answered, "I am not sure, my boy." He took another large gulp of nectar. "No one has ever been *uncorrupted.*"

Tah'quhal's jaw clenched, eyes burning into Komipea. "What about Tarik?"

The Chieftain walked to stand by his side and place a comforting hand on his shoulder, but Tah'quhal slapped it away, taking a sharp step back.

"Do. Not. Touch me." He seethed. "You have lied to me every single day of my life, and I have tried to let that go, but before we left for Earth, you made it sound like there was *hope* for Tarik. And *now,* you tell me no one has ever been saved from this?"

Komipea bowed his head, trying to hide the shame in his eyes.

Barry sprang to his feet, standing chest-to-chest with the fae warrior as he snapped, "What do you mean you want to save Tarik? He killed Izzy!"

Johnathan stood up. "Woah, easy there, buddy. This is new to all of us. We lost Izzy. Tah'quhal here . . . he is learning he most likely lost his best friend, too."

The heated stare between Barry and Tah'quhal lasted a few moments, each sizing each other up, the latter taking shocked note of the boy's height advantage. With that build and spirit, Tah'quhal thought he'd make a fine warrior. The sounds of clashing swords and laughter flashed through his mind, sending a pang shooting through his chest. Breaking eye contact, Tah'quhal wearily said,

"Just finish the story, Chieftain."

As everyone settled back down, Komipea continued,

"Very well. Torviid had tried to convince Malum what he was doing was wrong. One day, while Malum was toying with his dangerous magic, he disappeared in a burst of red essence. Many believed he had died, but some thought maybe he was transported to another dimension."

Mia recognized the heavy weight bearing down on Komipea, offering, "Chieftain, I can tell the next part."

The Chieftain gave her a grateful smile and nod.

Mia looked down at her tattoo and went on with the story.

"As Tah'quhal found out yesterday, there are other Keepers, so now would be as good a time as any." She took a deep breath. "I am the Keeper for Oceanus."

Johnathan almost fell off the log he was sitting on.

"What the hell do you mean you're a Keeper? Where is your staff? What is an Oceanus?"

She drew a circle in the dirt with her shoe, refusing to look up at anyone.

"Well, not all Keepers have a staff, and Oceanus is another fae city in Luminfae. My Keeper item is ashes of the first Chieftain of Oceanus. They are mixed into the ink used for my stigmata."

Barry's eyes twitched.

"Wait girl, so you like . . . you got a dead person *in* your tattoo?"

Mia let out a short giggle. "We can talk more about how morbid you made that sound later. Let's finish the story first."

The group was mostly silent, save for a couple agreeing mumbles and Johnathan's incredulous stare.

Mia went on, "After many years, Malum returned. His body had undergone a *crazy* transformation, red eyes, dark essence swirling around him, the whole nine yards. Torviid, of course, confronted him, but Malum didn't come looking for a fight. Instead, he really thought he could convince the fae of Laresque to join his cause. He wanted to dominate all the dimensions and place them under his rule. This creep *claimed* to have traveled to every dimension possible and asked for Torviid to join him."

Komipea walked over beside her, signaling he was okay to continue.

"Torviid turned his back to Malum in defiance. Malum vanished again, leaving an army of elves behind." The Chieftain's shoulders dramatically rose and fell as he took a deep breath. "They rained hellfire down on the city. The citizens of Laresque fought bravely, but by the time they finished off the small army, Malum was already off recruiting whoever he could. It was the start of the First Fae Wars."

Tah'quhal grew more and more agitated by the moment.

"You have mentioned the wars before, but so far, you have only described a battle."

"You're right, my boy," Komipea said. "Over the next hundred years, battles broke out all across Luminfae, thanks to Malum's twisted crusade. The final battle took place where it all began. Laresque."

The Chieftain grabbed another cup of nectar, staring into it as if he was seeing something long ago.

"Malum's army was massive, but Torviid had mustered plenty of allies over the years. Even still, nothing could prepare Laresque for the battle that would ensue. Family members turned against each other——brothers fighting brothers, fathers fighting sons, mothers fighting daughters. And when the dust finally settled, it was Torviid lying bloodied in the street with Malum standing triumphantly over him. According to witnesses, Torviid spoke an enchantment no one could understand, causing the two fae to be engulfed in white light.

"When the light mellowed out, they were both gone. Amidst the destruction and debris, the fae of Laresque came across a stone where Torviid's body should have been. They called it the Seer Stone when they discovered its ability to open a portal through an ancient arch in the town. As they worked to reconstruct their city, they renamed it Torvania in honor of Torviid, and cast a powerful spell to conceal themselves from the rest of Luminfae, hoping to keep anything like the First fae Wars from ever happening again."

An eerie silence fell over the group. They exchanged looks, trying to process everything they had just heard. Tah'quhal huffed and turned to walk away, but Johnathan asked,

"If Mia is a Keeper, how many more are there?"

The Chieftain responded, "I have plenty of information on that in the library. Perhaps you can come by in the morning and I can show you."

Johnathan cut his eyes to Mia, and then to Barry, and finally back towards Komipea. "I reckon that'll work."

Komipea tapped his fingers on his empty cup. As Chieftain, he had been entrusted with these secrets and knew that one day he would have to share them. After the emotional turmoil he knew he had caused, he suggested that everyone get some rest. Most of them agreed and headed off to bed. Tah'quhal, however, went out into the night once again to search for Trey.

The next four months seemed to stretch on endlessly, each day giving a glimmer of hope that Derek and Sarika would return. However, as the sun set, hope faded into the heavy realization that their friends were still missing. And the mystery of Trey added to Tah'quhal's troubles; he was like a ghost, always just out of reach but leaving traces of his presence all over the city.

The Cressida Library's walls bore witness to the group's quest to understand Luminfae. Komipea revealed as much as he could about the fourth dimension each day, hoping to help them not only find Derek and Sarika, but to find a way to stop the threat of Malum.

Most days enraged Tah'quhal, his world completely rearranged every morning as he discovered new information.

Johnathan grappled with the revelation that there may be multiple Keepers on Earth. His entire life, he had been raised to believe that his family was the only ones responsible for protecting Torvania, but now it seemed that they were not alone in their duties in the fourth dimension. He couldn't tell if he was relieved that he and his family were not alone in protecting Luminfae, or if it made him feel almost less special.

Meanwhile, Barry found comfort in Komipea's teachings, continuing his studies after each lesson. This new knowledge was completely foreign to him, but even though he was far from home in a strange place, he made the most of his time there. He longed to become attuned one day, but didn't think it would be right if he had to ask for it.

Early one morning, Mia yawned and rolled over, reaching her arms out towards the beams of sunlight filtering through her curtains. As she opened her eyes, a soft smile spread across her face at the sight of the room bathed in gentle morning light.

That moment of peace was ripped away by the realization that she woke up safe and warm, while Derek was still missing. She took a moment to steady herself before making her way to the common area of Komipea's home. Tah'quhal and the Chieftain were already sitting on the couch, sipping on nectar.

"Still no sign of Derek?" she inquired.

Komipea simply shook his head, indicating he had not seen or heard a thing. Tah'quhal reassured her that, even in Derek's disappearance, she still had Barry, Johnathan, and himself . . . even if Barry was always in the library or trying to train with the other warriors. Mia felt a sense of relief but still had concerns for Derek's safety. Komipea took a long swig from his wooden cup, then let out a hearty belch.

Mia, curious and slightly disgusted, gestured towards the cup in his hand and asked, "What exactly are you drinking?"

The old Chieftain chuckled and replied, "This is our traditional nectar——made from fermented berries and spices. It's quite strong for humans and I believe there is an age requirement on Earth for something like this, but given the circumstances, I don't think one sip would do much harm."

Mia's fingers curled around the intricately carved cup, her nose hovering over it as she inhaled deeply. The scent of fresh lemons and oranges filled her senses. She took a cautious sip, feeling the fiery liquid burn its way down her throat. A small cough escaped her lips, quickly followed by an exclamation of surprise. Despite the sharp taste, it was exactly what she needed in that moment——a burst of flavor and warmth to distract from the chaos surrounding her.

The rare serene moment was shattered by a piercing screech that sliced through the air. A violent boom followed, unleashing a shockwave that rattled Mia's bones and sent books flying off the shelves in the Chieftain's home. Barry came running down from upstairs, his eyes wide. Johnathan rushed from the cooking area, swiping his hand in front of him, as his Keeper staff materialized. Tah'quhal and Komipea slid their hands over their arms, readying their magic. The terror on everyone's face mirrored Mia's as she said, "I don't think that was Derek."

Chapter 15

Going Away Party

The roars of battle cries echoed throughout Torvania, their ominous sound casting a dark shadow over the city as the sky filled with hellfire. Corrupted fae and elves pounded at the gates, and as the defenders fought them back, new waves of enemies surged forward to take their places. From the surrounding hills, armies of twisted creatures launched fireballs that caused the walls to tremble. It was a battle on a scale not seen since before the city's fortifications were built.

The group reacted swiftly, converging on the entrance that was under the heaviest attack to defend against the advancing darkness. Standing before them was a familiar foe——Tarik, the mastermind controlling the attack.

The mere sight of Tarik sparked a blazing anger and grief within Tah'quhal. He now knew Tarik couldn't be saved, and he was furious with his Chieftain for not telling him that. He knew the fiend standing in front of him was no longer his friend, but how could he just forget all the good times they shared? All the times they trained together at the lake? Hesitating for just a moment, he forcefully swallowed and began chanting spells with such fervor that blue essence enveloped him, and he soared into the air towards Tarik, hardening his heart, even as he felt it breaking. He pushed his body harder, faster. Just as he was raising his hand for the attack, a darkness lashed into him, sending pain shooting through his body as he was violently thrown back.

The Chieftain's body froze, a cold sweat breaking out along his brow. He swallowed hard as he watched the shadowy form of Malum emerge from Tarik's body. He witnessed the shadow strike with a power that words couldn't describe, knocking Tah'quhal to the ground and leaving a large crater in his path. Just as quickly as it appeared, the shadow retreated back into Tarik, leaving Komipea's bravest warrior bruised and beaten in the dirt.

Komipea sent his fleetest soldiers to aid Tah'quhal, trusting that his unwavering spirit would soon rejoin the fight. The Chieftain marched towards the frontline, ready to join the defense of the walls, when he saw Barry peeking around the corner of a house.

"Barry, why are you hiding when your own are in danger?" He challenged.

Barry looked to Komipea, his shame overridden by the shaking in his hands.

"I . . . I don't know how to fight. I've only had a couple of lessons with your warriors. I don't even have magic. The only thing I can do out there is get people killed trying to protect me." He spoke softly.

The Chieftain's eyes were fierce but soft as he looked at Barry. "There was a fae from the wars who did not use magic. A loyal, brave warrior that let nothing keep him from defending his own——not even his fear." Waving his hand, a gleaming sword appeared in his grip. "He used items imbued with powerful magic, riding a mighty griffin to lead the front lines." Komipea held the sword out to Barry, placing the hilt in his hands. "When you are ready, take his sword and stand with us."

Barry gave a nervous nod as Komipea continued towards the walls of Torvania to join the fight. He held the sword tightly in his unsteady hands, admiring the design of the ancient blade. The silver metal gleamed under the faint light peeking around the house, its sharp edge reflecting the surroundings with a metallic sheen. Tiny, intricate engravings adorned the hilt, telling tales of forgotten battles and legendary heroes. Embedded in the crossguard, blue jewels glistened like drops of captured starlight, their glow intensifying with each passing second. As he steadied his hands on the hilt, a sudden warmth pulsed through his palm, and a flicker of flame danced along the blade.

He could feel the power coming from the sword, but he was still too terrified to join the fight. The stone walls of the house scratched his back as slid down to the ground. He let out a sigh and softly whispered, "What am I doing here?"

Johnathan, on the other hand, knew his role. He was the Keeper of Torvania, after all. Pushing towards the cracking walls, he slammed his staff into the ground, sending a shock up his arm. A protective shield of essence formed around the defending fae. He shouted,

"Why are they attacking?"

Mia came running with cupped hands from a nearby fountain, her stigmata shining a vibrant blue hue. She dropped the water towards the ground, whispering,

"*Ferrum.*"

The water began to swirl around her, and she pulled two dripping daggers from the stream. She looked at Johnathan.

"I'm not sure why, but I'm pretty sure I know *who*." Her voice was tight with fear. "We must defend the city. Derek has to have somewhere to find us. Besides, this is nothing a couple of Keepers can't handle, right?" Her false confidence was palpable.

Even though he knew she was only saying it to make them both feel better, it worked. She was right about Derek, but he had no idea if their combined magic would be enough to stave off this onslaught.

Komipea shouted, "Brace!" just before a massive fireball slammed into the main gate of the city. The stones crumbled, succumbing to the raging inferno, and left a crater in the city's defenses. John and Mia heard the deafening explosion a split second before they were sent hurting back into destruction and dust.

The ringing in Mia's ears was unbearably loud. Coughing, she tried to open her eyes, but everything around her was blurry. Broken pieces of stone and metal dug into her hands as she attempted to get to her feet, but her shaking only allowed her to make it to her knees. There was rock dust hanging in the air from the explosion, making it hard to breathe.

Through her doubled vision, Mia watched a figure battling against the enemy line. White orbs of light streaked through the air, colliding with the adversaries and sending them flying. Radiant waves surged forward, shoving the enemies out of the breach in the gate, the light shimmering and crackling with each pulse.

"Derek!" she shouted, scrambling forward to get closer to him, to see him. Her double vision gradually focused on the figure in front of her. As the two blurred fighters merged into one, the white light was only the hot edges of blue fire. It was then she realized——it was Johnathan.

A sharp pain pierced her chest. She had truly believed Derek had returned. At least, she'd wanted to believe. Tears streamed down her face knowing that he was still missing. He wouldn't show up to save her this time. Despite the sorrow weighing her down, the ache in all of her limbs, Mia found the strength to stand. She knew she had to protect the city, especially if she ever wanted to see Derek again. Whispering her incantation, she drew her blades, the familiar weight grounding her, and moved towards the battle, her resolve and speed growing with every steadying step she took.

Standing side by side with Johnathan, she sliced through her enemies with razor-edged spurts of water. Her daggers striking true every time a foe would get too close. The battle seemed endless, but they were holding their own at the hole in the gate, while the city guard did their best to fight outside the wall.

Two corrupted fae charged at Chieftain Komipea, their spears dripping with red essence. Mia watched as he brought his palms together at his chest before flinging his arms forward, knocking the spears from the fae's hands with a pulse. Unfazed, the fae continued their charge. Desperately, Mia hurled both of her daggers at them, but neither struck true. Horror filled her as the fae closed in on Komipea, but it quickly turned to delight as the Chieftain seized each Fae by the throat, his grip unyielding, and slammed them into the ground.

Barry brushed the dust off his pants from the explosion of the city's main gate. Still holding a death grip on the sword the Chieftain had given him, he watched as Mia rose to her feet and fought alongside Johnathan and Komipea, flinching as an enemy's spear narrowly missed Johnathan's side. Fear gripped him, but this time, it was not for himself. *"I have to help them. I can't just stand here and do nothing."* As the thoughts crossed his mind, the sword's flame ignited again.

Taking a long, slow breath, Barry closed his eyes, telling himself, *"You are Barry Grayson. You are a star athlete. You are capable of anything."*

He opened his eyes just in time to see Komipea obliterate the two fae that had charged him. A slow flicker in his periphery, at odds with the raging conflict around them, pulled his eyes to a sneaky little elf trying to hide in the debris. Nausea rolled through him as it pulled a dagger from behind its back and crept towards the Chieftain.

Barry launched himself off the ground. He hadn't even consciously decided to move but he was running as fast as he could, pushing his body harder than ever before. In the knick of time, Barry made it behind Komipea, swinging his sword down and deflecting the elf's attack. The Chieftain turned around and flicked his wrist towards the elf, sending it flying far over the city walls.

Tah'quhal fought his way back to consciousness, only to be met with the horrifying sight of his home, his *people*, under siege. Letting out a guttural bellow that shook the very ground beneath him, he summoned all his strength to unleash an explosive burst of blue energy that surrounded him like a fierce storm. With fury burning in his eyes, he reached out with an iron grip of magic and pulled Tarik to the ground, ready to put an end to the madness.

As Tah'quhal neared Tarik, he caught a glimpse of bright purple energy coursing through his enemy's body. Time seemed to slow around him. His fist flew towards Tarik's face when a dark figure emerged from Tarik, its red eyes gleaming through the ominous smoke as it locked its gaze on him. Trey materialized, a transparent form in front of Tarik, in a burst of vibrant purple light.

"Find Derek!" he yelled, his voice tinged with pain, before disappearing once more.

Time picked back up, and Tah'quhal could feel his knuckles crack as his punch landed squarely on Tarik's jaw, knocking him to the ground, and his head bouncing off a piece of rubble.

Mia and the others rushed to Tah'quhal's side, where he was now kneeling next to Tarik. They all watched as Tarik's stigmata slowly shifted from a corrupted red back to their natural blue. Tah'quhal hoped it meant his friend was fighting the corruption, but that was far from the truth. The tranquility was short-lived as Tarik's sinister grin warned them of a new danger approaching.

With swift and deadly grace, Tarik summoned a blade of crimson essence that seemed to pulse with malice. He lunged at Komipea's heart, lethal intent clear in his eyes. Before he could pierce Komipea's heart, Barry's sword sliced clean through Tarik's wrist. Blinking in shock at his own actions, he had the intrusive thought that he'd never been more grateful for the years he'd spent honing his reflexes on the football field. Tarik's now empty wrist poured blood, causing him to let out an agonizing scream that quickly turned into mad and deranged laughter. For the second time in the fight, Barry was able to save Komipea from danger.

Malum's dark shadow sprang forth from Tarik, looming over them all. Mia's trembling hand pointed out the swirling mass of darkness above them, and they could only watch in horror as it consumed Tarik's body. From his severed stump, pure blackness oozed out, transforming into a twisted limb controlled by the malicious entity that then possessed him once again.

Red essence erupted from Tarik's body as he stood up, animosity etched into his face.

"This isn't finished," he declared before taking flight towards Canter Mountain, a stream of shadows left behind him.

His followers vanishing into a cloud of pure darkness at their leader's departure. Left behind were the ruins of the city gate and settling dust over an otherwise untouched city.

While walking towards Komipea, an unsettling thought crossed Tah'quhal's mind. Since Tarik had seemed to fake beating the corruption, had his oldest companion truly been under Malum's control, or did he genuinely believe in their twisted cause?

Mia stared towards Canter Mountain and quietly asked, "Should we go after them?"

Tah'quhal placed his hand on her shoulder, whether for her comfort or his, he couldn't tell.

"I believe we should."

Johnathan interjected, "What if Derek shows up and we ain't here?"

The group fell silent for a moment as Komipea scanned the city, seeing the destruction, his citizens tending to wounded soldiers.

"I will stay behind and assist with the repairs to the city gate. If Derek and Sarika arrive, I will inform them of your departure."

Barry spoke up hesitantly, "Uh, guys? There may be another priority. Over the last few months, I've been doing some research in the library."

John, being slightly impatient, "Well, spit it out, buddy!"

A grin grew on Barry's face as he continued more confidently, "I read something about the *Hellfire Brigade*. They supposedly had similar magic to Malum. From what I can tell, the group was created in Terra. If we can learn more about them, then maybe we'd have an idea about defeating Malum."

Komipea tensed and his lips formed a slight frown at the mention of the Hellfire Brigade. He shared with the group what little he knew about them; they were a radicalized human group determined to carry out Malum's plans. He had not heard any rumors of them for the last hundred or so years, so he assumed they had either died or given up. If they had returned, it was possible that they were the cause of Malum's return, but in order to learn more, someone would have to make the journey to Terra, as Barry had suggested.

Tah'quhal interjected, "Tarik has fled to the mountain for a reason. Malum must have something there he needs. Mia and I need to get there and figure it out."

Mia nodded. "Tah'quhal is right, Barry. I'm sorry, but something is telling me that following Tarik is the move we need to make."

Even with the objections, Barry remained determined that someone had to go to Terra.

"I'll go," Barry said with gusto.

Doing his best to put on a brave face as he committed to a journey he knew was so far out of his depths.

Komipea looked at Barry with clear pride shining in his eyes.

"I knew I was not wrong to give you that sword. Keep it close, and continue to wield it with courage and wisdom."

The Chieftain swirled his hands and a leather sheath appeared. As he gave it to Barry, he said, "The sword's name is Everflame. Its original owner was a brave warrior, but sadly, he perished in battle many centuries ago. Even though that warrior is long gone, his bravery and spirit live on in the blade." Komipea leaned in close and whispered into Barry's ear, "Remember, magic is not the only power a warrior can wield."

Barry straightened his shoulders, face turning uncharacteristically serious. "I will carry it with honor, Chieftain Komipea."

Johnathan didn't want his friend to face this dangerous journey alone. "Buddy, you know I ain't letting you go without me. But how the hell are we going to get there?"

Barry's hardened face turned to a smile. "I know you always got my back."

Komipea materialized a small golden locket.

"You may find this last gift of particular use, Barry," said the chieftain as he handed him the locket and instructed him to open it.

To his surprise, a map was projected from the device. It depicted the entire realm of Luminfae, and when Komipea uttered the word "Terra," a line appeared showing the most efficient route to the city——through the Magia Forest and Ignis, the land of the succubi.

"This locket does not only contain a map. It will guarantee your safe travels beyond our borders." The Chieftain gave a close mouthed smile. "Although our great city has remained . . . cut off from the rest of Luminfae, myself and the other Chieftains have long kept in contact through *Torquewhirlers*."

Barry's eyebrow raised, "A what now?"

Mia laughed. "A magical carrier pigeon, Barry."

Komipea continued, "The other Chieftains will recognize my symbol and allow you to pass."

After finalizing their plan, Tah'quhal extended his hand towards the center of the group.

"Still I stand," he murmured.

Mia recognized the words from a story she heard about the First Fae Wars in Oceanus. She placed her hand on top and declared, "Until I fall."

Johnathan added his hand on top of Mia's.

"I will heed the lonesome call."

Barry, feeling a bit confused, looked at the group and joked, "I dunno what any of that meant, but let's do this thang!"

As the group laughed, a sense of camaraderie filled the air. Before they set off, Tah'quhal motioned for a local fae that was helping other soldiers to bring over some food and water. Mia walked up to Barry, snapping a piece of bread in half and handing it to him. They shared a look, but no words were needed, both understanding the gravity of what was to come. As they said their goodbyes, Tah'quhal gave Barry a firm handshake, while Mia and John shared a hug.

With her arms still tight around him in an embrace, Mia whispered to John, "If you see Derek before me, tell him how much I've missed him."

Johnathan gave her a reassuring smile as he released her and turned to join Barry. The two of them would head to Terra, while Mia and Tah'quhal were bound for Canter Mountain. Neither party was quite sure of the depths of the trials they were to face.

As they went their separate ways, Chieftain Komipea watched with equal parts fear for their safety and hope for their safe return. After he could no longer see them, he turned to his city to begin the long process of rebuilding. He had only taken a step when a sharp cough shook him. When he removed his hand from his mouth, there was a small amount of blood in his palm. Looking down at his chest, he noticed a tiny cut where Tarik's blade had grazed him. Blood began to trickle out and transform into crimson mist as it fell to the ground.

Chapter 16

Twist of Fate

The air was clean and cold, and the faint hum of fae voices could be heard off in the distance. Derek stood up slowly, taking in his surroundings. They were alien, yet familiar to him. He bent over and ran his hand through the grass, taking a full breath. Then it hit him. His nightmare flashed in his brain as he recalled the words he'd been cursed to listen to every night.

He clutched at his chest as his breathing became erratic. This place, this was the same field as in his dream. Derek was standing in the exact spot that he stood every night. To make matters worse, he realized Sarika was not with him. Frantically, he searched the area for her, calling her name. Derek was close to losing it when he heard rustling in the grass nearby and rushed over to find Sarika's unconscious body. He knelt beside her and gently brushed his thumb across one of her glowing markings, causing it to turn bright red for a fleeting moment before returning to its original color. Overcome with equal parts confusion and concern, he shrugged off the unease the red flash gave him so he could focus on helping Sarika.

She slowly regained consciousness and noticed the worried expression on Derek's face.

"What's wrong?" she asked.

"Are you okay? You were out cold." He asked.

"Yes." Sarika scanned her eyes over her body. "Yes, I am perfectly fine, actually. Are you okay?"

Derek shook his head, still unsure if what he saw was real. The only words that came out were,

"Did you really kiss me?"

Sarika giggled in response. "Is that a problem?"

Derek looked away sheepishly and whispered, "Mia."

Disappointment flashed across Sarika's face, so quick that her expression was the picture of nonchalance when Derek glanced back. Smiling, she reassured him, "It was just to distract you from jumping down a waterfall."

His eyes widened and his mouth flung open. "Jump? I didn't jump. *You* pushed me," he exclaimed.

"Well, yea. Hence the distraction," her giggle echoed.

At that light, gentle sound, Derek had to look away, scanning the scenery for a change of topic. Behind Sarika, a towering wall caught his eye, with a massive statue of a fae looming behind it. He noticed that the wall had been fixed recently. There wasn't very much wear and tear on the stones in that section.

"Is that Torvania?" he asked curiously.

Sarika stood up from her spot on the ground, following his gaze. "That is indeed my home."

In an attempt to lighten the mood and hide his lingering unease, Derek joked, "Looks like that statue could use some pants."

Sarika let out another light laughter at his remark and nudged his shoulder. "We could always suggest that to the sculptor," she played along, intertwining her fingers with his.

Derek glanced down at their joined hands, feeling a mixture of delight and anxiety about what Mia might think of them being so close.

Sarika sensed his unease and withdrew her hand with a light squeeze. "The kiss can be our little secret." Her heart gave a sharp pang as she said it, but she kept her voice as unaffected as possible. She wanted him to reciprocate, to choose to kiss her again. It was clear to her, though, that his heart was set on Mia.

Derek forced a smile. Between the changing stigmata and the kiss, his head was a mess. Derek wouldn't say it out loud, but he enjoyed it. He enjoyed Sarika. She just wasn't Mia. With that thought, his impatience to see Mia grew. He didn't want to keep her waiting any longer and took purposeful strides towards the gate.

As they neared the towering city walls, Sarika rushed to present her pendant to the guards. The gates, which seemed to be larger than life, slowly opened to welcome them in. But as the gates parted, Sarika's initial joy turned into shock and dismay. The once-thriving city of Torvania now was full of gloom. The streets just inside the gate were scarred from battle and a few homes still showed burn marks. The majority of citizens hiding inside, still too shaken to walk the streets freely.

"Who would have attacked the city?" Derek asked with a heavy heart.

She could only utter one word.

"Malum."

Derek wanted to ask her who exactly Malum was, but seeing the look on her face, he thought it might be best to wait until they found Mia.

Sarika whirled around to face the guards, demanding an explanation. All they could offer was a point towards Komipea's, cautioning her about his recent illness. Without any hesitation, she sprinted towards the Chieftain's home, Derek close behind. They raced through the empty streets of Torvania, swiftly arriving at the Chieftain's home.

Panicked, Sarika banged on the door. She waited maybe five seconds and then shoved the door open. Her eyes immediately fell on Komipea sitting on the ground, muttering spells in an attempt to fight his illness. As he heard the door slam open, he opened his eyes to Sarika and Derek standing before him.

A weak smile spread across his face as he greeted them, "Sarika . . . is that really you?" He coughed uncontrollably before continuing, "I was afraid you would never return."

Sarika furrowed her brow, confused by Komipea's words. "What do you mean, we have only been gone for a few hours? The Anchor transported us . . ." she trailed off as she glanced at Derek. "It brought us to a strange place, but it couldn't have been for more than a day."

Komipea turned to Derek, his gaze intense and searching. "You must be the young man that Tah'quhal and Sarika set out to find. Derek Stratum, I presume?" The Chieftain's face showed a mix of emotions——surprise, suspicion, and something else that Derek couldn't quite decipher.

"What exactly are you?" Komipea asked, but before Derek could respond, the elder fae was overcome with a body-wracking coughing fit.

Sarika hurried to his side and gently pressed her hands against the Chieftain's chest. "*Sana*," she murmured, as a bright blue light emanated from her palms.

The Chieftain expressed his gratitude, but he also urged them both to take a seat. He needed to share what had occurred during their absence.

Derek and Sarika listened attentively to the Chieftain's frail, yet resolute voice as he recounted the terrifying events of the latest battle in Torvania.

"Six months ago, your companions arrived here," the Chieftain began. "They informed us that you should have been with them, but you never arrived."

Derek leapt back to his feet. "What the hell do you mean six months?"

"Derek, do not curse at the Chieftain!" Sarika demanded.

Komipea forced a smile. "Sarika, no dear. It is okay. I am sure this is shocking. Please sit back down, and I will tell you everything."

Derek's eyes began to water. "*Six months,*" he thought to himself, "*I've been gone for six whole months?*" He slowly sat back down, not really because the Chieftain asked him to, but because he could not bear to stand any longer with how wobbly his legs had gotten.

He went on to tell them about Johnathan, Barry, and Trey's arrival, and how Trey disappeared soon after. Then he described Tarik's attack on the city, aided by Malum's shadow, and their assumption that Trey was somehow aligned with them because of his shady behavior and brief appearance on the battlefield.

Derek rose to his feet, anger boiling inside him. "How can you say that about my friend?" he yelled, unwilling to believe the accusation, despite how it explained Trey's odd behavior, his explosive anger.

Komipea looked at him sympathetically and reassured him that he had seen it himself. Derek couldn't fathom that one of his closest friends could be helping this Malum guy.

"Someone please explain who exactly Malum is? None of this is making any sense," Derek begged.

Through a few coughing fits, and dragged out breaths, Komipea told him much of the same information he had revealed to Tah'quhal and the others.

It all seemed like a surreal nightmare. Just this morning, he was getting ready for his senior year, and now he had already lost a friend, discovered another was the Keeper of a magical portal, fallen for a girl with ties to this realm, met two fae, kissed one of them, apparently was missing for six months. And now, he was learning that yet another friend might be entangled in this dark plot. He wasn't sure how much more of this he could take. His mind was spinning as Komipea continued his tale.

"Tah'quhal and Mia desperately pursued Tarik." The Chieftain turned his eyes to Sarika. "Although he was no longer the fae we once knew. He fled towards Canter Mountain, with Malum's shadow clinging to him like a helpless child." Focusing his gaze back on Derek, his eyes became haunted. "Unfortunately, I fear their efforts were in vain; it has been two months since then." The Chieftain paused to cough. "Johnathan and Barry embarked on a journey to Terra, hoping to find a solution to defeat Malum."

The walls seemed to be closing in on him. Derek squeezed his eyes shut before lurching out of his chair and making his way towards the door. "I . . . I just need some fresh air," he managed to say before stepping outside to be alone.

Komipea looked to Sarika and motioned for her assistance getting up. She reached out her hand and helped him to his feet.

As he stood, he began to speak, "Sarika, there is something I need to tell you——"

She cut him off, her words colder than the bottom of a glacier. "Tarik should have finished the job."

Her eyes turned a fiery red, mirroring the glowing stigmata on her skin. With a flick of her hand, a blade made of crimson mist materialized and pierced directly into Komipea's chest, phasing through his skin. When the blade disappeared, it left behind only a small mark on his flesh.

The Chieftain's expression was brutally empathetic. "It's not too late," he said with a hint of sadness.

Komipea's body went limp as the last bit of life drained from him. Sarika gently lowered him to the ground, her eyes and hands returning to their normal state. She gazed at his lifeless form with no expression, then walked over to his bookshelf. Picking up the prophecy page that Tah'quhal had read aloud during their last visit, she crumpled it up and stuffed it into her pocket. As she did, she caught a glimpse of the next page in the book and let out a humorless chuckle.

"Still I stand, Until I fall, I will heed the Lonesome call." she read out loud with amusement. "Ignorant fae will believe anything that gives them hope." She laughed once more before tucking the book back into its place.

After stealing another glance at the lifeless body of Komipea, Sarika made her way to the wash basin. She splashed cold water on her face and rubbed her eyes vigorously to create the illusion of tears. Taking a deep breath, she wrapped her arms around herself and let out a blood-curdling scream. Derek rushed back into the room to find the Chieftain lying dead on the floor.

"What the hell happened?" he asked, alarmed.

With disturbingly convincing sobs and sniffles, Sarika ran towards him, throwing herself into his arms.

"He started coughing again," she managed between sobs, "and then . . . he couldn't breathe anymore. My magic couldn't save him."

Derek hugged her tighter, allowing her head to rest on his shoulder as she whispered with a smirk, "I can't be in here . . . let's go outside and inform the guards."

The guards quickly arrived. She repeated her fabrication, even trembling slightly for good measure, before leading Derek to a nearby bench. Still maintaining her charade, she rested her head on his lap as he ran comforting fingers through her hair.

Derek was not quite as fooled as she might think; his thoughts were consumed by the chaotic events of the day, especially what he had witnessed in the fields earlier. The Chieftain hadn't looked *that* bad when he left moments before. *Could Sarika have been responsible for harming Komipea?* The thought lingered, but before he could contemplate it too long, Sarika sat up and emphatically declared,

"We must find Mia and Tah'quhal."

Derek hesitated, but ultimately relented. He was beginning to believe that this was all just a horrible nightmare and he would wake up at any moment. To test his theory, he dug his nails into his thigh, hoping it would jolt him back to reality. Unfortunately, the sharp pain only confirmed that this was not, in fact, a dream. If his suspicions about Sarika were correct, then Mia and Tah'quhal would be able to provide some much-needed guidance.

Derek gazed into Sarika's tearful eyes, aching for her pain, even though he wasn't sure anymore how much of it was real. The path before them was now filled with unknown risks and hazards, and the responsibility of saving their friends, Torvania, and … he didn't want to think of how great the stakes were if Malum had really returned. And to add to his worries, he still had no clue where his magical abilities came from or why he was plagued by the same nightmare.

The two gazed at Canter Mountain, looming far in the distance beyond the city walls, before heading towards the main gate of Torvania. With each anxious step, Derek clung to the desperate hope that Mia would be okay until he found her. And he *would* find her.

Chapter 17

Friend or Foe
Two Months Prior

At the base of Canter Mountain, a gaping cave mouth loomed. The once vibrant honey-colored grass at its edge lay wilted, the blades brittle and gray. Though the sky above remained an unblemished blue, a chill clung to the air, carried on a lifeless breeze that seeped from the cave's depths.

Mia hugged her arm as she asked, "So, you think he went in there?"

"I believe so," Tah'quhal grunted, his stigmata starting to glow.

Mia watched, slightly envious of his confidence, as the Fae walked into the cave without hesitation. She did her best to put one foot in front of the other to follow him. The further they stepped into the cave, the more light they lost. Darker and darker, until the only light around was the faint glow of Tah'quhal's stigmata.

Mia ran two fingers along the top of her left wrist, all the way to the end of her middle finger as she whispered, "*Lux.*"

Her spiral tattoo began to put off a bright, yellowish light, illuminating the long corridor of the cave. The walls became more structured the further they walked in. Rough stone turning to chiseled cobblestone on the floor.

As they reached the innermost chamber, Tah'quhal raised a fist in the air, signaling for Mia to stop. As she came to a halt, she ran her palm over her tattoo, putting out the light.

Tah'quhal whispered, "He is here. I can feel his presence."

"What exactly is . . . here?" Mia asked.

"This is the dungeon below the mountain's castle. Thanks to Komipea's lies, I am uncertain if the stories are true, but this is where it is said that Malum perfected his Odium magic." He explained.

"So Tarik is hid——"

Mia's words were cut off by a familiar voice echoing down the hall.

"Ahhh, Tah'quhal, I figured you would come . . . and you brought my plaything." The chilling voice of Tarik rang out.

His feet slammed against the stone floor as Tah'quhal dashed towards the sound of his old friend's voice. Mia managed to match him, taking three steps for every one of his. As they ran down the main hall, they followed the echoes of Tarik's voice.

"Ohhh, you're getting warmer."

They turned down a smaller hallway that opened up to a large, circular room that was dimly lit by torchlight. In the middle of the room stood Tarik, his back facing the duo.

"There you are, old friend. Come over here and give me a hug."

Tah'quhal's shoulders were stiff, his hands curled into white-knuckled fists at his sides as he bellowed, "Turn and face me!"

Tarik never moved. Not even the slightest flinch. Tah'quhal would typically curl his upper lip at the dishonorable notion of attacking a man who had his back turned, but he was done playing Tarik's *games.* He let out a growl, wanting Tarik to know he was coming, as he began to sprint towards his friend. "*Flamma percutiens.*"

His right hand engulfed in flame, he swung with all of his might at the back of Tarik's head. As his fist landed, the body erupted in flame. Tah'quhal stood, chest heaving, over a pile of ash. He spun on his feet, searching the dimly lit room.

"What is this trickery, Tarik?"

Mia rushed to his side. "Was that not him?" she asked in a panic.

Her question was answered by a puff of red essence shooting up from the pile of ash. The two of them choked on the thick, blinding haze. Tah'quhal reached out a searching hand for Mia, only to find one of two stone pillars that had risen in front of them. A gust of wind rushed past them, slamming their bodies into the pillars they now found themselves chained to.

Tah'quhal grunted, muscles looking like they might pop as he tried to break his bindings. "This won't hold me forever!"

No matter how hard he tried, the chains would not break. Furiously, he attempted speaking an incantation. Nothing. Mia's blood ran cold when no essence would form. With dread coiling in her stomach, Mia tried one of her own, but just like Tah'quhal, nothing happened.

Tarik's laughter rang out in the chamber. It was the kind of laughter that no one could enjoy. It just kept going . . . going . . . going. Then, silence.

Mia sniffled as she choked out, "Why are you doing this?"

"Because he is *corrupted*, Mia." Tah'quhal replied, pain evident in his voice. With the haze, she wasn't sure if it was the physical kind.

The laughter rang out once again, this time short and sweet, as Tarik emerged from the now dissipating smoke,

"Oh, my. Oh, my, you still believe the old Chieftain's lies?"

Tah'quhal seethed, "I can see it, Tarik! They are not lies!"

Tarik's lips curled into a smile as his fingers toyed with one corner of his mustache. "This is not corruption, you fool——this is power."

Slamming his chains against the pillar, Tah'quhal tried again to break free. He tried to channel his magic, but his stigmata only flickered in and out.

"It is no use, Tah'quhal. Those chains come from Mythos. A realm that can give great power and can take it all away." Tarik mocked.

Tah'quhal gritted his teeth and let out a weary sigh, calming his tone. "When I get out of here, I *will* save you. Then you, me, and Sarika can figure all of this out."

"There is no saving me! I already told you, this is not corruption. My soul is clear. I have prepared for this my entire life!" Tarik hissed.

"You know not what you speak of. It is Malum's dark magic doing this to you," Tah'quhal replied, sounding as if he were convincing himself.

Tarik slammed his still flesh-covered fist into the side of Tah'quhal's pillar, "Don't be so damn naive! Malum has not corrupted me. We were raised to follow this path. This is our destiny."

"We?" Tah'quhal breathed. Inside, he knew what it meant, but he needed to hear Tarik say it.

"Of course, *we.*" Tarik dragged out tauntingly, "Sarika, and I have bided our time, waiting for this moment." Tarik looked down at Mia, drinking in the sight of her trembling fear. He continued, piercing her with his gaze, "And now she is all alone with Derek. Who knows what kind of mess she has planned for him?"

Mia let out a strangled, "Derek." She wiped her eyes on her sleeve, not wanting to give this monster the satisfaction of her fear. Her voice flattened, "Whatever she does to him, I will do so much worse to you."

"Oh, you promise?" Tarik laughed. His eyes took on a harder edge when he turned his attention to Tah'quhal. "I have wanted to do this for a very long time."

Tah'quhal's face stung with the harsh punch Tarik landed on his left cheek.

"You've always thought you were better than everyone. Better than *me.*" Tarik sneered, delivering another precise strike to Tah'quhal's face. "Look who is better now."

He pulled Tah'quhal's head back by a fistful of hair. "If it were up to me, I would end you here and now." He spat. "Lucky for you, Malum wants to take care of you himself." He finished his speech with a nose breaking punch.

Spitting blood onto the ground, Tah'quhal asked, "Why would Malum want me?"

"Oh boy, do I need to give you a history lesson?" Tarik chuckled, "You strut around Torvania, telling anyone that will listen that you are Torviid's descendant. I will admit, I do not know his plans for you, but I am positive it will be . . . painful."

Mia pushed down her horror, her gut clenching in equal parts anger and fear at their helplessness. As she saw the blood begin to run from Tah'quhal's nose, she snapped, "That's enough! Leave him alone!" She regretted it the moment he froze.

Tarik slowly turned his head to stare down at her. "Oh, don't worry. You're next, and there is no Derek here to save you now . . . *Dolor*" Searing, blinding pain engulfed her.

Mia opened her mouth in a silent scream, the blood in her veins seeming to boil, as if liquid fire had been injected into her bloodstream. Her body was torn between going limp and thrashing. Whatever would make it stop.

Tarik knelt next to her, whispering disgustingly gently, "Fear not, you will not die . . . it just hurts . . . a lot. I wouldn't dare let you perish without Derek here to watch."

Mia's vision began to fade, dark circles closing around everything she could see. The last thing she saw as her consciousness slipped away was Tarik sauntering out of the dungeon.

The clang of metal on stone jolted her awake. A tray with something resembling mashed potatoes lay in front of her. They smelled more like rotten eggs, but her stomach was growling. "*How long have I been asleep?*" she thought to herself.

Tah'quhal's foot slid the tray closer to her. "You need to eat," he grunted as he stretched out. "Who knows when he will feed us again."

Mia reached her face out towards the tray, still too weak from Tarik's magic to use her arms. Doing her best not to breathe through her nose, she lapped up the mushy food. She gagged. The stench was one thing but the *taste*, it was like eating garbage. She forced the food down her throat with a loud gulp. "What is this?"

"What isn't it? If I had to guess, I'd say he just mixed whatever scrap food and herbs he had together and threw it down for us." Tah'quhal stared at the food in front of him. He took a long breath. "I am sorry."

"Why are you sorry?" Mia asked.

"I let my pride get us into this mess." Tah'quhal whispered.

"No Tah'qu——"

"Do not make excuses for me. My entire life, I was told I was destined for greatness because I was Torviid's descendant." He stared at something far beyond this dungeon. "But what about my father? What about my father's father? Why were they not destined for greatness?" He looked back down at the gruel in front of him. "I let it all go to my head. Tarik was right about one thing; I thought myself better than everyone."

From her position curled up on the floor, there was not a lot she could do to help him. She was not even strong enough to grab his hand in support. So, she gave him the only comfort she could——she listened.

"At the very least, I should have known this would be a trap . . . one of Tarik's tricks." He spat in frustration.

Mia almost expected him to send his tray flying; that was the Tah'quhal she had become accustomed to.

He merely set his food down and continued, voice thick with emotion she'd never heard from him. "We trained together our *entire* lives. If I had only ... I was impulsive. I was rash, not just here, but in Torvania, on Earth, too. And now we are stuck here in this decrepit dungeon. I failed you."

Mia held onto his last words. The guilt she could hear in his voice made her feel like she wasn't the only "you" he was referring to. It was clear he carried the burden of Izzy's death and false responsibility over his friends' betrayals. But it also seemed like he was admitting they might not ever get out of here.

Each day that came, Mia forced herself to eat more, trying to keep her strength in hopes she and Tah'quhal could devise a plan to get free. Even though she had never been the type to need saving, she still held onto hope that Derek would show up. Something about his presence comforted her. Almost two months had passed, but she held on strong. Passing the time that she was awake by trading stories with Tah'quhal.

One day, as they waited for their usual entrée of garbage to arrive, the ground beneath gave a violent shake. Mia and Tah'quhal looked at each other, their eyes wide as the trembles sent gravel and dust falling from the ceiling.

Tah'quhal tried to keep Mia calm. "Pull on your chains. Maybe the tremors have weakened the stones?"

"But it could be someone coming to help." She gave a half hearted grin before yelling out, "Help! Help us!"

A faint white light began to light up the hallway in front of them.

Tah'quhal, momentarily disregarding every instinct in his body, hoping a change in his demeanor would manifest a better outcome, grunted, "Can anyone hear us?"

A large chunk of the ceiling fell behind them, hitting the ground hard enough to make them buckle to their knees.

She drew in a breath to call out some more, but it got stuck in Mia's throat as a bright white light emanated from the entrance to the dungeon. The air rushed out of her as she voiced the hope that had been echoing in her heart for months, "Please be Derek."

Chapter 18

The Forest

Two Months Prior

Sweaty from walking all day, Barry's curse reverberated through the thick foliage as he and Johnathan cautiously ventured deeper into the heart of the Magia Forest.

"I didn't think anything could be worse than Earth's mosquitoes, but these magical bloodsuckers are relentless!"

Johnathan couldn't help but grin as he twirled his keeper staff with a flourish. A sharp snap cut through the air, making the swarm of annoying insects vanish without a trace. Barry's disbelieving expression slowly turned towards Johnathan.

"Seriously?! You let these little devils feast on me for an entire *hour* before deciding to use your magic stick and make them disappear!"

Johnathan couldn't contain his laughter and was bent over, struggling to stay standing. Barry's fuming expression only seemed to intensify his laughter. Eventually, Johnathan pointed at Barry's arm, where a large bump could be seen from the recent mosquito attack. Despite being a six foot seven jock, Barry let out a scream that could have shattered glass.

"Oh, my god! I'm going to die from alien bugs and it'll be *your* fault!"

Johnathan's laughter echoed through the forest, tears streaming down his face from the cathartic fit. Still snickering, he lifted his staff once more and made a small motion with it. A tiny puff of blue mist appeared from the tip of the staff and landed on Barry's bump. As soon as it touched, the itching mass burst like a bubble, leaving Barry staring at his arm in a mixture of shock and relief. He let out a deep sigh, his expression changing from fear to comical seriousness.

"That was a close one. I think that lump was about to ask for my name and number."

Johnathan wiped a stray tear from his cheek and composed himself, finally calming down from his fit of laughter. "I'm happy I could rescue ya from the seductive powers of a bug bite. Can we continue on now, oh brave hero?"

Barry playfully saluted him. "Lead the way, magical mosquito banisher!"

Before they could continue their journey, a strange laugh echoed through the air. Barry and Johnathan looked around nervously, unable to pinpoint the direction of the delicate, tinkling sound. Just as Barry reached for his sword, a tiny figure appeared from behind a nearby tree. It was a pixie, no larger than the span of their hand, fluttering around them with graceful movements.

Barry's discomfort was evident as he blurted out, "Oh, for the love of . . . you're not going to bite me, are you?"

The pixie let out a bell-like laugh and shook her head. Johnathan held out his keeper staff, and the small creature gracefully landed on it. Barry and Johnathan leaned in for a closer look, marveling at her dress made of shimmering leaves with a corset crafted from intricately tooled leather.

"And what do we have here?" Johnathan asked.

The tiny pixie gave a beatific smile before announcing herself, "My name is Tae. I am the ruler of all things in the Magia Forest!"

As Barry and John exchanged anxious looks, Barry tightened his grip on his sword, anticipating a battle with this self-proclaimed monarch of the woods. But before the tension could escalate, a deep voice, with what sounded like an Australian twang, echoed from behind the trees.

"Tae, don't go telling tall tales now."

Out stepped a towering orc, his skin the color of forest leaves, with sharp tusks protruding from his lower jaw, and a mane of black and gray hair. Adorned on his body were blue and red stigmata.

"The name is Ortug. Who might you two tiny fellas be?" The orc boomed, his body radiating intimidation, despite his friendly words.

Johnathan and Barry couldn't help but notice the massive size of this being as he approached them. It was the first time Barry had to physically look up during a conversation.

Ortug's eyes flickered with a mix of anger and curiosity as they landed on Johnathan's Keeper staff. The stigmatas covering his body glowed brighter the closer he got, prompting him to demand an explanation for the relic's presence as he reached out to touch the staff.

Johnathan quickly regained his composure, his expression betraying no emotion. After the battle in Torvania, he wasn't willing to let anyone or anything touch his Keeper staff. He plunged the staff into the ground with a purposeful thrust. A powerful gust of wind erupted from it, sending the two woodland creatures flying backwards.

Ortug and Tae were knocked off their feet by the shockwave, the orc deftly catching Tae as they tumbled backwards.

The orc's smug expression turned to one of surprise, with a note of what Johnathan could swear was respect. "Looks like you're not so small after all," Ortug gruffly remarked to Johnathan.

As Ortug regained his balance, Tae began to hum a sweet melody, her voice resonating in the air. Slowly, the small pixie started to expand, growing taller and filling out until she was the size of an average human woman. Her eyes glowed a vibrant green hue, and even her outfit changed to match her transformation. No longer wearing a modest leaf dress, Tae now donned a more alluring ensemble that showed off her curves. With a graceful gesture, she summoned leaves to swirl around her, forming into a powerful storm of sharp winds.

Taking a nervous gulp, Barry unsheathed his sword while Johnathan pulled his staff from the ground. Just as the tension reached its peak, a wooden spear thudded into the ground between the opposing parties.

Barry mumbled to Johnathan, "Oh, come on man! What now?"

His question was answered in the form of a woman descending gracefully from the treetops, a vision of beauty that took his breath away. She landed next to the spear with poise, leaning casually against it like a natural extension of her being. The rustling leaves and whispering breeze seemed to harmonize with her presence, giving her an air of confidence and grace.

Her blonde hair cascaded down her back in intricate braids, one side shaved close to the scalp, giving her an edge. With blue eyes that sparkled like a rushing river and possessed the same coolness, she seemed to hold the secrets of the ancient woods within her gaze. Her attire mirrored her surroundings, donning rich, brown leather leggings and a matching crop top that hugged her lithe figure.

But it was her skin that told the tales of magic and communion. Numerous shimmering bands of blue stigmata etched upon her flesh in intricate designs, each tattoo representing a mastery over an incantation or ancient ritual. Her lips were painted a dark red, exuding both enchantment and defiance, in perfect sync with the untamed beauty of the forest.

It wasn't just her physical appearance that left an impression——it was also the aura she emanated. A mixture of allure, wisdom, and wildness that embodied the natural world around her.

As she retrieved her spear from the earth, their gazes locked with an intensity that seemed to carry the weight of time itself. In her presence, Barry felt a deep admiration, a reverence. She *was* the forest, and Barry couldn't help but be captivated by her in a way he had never felt before.

"Ortug, haven't I instructed you to bring all newcomers to me?" she demanded, her sharp gaze fixed on the orc. Even when angry, her voice was tinged with a low, honeyed tone. With confidence and control, she introduced herself. "I am Caldera." Barry blinked and her spear was pressed against his throat. "That locket around your neck. How did you come across it?" she questioned sternly.

"I . . ." Barry stuttered out, "I got it from Komipea!"

Johnathan's grip on his Keeper staff tightened, ready to take action. Caldera, without even sparing him a glance, waved her hands to materialize a cage of leaves and twigs around him. He attempted to use the staff's magic to break free, but it was no use.

Caldera's eyes bore into Barry's, and he couldn't look away, not even to check on his friend. He was caught in a war of emotions. Along with the undeniable attraction, he'd be a fool not to be terrified of the *very* pointy metal currently hovering over his carotid artery.

"What name did you just say?" Caldera asked.

At Barry's nervous, "Komipea," Caldera removed her weapon and released Johnathan from his leafy prison.

Johnathan was growing frustrated by the constant danger they seemed to encounter. "Dadgummit! Why does everything and everyone we've come across in the last few months try to kill us?" He exclaimed, his voice filled with annoyance. Caldera paused, somehow looking strict and amused at the same time.

"It's imperative that we reach Terra." Barry blurted out, hoping he read her right and she'd appreciate him being blunt.

Caldera turned towards him, her eyes locking onto his once more as she searched his gaze for intent. Barry thought he might have seen a glimmer of approval in her blue irises.

"Now who exactly is a Komipea, and why would they send you twos to Terra?" Ortug cut in.

Caldera and Tae exchanged a quick, concern-filled glance.

Caldera interjected firmly, "If Komipea has sent two humans——their city's keeper being one of them——then the situation must be dire."

Johnathan and Barry's grave faces reflected the truth of her statement.

With a formal introduction, Caldera presented herself and her companions to Johnathan and Barry. "I am known as Caldera, the Chieftain of the Magia Forest," she announced. "This is Tae, my trusted guide since I was young. And this is Ortug, my muscle. He often allows his brawn to do more thinking than his brain." She said pointedly, referring to his earlier aggression. Caldera suggested they take this conversation back to her village, although it sounded more like a demand. Once they arrived, she promised to listen to their story, explain her own position, and potentially offer assistance in their cause.

After exchanging a few quiet words, Johnathan and Barry nodded in agreement with Caldera's proposition. Ortug was still visibly confused, much like Tah'quhal after discovering Chieftain Komipea's deceit. Caldera instructed Tae to explain everything to Ortug on the way to their village.

As the odd group of tentative allies made their way towards the village, Barry leaned in close to Johnathan and whispered, "I think I'm in love, bro."

Laughing, Johnathan quipped, "Okay Mr. Hotshot."

Caldera glanced back at them with a slight smirk. Barry gave a confident smile. "She digs me! I'm definitely sliding into the magical equivalent of her DMs."

Chapter 19

The New Journey

Johnathan and Barry marveled at the village before them that looked like a natural extension of the forest itself. The forest throughout the village remained undamaged, with every tree still standing, innovatively repurposed instead of being chopped down. Houses were intricately carved from the trees, connected by bridges that seemed to be woven into a magical web. Fallen branches had been transformed into benches and seating areas. The bustling atmosphere of the village gave them the impression that they were in a metropolis, rather than the ancient forest they were standing in. Orcs, fae, pixies, and even humans could be seen walking the streets, their glances a mix of wariness and curiosity. Johnathan and Barry exchanged cautious yet friendly waves, earning a few tentative smiles.

Making their way to the large tree house in the center of town, Caldera waved over two fae that were wearing almost ceremonial armor.

"I need to discuss some things with my new friends here. Call for the town to meet underneath my balcony. I will address them soon."

The two fae nodded their heads in unison, then marched towards the barracks to inform the others.

Once settled, Caldera gave her full attention to Johnathan and Barry, listening as they recounted their long journey. After they'd finished, Ortug turned to Caldera, brow furrowed.

"If all this chaos is happening in our realm and on Earth, then where is Codi?"

Anticipating Johnathan and Barry's confusion, Caldera clarified that Codi was the Keeper of the Magia Forest's portal.

Caldera pointed out, "If Codi has not alerted us, she may know nothing of what is happening."

"Maybe that means Malum ain't done nothing else on Earth yet. Maybe it's all just at Riverrun." Johnathan nervously suggested.

Tae said, "We should reach out to Codi. She can help."

But Caldera was insistent, "Not yet. We should not interrupt her unless it is absolutely necessary. Her job as Keeper is to keep our portal safe on Earth. Not to come running at our every call."

"Wait just a minute now, is it possible that we might've met Codi?" Johnathan asked.

Caldera gestured towards Tae, who quickly retrieved a copy of the book of Keepers. She told him exactly what it was, but try as he might, Johnathan struggled with the book's bindings, causing confusion among those around him. It should have been a simple task for him to open it, since only keepers could, but he seemed to be struggling.

After a few moments, Caldera's eyes narrowed, and she asked, "Who exactly gave you your Keeper staff?"

Johnathan's brow furrowed. "My father."

Relaxing slightly, Caldera asked, "I hate to be this blunt, but your father is still alive, correct?"

Johnathan's eyes stung. He hadn't seen his father in four months.

Barry placed his hand on his shoulder, giving a slight squeeze, "Hey man, I'm sure he's okay."

Caldera affirmed, "The book would not update unless the previous Keeper made the change themselves, or if they had perished. The fact that you can not open it proves your father still lives." She spoke with such assuredness that Johnathan's shoulders relaxed.

Johnathan and Barry shared a moment of recognition for all that had changed or been lost, the unspoken weight of the feelings this conversation stirred settling between them. It had been so long since they last saw their families. The thought that Barry's family did not even know why he vanished constantly pricked at his mind, but was rarely acknowledged between them. They also realized that it had been more than four months since Izzy's death at the hands of Tarik. With everything that had happened since then, Johnathan hadn't taken time to properly grieve. But before the melancholy could fully set in, Barry gave his friend a sad smile,

"They're why we have to keep moving forward."

Johnathan met Barry's understanding gaze and nodded in agreement.

Caldera felt like an intruder as she observed the deep grief and worry pass through these two humans, and in that instant, she affirmed her decision to join them. She could sense the courage and potential for leadership that Komipea saw in Barry. A soft smile grazed her lips as she gazed at him, and when Barry caught her eye, she happily said, "I know the fastest way to Terra, and I know the paths of who you will cross to get there. If you two would have me, I would like to accompany you."

Barry, full of excitement, playfully put his arm around Caldera. "Don't worry, I'll protect you, gorge—— ouch." Barry said from the ground Caldera had effortlessly flipped him onto.

With a serious expression, she leaned down and whispered in his ear, "It's not going to be that easy."

Despite the laughter from everyone, Barry stood up smiling, body slightly sore but eyes twinkling from Caldera's flirtatious challenge. Determined to not let Barry attempt another move, Caldera stepped out onto the balcony.

"Listen, my friends. Our world is usually calm and tranquil, but trouble is brewing. I must leave to assist our two new human companions, but fear not! Tae and Ortug will protect and guide you in my absence. Tae will keep watch on the skies for any urgent messages from me. If one comes, it means we need everyone's aid."

After the crowd cheered for their Chieftain, Caldera strolled over to Barry and stared into his honey-colored eyes. "This journey won't be without tribulations," she warned. "We'll need transportation."

The two boys exchanged a look, and Johnathan asked, "Do you have cars in Luminfae?"

Caldera chuckled as she led them towards the exit. "I'm not exactly sure what a *car* is, but I know just the creature to help us out."

Barry and Johnathan shared a puzzled glance, but trailed after Caldera as she started out the door. On his way out, Barry spotted a book lying discarded on the floor. The title "Legends of Luminfae" printed on its cover compelled him to pick it up. He curiously skimmed through it until his eyes landed on a page that read, "Still I stand, Until I fall, I will heed the Lonesome call." He remembered Mia, Johnathan, and Tah'quhal saying that before they all set out on their mission, and he was eager to learn what exactly it meant. Looking around the room, he noticed a satchel sitting on the table. Without hesitation, he shoved the book inside, put it on his back, and hurried to catch up with his party.

Caldera led them to a large clearing in the woods outside of the village. The boys watched as she moved the braids out of her face and kneeled down on the ground. The stigmata on her body brightened as she hummed a soothing melody. Branches whipped and leaves twirled as the wind sent the trees into a wild dance around them before a resonant, yet chilling noise echoed from the bushes in front of them.

Johnathan gripped his staff, ready for anything, but Barry was mesmerized by the tune Caldera was humming. He was *so* mesmerized he didn't even notice a magnificent beast emerge from the thickets. Johnathan gave him a slight, but insistent, nudge, and when Barry finally looked up, his jaw just about hit the forest floor.

The boys stared in awe at the elegant creature before them, its appearance both grand and otherworldly. They thought it was a griffin, but unlike any they'd seen depicted. It didn't have the traditional wings atop its lion-like body. Instead, it boasted a streamlined and formidable build, its muscles flexing beneath a coat of rich brown fur. It held its head with an air of royalty, and its striking golden eyes surveyed them with sharp intelligence. Its graceful gait came to a halt as it assessed them. Despite not having wings, it exuded an air of grandeur and strength that demanded admiration.

Caldera said, "Meet Eirene, a Grand Griffin who lost her master during the First Fae Wars."

Johnathan asked, "No wings? I thought griffins were supposed to have wings?"

"Griffins only grow wings when they are truly bonded with their rider. Sadly, Eirene's rider perished in battle. Her wings molted away shortly after." She paused for a moment in empathy for the griffin's loss. "Even so, she is still the swiftest mount around."

Barry remembered what Komipea had said about the sword belonging to a warrior who rode a griffin to battle and questioned if it had once belonged to Eirene's rider. Not wanting to startle the magnificent creature, he cautiously unsheathed the sword and softly spoke its name. "Everflame."

The griffin's gaze zeroed in on Barry and the sword, slowly approaching him with its head held high. As the beast moved closer, Barry thought to himself, "*Am I about to get mauled?*" Trying to hide his nervousness, he pushed down the lump in his throat. He refused to look away or show cowardice. The griffin let out a proud screech and bowed its head in submission. He tentatively reached out and stroked her head. The griffin rumbled in approval, and Caldera tenderly remarked,

"Looks like she's taken a liking to you."

Caldera gestured for Barry to climb onto Eirene's back. Internally crossing his fingers in hopes that he wouldn't get bucked off or have his eyes pecked out, Barry hoisted himself onto the griffin. Eirene stood tall, waiting for Barry's instructions. Caldera beamed at Barry as she joined him on the griffin's back and wrapped her arms around his waist. Johnathan quickly followed suit, settling in behind Caldera.

She leaned into Barry and explained, "To get to Terra, we have to pass through Ignis. Just direct Eirene where you want to go; she knows the land better than anyone."

Barry gazed down at the real life, actual griffin he was sitting on and exclaimed with a giddy grin, "To Ignis!"

With a powerful roar, Eirene took off, zooming through the forest with incredible velocity. The unlikely trio held on tight as they sprinted towards their next destination, guided by their new ally. For the first time, they felt ready for whatever was to come next.

Chapter 20

Fire

Eirene stretched out on the ground, using a rock for a pillow while she gnawed on a skrellux bone from their successful hunt. The fire in front of her popped and hissed as Caldera regaled Barry and Johnathan with stories from her time as Chieftain of the Magia Forest.

Barry hung on to every word Caldera spoke, completely enamored by her. It wasn't just her words that captivated him, but also the way she carried herself and took care of those around her. She kept a watchful eye on Eirene, looking for signs of exhaustion and making sure the griffin hadn't pushed herself too hard. Caldera made sure there was enough food not just for herself and the two boys, but also for their new furry friend.

Barry examined the fine-grained meat in his hands and couldn't help but unabashedly ask, "What exactly are we eating?"

Caldera chuckled, having momentarily forgotten she was traveling with two humans who were unaccustomed to Luminfae.

"The closest proximation would be your Earth rabbit," she said before casually adding,

"Well, if that rabbit had wicked eyes, longer legs, razor-sharp teeth, and a long tail that serves as a weapon. We call it a skrellux."

Barry's expression turned horrified. He gasped, "So we *ate* that?"

Caldera's lips tilted in a wry smile. "But it tasted good, right?"

Johnathan nudged Barry and teased, "Didn't you see it when Caldera brought it back to camp?"

Barry blushed, avoiding eye contact as he replied, "I may have been distracted at the time . . ."

Johnathan playfully poked fun at him once more. "You were too focused on something else, huh, buddy?"

Barry lightly pushed Johnathan and said with a laugh, "Shut up, dude!"

Caldera grinned at Barry and playfully winked at him. "We'll be arriving in Ignis tomorrow. It would be wise to get some rest tonight. And keep your senses alert for any potential dangers." She got up from her seat and gently patted Eirene's head, her voice growing serious and weighted. "Ignis can be a treacherous place. Don't trust anyone or anything we encounter."

With that, she headed to her tent to retire for the night.

The next morning, the team assembled on Eirene. They emerged from the lush forest and into the desolate outskirts of Ignis. The air was heavy with a burnt smell, and the once vibrant plant life of Magia Forest had been replaced by a harsh terrain of sulfur and molten rock. Caldera caught Barry's tensed posture as they continued deeper into the barren land.

She leaned into him and asked, "Are you feeling okay?"

Barry's response was a tight mixture of anxiety and vulnerability. "I can't believe it . . . this is all just *unreal*. I never thought any of this wild stuff could actually exist, but here I am, riding a griffon straight into the depths of what might actually be Hell."

Caldera's heart warmed with a sense of tenderness as she saw Barry stripped of his tough facade, his fears exposed. She wrapped her arm around him and reached for his hand, hoping to offer some comfort. A pleasant rush went through her when Barry's strong grip pulled her tighter against him, instinctively responding to her, even as his eyes widened at her touch. Caldera could still feel the muscles in his body tensing, though. To distract him, she asked, "How old are you, Barry?"

With a playful smile, he replied, "Old enough to know all the best places to take a beautiful woman on a date back on Earth." He sort of chuckled before continuing, "Don't judge me, but I'm twenty. Maaaybe I had to repeat kindergarten once . . . or twice."

Caldera made a pondering sound. "Well then, here's a deal for you. If we make it through this journey to Terra, and whatever comes after, *and* if you can guess my age," she said with a skeptical brow that implied she didn't think it was likely, "perhaps I'll let you take me out."

Barry, without a doubt, had the dimension's goofiest smile on his face. He was eternally grateful Caldera was seated behind him on the griffin. That grin would have ruined things for sure.

Johnathan's sharp laughter broke the flirtatious tension between them, causing both Barry and Caldera to turn and look at him in surprise.

Barry raised an eyebrow, silently questioning what was so amusing that he'd interrupt them when he'd *actually* been getting somewhere.

Between his chuckles, Johnathan asked, "Just how focused were ya when Komipea told us how long he had been Chieftain?"

Confusion flickered across Barry's face. He stumbled over his words, saying, "Uh, yeah, he mentioned something about hundreds of years, but I thought it was an old man telling tall tales."

Caldera slyly added, "Oh sweetie, fae have much longer lifespans than humans."

Barry's confidence waned. He asked, a little higher pitched than he intended, "How long have you been the Chieftain of the Forest?"

Caldera playfully shook her head in response, indicating that she wouldn't reveal that information.

Ahead of them, a single drawbridge stretched over a moat of bubbling lava, serving as the only entrance to their destination, a looming castle that dominated the landscape. The trio dismounted and instructed Eirene to stay put until they gained permission to enter the city. As they approached the molten river, Caldera gripped Barry's hand tighter in reassurance.

Johnathan nudged Barry, making him jump, tension coiled tight in his body. "This is absolutely terrifying," Johnathan whispered, "And Komipea is nine hundred and fifty-two years old."

Barry, trying to hide his fear, joked, "Well, Caldera, I'd say you're not a day over nine hundred and fifty-two, but you still look like you're twenty-one." He then turned his attention to the daunting castle ahead, holding onto Caldera's hand like a lifeline.

She bit her lip, "Close enough." Coyly, she leaned in and kissed his cheek before adding, "Actually, it's nine hundred and eighty-three. You can be assured that all of those years of knowledge will help us navigate Ignis successfully."

Leading the way, Caldera stepped onto the drawbridge with Barry's hand in tow and Johnathan close behind. As they approached, the massive gate at the other end creaked open.

Johnathan and Barry found it difficult to take another step, both captivated and disturbed by the scene before them. The inhabitants resembled the fae, but their features were uncanny——their skin dyed in shades of deep red, royal purple, electric blue, emerald green, and even jaundiced yellow. Pointed ears were accompanied by curled horns atop their heads, and some even sported long, snaking tails. Their clothing left little to the imagination, almost designed to prevent you from looking away. While most were female, there were a few males among the crowd. Within the masses, a small group of humans could be seen. By the defeated looks on their faces, it was clear they weren't exactly happy to be there.

Caldera turned her head back to the boys, her voice low but full of warning. "These are the succubi. The humans you see here are slaves to them. They will try to charm and enchant you, hoping to trap you within their seductive hold. Be on guard."

Johnathan and Barry gave stoic nods as they navigated through the eerie cityscape.

While they walked, the alluring whispers of the succubi reached their ears. As Caldera had warned, they enticed them with promises of wealth, authority, and desire. Johnathan instinctively covered his ears, while Barry kept a vigilant gaze on Caldera, refusing to be swayed by any of the temptress' empty promises.

Just as they were nearing the end of the city, a burst of fire erupted, creating a blistering circle that trapped them inside. Johnathan raised his Keeper staff to meet the threat, while Barry drew his sword and Caldera poised her spear for battle.

From a looming tower set in the center of town, a haunting voice called out with a sensual pout.

"Leaving so soon?"

The ring of flames parted, revealing a fiery path that seemed to beckon them towards the tower. With no other options, they followed the trail. The door behind them slammed shut the moment they stepped through, trapping them within its walls. Descending from a spiral staircase was Talissa——a succubus whose gaze was fixated on Johnathan. As she neared him, her fingers brushed intimately against his skin.

Talissa's muted red complexion was adorned with dark crimson markings. Her dress clung to her curves and bore strategic slits up to her hips, open sides, and a deep cut neckline. The deep purple of her lipstick matched the exact shade of her eyes. Everything about her oozed carefully calculated seduction. She was a nightmare wearing the guise of a fantasy.

Johnathan's voice was shaky, but not meek, when he declared, "I am the Keeper of Torvania, and we require passage through this land."

Talissa, her fingers now digging into Johnathan's face as she cupped it, replied with a hint of sarcasm, "A powerful Keeper you must be. And what is the destination of your quest?"

Caldera cleared her throat, and Talissa cocked her head in acknowledgement of the other leader. "Talissa, it's been quite some time," Caldera remarked without warmth.

"Oh, yes. Yes, it has." Talissa dragged her eyes over Caldera. "If you're with these heathens," shooting Johnathan and Barry a disparaging look, "then your business must be serious."

Caldera explained their mission, but unlike others who had heard their story, Talissa showed no change in her demeanor. In a bored voice, she drawled, "You're familiar with the toll required for passage through Ignis. Pay it, and you and this scum can continue on."

Caldera gave a slight nod before rummaging through her bag. But Talissa stepped closer and slipped her hand into Caldera's pocket, their eyes locked in a tense standoff. She searched around all the pockets she could find on her before reaching into Caldera's bag herself and pulling out a handful of leaves from the Magia Forest.

Barry's grip tightened on his sword, ready to intervene at Caldera's discomfort. Caldera noticed Barry's reaction and shook her head at him, signaling for him to stand down.

"This will do, and make sure your guard dog knows to be careful with that sword." Talissa forcefully kissed Caldera, reveling in the angry waves pouring off of Barry, before disappearing in a burst of flames.

The door to the tower swung open, revealing the trail of fire once more to lead them towards the exit.

Just outside the tower, Jonathan asked, "What was that with the leaves?"

She explained, "The flora of the Magia Forest fuel the everflame portal in Ignis. The leaves I just gave her will keep it open for at least two hundred years." She paused and took a deep breath. "Ignis will one day seek to expand further into the forest to keep their access to Earth open. This . . . arrangement might at least buy us time."

Barry's attention turned to his sword, and he mumbled, "Ever-flame?" Then, even quieter to himself, "Could that be where the name of his sword came from?"

Caldera pivoted to face him. "That is the second time I've heard you mention that name——"

Before she could finish her thought, Eirene arrived in a rush through the streets of Ignis. The griffin stopped beside Barry and knelt down for him to climb onto her back. Barry turned towards the griffin, hiding his face from Caldera as he pretended to fuss over the mount. He knew he had no right to be jealous, but he couldn't keep his tone quite as nonchalant as he intended when he asked,

"And the kiss?"

Caldera staunchly admitted, "We have a history——about a hundred years ago." She placed a reassuring hand on the middle of Barry's back, "That's all it was, history."

Barry felt better, relaxed even, after Caldera's last statement. He helped her climb onto the back of Eirene, trying to find a way to ask her the questions on the tip of his tongue. Before he could, Johnathan climbed on the griffins back and urged them to leave the city while they still had the chance.

Barry nodded in agreement. He'd never been so happy to get out of a place as he was to leave that city behind. Once they had passed through the far city limits, they could see a vast mountain range in the distance. Their destination was just beyond those mountains. They were getting closer, yet it still felt like a long journey ahead.

Chapter 21

Terra Rising

B arry and Johnathan soon realized that their journey to Terra was going to take *much* longer than they had originally anticipated. They had consulted Komipea's map and estimated it would only be a week's journey, but more than a month had gone by since they left the city of Torvania. It became apparent that Luminfae was far greater in scale than they had imagined.

As they continued their journey from camp through the monotonous desert of brimstone and fire, Caldera tried to lift the spirits of the tired humans by assuring them that Terra was not far away.

"We only need to pass through Dragoon Pass and Terra will be on the other side."

Barry's voice rose an octave. "Dragons?!"

Caldera couldn't help but grin as she corrected him, "No, no, not 'Dragon Pass.' It's called *Dragoon* Pass——it's a tunnel carved through a mountain. It got its name from the First Fae Wars when a legendary group of fae known as the Dragoons helped build it as an escape route for the enslaved in Ignis to reach Terra." Seeing Barry relax, Caldera let out a small laugh. "No dragons here; don't worry. Beyond Oceanus is another story."

Johnathan joked, "Hey Barry, maybe we can plan us a vacation in Oceanus once all this is over!"

Barry shot him an exaggerated glare, but Caldera continued to chuckle.

She reached out and took Barry's hand, saying in her best impression of him, "Don't worry, I'll protect you, gorgeous."

Barry was still blushing as they neared the tunnel where a warning caught their attention on the mountain above:

"Terra Marked By The Gods – HB."

Barry brought Eirene to a halt and squinted at the message. "What could that mean?"

Trying to inject some optimism into the situation, Johnathan suggested, "Maybe that's just a way of saying Terra is a safe haven."

"Not likely. I would imagine that 'HB' stands for the *Hellfire Brigade*. Their leader believes himself to be a god, much like Malum." She let out a sarcastic laugh. "They have even claimed to travel to the *Sacred Dimension*, but in all reality, he is just a human that convinced other humans to follow Malum's twisted ideologies."

Barry asked, "What if he really did go to that dimension?"

"The Chieftains of Luminfae have long debated that very question. To be honest, we don't know. The only fact is, they are a dangerous group." Caldera answered, while she wrapped her arm around Barry again.

Johnathan spoke up, "Well ya learn somethin' new every day. I'll admit, that doesn't sound very sunshine and rainbows, but we need to get to Terra, anyway."

The trio set off into the Dragoon Pass on the back of Eirene, beginning what would be a long day's trek to their destination on the other side.

Once through, Barry breathed in the abundant fresh air, enjoying the distinct lack of sulfuric odor. The surrounding trees were adorned with lush, green leaves, providing a stark contrast to the barren landscape they had left behind. Ahead, they could see the bustling city of Terra, a welcome sight after their long trek. They neared the city gate and two fae stepped out from behind a small door, greeting them warmly.

"Welcome to Terra, travelers! What brings you to our home?" said the first fae.

"Might we offer you some elixirs of rejuvenation to aid your travel weariness?" added the second.

Caldera accepted the offer for the three of them as they dismounted.

Barry wasted no time in downing his potion, feeling a burst of energy surge through him that made him want to beg for the recipe.

Johnathan sipped his more cautiously but responded with the same enthusiasm.

Noticing their impressed faces, the first fae explained, "It's a simple mixture of Torry Seed tree leaves and Torrig Scat."

At Barry's blank look, Johnathan theatrically whispered to him, "I would imagine that a Torrig is some type of creature, as 'scat' typically refers to poop."

Barry's face went pale, and his stomach churned with disgust.

Caldera threw her head back in laughter at his expression before composing herself to face the fae. She informed them that she and her companions were seeking an audience with Chieftain Serene, showing them the locket hanging from Barry's neck.

The two fae signaled to the gatekeepers to open the gates. Eirene was escorted to the stables while Johnathan and Barry moved further into the awe-inspiring city of Terra. It was unlike anything they had ever seen in Luminfae.

The structures resembled those on Earth, and both fae and humans alike were using modes of transportation that closely resembled bicycles. In the center of the city stood a towering geyser that stretched up into the sky. Behind that was the most crystal-clear lake they had ever beheld.

Vast gardens surrounded the lake that extended as far as the eye could see. The tranquility of this place was tangible, making it the most peaceful location they had encountered on Earth or Luminfae.

The group was directed towards the gardens, where Chieftain Serene was waiting for them. While walking, Caldera told the boys,

"Before we get here, I just want you two to know that Serene is part of the 'Old Guard.' Meaning, she was around for the First Fae Wars. Torviid helped her defend their geyser against Malum's forces."

Stunned, Johnathan replied, "I'll be a monkey's uncle! I knew fae could live for a long time, but I had no clue it could be that long.

"She is currently three thousand four hundred and seventy-two years old." Caldera looked at Johnathan with a hint of concern in her eyes. "We don't live that long anymore. No one really knows why, but our lifespans seemingly shortened after the final battle between Torviid and Malum."

Barry made it his mission to keep that look of worry off her face. "Okay, cool! So we finally get to meet a grandma fae," he joked.

No sooner had the words left his mouth, when an energetic and youthful voice resounded from the nearby fields,

"Oh, my goodness, Caldera! It's been ages since I've seen you!"

The group turned towards the voice as Caldera eagerly rushed to meet the figure.

Johnathan nudged Barry with a mischievous grin on his face and teased, "Uh-oh! Might be another ex!" To which Barry playfully pushed him and told him to be quiet.

Caldera introduced them. "This is Serene, the Chieftain of Terra."

He was stunned; *this is the three thousand year old fae?* She appeared to be the same age as Caldera, with a sleek, jet black curtain of hair, intricately woven with vibrant purple flowers. Her long, flowing yellow dress accentuated her striking, cornfield colored eyes.

Johnathan couldn't help but exclaim, "That ain't no ordinary grandmother."

Caldera gave him a stern look at the same moment Barry smacked Johnathan on the back of the head in reprimand.

Serene just laughed and replied, "It's okay. We rarely have visitors here, but when we do, they all react the same way. This place sustains us and allows us to live long and meaningful lives." Her gaze turned serious. "But please, if I know Caldera, there must be an urgent reason she brought you here."

Johnathan quickly filled Serene in on all the details leading up to this moment. As she listened, her expression grew weary with the weight of the story. When he mentioned the Hellfire Brigade, Serene's reaction was almost visceral.

Noticing her reaction, Barry said, "Please, if there is anything that you could tell us to help defeat Malum, we need to know."

After a brief pause, Serene collected herself and instructed,

"Barry and Caldera, go grab three vials from that stand over there." She pointed to a cart nearby. "Bring them to the cave beneath the geyser and fill them up. Once you're done, meet me and Johnathan back at my house."

Barry and Caldera exchanged slightly puzzled glances before the latter tried to question why, but a meaningful look from Serene shut her down. As they made their way towards the cart, Barry took advantage of the moment alone to ask, "Since we dunno how this will all play out, can we consider this our first date?"

Caldera hesitated for a moment, weighing her reserves against her interest, before replying, "I would like that very much."

Barry pumped his fist close to his chest, whispering, "Yes!"

Caldera looked coyly over her shoulder. "You're going to have to keep up." With a wink, she grabbed the three vials and raced off, keeping just enough of a lead on Barry to have some fun.

Johnathan basked in the peaceful atmosphere of Terra as Serene led him into her home. As she retrieved a few books from her shelf, she invited him to sit down.

"Would you like something to eat or drink?" she asked politely.

Johnathan declined with a shake of his head. Serene placed the books on the table and sat beside them, pulling out a piece of parchment from one of the books.

"So you are the keeper of Torvania?" she inquired.

He nodded silently.

"Then allow me to share what I know to be true."

Johnathan listened intently as Serene began, despite how far-fetched what she said seemed.

"There are countless dimensions in the universe. The Start, Mythos, Earth, Luminfae and Oblivion are ones that have been documented to some extent. However, the most important one for you to know is the Sacred Dimension. To my knowledge, only three beings have claimed to have been there."

"Three?" Johnathan interjected. "I thought Malum was the only one who said he had gone there."

Serene gently shook her head before continuing, "Most stories only mention Malum's journey. They often portray the Hellfire Brigade as his minions. But they are wrong. In truth, these three individuals all sought out this realm for their own purposes. Malum, of course, sought ultimate power, but it is the second traveler who will surprise you . . . Torviid."

Johnathan's breath caught in his throat as he asked, "What do you mean, Torviid?"

Serene calmly handed him a piece of parchment. "On his journey, Torviid wrote an account of how he successfully navigated the Sacred Dimension. He left it with me, in case a threat like Malum ever resurfaced. When he returned, he was consumed with the sole purpose of banishing Malum. The beings in the Sacred Dimension pledged to help him, using their immense power to keep Malum confined, on the condition that no other entered their realm."

A knot grew in Johnathan's stomach at the direction he sensed the story taking.

"These beings were known as the Deus," Serene continued, "or 'Gods' in your language. They kept their promise until Helian, of the future Hellfire Brigade and the third traveler to the Sacred Dimension. When I first met him, he had escaped from a succubus in Ignis and sought refuge here on Terra."

Serene's eyes became haunted as she recounted the events. "Helian took an interest in learning about Luminfae's history once he was freed from Ignis. I will admit, I indulged his curiosity a bit too much. At the time, I did not realize he'd become obsessed with traveling to the Sacred Dimension.

"If only I'd known he had an almost pathological need to explore. To always be on the run after he had been held captive for so long . . . I had granted him access to my personal library, and he found my vault. Late one night while I was asleep, he and some of his cohorts found a way in, discovering the note Torviid had left me."

She paused, her voice laced with sadness. "His curiosity sparked a chain of events that I couldn't control. Helian and his companions embarked on a journey to the Sacred Dimension, where they faced Sarissa, the Hellfire Queen of the Deus. Despite her anger at their intrusion, she invited them to a feast."

Screne took a deep breath, collecting herself before speaking. "The feast was extravagant, and as they indulged in the delicious food and unique green beverage offered by Sarissa, something changed. Helian and the others felt an unprecedented power coursing through their bodies."

Tears streamed down her face now, the weight of her memories pressing heavily on her.

"In a moment of doubt, Helian questioned Sarissa's motives for giving them such a gift. She snapped her fingers, and in an instant, the once-celebrating group burst into flames . . . all except for Helian. They were reduced to nothing but ash and bones. Sarissa informed Helian that the drink she provided was mixed with *hellfire*——a substance made from her own blood that gave her the ability to instantly end the life of anyone who had consumed it. She told him that he was now bound to her, having broken a thousand-year peace treaty. And so, the Hellfire Brigade came into existence. Helian became her enforcer, once again a captive thanks to the hellfire he ingested, but granted access to dark magic with the purpose of wreaking havoc in Luminfae for breaking the truce."

Serene wiped away her tears and composed herself again.

"When Helian returned, he dove into the geyser. He sought out those on Earth who would listen to him and used Malum's words as a guise to attract attuned humans to his cause. Upon returning to Luminfae, he attempted to do Sarissa's bidding, but it was evident that he had another agenda. While Malum wanted to dominate all dimensions, Helian only desired to return to the Sacred Dimension and defeat the Deus.

"He knew he had to bide his time and make small attacks on Terra in order to appease Sarissa. I still do not know why he eventually stopped attacking, but one day, he led his brigade into Terra, demanding that we stop practicing magic altogether. He declared that any detectable use of magic would result in the death of five fae."

Her hands began to tremble as she continued, "We tried to fight back, but a colossal battle ensued. In the end, Helian and his brigade emerged victorious, taking five fae with them. During the battle, his satchel had been knocked off. Inside, we found a journal detailing what he had seen in the Sacred Dimension." She pointed to the journal on the table.

With a touch of shame, she confessed, "Since then, Terra has refrained from using any noticeable magic, and Helian has yet to return."

Her ears twitched, and she swiftly passed the journal to Johnathan, who carefully tucked it into his own satchel. Just as he was about to ask what had changed, Serene leaped out of her seat.

"Hurry, go to the cave and bring Caldera and Barry here immediately!" she exclaimed, pushing him towards the door. Her dress transformed into regal armor, bearing the same hues as her previous attire.

Without hesitation, Johnathan raced towards the cave.

Barry was captivated by the stunning beauty of the cave they had just entered. The walls glowed with bioluminescent flora and fauna, and the geyser continued its journey deep into the cave. Caldera brought him to the water's edge, saying,

"This is where the Fallen River flows in Mythos, a place that few return from. It's a cautionary tale for young fae that warns them against venturing here. But in this cave, it transforms into something magical: a geyser that brings hope, success, and magic to those who stand by it." With a flick of her wrist, she levitated the three vials effortlessly into the air, showcasing her magical prowess. The vials flew towards the geyser and filled with its water before returning to her waiting hand.

Barry tried his best to focus on Caldera's words, but he found himself entranced by how expressive her face was, how passionate she was for this place. The luminescent flowers cast a soft glow on her skin, highlighting the intricate markings that seemed to dance in the light. She was the most incredible sight he had ever seen.

Caldera let her words trail off when she noticed his less than subtle stare. She turned towards him with a playful quirk of her brow.

"Are you listening or are you too busy being mesmerized by me?"

Barry grinned at her unabashedly, simply saying,

"Yes."

Caldera took a step closer, running her hand along his cheek. Her gaze pierced through his own as she whispered, "Kiss me."

Barry didn't have to be told twice. He lifted her up to meet his lips, and she instinctively wrapped her legs around his waist, arms encircling his neck. They pressed together in a deep and passionate kiss, everything else fading away in that one perfect moment. Barry was lost. Caldera moved her hands to his hair and he felt everything intensify, wrapping his arms around her tighter and——

"Y'all, we need to——Oh! My bad,"

Johnathan exclaimed, sharply turning away from the scene he'd just burst into.

Caldera gracefully untangled herself from Barry's embrace, maintaining her composure.

"What's the matter?" she asked calmly. Barry shot a frustrated glare at Johnathan, who had turned back, looking embarrassed and flustered.

Still red, Johnathan answered, "Something's happened to Serene. She transformed her dress into armor and sent me to get y'all."

Caldera tightened her grip on Barry's hand as they hurried out of the cave, swiftly ascending to the surface. When they emerged, fae were rushing about and arming themselves, tension thick in the air.

Caldera rushed to Serene's side, urgently asking, "What's happening?"

Serene rushed through her explanation.

"The warning you saw above Dragoon Pass was no jest. Someone here must have used magic, because the Hellfire Brigade was just spotted on the outskirts of town."

Caldera's face turned pale.

"Serene, I'm so sorry. This is my fault," she said earnestly.

Serene smiled tightly and replied, "It's alright, dear. You did not know."

Serene gestured towards the vials that Caldera had filled. "If the Brigade does attack, break those vials upon your chest and visualize where you want to be. Anything and anyone you are touching will instantly be transported there." Another fae hurried over, carrying harvested plants that resembled tiger lilies.

"Chieftain, it appears that twenty of the plants have blossomed," the fae reported.

Serene explained, "These plants can be crushed and turned into an elixir that has powerful healing properties. However, they are rare and should only be used sparingly."

With a smile, she handed the plants to Barry, who carefully placed them in his satchel.

A cloud of green mist erupted from the city gates and a frail, ancient voice echoed,

"Serene, you have disobeyed your promise and used magic. As punishment, five fae lives will be taken!"

Johnathan twirled his Keeper staff and summoned a gust of wind that dispersed the mist, revealing four figures dressed in black with accents of red and gold. Among them was an elderly man with a gray beard and hooded robe, a domineering woman in full armor that had leather accents and sharp edges, a muscular man with armor and vials of the same green haze, and a young girl around Barry and Johnathan's age. The younger girl wore black leggings with red camouflage and carried a bow and arrow similar to Johnathan's Keeper staff in markings and style.

"Codi?" Caldera exclaimed, disbelief evident in her voice.

The young girl avoided eye contact, attempting to conceal her identity.

The elderly man stepped forward and introduced himself. "I am Helian. I have been blessed by the Hellfire Queen herself," his eyes falling on Serene, "You have brought this horror upon yourself. Retribution will take place."

Barry drew his sword, took a step in front of Caldera, and whispered, "Everflame."

Before the sword could begin to glow, Helian flicked his wrist and sent Barry flying into Caldera, sending them both crashing onto the ground.

Eirene came running down the street and stood in front of Barry and Caldera for protection.

Johnathan readied his Keeper staff, preparing to act, but Serene sharply commanded,

"No! Get your companions and leave. You have a far more important battle to prepare for."

They shared a brief, tense look before Johnathan reluctantly agreed with a terse nod. He rushed to Barry and Caldera's side. "Smash your vials and think of Torvania!"

Barry scrambled to his feet, pulling Caldera up with him. He tried to run towards Eirene with his hand holding onto Caldera's arm, but she would not budge. Her eyes were fixated on Codi. Barry knew they did not have time to waste. Crossing his fingers that she wouldn't stab him for it, he picked her up and sat her onto the griffin. Jumping on Eirene, he broke his vial between them, shouting, "Torvania!"

In a flash, they disappeared.

Johnathan turned to look at Serene, who nodded reassuringly. Armed with his vial, he moved to smash it against his chest. A piercing pain shot through his left shoulder where Codi's arrow was now embedded in his flesh.

Dropping to his knees, he crushed the vial, uttering a strained "Torvania."

Chapter 22

Reunion

Present Day

Derek fought the urge to run towards the city gate. Sarika, however, showed no such anxiety to get to Canter Mountain, strolling leisurely beside him. A small fae darted towards Derek and tugged at his pants leg, breaking him from his irritation. The child's voice was shaky as he looked up at Derek, pleading for help.

"Excuse me, sir, have you seen my father?"

Derek knelt down, concern pinching his brow. "I haven't, but maybe I can help you find him."

An adult female fae ran out of a nearby house towards them, calling for her son.

"Zaer! Zaer! Time to come home!" She stopped when she saw Sarika. Turning to Derek, she said stiffly, "I'm so sorry. My husband . . . he joined the fight when *her* brother attacked our city. He ran out of the gates to push back the invaders and . . ." She trailed off, looking at Sarika with disdain. "He never returned." Tears welled up in her eyes as she turned away with her son in tow.

Derek's face contorted in horror as he *really* took in the devastation surrounding him——what it meant for those who lived here. The weight of it all crushed down on him. In the last day, he's been terrified to his core, confused to the point of insanity, and ripped away from everything he thought he understood, but *this* . . . this might be too much to bear. His own grief, still fresh and bleeding, was an echo in comparison to the utter agony he glimpsed in her eyes before she ushered her son away.

A surge of emotions washed over him, tightening the knot in his chest even further, as he realized that his family had no idea where he was or what he had been through. He felt his magic trying to stir, his arms beginning to burn, but this time no white light accompanied them. Rapidly clenching his fists and shaking his hands, he let out a desperate,

"Ugh!"

The young fae and his mother turned back, startled by Derek's outburst, and quickly fled from the scene. They were not so much afraid of the noise but rather the way Derek's arms seemed to flicker with small blinks of white light. The burning started to reach the point of pain and he furiously started rubbing his arms, hoping for any relief. After a few moments, his arms burst with bright light and the pain slowly started to fade. Devastated and defeated, Derek yelled,

"What the hell is going on? Why does this keep happening?"

Sarika approached him cautiously, her calm and steady voice acting as a lifeline.

"Derek, I believe we can find answers to your questions, but I need you to trust me," she reassured him.

Derek sought out her gaze, eyes wild, and his arms still burning with light.

Sarika knelt beside him and gently placed her hand on his chest, her touch a soothing balm.

"Breathe, Derek," she instructed calmly.

He followed her lead, taking deep breaths; he hadn't even realized he'd been hyperventilating. With each inhale and exhale, the intensity in his heart began to fade away.

"Again," Sarika urged him, and he complied, watching as the glow in his arms slowly dimmed. Once Sarika had helped him regain control, she suggested that they visit Komipea's section of the Cressida Library before heading to Canter Mountain.

"But we can't let anyone see us go inside," she whispered to Derek. "Maybe we can find some answers there."

Derek's instincts were telling him he needed to get to Mia, but he thought to himself, "*I won't be any good to her if I don't know how to manage what is happening to me.*" Sarika's confident demeanor gave him a glimmer of hope.

He followed her lead, desperate for any clues, any answers. They made their way into the library, where Sarika positioned herself in the center of the room. After taking a deep breath, her stigmata began to glow, illuminating their surroundings. In response, a section of the floor slid open, revealing a spiral staircase.

Derek's body stiffened. He felt a chill run through his spine, almost like something was telling him to run. He pushed away his suspicion as Sarika extended her hand towards him, smiling in the way that always managed to ease his worry. Taking her hand, they descended the stairs.

Derek shot Sarika a curious look as they entered the library vault below.

"What *exactly* are we looking for down here?" he asked.

Sarika wasted no time grabbing a map from a nearby shelf. She unrolled it, and Derek caught a sharp whiff of the musty scent that seemed to permeate everything in this place. The map revealed a detailed layout of Torvania, and with a wave of Sarika's hand, it expanded further.

"How is a map gunna help us?" Derek questioned, slightly irritated that they delayed their trip for this.

Sarika stayed focused on the expanding map. "You see, most fae in Torvania are ignorant about Luminfae," she explained matter-of-factly.

When he inquired why, she told him, "Komipea liked to hoard information. He thought it best that Torvania continued on in blissful ignorance." Touching Derek's shoulder, she put a convincing smile on her face. "He trusted me with some of this information, and now I am trusting you."

The pressure of Derek's headache returned as he struggled to piece everything together.

Sarika stepped so close to him their faces were almost touching, and Derek could hear his heartbeat in his ears, forgetting about his headache entirely. Leaning closer still, she reached behind him and pulled a book off the shelf, placing it on a nearby table. A nervous chuckle escaped Derek as he admitted,

"I thought you were about to kiss me again there for a second."

Avoiding eye contact, he took a closer look at the book in front of him. Its title read "Keepers." He murmured to himself,

"Like Johnathan?"

Sarika turned back to him with excitement in her eyes.

"Exactly," she confirmed, playfully adding, "Did I hear something about a kiss?"

Derek blushed and quickly changed the subject to prevent further embarrassment.

"So, what is this book about, exactly?"

Sarika brushed her arm against his as she explained that each city in Luminfae had its own keeper on Earth. The book contained the names of these keepers, who held great power.

"Typically, only a Keeper would be able to open this . . . but we know you are different. I'd love to know if you can open it."

Derek stared at the book on the table, reaching his hand out towards it. He stopped and asked, "You said there could be something about me down here. Is this what you meant?"

Sarika stepped behind him, her finger tracing a circle on his shoulder.

"It won't be able to tell us what exactly you are or how you have your magic. *If* you can open it, then after all this is over, I will take you to the grand library in Oceanus." She squeezed her hand around his arm. "The scholars there will be able to answer any questions you have."

Her words sat heavily in his stomach. It felt like she was bribing him, but he needed answers. Derek reached out to touch the book. As soon as his fingers touched it, his arms started to glow. The book opened with a pop, revealing its secrets.

Sarika beamed ecstatically as she turned Derek around, grasped his face, and kissed him deeply. In that moment, all of Derek's thoughts calmed. He could *see* how cracked the walls she had put up had become. If he just pushed a little harder, he would be through and could finally see what she was hiding. Almost as if she could sense his intentions, she pulled back.

When they broke apart, Derek's mind stayed focused on the falling walls he could see. Sarika's kisses started to feel calculated, like they were always coming at a time when he was compelled to ask questions. This time, he wasn't flustered. Of course, he enjoyed the calming feeling it brought him, but even that was starting to feel fake. Artificial. He was confident she was hiding something from him.

"What's wrong?" he asked, as Sarika pulled away and closed the book.

"Nothing! But we need to take this book and find Tar . . .Tah'quhal and Mia," she exclaimed.

Derek's eyes widened at her slip of words, a sense of wrongness sinking deep into his gut. He decided it was time to put his own walls up. Time to be cautious until he and his real friends were reunited.

He reluctantly agreed, his gaze lingering on the closed book. Knowing that he would need to not act any differently around her, he said, "I can finally see Mia again."

Sarika ignored his comment completely, stashed the book in her bag, grabbed Derek's hand, and hurriedly dragged him out of the library.

As they bolted out of the building, a massive vortex of water materialized in the middle of the street. A magnificent griffin emerged from the water with two individuals perched on her back. The water cleared enough for Derek to make out the faces of an unfamiliar female fae and——

"Barry!"

Derek exclaimed with joy, running towards his friend. Caldera, still running on battle adrenaline, lept off Eirene's back, leveraging her spear to defend Barry against Derek.

Fortunately, Barry quickly jumped down from the griffin, placing soothing hands on the death grip she held on the spear.

"Take it easy, girl," Barry said in a reassuring yet exasperated tone. "This is Derek, the friend I mentioned."

Caldera gave Derek a quick apology before turning her anger to Barry, giving him a firm smack on the head.

"Why did you do that? Serene . . . Terra needed us!" she scolded, her frustration evident.

Barry tried to explain. "Johnathan told us——"

As if in response to his words, another whirlpool appeared, dropping out Johnathan. But the relief of their reunion was short-lived. The arrow that had struck him in Terra was still embedded in his shoulder. On his knees, he tried to muster a semblance of humor.

"Well hey there, buddy. I was starting to think I'd never see your ugly mug again," he managed to say to Derek, before a bout of coughing spewed blood from his lips.

Derek's body locked with dread as painful memories of Isabella's death flooded his mind. His panic gripped him and he couldn't move, not even to help his closest friend.

Barry lunged forward to catch Johnathan before he hit the ground. Caldera and Sarika quickly went to inspect the wound, and Sarika started weaving incantations. Sarika lifted her hands to press against Johnathan's wound, but Caldera's urgent cry stopped her.

"The arrowhead could be poisoned! He is coughing blood, but the arrow is in his shoulder. My guess is slinake venom. Magic would only make things worse."

Sarika scoffed and assured them that the Hellfire Brigade doesn't use slinake venom on their weapons.

Caldera's ears twitched. She thought to herself, "*How would she know that?*" Another cough made her push her thoughts aside to focus on Johnathan.

"No, but Codi does. We need to stabilize him." Caldera firmly directed.

Barry frantically demanded, "Someone go get Komipea. He can help."

"You can't." Sarika said softly.

"What do you mean, his house is right there?" Barry asked, pointing to a nearby home.

Derek, still frozen in place, shakily said, "He's dead."

Barry stared back in shock and Caldera turned to Sarika, eyes narrowed. "What does he mean, *dead*?"

Sarika gave no answer. She just looked to the ground, letting a tear fall from her eye. The silence was broken by another round of Johnathan coughing. At the sight of more blood, Barry lifted Johnathan into his arms, careful not to jostle his wound.

"We can talk about Komipea later. We need to save John right now."

Barry raced towards the library, kicking the doors open, while Caldera hurried to brush the contents off a table inside. Sensing his rising panic, Sarika walked towards Derek, stretching out a hand towards his shoulder.

Derek swatted the fae's hand away. He slowly turned and tried to walk towards the library, but couldn't. All the trauma and disaster of his last twenty-four hours raced through his mind, choking the breath out of him: the red and blue essence, watching Izzy die, Komipea dying before he could get any kind of answers, and now, seeing his best friend knock on death's door. His mind wanted to shut down. He wanted to help . . . he had to help . . . he was going to . . .

Chapter 23

Save Me

An all too familiar voice rang through Derek's head.

"In his hands, the fate of all appears."

Derek swayed on his feet.

Sarika approached him, brows furrowed.

"What's wrong?"

Placing her hand on his chest, Sarika could feel his thundering heart. She tried to use her magic to calm him, but Derek's inner turmoil was too intense. He also seemed more ... resistant to it.

Uncertainty, panic, and relief fought for dominance in his head. *This is all part of my stupid nightmare.* He dug his nails into his palm, and although he registered the pain, he told himself it didn't matter. He *knew* he was dreaming. This was just him refusing to wake up. Muttering under his breath, almost deliriously, he whispered,

"You're not real."

Sarika took a step back, her confusion evident on her face. "What do you mean, I am not real? I am right in front of you."

"None of this is *real*," he insisted, his voice trembling. "If this were real, I wouldn't be able to do this!" he exclaimed, raising his hands that were, for once, glowing bright white at his command.

"Or this!" he cried out. His power rushed through him in a way that seemed *too* real for his loosely tethered sanity as he summoned a bolt of lightning. It struck a nearby house, setting it on fire.

The fae family who lived there immediately ran for safety, their terror palpable. Derek continued his dramatic display, his voice dripping with sarcasm.

"You're really scared of a man with supposed magical powers, aren't you?"

His stomach rolled with nausea that he tried to ignore as the small, uncertain part of himself recoiled at the possibility that he'd actually done that.

Sarika had an odd sense of satisfaction as she watched Derek's breakdown become more and more dangerous, not only putting himself at risk, but those around him.

Desperate to prove this was a dream, he declared, "I bet I can even fly!"

Despite Sarika's warnings, Derek dashed towards a nearby house, climbing an attached trellis onto the roof. He stood atop it for a moment, fists pressed against his eyes, fighting with everything he had to wake up. The voice of his nightmares still echoing in his head, he lept.

Sarika, who had readied her magic to soften his landing, gasped in astonishment when Derek jumped, but did not fall. Brilliant white light burst from his downward extended hands to the ground beneath, keeping him suspended in mid-air. He hid his own amazement, still convinced he was only in a dream.

In the haven of the library, Barry and Caldera worked together to stabilize Johnathan while chaos raged outside.

Caldera told Barry, "Stay here with Johnathan. I'm going to see what is taking them so long."

Her steps faltered when confronted with the sight of Derek, suspended in the air by a blinding, radiant light. She never imagined she would see one in the flesh.

"*Semideus*." she whispered in concern and awe as she stepped next to Sarika.

Sarika whipped her head towards Caldera in disbelief. A semideus——a being from ancient myths, believed to be extinct or hidden away in another dimension.

"Are you sure?" Sarika demanded.

Caldera snapped, "There is no time for this. Johnathan's life is on the line, but if Derek is semideus, then he can help."

Sarika barked back, "Caldera, you will be able to get through to him. His mind has broken. He thinks this is all a nightmare."

Caldera took a deliberate and slow breath, then with desperation evident in her voice, she called out to Derek.

"I know you think none of this is real, and I can't imagine what you've been through. But if you want to save Johnathan, we need your help!"

Her words hung in the air as Derek stopped mid-flight, gazing at the two fae women beckoning him to pause.

"This is all just my mind playing tricks on me!" Derek argued.

Caldera urged, "Think of Johnathan!"

He gave no response, his mind made up.

"Derek, look at the destruction you are causing around you. Tell me how that is not real?" Caldera begged.

Two fae children were standing in the street crying as their parents hopelessly tried to put the blaze overtaking their home out.

He rapidly blinked his eyes, trying to flush out the tears that were forming. Even if this was a dream, he didn't want to cause anyone pain. He didn't want to be someone else's nightmare.

Slowly, Derek descended back down to the ground.

"Fine. What do you need me to do?" He relented.

Caldera gestured towards the library, and Sarika reached for Derek's hand. He once again refused her touch, noting the sharp look in her eyes. His mind was a scattered jigsaw puzzle, and exhaustion now threatened to pull him under, but he was certain of one thing——Sarika was hiding something.

Once inside the library, Caldera commanded, "Barry, stay back." She looked at Derek. "Place your hands over Johnathan. Focus on your friend. Summon your magic, and picture him healed and healthy."

After a few hesitant seconds, he tried. When nothing happened, he growled in frustration, the bitter helplessness returning. It was easier to cling to this being a dream than admit that even with all this power, he was *useless*. He shrugged his shoulders and looked back at Caldera.

"Looks like my magic well has run dry," he quipped sarcastically.

Barry's worried face turned stormy. "What the hell is wrong with you? Johnathan is *dying*!" he yelled.

Sarika whispered, "He thinks he is dreaming."

Barry strode towards Derek with his fist clenched, anger boiling in his veins.

Barry delivered a solid punch to Derek's left cheek. "Still think this is all a dream?"

Derek stumbled backwards, clutching his throbbing face. The pain was real, and it seared through him. Shame pulsed in time with his cheek as the last of his denial bled away, giving him his first real semblance of clarity since this mess started. Amidst the ringing in his ears, he could hear Sarika scolding Barry.

One hand on Barry's chest, restraining him, Caldera met Derek's gaze, her command firm and steady, grounding, "Help him, Derek. Now."

He forced himself towards Johnathan, and despite his stumbling steps, his arms began glowing once again. Everyone's words faded into the background as Derek reached Johnathan's side. He placed his radiant hand over Johnathan's wound, remembering what Caldera had said. "*Picture him healed and healthy.*"

The light grew brighter, forcing everyone to shield their eyes. Derek felt his strength waning, and in a pained cry of desperation, he dragged out a final surge. And then, the light disappeared, leaving Derek on his knees, tearfully saying,

"I . . . I promise I tried."

Sarika rushed to comfort him. Caldera and Barry cautiously approached Johnathan's motionless body, preparing for the worst.

"Who died?" Johnathan's voice rang out, rasped and barely more than a whisper.

Derek's eyes darted to Johnathan, and a wave of relief crashed over him. He pulled his friend into a tight hug, causing Johnathan to wince a little. Barry joined in, embracing them both. Sarika discreetly tucked a piece of paper deep into her pocket before approaching and placing a comforting hand on Derek's back. Choking back sobs, Derek apologized.

"I'm so sorry. My mind . . . I thought I was . . . I thought I was stuck in the nightmare I have every night."

Barry raised an eyebrow. "What nightmare? You've never said anything about it before."

Derek took a deep breath. He looked at John and then back at Barry. "I never wanted anyone to think I was insane. I told John about the dream when he first showed me the Anchor."

He summarized his nightmare to them.

"I get that it sounds crazy, but when Sarika and I got here, I recognized the fields outside the city as the same fields from my dream. And outside earlier? I heard the voice from my dream saying 'in his hands, the fate of all appears.'"

Caldera's breath caught in her throat before she softly recited, "With courage, he'll mend what's torn inside. The realms tremble as the battle draws near. In his hands, the fate of all appears."

Derek's muscles tensed at the words. "Yes!" he shouted, "That is exactly what I hear. What does it mean?"

"I am not sure why those words echo in your dreams, but they are a part of a prophecy passed down since the First Fae Wars." Caldera walked towards Derek, staring at the white bands on his arms. "Serene, the Chieftain of Terra, would have more information . . . and she could tell you about what you are."

Derek smiled. For the first time since this started, he felt like he was actually getting closer to answers. He softly spoke, "I'm sorry. You all probably thought I was crazy and . . . well, I'm sorry."

Barry walked to Derek, extending his hand. "About that punch, man."

"I needed it dude." Derek cut him off, grabbing his hand and pulling him in for a hug.

The group readily forgave him, and the tension began to dissipate.

Derek turned to Caldera. "Well, since we didn't really get a proper introduction. Hey, there. I'm Derek."

Caldera smiled at Derek with a tone of respect in her voice, "It is an honor to meet a semideus."

Derek's brows pinched in confusion.

"The Chieftain of the Magia Forest here thinks you are semideus solely based on seeing your magic," Sarika explained.

Caldera cut her eyes to Sarika. "And how do you know who I am?" she asked.

The air crackled with tension. Derek nervously interjected,

"Komipea taught Sarika all he knew about Luminfae. In fact, right before you arrived through that water portal, she was showing me what she learned in the vaults below."

His explanation only raised more questions for Caldera. "What all do you know about the Sacred Dimension?"

"The what?" Derek asked.

Johnathan spoke up, his voice still weak, "Well now's a good a time as any. I learned a *lot* from Serene."

He recounted their journey in Luminfae and all the information Serene had given him. Johnathan noticed his satchel laying on the ground next to the table he had been laid on. He pointed to it and Barry picked it up, the journal inside falling to the ground. Before he could explain its significance, Sarika scooped it up and gasped,

"Helian. How did you get this?"

Caldera narrowed her sharp gaze at Sarika's reaction. "Again, you know of things you shouldn't."

Sarika quickly responded, "Komipea revealed copious amounts of information to me. The years of keeping secrets weighed heavily on the old fae. Helian's story was one of those secrets."

Barry furrowed his eyebrows and exchanged a concerned look with Caldera. This was a surprising revelation, as Barry had not come across any mention of the journal in Komipea's secret library.

Caldera ignored Sarika's weak excuse, instead explaining to Derek, "Semidues are believed to be the descendants of the rulers in the Sacred Dimension, or at the very least, share their bloodline."

Derek's mind spun as he took a step back, feeling the ground beneath him shift yet again. He stammered, asking about this *sacred dimension*, but Caldera's response was uncertain.

"Some fae, like Malum, think it is the realm of *gods*. Even in fae folklore, the concept of the semideus is shrouded in human legends." She paused to gather her thoughts. "I'm sure you have heard some of the stories. Heroes like Hercules, Achilles, Sigi, Skiold, and Imhotep."

Johnathan's shocked whisper filled the air. It was barely audible, but it was clear enough for Derek to hear.

"Demigods?"

He felt the urge to panic again as the realization sunk in. How could *he* be connected to something as extraordinary as demigods?

Caldera continued, "If the legends are true, then you, semideus," she looked at Derek, "would have a portion of the magical power that the beings of the sacred dimension have."

Derek stared at his arms, flickers of light coming from them as Caldera went on more contemplatively, "Of course, I've never met them, but if they truly are as powerful as the stories say, if your healing abilities are but a mere fragment of theirs . . . then why have they not intervened in the wars, famines, and disease that other dimensions have suffered?"

Sarika's bitter response cut in, "Because they think they are better than us. They have abandoned the lower dimensions."

Derek caught the concerned glance exchanged between Barry and Caldera. Sarika's reaction did seem peculiar.

Seeing their discomfort, Sarika quickly changed the subject, urging Derek.

"These answers are important, but we have lingered long enough. We have to make our way to Canter Mountain before it is too late."

Despite his eagerness to understand his new powers and origins, Derek knew he needed to find the rest of their friends. They needed to come up with a plan for their next move.

Sarika again reiterated the need to go to Canter Mountain, but Caldera interjected, "John will not be fit to travel any time soon. He needs to heal."

"Caldera is right. There is no reason to put him in harm's way right now," Barry murmured, his tone filled with unspoken worry.

He crossed his arms tightly over his chest, a deep crease forming between his eyebrows. "I think we need to go to Oceanus. We need more information about Malum that we might be able to find in their library."

"I hate to disagree, but finding Mia and Tah'quhal is more important," Derek challenged, lips pressed into a tight frown.

After a few moments of debate, Derek's arms began to shine and an eerie silence fell on the library.

Nervously, Johnathan asked, "What's going on, buddy?"

Derek's eyes scanned his shimmering arms. "I have no idea. So far, it only happens when I'm panicking or——"

An explosion boomed from outside, shaking the ground beneath them. Barry instinctively reached for his sword as he and Caldera rushed towards the door, with Sarika following close behind.

Johnathan gave Derek a reassuring nod that he'd be fine, and Derek was off. The four of them hurried out to find a thick cloud of black smoke, occasionally lit up by bursts of blue and red essence. Derek's arms began to shine brighter as he aimed his hands at the cloud, dispelling the darkness with a brilliant light. And there, standing in the midst of the dissipating smoke, was Trey.

Derek's heart swelled with relief as he ran towards him. But his excitement came to an abrupt halt at Trey's authoritative,

"Don't come any closer!"

Derek dug his shoes into the ground, confusion written all over his face. Trey's voice cut through the tense air.

"For years, I have stood by your side," Trey spoke, his words heavy with a burden that seemed almost impossible to bear. "I know exactly what you are, and I have kept the reaper at bay, but I'm not sure I can do it much longer." The strain and urgency in Trey's voice were palpable. He pushed on, determination etched into his face, despite the visible struggle. "I wish there was another way, but these are the cards we've been dealt."

Trey's hollowed eyes locked onto Derek's. The storm of worry, fear, and resolve in Trey's eyes nearly brought Derek to his knees.

With gravity, Trey said, "Malum's army grows stronger each day in Oblivion, and they are an overwhelming force." Trey's voice trembled. "You will need more allies. You will need Mia and Tah'quhal."

The words hung heavily in the air, carving themselves into Derek's mind. "Mia and Tah'quhal are being held captive inside Canter Mountain," It now looked as if it caused him physical pain to speak. "Once you rescue them, gather the broken stones from the castle atop the mountain and use them at the Anchor to journey to Oblivion."

Trey's words echoed like a call to arms, each syllable charged with a sense of criticality that sent shivers down Derek's spine. He tried to move towards his friend, but Trey's outstretched hand released a gust of wind that knocked him to the ground with unnerving strength.

"I've done all I can," Trey's voice broke. "The rest is in fate's hands now. I don't know what all you've learned." He paused. "It pains me to say this, but make no mistake, we are on opposing sides. War is inevitable." Trey gritted out the last words, visibly shaking with the effort.

With another thunderous explosion, the thick smoke returned, enveloping them, and just like that, Trey was gone.

Trey's words hung heavily in the air. Derek's heart ached, not just for losing his friend, but for Trey's clear suffering. He couldn't afford to lose focus again; they needed to confront the threat head-on, starting with finding Mia and Tah'quhal. Glancing at his companions, Derek saw the same conviction reflected in their eyes.

Derek strode past his group of friends, heading straight back to the library to catch Johnathan up, Barry immediately following behind. When he shared Trey's warning that they were now on opposing sides, Johnathan signaled for Derek to come closer, his voice lowered in secrecy.

"I've always sensed something off about Trey, but he *is* our friend. Whatever he said out there, someone's gotta be controlling him."

Barry added, "John's right. You could see the pain in Trey's eyes. He doesn't want any part of this. It has to be Malum's influence."

As Caldera and Sarika joined the rest of the group, Derek took charge with newfound confidence. "I feel like I'm back on the mound deciding what pitch to throw." He looked at Johnathan steadily, mind clearer than ever. "I'd love for you to go with us, but I don't think you're strong enough just yet."

John turned his head to look away from his friend. He knew he was right, but he wasn't willing to admit it out loud.

Derek's voice was unwavering as he spoke. "John, your priority now is to rest and recover. But once you are fully healed, I need you to gather any remaining fae here in Torvania who are still willing to fight."

He turned to Caldera and Barry next.

"Head back to the Magia Forest, Ignis, and Terra, and convince 'em to join our cause. Tell them to meet us here in Torvania, where they will find Johnathan waiting for them."

Caldera quirked her eyebrow, nailing Derek with a frightening look.

"Uh, if that sounds good to you, Caldera." He quickly added.

Caldera gave him a quick nod, her features slightly softening.

Derek then turned his attention to Sarika.

"We will journey together to Canter Mountain to rescue Mia and Tah'quhal. After that, we'll move on to the other cities of Luminfae before coming back here to Torvania with everyone else." Locking eyes with each of them, he stressed, "This has gone on long enough. Malum is a threat that needs to be stopped. He has flipped all of our lives upside down, and I don't know about y'all, but I'm tired of it."

The group hung on to every word Derek spoke, moved by his unwavering grit and newfound sense of purpose.

Caldera leaned towards him, "It would be smart to remember that I am the Chieftain of the Magia Forest. I *give* orders, I do not take them. Keep that in mind, lest you figure out just how sharp my spear really is." She gave a quick pat on his shoulder. "Now, may I get a moment with you outside?"

Once outside, she cautiously said, "Derek, I know you have only just met me . . . but there is something off about Sarika. She knows things she should not."

Derek agreed, "I have felt something strange about her, too, but so far she hasn't given me a real reason not to let her come. Besides, we all have our new tasks, and I can't make it to Canter Mountain alone."

"Just be careful. Keep a close eye on her," the Chieftain of the forest pleaded. "I care for Barry, and he cares for you."

Derek raised his eyebrows at that, a small grin on his face. "You betcha. I'll keep my eyes open for anything." He turned to walk back inside but paused, looking back over his shoulder. "Keep Barry safe."

Caldera nodded in response as she followed him back inside the library.

They found Barry and Sarika ready for their assigned tasks when they returned.

Barry locked eyes with Johnathan, and they shared a heartfelt embrace, unsure when they'd see each other again. Derek joined in the hug, treasuring these last few moments with his best friends. Sarika, ever practical, cut through the moment with a blunt,

"It's time to leave."

Caldera offered a final warning to the group, "If our path takes us to Oblivion, know that it is a dark and malevolent realm. Malum chose that location for a reason——dark magic thrives there. The very landscape may trick and deceive us, and every element will pose a danger. Keep this in mind as we prepare for the journey."

Barry, Caldera, and Derek discussed their plans, deciding that the former two would go back to Terra first, using the last vial from the geyser. Hopefully, they could obtain more vials while there to quicken their journey.

"Barry, we need to be careful. The Hellfire Brigade could still be in Terra." Caldera warned.

Barry shuddered at the thought, recalling how they had left in the middle of a battle. Derek watched as the two mounted the griffin, shattered their final vial, and vanished into a watery vortex.

Derek faced Johnathan with vulnerable sincerity. "Get better and get better fast. We are going to need you at your best. And I need my best friend with me for this," he urged. Johnathan nodded firmly, eyes shining with promise. With that, Derek and Sarika embarked on their journey towards Canter Mountain.

Chapter 24

Canter Mountain

After a long day's trek, Derek looked up at the jagged fortress above, his heart galloping like a wild stallion. Familiar panic began to twist in his gut at the fear that he may have come so close, only to fail. Even so, his magic remained calm. His arms, once unbridled channels of strength, now felt more controllable, a promising indication of his increasing command over his powers.

Sarika pulled his gaze, her eyes brimming with secrets that seemed desperate to get out. Taking a deep breath, she hesitantly opened her mouth to speak, her voice carrying the weight of everything unspoken.

"There is something I need to tell you," she began. Before she could continue, the ground beneath them began to tremble and quake in rippling shockwaves.

"What's going on?" Derek shouted over the noise.

Sarika's calm response broke through the chaos. "The mountain is directly connected to Oblivion. Something . . . or someone, knows we are here."

Whatever she'd been about to say slipped away, her cool face betraying nothing of her emotions.

Derek's eyes narrowed as he looked at Sarika. How did she know such intricate details? He knew Komipea had shared secrets of Luminfae with her over the years, but if they were headed to Canter Mountain, why hadn't she mentioned this before? Derek was about to question Sarika when a faint, desperate voice obliterated any focus or reason he may have had.

"Help!" The sound seemed to come from within the walls of the mountain, echoing through the arched doorway carved into its side.

"Mia." Derek breathed.

Running on adrenaline and instinct, he sprinted towards the archway.

He had to find Mia.

As he reached the archway, Derek realized that the interior of the mountain had been excavated and transformed into a magnificent castle. Darting down different hallways, he desperately hoped for Mia's voice to call out again so he could get his bearings in the maze.

Sarika soon caught up to him, "Derek, I really need to——"

"Help!"

Mia's voice was quickly followed by a second voice calling out desperately,

"Can anyone hear us?"

Derek exchanged a worried glance with Sarika before pointing towards a hallway on his left.

"That's Tah'quhal!" he proclaimed with confidence, before launching himself down the corridor. As they left the fading daylight behind them, Derek's arms began to shine, illuminating their path through the darkness.

This time, Sarika didn't match his cadence with her own frantic pace. Instead, she kept a steady jog behind Derek, using the glow from his arms as a guide.

After several dead ends and seemingly endless corridors, Derek came to a halt in front of a dungeon chamber deep within the castle's walls. There, he found Mia and Tah'quhal bound to two stone columns at the center of the room. Sarika stayed back at the entrance, her aura acting as a silent guard.

Derek quickly scanned his eyes over Mia, knees nearly giving out in relief when he didn't spot any obvious signs of injury. Despite her disheveled appearance, her eyes were lit up with surprise and hope. Covered in dirt, their clothes torn, it was clear that they had endured much during their capture. Derek felt like he couldn't get to her fast enough.

"Derek?" Mia whispered.

Channeling his magic into his hands, Derek tore off the chains imprisoning Mia. "We really have to stop meeting like this," he half heartedly joked. She immediately embraced him, wrapping her arms around his neck. Derek pulled back to look into her eyes, needing to see that she was ok. He held Mia's gaze for what felt like an eternity before she leaned in and softly kissed his lips. They were interrupted by Tah'quhal's throat clearing.

"Ahem . . . I'm still tied up here!"

Derek chuckled and made swift work of Tah'quhal's restraints.

Tah'quhal reached out his hand to clasp Derek's. "I'm glad to see you again."

Mia massaged her own arms, twisting her wrists to work out the stiffness, as she asked,

"How did you know we were here?"

Not wanting to spend too long lingering in the dungeon, he rushed through his explanation. "When we went through the Anchor, instead of ending up in Torvania as planned, we found ourselves in Mythos."

"Mythos!" exclaimed Tah'quhal.

"Yes," Derek continued, "when we finally made it out and to Torvania, Komipea was telling us of everything that had happened and then he . . . his sickness . . ."

Tah'quhal's head slightly cocked to one side. "Sickness? What sickness?"

Derek avoided eye contact, staring at a fixed point on the ground. "Tah'quhal, I don't really know. I had stepped outside and left him alone with Sarika and then I heard her scream and . . ."

Mia grabbed his hands, her eyes wide. "Derek. Sarika can *not* be trusted. She and Tarik have been working for Malum for years. Please tell me she is not here with you."

A chilling laughter echoed through the dungeon, filling the air with a sinister symphony that seemed to emanate from the walls.

"Oh, Mia, my dear," the voice taunted, freezing their blood.

A surge of wind accompanied by red essence enveloped the chamber, forcing Derek, Tah'quhal, and Mia to the ground.

Derek's eyes darted to Mia, silently asking if she was alright. Tah'quhal propelled himself to his feet with a powerful grace, as if he had spent the last several weeks building his power inside of him.

The atmosphere in the dungeon crackled with tension.

His stigmata glowed fiercely on his skin, almost in defiance of his caged magic. His long, black hair and now wild beard gave him a savage look as he stood amidst the cold stone walls of the dungeon, every bit the image of the vengeful warrior.

Before him stood Sarika, her sultry smile and long blue hair no more than a beautiful deception. Those same stigmatas of lace Tah'quhal had been jealous of burned red, a cruel mockery of their shared past. The truth that their friendship, relationship, had been built on betrayal now hung between them like a specter. Her once-comforting eyes now gleamed with a chilling crimson tint that shook Tah'quhal to his core.

The silence in the room was oppressive, the air charged with an impending clash of powers. Tah'quhal's body was tense, his fingers itching with restrained energy. Without breaking his gaze away from Sarika, he thrust his hands forward, summoning a thin blue mist that materialized into two gleaming swords.

"I knew there was something off about you." Derek's angry voice rang out, breaking the silence.

Sarika laughed sardonically. "Well, if you were *smart*, you would have done something about it before now."

Derek's arms ignited in a blazing intensity, the white glow brighter than ever before. He took a stance next to Tah'quhal, ready to stand with him in this fight.

"No, Derek Stratum, this fight is mine and mine alone. Stay with Mia." Tah'quhal spoke firmly.

Derek was torn as he looked between him and Mia, who had already moved to fight beside them. "Are you sure?"

Tah'quhal brow set in a hard line. "I need to do this."

The corners of Sarika's mouth lifted into a mischievous grin as she watched Mia and Derek hesitantly step to the side. As if accepting Tah'quhal's challenge, a gust of wind whirled around her, lifting her hair to sway with its movement. With a flick of her wrist, flames formed into a sharp sword. She looked ethereal. Deadly.

Their swords clashed, sending pulses of magic through the dungeon. The longer they fought, the more the rhythm of their sparring subtly shifted. Sarika's movements took on a seductive grace, each calculated step and motion luring Tah'quhal to the edge of her blade. Her gaze never left his, speaking of heated encounters and stolen caresses, even as they fought.

"Tah'quhal," she purred, her voice a sultry whisper amidst the clash of metal. "We were once so close, remember? All the long nights we spent together? Can you deny what we shared?" Her questions took on the trembling pout of a heartbroken lover, striking Tah'quhal harder than any blade.

Tah'quhal's grit faltered as he was flooded with memories of their past. Sarika took advantage of his momentary distraction, sending a gust of fiery wind rushing towards him. Derek outstretched his arms, forming a shield of radiant light that extinguished the flames and calmed the winds to a gentle breeze. The gratitude in Tah'quhal's nod spoke volumes about how close of a call that had been.

Even with his defense, Derek noticed a deep burn on Tah'quhal's leg, his pants torn and singed from where a piercing shot of Sarika's fire had gotten through. He ran toward Tah'quhal, placing his hand on the wound and focusing his light on it,

"You may not want me to help you fight, but at least I can help keep you going," Derek said with a half smile.

Sarika laughed. "Go ahead, heal him. I'm having too much fun for this to end."

With renewed vigor, Tah'quhal returned to his battle against Sarika. Their powers clashed relentlessly, filling the chamber with flashes of essence and elements.

Sarika spun away from Tah'quhal's blade as if they were dancing, her laughter ringing out like a haunting melody.

"You *see*, Tah'quhal? Power is not the only thing that binds us. There's a chemistry, a fire between us that even your essence cannot extinguish."

Tah'quhal tightened his grip on his swords as he blocked out the feelings she'd always been able to stir.

"Your words won't sway me, Sarika. Betrayal has severed whatever bond we once had."

Undeterred, she closed the distance between them once more, moving like a cat about to pounce or play

"We both know how good you are at hiding what you really feel. Always the brave soldier. Deep down, you crave the connection we shared. The way our powers complemented each other. The way our magic intertwined." She dragged the last word out suggestively and leaned closer, her voice low and breathless. "You cannot deny the passion that still simmers between us."

Tah'quhal's resolve wavered as her words wormed their way into his mind. She has always possessed a hold on him, ever since their first day of training. His heart, still raw from her betrayal, wanted to be swayed by her words. Wanted to believe she was still the woman he had loved for the last century.

"You're right, Sarika." He said, stepping closer to her, voice low and gruff.

Her eyes widened at his admission, at the way his sword hand relaxed as he stepped closer to her. Her cunning eyes twinkled as she watched him fall effortlessly into her web. Arching an eyebrow with a triumphant, "Oh?" she allowed him to approach, still deciding if she'd strike him or take him with her.

Sarika savored the moment, the victory. Derek and Mia let out pleas and warnings, but Tah'quhal was already close enough to embrace or kill.

Tilting his head towards her, eyes fixed on her lips, he whispered, "I *have* always been good at hiding how I feel."

Then slid his blade through her stomach.

Sarika stumbled back, her laughter now tinged with bitter surprise.

"Oh, my, I did not expect that," she gasped, pain, and maybe a little pride, evident in her voice. She closed her eyes, the wind around her picking up speed, and whispered, "*Finis.*"

Tah'quhal backed away from Sarika, moving towards Derek and Mia. When he turned his face towards them, Derek noticed his skin was pale and ashen, like his blood was seeping out with Sarika's. Tah'quhal's face tightened, every muscle locking as if bracing for an impact.

"Take cover," he shouted.

Sarika ripped the sword from her stomach, screaming in agony, and covered her wound with her free hand, holding back the flow of blood with her magic. She slammed the sword into the ground. A maelstrom of red essence erupted from the slung blade and the ground quaked beneath their feet. Sarika's hands ignited in flame as red essence poured from her nose.

She aimed her hands at Mia, and a spear formed out of the flames. With one swift movement, she hurled the spear at her unsuspecting form.

Time slowed as the spear flew through the air. Tah'quhal looked back to see it closing the distance, eyes widening as he realized he was not the target.

There was nothing but light. It burned through the spear, the red essence, even the explosive shock wave Sarika sent out. The only sound that could still be heard was the half laugh, half cry of Sarika's voice.

"We would have made a wonderful team," she whispered as she snapped her fingers and vanished.

As the white light dimmed in the dungeon, Derek stood untouched in front of Mia, his arms still faintly glowing with a residual ethereal shimmer. In a heartbeat, Derek had thrown himself in front of her.

"I thought the spear would strike Mia. You have grown since we last saw each other, Derek Stratum."

Derek's heart twinged. Hearing Tah'quhal say his full name reminded him of his first actual conversation with Sarika. "Just Derek is fine."

Tah'quhal nodded his head. "Very well, Derek." He looked at Mia as she ran up behind Derek and wrapped her arms around him. "I figured the Keeper of Oceanus would have been more eager to join the fight."

Derek raised one eyebrow. "Keeper?"

Mia ran a hand through her tangled, dirty hair, looking to Tah'quhal, "I'm pretty sure you're the one that told us not to get involved." Her eyes shifted back to Derek's expectant face. "Yeaaa, I promise I will explain all of that later, but for now can we get out of this creepy dungeon?"

Derek admitted, "I would love to get out of here, but we have to find something first." He quickly told them of Trey's arrival in Torvania, his cryptic warning, and about the stones he needed to retrieve.

Tah'quhal said, "The castle is directly above us, but I doubt it will be easy to locate these stones. Perhaps you two can search the upper floors while I search the lower ones."

He cracked his knuckles and waved one hand in the air. "You two look after each other. I can handle my own if I run into trouble." Tah'quhal grabbed Mia's arm, saying, "*Signum.*" The stigmata under his eye flickered blue, and Mia's tattoo did the same. "Do you feel that? If either of us finds the stones, just whisper the same incantation so we know to meet outside."

Mia and Derek nodded in understanding, and Tah'quhal began his search.

As Derek and Mia climbed the spiral tower, their hands tentatively intertwined. They searched countless rooms. Mia cast nervous looks to Derek, worried he wasn't happy to see her. She could clearly see the distress in his eyes.

Derek was doing his best to steel his nerves. He explained everything that had happened to him since they were separated . . . almost everything. He knew that he would need to tell Mia about Sarika, he just didn't know how.

When they reached the top of the tower, they finally found exactly what they were looking for: a shattered amulet encased in glass. Mia moved towards the case to retrieve it, but Derek remained still, holding onto her hand.

She turned to him with concern and asked, "Derek, what's wrong?"

His gaze stayed fixed on Mia, his hands shaking with anxiety.

She closed the distance between them and took his other, trembling hand firmly in hers, asking again, "What's wrong, Derek?" Her eyes showed genuine care and worry.

Taking a deep breath, Derek explained with quiet intensity. "I need to tell you some things about Sarika," he started, his voice heavy with resignation. Mia's open and patient face gave Derek the courage to keep talking.

"There was a connection between us that I can't fully explain. She . . ." Derek paused briefly before blurting out, "She kissed me." His face flamed with regret, bracing himself for her scorn, to lose any chance he might have had with her.

Mia stood silently for a moment, processing his confession. Her intense gaze never left Derek's face as she searched his eyes. Seeming to find what she was looking for, her muscles relaxed. When Derek almost couldn't take the silence anymore, she spoke, her voice empathetic.

"For me, it has been six months. But for you, it's only been a little over a day. You were thrown into this mess, and Sarika was the only one by your side. Technically, you've spent more time talking to her, being with her, than we ever got the chance to. I can't blame you for connecting with her when she's the only person you had here . . . even if she ended up being an evil bitch." She added disdainfully.

Derek managed a small chuckle at her choice of words, and Mia's lips curved into a half-smile.

Softening her tone, she continued, "I'll admit, I have had a crush on you for the better part of our Junior year. I'd kinda watch you hanging out with your friends and teammates and hope you would come talk to me. It was adorable back at the school, when all you could manage to say was 'Lavender.' I've seen your growth in this world, and honestly, it is pretty amazing. Life is full of unexpected events, especially during what might literally be the end of the world. But what truly matters is that you are here now, telling me about all of this."

Derek let out the breath he'd been holding, a mixture of relief and gratitude evident on his face.

"Mia, even through everything that has happened, my thoughts have always gone back to you. You've taken up most of my thoughts since the day you transferred to Riverrun," he confessed.

Mia gave him a shy smile and gently squeezed his hands. "Thank you for telling me, Derek. We're in this together now, and that's what matters."

"Together," Derek agreed.

Feeling lighter than he had since all of this began, Derek's attention shifted to the glass case holding the amulet. He took a deep breath and raised his arm towards the case. His radiant energy surged forth, effortlessly dissolving the glass. Derek shot Mia a half grin that sent a swarm of butterflies off in her stomach.

"But did you really *have* to bring up the lavender thing?"

Mia smiled playfully, quirking her brow. "I'll never not bring it up."

With the protective case now gone, Derek reached out to retrieve the broken amulet. Together, they ran toward the exit, Mia whispering, "*signum.*"

Once all three were outside, Derek said, "Well, I guess it's time to head to Neutrale and Oceanus."

"I can not go with you," Tah'quhal gruffed. "There is something I need to do . . . for me. You have both seen the statue of Torviid, but there is also a small shrine just on the outskirts of town. I feel something calling me to go there, but I promise, once I am finished, I will meet you in Torvania and I will be ready to fight."

Derek asked, "Are you sure about this? I really don't want you to be alone."

"It is the first thing I am sure of since I met you." Tah'quhal answered.

Reaching his hand out, Derek said, "Then good luck, friend. We will see you soon."

Tah'quhal nodded and planted his hand firmly in Derek's. With that, he turned and set off on his own.

Turning to Mia, Derek asked,

"You don't know the fastest way to Neutrale, do ya?"

Mia smiled and traced her tattoo with two fingers.

"How about we make a stop at Oceanus first?" At his nod, her tattoo began glowing and Mia grabbed onto Derek's hand. A shower of blue essence formed above their heads and they were gone.

Chapter 25

Oceanus

The first thing to hit their senses was the sharp smell of brine. As the blue mist cleared, Derek and Mia found themselves standing before a colossal stone gate with walls that stretched beyond their line of sight. Behind them was an endless ocean. Derek blinked, struggling to comprehend the sudden change in scenery.

Mia let out a small giggle. "There are definitely perks to being the Keeper of Oceanus. If I had been able to break free from my bindings on Canter Mountain, I could have teleported Tah'quhal and myself here."

Derek turned to her, "Wait, so you mean this whole time you could have come here and gotten help?"

Mia's smile faded. "It's not that simple, Derek."

Frustrated, Derek exclaimed, "What do you mean, it's not simple? You've been here for *six* months! You could have come to Oceanus and asked for help before heading off to Canter Mountain!"

Mia pleaded, "Please, just come inside. Karrent can explain everything."

Derek stiffly asked, "Who the hell is Karrent?"

The answer didn't come from Mia, but rather from the sound of the huge gate slowly sliding open. The metal groaned as the heavy iron bars retracted into their stone housing.

"That would be me," replied a tall man with long, wavy turquoise hair. "I am Karrent. I suspect you have some questions that require rather immediate answers. Please follow me, and I will do my utmost to provide them."

Derek's gaze lingered on the peculiar fae in front of him. His complexion was almost translucent, and his eyes were lighter than the sky above them. He was dressed in flowing teal robes. Everything about him, the colors and grace, felt like staring at the ocean tide. Derek had become accustomed to the intricate markings on the skin of fae, but Karrent's were different. They consisted entirely of blue spirals, similar to Mia's tattoo, but covering his entire body.

Then Derek noticed his ears. While all the fae he had encountered had pointed ears, Karrent's looked closer to fins.

"Never mind who you are," Derek said with a raised eyebrow, "*What* exactly are you?"

"Derek!" Mia interjected.

Karrent flashed a smile, revealing one sharp tooth amidst a perfect set. "That is one question I can most certainly answer," he replied calmly. "I am a natare——cousins of the fae, but better adapted to living near and in the waters of Luminfae and Earth."

Derek turned to Karrent with a curious expression. "Earth?" he asked.

Karrent let out a laugh. "Have you never heard of Atlantis, my dear boy?" He then gestured for Derek to follow him and Mia through the gate to the grand library of Oceanus.

Derek followed hesitantly, his eyes widening as he took in the sight of the massive city. Torvania may have seemed like a large town, but compared to Oceanus, it was just a small village. If Torvania was home to thousands of fae, Oceanus could easily hold tens of thousands.

The busy market square was filled with a lively mix of beings from all corners of Luminfae. A gentle sea breeze brushed against their faces, carrying the scent of salt, smoked fish, and rich spices. Children darted between stalls, chasing each other over the cobblestone streets. Amidst the bustle, no one seemed to be concerned about the looming threat beyond their protective walls.

Derek followed Karrent into the library, agitated for reasons he couldn't quite put his finger on.

He tried not to gawk when he finally stepped inside. The library building may not have appeared very large from the outside, but inside, the shelves stretched as high as he could see and were overflowing with books, tomes, and scrolls.

"What is all of this?" Derek's awed voice asked.

Karrent proudly replied, "This is Luminfae's history, present, and future. Oceanus was constructed around this library, and it is here that I, with the assistance of Mia and her family, uncovered Malum's plot. Well, the beginning of it, at least."

Derek's interest piqued again when Karrent revealed an old tapestry depicting the First Fae Wars. It detailed how Oceanus stood as a key defender against Malum's power and influence. Derek's mind was drawing a blank, and his face showed it.

The Natare gazed at him inscrutably before continuing. "Luminfae used to be a peaceful realm until the First Fae Wars erupted. Just like Earth was peaceful until Adam and Eve ate the forbidden fruit. All dimensions were peaceful until a pivotal moment changed everything." Karrent paused and looked out the window by the door. "Luminfae eventually returned to a state of peace, but then Malum came back. Earth was mostly peaceful, too, until something changed. That something was your birth, Derek."

Derek was getting really tired of feeling like his world was turning upside down.

"What do you mean by 'my birth'?" He asked, taking another step back from the natare. Mia held his hand tightly, trying to convey reassurance.

Before Karrent could respond, the doors of the library swung open, and a hooded figure entered. Karrent referred to this individual only as 'V.'

V walked over to the table where they were sitting, placed a scroll down in front of them, and then swiftly exited the library.

"Thanks, V! We must do this again soon, but maybe next time try to keep it shorter," Karrent said dryly, before turning his attention to the scroll. "This is what I've been waiting for. Come with me to the backroom, Derek, and I'll show you everything."

Inside, Derek took in the sight of numerous scrolls and notes plastered onto the walls. A quick glance showed that most of it seemed to pertain to Malum. Karrent unrolled the scroll V had brought on a long wooden table in the center of the room. Derek and Mia waited anxiously while Karrent examined the text. After a few moments, Karrent exclaimed, "This doesn't make any sense, no sense at all."

Mia inquired, "What do you mean?"

Karrent hesitated and scratched at his head before replying, "Perhaps V brought me the wrong thing. Come over here, Derek, I'll show you."

Derek looked at the scroll, but nothing on it made any sense to him. It was written in a language he could not read, and the drawings just seemed like scribbles.

"See? You see here?" Karrent asked as he put his finger in the middle of the scroll. "V told me this scroll would reveal Malum's endgame. All this parchment tells me is that Malum has a plan." He picked the scroll up and brought it close to his face. "A plan to make everything one . . ."

Karrent plucked through scrolls on the walls like he was looking for something specific. Derek squinted, his eyes narrowing in a puzzled gaze as he thought to himself, "*What is this guy on about?*"

The natare continued, "The universe is composed of numerous dimensions, as you now know. Most from Earth remain ignorant of this, but it has not always been that way. Many years ago, even before the First Fae Wars, Earth had equal access to magic as Luminfae and other dimensions."

Derek's forehead creased. "So, what happened?"

Karrent smiled wistfully, "*That* is the question we have been trying to answer. You see, many assumed that Torviid and Malum's war was a struggle for ultimate power and magic. However, some scholars in Oceanus had a feeling there was more to it. They were aware of other dimensions and knew that both Malum and Torviid had traveled to the so-called 'Sacred Dimension.' There were even rumors of a human who had journeyed there."

Derek turned to Mia and silently mouthed, "Helian?"

Karrent nodded, "Yes, Helian. While the scholars knew very little about the Sacred Dimension, they knew that whenever someone returned, major changes followed. So they decided to delve into the past in order to better understand their present and possibly predict the future. These scrolls revealed that humans and fae co-existed freely on Earth, Luminfae, and other dimensions before the First Fae Wars. Something must have happened to sever this connection."

Karrent paused for a moment and rubbed his jaw. "Unfortunately, the researchers never completed their work, and we are left wondering why. In my own research, I stumbled upon V, who promised to provide me with more scrolls. But what they brought me makes little sense."

Derek, patience growing thin, interjected, "Can we pause the history lesson and get to the point?"

Karrent nodded in agreement. "Of course, you're right."

He sat down on top of the table in front of Derek holding a scroll in his hand, one leg crossed over the other, "This one details Malum's visits to Earth during the wars, but it also reveals his motivation: he had found a human lover. When we discovered this, we searched for traces of magic on Earth, which led us to Riverrun. We knew whoever it was couldn't be Malum's offspring, but possibly a descendant. Mia's grandfather transferred his Keeper status to her so she could attend your high school and investigate what was happening."

"Wait," Derek turned to Mia, his eyes slightly squinted. Hurt made his voice soft. "You were only there to spy on me?"

"No!" Mia shouted. Drawing into herself, she grabbed her elbow. "Not exactly . . . I was there to investigate, but then I saw you. I watched you from afar and . . . and you were sweet and kind, and you even saved me . . ."

Derek stood up, taking a few steps away and running his hands through his hair. "I'm sorry, this is all just so damn much."

Turning to Karrent, Derek's voice rose in agitation "Wait . . . you think I'm related to Malum?"

"No, my boy . . . well, not any longer. We now understand that you are a descendant, but not his. You are a semideus——descended from one of the beings from the Sacred Dimension." Karrent explained calmly. He continued, "When Mia approached you, she sensed an immense amount of magic emanating from you. Magic like she had never experienced before. Before she was captured by Ivan, she was able to send a message back to us, and I immediately delved back into my research."

Derek flinched at the mere mention of Ivan's name. "Was he Malum's descendant?" He asked.

Mia tried to lay her hand on Derek's shoulder, but he pulled away. She could see the hurt and confusion in his eyes.

Karrent spoke softly, "Yes, he was. But so is your friend Trey."

Derek's heart gave a painful squeeze. The warning Trey had spoken to him when he appeared in Torvania echoed in his mind:

"*I'm keeping the Reaper at bay.*"

Derek questioned incredulously, "If Trey is Malum's descendant, then why is he trying to help me?"

Karrent continued, "I'm not sure about Trey's involvement, but based on your strong emotions towards him, I can tell he was a dear friend to you. It's possible that he may have been fighting against Malum's orders. However, it is no coincidence that you and Malum's descendant formed such a close bond——it may have been part of a larger plan. And let's not forget the Keeper of Torvania, who was also part of your inner circle. It's clear to me that you hold a significant role in all of this."

Karrent stood up from the table, staring at the wall of tomes and maps. "That is why I had hoped the scroll that V had brought would tell us more. We already know that Malum wants to be the *one* ruler of the dimensions."

Karrent turned back to face Derek. "I must urge caution; this has all been too carefully orchestrated. Expect Malum to be anticipating your every move."

Derek inhaled deeply, trying to calm his racing thoughts. He was feeling completely overwhelmed and unable to make sense of the chaos around him. Just as he felt himself on the verge of breaking down, Mia calmly took hold of his face and locked eyes with him. No magic, no games, just Mia, her voice, and the smell of lavender that he was starting to think was just *her*.

"Derek, I'm here for you. I always have been, even if I didn't know it. Our paths were meant to cross."

Sensing they needed a moment, Karrent took this opportunity to slip out and grab an artifact they would need for their journey, sighing, "Young love," as he went.

Derek turned to Mia and confessed, "I *really* like you, Mia. But these past few days have been chaotic for me. I thought it was just the first, last day of high school, and I finally had the courage to talk to you. But then everything changed. My mind has been constantly fighting itself since I saw that first streak of blue. I want to believe your feelings are genuine . . . but after what Karrent said, and everything that happened, how can I be certain?"

Her lips curled into a smile, but it didn't reach her eyes. She turned away, not wanting him to see the glisten of unshed tears.

"Six months, Derek," she said, voice wobbling. "I spent *six* months wondering where you were." Mia looked back at Derek, the vulnerability and regret in her eyes hitting him in the gut. "Yes, I was initially at Riverrun to search for Malum's descendant, but after seeing you, I was . . . well, I was smitten." She said with a soft smile. "It may have been your magic that drew me to you, but it was *you* I thought about, you I worried about every day you were gone. It might sound cheesy, but it feels like I've always been searching for someone like you, and in the blink of an eye, it almost disappeared."

Mia's choked voice broke off as she turned away again, harshly swiping at her cheeks. Derek watched her, his heart aching, and he wanted to kick himself. "*What the hell is wrong with you, Derek?*"

All he wanted to do was reach out to her, to wipe away the tears he'd caused.

In a hushed tone, he reassured her, "I trust you."

Mia stilled. "Say it again, Lavender."

More firmly, he replied, "I trust you. I believe y——"

Mia fell into him, pressing her lips to his in a passionate, lingering kiss. They poured every emotion they'd built up into this kiss. The months of Mia missing him, the confusion, the terror that they might have lost one another. This kiss was healing. It was a beginning.

"Oh dear, I am very sorry for the intrusion, but I have something for the two of you." Karrent's amused voice rang out.

Breaking apart with a start, they turned to face him, their cheeks slightly flushed. The natare presented them with two objects: a sealed letter, intended for Nidalle in Neutrale and an enchanted necklace. The necklace was crafted from gold and adorned with the emblem of Oceanus. Karrent explained that it had the power to transport them anywhere in Luminfae by touching a map and the pendant simultaneously. However, there were only three uses available, as charging the magic inside is a time-consuming process.

Derek asked, "The city seems unbothered by everything happening. Can we count on Oceanus' support in the fight?"

With confidence, Karrent declared, "Oh. do not worry. Oceanus will answer your call. There are songs and stories aplenty of our warriors and healers. The common folk need not deal with such a catastrophe. I will personally lead our army to meet you in Torvania." Nodding towards Mia, he continued, "I am fairly certain our Keeper will join your ranks as well."

Mia beamed. "Of course I'll be with you."

Derek mirrored her smile, almost giddy, despite the fact that they were making literal war plans. Not quite the first date he had in mind. "Then I guess we should test out this necklace and head to Neutrale."

"Before you go, there are two more things I need to tell you." Karrent said. "The first is that, while we know you are a semideus, we still don't know all the powers and abilities that come with it. So be cautious in how you use your magic until you fully understand how it works."

Derek nodded, signaling his understanding.

"And secondly, Neutrale is known for their unique customs and beliefs. Their leader, Nidalle, is an ancient fae who may have more info on the semideus. Just make sure to listen and stay on her good side."

Derek nodded in understanding once more before turning to face Mia. She gently placed the necklace over his head, and he asked, "Are you ready?"

She nodded and pointed to Neutrale on a nearby map. Derek walked over to stand beside her and took her hand in his. They both touched the pendant hanging from Derek's neck and disappeared in a flash of bright white light.

Chapter 26

Tah'quhal

Tah'quhal breathed in the crisp air as he made his way through the outskirts of Torvania. His whole life had fallen apart. Growing up, he thought he knew Sarika and Tarik well, better than any other, but he never could have fathomed their involvement in something so sinister. So many emotions swirled in his mind. Angry at himself for not knowing. Heartbreak due to his relationship with Sarika. Even a bit of guilt for hurting her.

His every instinct urged him to flee, to leave this place behind as quickly as he could.

Jaw clenched, Tah'quhal wrestled with a furious self-disgust at all the years he wasted living what he knew to be a lie, and a bone deep exhaustion as the weight of those years pressed on his soul. He could grind his bones beneath the weight of his regret.

"Dammit!" His voice echoed through the open fields around him.

He wasn't supposed to be overcome with so many emotions. He was supposed to be a shining light, a guide for Derek. Instead, he felt like he was folding into himself, becoming a terrified man.

A single tear fell from his face and he watched it splash in the dirt below him. He was meant to be a *warrior*. The idea was laughable to him now. He protected no one. He had helped *no one*. The pain, the self-hatred, it all built up until he gave voice to the blame that echoed in his heart,

"Komipea could still be alive if I had stayed." He dropped to one knee and slammed his fist into the ground. Expecting to feel pain in his hand, he sighed. All he felt was numbness. He wanted his words to be true, but he knew that he would have had to have known about Sarika and Tarik's deception in order to stop any of this from happening.

Rising back to his feet, he noticed Torviid's shrine in the distance. He had been so lost in thought, he hadn't realized how close he was to his destination. Taking a deep breath, he balled his fists at his side and walked towards the shrine. With each step closer, his stigmata began to glow brighter, the magic here resonating with him.

His steps became cautious, unsure of what he would discover. He took a moment to study the small statue, an exact replica of the one towering over Torvania. It seemed to be drawing him in. Even while he was held captive on Canter Mountain, this shrine seemed to beckon to him.

His gaze fell upon the inscription at the base of the statue:

"For our Hero. For our Protector.

Still I Stand. Until I Fall.

I Will Head the Lonesome Call."

Protector. That word was like a punch in the gut. A legacy he couldn't live up to. Tah'quhal took a step back, his mystical bands radiating with energy as tears streamed down his face. A wave of emotions rushed over him like a tsunami. Confusion, anger, sadness, happiness——some were familiar to him, others he had not felt in quite some time.

Staring into the eyes of the statue, he cried out,

"How did you do it? How did you bear the weight of all the innocent lives taken in a war you could have prevented? Teach me because I cannot understand. I cannot understand how you could choose Malum over humanity. Why I now have to choose duty over love. Why I have to lose EVERYONE . . . because you could not end it three thousand years ago."

The sky roared with thunder, a powerful bolt of lightning striking the statue before him. Tah'quhal stumbled back in shock as a spectral figure emerged from the statue. Staring at the specter, Tah'quhal thought he was back at the river staring at his own reflection. The only defining difference was the scars on the figure's face. It was clear in his time alive, he had fought many battles.

"Tor . . . Torviid?" he stammered.

The ghostly form responded, "Tah'quhal. You possess my blood-line, my strength, and my sense of pride. And it appears you also have inherited your great-grandmother's emotions."

Breathless, Tah'quhal started, "I have so many questions! What am I supp——"

"There is no time for that." Torviid snapped.

Irritation and confusion flashed across Tah'quhal's face. This was the first person who might have answers, who could help him make sense of his raging mind, and he wouldn't even get the chance to ask.

Torviid approached him and placed his translucent, yet tangible, hand on his shoulder. "I cannot linger here for long. I should not even be here now. But I managed to make one last deal so that I may speak with you."

Tah'quhal's confusion only grew deeper. "What kind of deal? And why is it your last?"

"Enough questions!" Torviid yelled, causing Tah'quhal to stiffen and pull away from his grip.

Torviid ran a hand down his face. "I apologize for my outburst. Time is of the essence here." He stressed, looking towards Torvania. "I have something to give you and something to tell you. Whatever the outcome of the coming battle, I need you to promise me that you will protect that city at all costs."

Tah'quhal clenched his jaw, insulted that Torviid doubted he would. "I promise. But why are you appearing now? Where have you been all this time?"

Torviid's lips twitched up. "You are an inquisitive one, but I doubt you would believe me if I told you. I wish I could join you in this war, but my past actions have sealed my fate." His voice became fervent as he bore his gaze into Tah'quhal's.

"Listen closely. When I depart, the hidden compartment in the shrine will open and reveal the enchanted armor I wore in my final battle against Malum. It protects against his mind control magic. Use it as you see fit. And when you see Derek, warn him to be cautious of who he trusts. Someone from Earth is responsible for all of this, someone who knew exactly who and what Derek is. Derek is the key. He is more than just any other semideus."

Tah'quhal didn't fully understand, but he hung on to every word.

Torviid continued, his voice carrying an ancient sorrow. "Love is what sparked this conflict . . . the love of power. The love of a brother, however misplaced you may deem that love to be, is what made this conflict yours. But love can also be powerful enough to end it. My brother did not always have such twisted ideals. No creature is born good or evil, it is not that black and white. Some events have been set into motion that may be unstoppable. But if you and your new friends can find the courage, the knowledge, and heart, then there is still hope."

As Torviid's body began to fade away, he added, "To answer your earlier question . . . I do not carry their deaths lightly. Every one sits like a stain upon my soul. But I saved lives, too. Being a protector does not mean you are infallible. It does not mean you will not fail.

You simply vow to try. Until you fall." And with that final message, Torviid vanished into thin air.

Tah'quhal gazed up at the vast expanse of sky above him. He knew Torviid was right. He wanted more time, he had more questions, but now he understood why Torviid made the decisions that he did.

The only response was the sound of a stone falling to the ground with a loud thud. He turned around and saw that a small opening had appeared at the base of the statue, revealing Torviid's armor. With trembling hands, Tah'quhal picked it up, his heart filled with more purpose than he had felt in quite some time. He leaned his head over and wiped his sweat on his sleeve.

As he stood in front of the statue, he slowly began to remove his clothing until he was left with only his undergarments.

"Torviid, if you can hear me," he spoke to the statue as he started putting on the armor, "I will do as you said. We will prevent whatever we can and fix any mistakes we have made. We will not let Malum use us as a stepping stone; instead, we will be the shield that blocks his evil plans. And I vow that I *will* protect Torvania." Fully clad in his great grandfather's armor, a surge of magical energy coursed through him, exhilarating and unfamiliar. Moving his arms in a circular motion, a gust of wind erupted from them.

The armor itself was a sight to behold: golden chainmail intricately crafted with ethereal engravings of twisting ivy and glowing fae blossoms. The craftsmanship and artistry spoke of ancient times and the fae race's connection to nature. Fae runes adorned the design, emitting a soft glow of arcane magic that offered protection against the darkness beyond Torvania's borders. Embossed pauldrons and greaves shimmered like stars in the enchanted light, paying tribute to the fae's celestial origins. Adorned with a regal crest and delicate accessories, it embodied Torviid's essence——elegance, magic, and unyielding strength——a fierce protector of Luminfae and its inhabitants.

Not only was the enchanted armor imbued with magical abilities, but the intricate runes etched into the pauldrons amplified and channeled the wearer's own prowess. With gratitude, he gazed up at the sky, almost believing Torviid gazed back. He murmured a quiet, sincere, "Thank you."

To his surprise, a clap of thunder echoed in response. A satisfied smile spread across Tah'quhal's face as he turned to face Torvania. As he took a step forward, he heard a faint whistling sound akin to an arrow soaring through the air. Turning back just in time, he watched as a spear descended from the sky and embedded itself into the ground near Torviid's shrine.

Cautiously approaching the spear, he saw that it had a note attached to it with the words "*One more gift*" scrawled on it.

Tah'quhal plucked the spear from the ground and immediately felt its energy harmonize with his armor. A delighted laugh escaped his lips as he exclaimed, "Unfortunately, I am accustomed to swords," prompting the spear to levitate out of his hands and emit a low hum. A blinding purple flash illuminated the area and two perfectly balanced swords materialized before him. With a grin,

Tah'quhal scooped the swords out of the air and declared, "Now I can work with these."

Tah'quhal secured the swords on his back and turned to face Torvania. He knew that soon, his companions would join him there, but he needed to speak with Derek alone before they continued their journey.

Taking his first step toward Torvania, everything went dark. Panic rose in his chest as he called out, "What trickery is this?" But all he could hear was the sound of his own voice echoing back at him.

After a few moments of silence, Tah'quhal took a deep breath and focused on his magic. Drawing upon its power, he simply thought of his swords in his hands and they were there, radiating a bright purple light. He could feel his feet on the ground, but it seemed like he was floating through the darkness.

Desperate for answers, he shouted once more, "Whoever is doing this, face me!"

"It seems Torviid is still a thorn in my side," the voice jeered. "But it will not matter whether you don his armor or not. Your little resistance, like your pathetic attempts to be a warrior worth remembering, is destined to fail."

The voice was powerful and authoritative, instantly capturing Tah'quhal's attention. He expected the voice to continue but was instead propelled through a blinding tunnel of bright light, his body hurtling at seemingly impossible speeds. And just as quickly as it had begun, it was over. He found himself standing in the same spot as before, disoriented and bewildered.

Once more, he heard a faint whistling sound. An arrow shot by, narrowly missing him, and embedded itself into the ground. Attached to the arrow was a note that read, "Torviid is not the only fae capable of making deals."

Tah'quhal scanned the area for the archer, but there was no one in sight. The whistle of an arrow zipped past his head once more. This time, no note was attached. Then again, and again, until arrows flew all around him.

"I grow tired of these games!" he shouted.

The arrows ceased. The accompanying silence was broken by a low and long rumble of thunder. He looked to the sky to see a single cloud above him that twisted and took on a greenish hue. His eyebrows scrunched as his knuckles popped from gripping the hilt of his swords.

"Whoever you are, show your face," he demanded.

In response, the cloud began to drop green rain that ignited the grass around him in hellfire. He surveyed the area, thinking to himself, "*This is all an illusion.*"

The same voice as before echoed from the skies. "The realms tremble as the battle draws near, In his hands, the fate of all appears."

"*I know those words, they were in the book I found in Komipea's home,*" Tah'quhal thought to himself.

The voice hissed, "Ask Derek about what you just saw and heard. That should be a fun conversation, great grandnephew."

Thunder clapped from the skies. As it trailed off, Tah'quhal could hear a sickly laugh floating in the breeze.

He didn't waste his time waiting for a response and took off towards Torvania. He knew he needed to get to Torvania and find his friends as soon as possible.

His thoughts were racing at the same speed as his movements. If that was really Malum speaking to him, then he must be more powerful than Tah'quhal had thought. Malum was already two steps ahead.

His only concern now was reaching Torvania as quickly as possible. He *needed* to talk to Derek and brace him for whatever was to come next. His heart was still heavy from his actions, but his purpose was renewed. He was ready to do *whatever* was necessary to prove that he was a true fae warrior.

Chapter 27

Old Paths

The sound of the whirlpool echoed through the streets of Terra as Barry and Caldera emerged from its swirling waters on the back of Eirene. Barry quickly dismounted, sword drawn in anticipation of a confrontation with the Hellfire Brigade. Instead, they were met with Serene's weary and surprised face.

"I was not expecting you back so soon, and with one less companion."

Caldera wasted no time. "Johnathan is recovering from his injuries." Steeling herself, she beseeched Serene, "I cannot imagine what has occurred in our absence, and I know you are facing your own challenges, but we need your help, Serene. Malum has returned and war is upon us."

"How can you be certain?" Serene asked.

Caldera quickly explained Malum's resurgence and the revelation that Derek may be a semideus, detailing Derek's newfound abilities and how he could access powerful magic without any attunement.

The silence that enveloped Serene seemed endless, her distress palpable. Finally, after what felt like an eternity, Serene said, "If what you speak is true, we must act quickly. Follow me to my home." As they made their way to the Chieftain's home, Serene continued, "Helian and his brigade left after you vanished. They disappeared in a haze of green smoke almost immediately after Johnathan went down. I'm not sure why they retreated, but we have been preparing for when they return."

Barry and Caldera quickly followed the Chieftain. Once inside, they listened intently. They nodded along, having heard a similar story from Johnathan, until Serene said, "Torviid could have easily asked the Deus to put an end to Malum once and for all, but he couldn't bring himself to do it to his own brother." Barry and Calder's eyebrows shot up.

"Brother?" Barry asked.

Serene nodded. "Yes, they were brothers. Twins, actually. Because of that tie, Torviid could not bring himself to have Malum killed. He instead chose to banish Malum. However, choosing *which* dimension was no light feat. The Start was out of the question, since it's a gateway for magic to flow into other dimensions. Mythos was a close second, but Torviid knew that the creatures who inhabit it would follow Malum and potentially set him free. Earth was not an option either, and Luminfae was where Malum already resided. The only other place Torviid knew of was Oblivion——the realm from which Malum's dark magic originated."

Caldera interjected, "But I thought Malum created Odium magic?"

Serene chuckled softly. "My dear, Odium . . . Bonum . . . Libra. These are just names fae use to classify different forms of magic. While Malum may have been the first to fully control Odium magic, it has always existed."

Barry turned to Serene with a puzzled expression. "Serene, forgive me if I'm being impolite, but how does this help us?"

Serene narrowed her eyes at Barry. "Knowledge is power! Understanding what happened in the past will allow us to strategize for the upcoming battle." She walked over to her bookshelf and retrieved an old tome. "This is a lineage book. If Derek truly is a semideus, he may be able to trace his bloodline with this. But be warned, he may not like what he finds."

She handed the book to Barry and continued, "Before the First Fae Wars, the scholars of Oceanus were researching what happened to magic on Earth. They stopped their pursuit of this knowledge once Malum attacked, instead focusing their efforts on stopping him. After the war, those who survived never resumed. However, they did find that part of the reason magic was lost had to do with the Ancient Keepers."

Serene then turned to Caldera and added, "If war is indeed on the horizon, you will need more than just support from your allies. To have a chance at victory, you must also gather the Keeper from each city in Luminfae to join your army."

Barry and Caldera exchanged quizzical glances."If we need the Keepers, then we need Codi. Why was she with Helian before?"

Serene's response was filled with a somber understanding. "Helian is a master of manipulation. If he knew of even one weakness in Codi, then he could exploit it. Once he uses his words to worm his way in, his green elixir keeps them bent to his will."

Barry asked, "If she's now working with the Hellfire Brigade, can we really trust her?"

"Serene! We need to talk," a lively, redheaded woman exclaimed as she burst into the house. Realizing there were guests, she blushed, stammering, "Oh! I'm sorry, I didn't know you had company. Wait, Caldera?"

Caldera greeted the woman with a smile. "Hello. Stella, how have you been?"

Stella's face was apologetic. "I'm sorry, Caldera, it is really good to see you, but I need to speak with Serene."

Serene gestured for Stella to follow her into another room while Barry and Caldera stayed behind. Caldera turned to Barry with a mix of emotions.

"All this information, Bear . . . I don't know what to make of it. Convincing Ignis to join us was already going to be a tall order. Now we need their Keeper, and we have to find a way to free Codi." He took her hand, a hint of sadness in his eyes.

"My mom is the only other person who calls me 'Bear.' It's been over six months since I've seen her."

He hadn't thought about home before starting their journey. What would he come back to once this was all over? How did his parents think he disappeared? And what had happened after he and his friends left? Caldera could see the sorrow creep into his eyes and placed a comforting hand on his cheek.

"If you don't want me to say it again, I won't," she said softly. Barry eased at her touch, giving her a gentle look.

"No, I loved it."

Their tender moment was interrupted by Serene and Stella rushing back into the room.

"Terra will join you, but we need your help first," Serene announced urgently. "The Hellfire Brigade is on their way back."

Barry and Caldera did not hesitate, drawing their weapons as they stood.

Serene quirked a smile and said, "I'll take that as a yes."

Stella flit her eyes over Barry. "You're not attuned, are you?"

Barry shook his head no. Stella shot a worried look at Serene, the latter responding, "Go and get the Braven." A few moments later, Stella returned with a peculiar bracelet and placed it on Barry's wrist.

She explained, "This bracelet has a magical enchantment and will serve you well. Simply say the word 'Braven' and it will activate."

Barry repeated the word, and the bracelet began to glow, transforming into a round shield made of metal with an ethereal blue glow around its rim in his hand.

Screams echoed from outside, forcing Barry to tear his gaze away from the magnificent craftsmanship of his new shield. Stella and Serene were the first out the door, with Barry and Caldera close behind. As they stepped outside, they saw the Hellfire Brigade's telltale green mist creeping towards them. And through the mist, stood the same four figures as before: Helian, Mckinna, Scab, and Codi.

Serene was prepared for their inevitable return and had formulated a plan. She swiftly signaled to her fae archers, who unleashed arrows with enchanted nets towards the group. Codi was the only one who reacted quickly enough to evade it, rolling to the side and out of the net's path. The remaining three members of the brigade were ensnared by the magical webbing, and Serene's fellow Terraians chanted incantations to keep them pinned to the ground.

Caldera took this opportunity to reach out to her Keeper, pleading, "Codi, it does not matter why you've chosen to align yourself with these villains. It is not too late. We *need* you and your skills on our side. Leave this darkness behind and come home to us."

Codi's bow——crafted from her own keeper staff——pulled taut, an arrow fixed towards Caldera. Tension crackled in the air, but Caldera's voice was unwavering.

"If you believe I deserve death, let the arrow fly. End it here and now, Co."

Codi adjusted her aim and let the arrow fly, directing it towards Serene with an intent to kill. Barry, who had been intently watching in dread, saw the moment she moved. Heart in his chest, Barry lunged through the air, his arm stretched out in a desperate attempt. The arrow caught on the edge of his shield, deflecting the incoming arrow.

As he regained his footing, he yelled, "Everflame!"

Eirene came barreling through the streets of Terra. The sudden chaos diverted Serene and her allies' attention from the magical barrier trapping Helian and the others. With the binding spell unfocused, Helian broke free from his mystical imprisonment and rushed to Codi's side with a satisfied grin on his face.

"Well done, Codi." Helian praised. He stepped forward, his voice aged but demanding authority. "I was chosen by the Hellfire Queen." He flexed his hands and green slime oozed from his fingertips, hissing with steam as it hit the ground. "Chosen to sow the seeds of chaos, a punishment for breaking order."

Serene stood tall, lifting her chin. "We know who you are, and you are not welcome here. Terra has bowed down to you for long enough. It ends today!"

A half cocked smile graced Helian's face. "Oh, Serene. You never bowed to me . . . you *cowered*. I set forth one simple rule. No magic in Terra, and for years, you obliged."

Caldera, cracking one knuckle at a time, "Enough talking! Leave or fight!"

"All in due time, protector of the forest." He glanced at Caldera before turning his stare back to Serene, his eyes starting to glow with an eerie green hue. "That rule was only set in place so that your magical essence would build up inside your blood. That essence is to be harnessed and unleashed on the Hellfire Queen, breaking her hold on me and all others in the lower dimensions. Now, I offer you peace. Join me. Journey with me back to the Sacred Dimension. The rest of the Terraians will be free to live peacefully or fight Malum. I have no concern for them. "

"Never." Serene sneered.

Helian slung open his robe, reaching for two glowing green orbs. "You misunderstand. I do not need you alive."

Serene gazed at her homeland of Terra, her expression turning fierce as she declared, "If you seek my blood, then you must be prepared to spill it."

Helian simply smiled in response. "As you wish."

He slammed both of the orbs to the ground, and in a noxious cloud of green smoke, Scab and Mckinna were transported beside Helian. As the three of them stood together, Helian turned his gaze to Codi, his words carrying an air of prophecy.

"It's time to end this, my dear. The Sacred Dimension awaits, ready to welcome you."

Magic crackled in the air, and the sun hung low in the sky, casting long shadows over the terrain as warriors from both sides prepared for the coming storm.

At the forefront of the Hellfire Brigade stood Helian, master of hellfire magic. His eyes glowed with an unnatural intensity, and his very presence seemed to ignite the air around him. Green flames danced at his fingertips, poised to unleash their destructive power. By his side was Mckinna, a blur of motion with unmatched speed. She could dart across the battlefield like a ghost, striking her enemies from unexpected directions before disappearing again.

Scab, towering over everyone else in the Hellfire Brigade, radiated with pulsing veins that gave off a preternatural green light. He downed another vial of the elixir that granted him immense strength and rolled his shoulders while cracking his neck. And then there was Codi, unnervingly calm and armed with a bow imbued with Keeper magic. Her arrows were precise and deadly as they flew towards their targets with unerring accuracy.

On the opposing side stood a mismatched bunch of allies. Barry and Caldera were poised to defend this town, the latter focused and collected the way only a seasoned warrior could be. Barry, on the other hand, stared at his sword, hearing Komipea's words over and over again in his head,

"A loyal, brave warrior that let nothing keep him from defending his own——not even his fear."

Serene and Stella put on a facade of bravery, while the citizens of Terra prepared for whatever sacrifices they may have to make. The former bearing the weight of responsibility of bringing this fight to her town.

At Helian's whispered command, Mckinna disappeared in a blur, reappearing behind Stella with a dagger pressed against her throat. Barry spun to face them, brandishing his sword, but Serene stopped him with a calm warning.

"You won't be fast enough."

Mckinna gave a smug smile as she taunted, "Go on, Serene. Take your place by Helian's side."

Stella was openly crying, but her voice rang with steely resolve as she begged, "No! Don't listen to her."

Serene looked at her friend, watching her clamp down on her own fear for her sake. Her face hardened. She squared her shoulders and started walking towards Helian.

Barry shouted, "There has to be something we can do!"

Never turning back, Serene continued her somber walk towards Helian. Eirene bravely stood between her and Helian, trying to halt her progress. Annoyed, Helian coldly commanded Scab to eliminate the creature.

Scab barreled towards Eirene, fueled by ruthless intent, his arms pulsing with veins of sickly green light. He raised his arm to deliver the blow. But Barry was already moving. He rammed Scab with his shield just in time to intercept the deadly blow. Gritting his teeth past the painful shock the hit sent up his arm, Barry frantically urged Eirene to escape while she still had a chance at survival.

Barry's perseverance was put to the test as Scab relentlessly pushed against him. He could feel himself getting closer and closer to the ground, knowing that if Scab brought him down completely, he would be crushed like a bug. His mind replayed all the times he was taken down by a two hundred pound linebacker, or when a massive lineman slammed him into the turf, trying to think of anything that might get him out of this situation alive.

Eirene's roars grew louder and more frantic as she tried to help, while Caldera attempted to calm her down. Eirene stopped and looked up at the sky, letting out a long and powerful roar. In one swift motion, she leaped into the air, momentarily tearing Scab's gaze away from the battle.

Taking advantage of the distraction, Barry lunged forward and pierced his sword through Scab's midsection. He yanked his sword out and Scab stumbled backward, clutching at his stomach.

Eirene swooped down from above, snatching Scab in her talons and carrying him high up into the air.

"Barry! She has bonded with you! Eirene has her wings!" Caldera exclaimed.

Barry was astounded as he watched Eirene drop Scab from a height of at least sixty feet. He braced himself for what was sure to be a gruesome landing, but just before impact, Helian conjured a bed of green ooze to cushion Scab's landing.

"That's enough!" Helian shouted in frustration.

Upon hearing Helian's words, Codi notched three arrows into her bow. As she released them, she whispered, *"Reperio scopum meum."*

Each arrow flew towards a different target. Barry barely raised his sword in time to slice his in half. Caldera, however, easily deflected hers with a spin of her spear. The final arrow headed straight for Stella, who still had a dagger pressed against her throat. She buckled her knees at the last moment, causing Mckinna's dagger to scratch her throat as Codi's arrow struck Mckinna in the shoulder. Mckinna let out a curse as she felt the sharp pain, but it was not nearly enough to kill her.

Helian, frustrated by yet another failure, spat, "I'll do it myself, starting with this one!"

He pointed directly at Barry with his finger. He scoffed. "Do you really think a mere *boy* can stop me?" As he spoke, green hellfire dripped from his fingertips.

Barry raised his shield as the deadly flames rushed towards him. The fire engulfed his shield, but some of it managed to seep around as searing pain licked at his arm. Barry cried out in agony as his flesh melted towards the bone beneath.

Caldera felt her heart stop. She couldn't breathe as she watched Barry writhe in pain. At his broken cry, she tried to rush to his side, but Mckinna pulled the arrow from her own arm and stabbed it into Caldera's leg.

Through his haze of pain, Barry could see Caldera struggling to pull herself closer to him.

Eirene landed in front of Barry, roaring at anyone that looked his way.

"No ... protect ... Caldera," Barry managed to grunt out through the pain.

Though the griffin looked at him with concern, she obeyed his command.

Helian leveled his sinister stare at Serene, stating, "This is your last chance. Surrender yourself and I'll spare your precious Terra. Refuse again and I'll stop being nice."

Serene looked at her people, her brave allies, and felt her resolve harden. She locked her stormy gaze with Helian and lifted her chin in defiance.

"No."

Helian flicked his eyes to Codi. "Don't miss this time."

Codi nodded and readied another arrow towards Serene. As she started to release the arrow, Eirene let out a powerful roar. Codi's concentration broke as she looked at the griffin in surprise and her arrow narrowly missed Serene's head, slicing off a piece of her hair instead.

Helian's rage reached its peak as he shot a glare at Codi. Without uttering a single word, he snapped his fingers and her eyes went blank. She lowered her bow and stood motionless, her stocky figure staring straight ahead. She seemed to be a mindless pawn, a toy soldier at Helian's disposal.

Caldera screamed for her friend. "Codi! No, what did you do to her?"

Helian remained silent as he stalked towards Barry.

Caldera continued to try to get through to Codi. "Do you remember when you first became the Keeper of the Forest? You were so excited to inherit your bow from your grandmother. You said you had dreamed of that day your entire life." She continued to try and crawl towards Barry.

"Codi, I was there for you when she passed away. We spread her ashes in the portal, so that you would always feel close to her." Tears began to fall down Caldera's face. "No matter what he has promised you or what you have done, *I* will always be there for *you*."

Barry lay on the ground in agony, every nerve ending in his arm raw and exposed. Helian loomed over him, seething with fury.

Helian sneered at him. "You were never meant to survive in this world." The fiery droplets from his hand sizzled against Barry's forehead as he prepared to deliver the final blow.

He raised his hand above Barry, ready to take the final blow.

"Aghh!" Helian cried out in pain as an arrow struck him in the back. He hunched over, turning to see Codi pointing her bow at him from her knees.

"You despicable scum," she cried out. "You twisted my mind and controlled me." Her hands shook violently as she stared at Helian.

In response, Helian merely laughed. "My dear, Codi," he said with a hint of malice. "I could have brought——"

His words cut off as a sharp pain slashed through his side. While Helian was distracted, Barry mustered what little strength he had left to swing his sword at him.

Time seemed to freeze as their fates collided. Helian's aura flickered as the sword made contact with his body. He stumbled back, a mix of disbelief and genuine fear on his face. Though the wound was not fatal, it was enough to break through his arrogance.

As Helian's flames flickered and faltered, Mckinna rushed to his side in a blur of motion. She shielded him with her body, determined to protect her leader at all costs.

Helian let out a hacking cough, blood splattering from his mouth. "Fine. You may have won this battle, but the war is far from over. None of you have any idea what's coming." He turned to Barry and added, "Just remember that I tried to prevent it."

A dense cloud of green smoke engulfed them. When it cleared, Helian, Mckinna, and Scab were gone without a trace. The only remaining member of their brigade was Codi.

Serene's shouts for healers brought fae from all corners of the city to attend to the injured. As soon as Caldera was able, she rushed over to Barry, swearing she would kick his ass if he tried to die on her. She placed both hands over his wound, whispering, "*Sana . . . Sana . . . Sana,*" over and over again as blue essence formed around his wounds.

A cooling, ethereal bandage formed around Barry's arm as he looked to Caldera, still able to smell the charcoal-like scent of his charred skin.

"Thank you," he said softly.

Caldera half-joked, "If you ever do that to me again, I'll find a dragon to feed you to." She leaned down and kissed him tenderly.

Despite his arm feeling like it had the world's worst sunburn, he assured her he would be okay. Only then did Caldera turn her attention to Codi, who was still on her knees.

Stella and Serene helped Codi to her feet and guided her towards Caldera and Barry.

Codi's eyes were swimming with remorse. "Caldy, I'm so sorry. I was weak." Her eyes shone with tears. "Helian came to me. He told me he could bring Grammy back. He told me all I had to do was drink his stupid elixir, and we could go to the Sacred Dimension and bring her back."

Caldera sighed and placed her hand on Codi's shoulder. "You should have come to me before ever listening to the words of a stranger. You know your grandmother would have never listened to the twisted words of a power hungry fool." She pulled Codi in for a hug. "I forgive you. But in order to regain my trust . . . everyone's trust, you will need to join us against Malum."

"Of course, Caldy. Whatever it takes." Codi responded through held back sobs.

Serene added, "Terra will stand with you against Malum. We will make sure Codi is ready for battle. But you, Barry, and Eirene must continue your journey. We will meet you in Torvania."

Barry stood up and walked over to Eirene, gently caressing her new wings with his good arm. Turning back to Caldera, he said, "Serene is right. We need to get to Ignis."

Stella reached into her satchel and handed them four vials filled with water from the geyser. "Use these if you get into trouble."

Caldera nodded and took the vials before walking over to Barry and Eirene.

"Shall we fly?" asked Barry with a smile.

Caldera drank in his easy expression, the tension leaving her body for the first time since he went down.

"One thing first." She replied.

Caldera lifted her hand towards the sky and whispered an incantation. A small blue bird materialized from her fingertips. "Meet us in Torvania, bring anyone that will fight." she instructed before the bird flew off towards the Magia Forest.

Barry and Caldera mounted the griffin, giving a gentle pat on Eirene's head before taking off into the sky. They didn't have time to process everything that had happened. There were far more pressing matters at hand. But they both knew that their experiences in Terra would never fully leave them. Barry stared at his bandage, picturing the scars beneath, serving as a constant reminder that he'd never be the same. When Caldera kissed his shoulder, looking at him with fierce pride, like he'd proven something today, it didn't seem like such a bad thing. Smiling to himself, Barry thought, *that's not so bad at all.*

Chapter 28

Neutrale

Derek and Mia appeared in a blinding flash of white light just outside the village of Neutrale. Derek turned to Mia with a smile.

"This teleporty magic would have been useful when I was stuck in Mythos."

Mia chuckled and teased him. "Who knows, maybe since you're a fancy-pants semideus, you'll figure out how to do it without the necklace."

Derek pretended to be considering it. "That would be incredible. I'd never be late again," he said before smacking into an invisible barrier at the edge of the village. He reached for his face, rubbing his nose as his cheeks flamed with embarrassment.

Mia let out a cackle and clapped her hands together. Still looking back at Derek, she also slammed into the barrier.

Through his laughter, "Well, at least I'm not the only one."

Derek took a moment, just a moment, to enjoy the simple pleasure of laughing with the girl he has had a crush on for ages.

"Karrent didn't mention anything about a barrier," Mia said.

Exchanging worried looks, they scanned their environment. Mia nudged Derek, pointing towards a diminutive man running towards them from the nearby village.

He yelled an out of breath, "Hold on for just a moment, travelers! I'll be with you shortly!"

The small being approached them, barely rising above Derek's knees. Derek couldn't resist, letting out a little chuckle as he mumbled, "*Shortly* was right."

Mia shoved her elbow into his side, causing him to cough through his laughter.

Indignant, the man declared, "There is no need for jokes about my stature, good sir. My name is Gregarious Starius Tokonous Frederick Senderson, the third. You may call me Mouse, ma'am." Narrowing his eyes at Derek, "And *you* can call me Gregarious."

Again, Derek could not contain his laughter, and, again, he caught an elbow in his side from Mia. Trying to compose himself, he asked, "Why Mouse?"

Mouse huffed. "That is none of your business."

"I'm sorry," Derek apologized. "I didn't mean to offend you. Could you please tell us how to get into the village?"

Slightly mollified, Mouse replied, "In response to unscrupulous visitors, and those disrespecting the ways of Neutrale, Chieftain

Nidalle has ordered a lockdown. Only those with official business may enter."

Mia showed the man the seal on the note from Chieftain Karrent of Oceanus and explained that they had an urgent matter to discuss with Chieftain Nidalle. After looking at the seal through the barrier, Mouse exclaimed,

"Very well! I will go fetch Abhaya and the Chieftain immediately!"

Before Derek or Mia could say anything else, Mouse was already scampering back towards the village.

Derek looked at Mia. "Come on, you know that was funny."

She tried, and failed, to suppress a grin. "Shut up, Derek." She playfully shoved him, and he grabbed her arm to pull her into a hug, stealing her breath. She looked into his eyes, getting lost in their icy blue depths. "You make things easy, ya know?"

"What do you mean?" Derek asked through his awkward smile.

Mia placed her hand on his chest. "From the first day I met you, being around you has been . . . well, it's just been easy."

"Wow, I'm shocked." Derek said.

"About what?" Mia asked in confusion.

"You just gave me a compliment," Derek joked.

"Yeah, well, don't get *too* used to it." Her eyes twinkled with laughter.

Derek reached for her hands, taking them tightly in his. She leaned in and gently kissed him, a small gesture that spoke volumes about how they felt for each other. Derek couldn't help but feel grateful, despite the approaching battle. After years of searching, Derek had finally found where he fit, and he had Mia by his side. Doubts still lingered in the back of his mind, knowing that everything could change in an instant. But for now, he wanted to cherish every moment he had with Mia.

A few minutes later, two women from the village appeared in the distance. Mia gestured to the one approaching on the left side and said,

"That's Abhaya, the Keeper of Neutrale. And the fae next to her is Nidalle, the Chieftain."

As they neared the barrier, Abhaya stepped forward and asked, "Why have you come here?"

Derek stared at the Keeper, slightly intimidated. She radiated authority, a certainty that she possessed more knowledge than anyone in the room. On her, however, that confidence did not feel arrogant; it was simply a fact. Her name, Abhaya, meant "fearless" in Sanskrit, and perfectly captured her unshakeable spirit and profound wisdom. She was draped in flowing robes of regal amethyst that seemed to sway with the magic she commanded. Intricate stigmata adorned her skin in a vibrant purple spiral, detailing her mastery over the arcane arts.

Her sharp eyes shone in a captivating shade of blue. In the right light, they even looked purple. Though she did not look her sixty-eight years, strands of gray in her black hair spoke of experiences beyond measure. Her timeless beauty defied age. A yellow bindi adorned her forehead at the focal point of her ajna chakra.

Everything about her spoke of her perception, inner wisdom, and centered energy.

For the last time, she asked, "Why have you come here?"

Derek's words tumbled out in a rush, explaining the brewing war with Malum. Abhaya scoffed at the idea of him knowing anything about it. But before he could say more, Mia presented a note from Karrent, stating that it was meant only for Nidalle's eyes.

Seeing the seal, Nidalle emerged from the barrier, a fae of unmatched beauty and age. She exuded elegance in a gown of cascading silk folds that clung to a tall, slender frame. Its purple hues were richer in color than Abhaya's robes, mirroring the twilight sky. Her golden jewelry glinted off her metallic stigmatas that scrawled across her skin like a dead language.

Her kohl lined, bright purple eyes were ringed with a black as deep as the obsidian waterfall that hung to her waist. The contrast was magnetic and unnerving. Predatory, like a cat.

But what truly set her apart was her age——three thousand one hundred and eleven years old and part of the "old guard," a living bridge between fae epochs.

Nidalle's intense gaze was locked onto the strangers, staring until they wanted to squirm.

"Well, hand it over," she purred.

Mia handed the note and waited anxiously as the Chieftain read it, her face impassive. Nidalle paused and turned to face Derek.

"Are you a semideus?" she asked pointedly.

Derek gulped nervously. "Um . . . yes?" It came out as more of a question than he intended.

Arching an eyebrow, Nidalle calmly demanded, "Prove it."

Despite his improving skills in wielding magic, Derek hesitated. He feared he wouldn't be able to make it work this time, or he would accidentally do something wrong. To calm himself, he took a deep breath and closed his eyes, focusing on Mia's face in his mind. As he concentrated, his arms began to emit a bright glowing light, followed by his eyes and hair. He could feel himself rising slightly off the ground, but not recklessly, like he had done in Torvania. He could feel the flow of magic inside himself, more in control than ever before.

Mia looked at him in amazement. She couldn't believe how much his magical abilities had grown in such a short time.

Nidalle and Abhaya were equally mesmerized. They had never witnessed anything quite like this before. Nidalle's eyes lit up; it was rare for her to experience anything truly *new*.

Pleased, Nidalle said, "That's all the proof I need."

Derek gently landed back on the ground as the bright light started to fade. "War is imminent, and we are here to ask for your help," he declared.

Abhaya and Nidalle exchanged a glance before simultaneously moving their arms in a complex pattern, lowering the barrier so Derek and Mia could enter their village.

Nidalle and Abhaya led the way into the village, with Derek and Mia in tow. But as they approached, Abhaya stopped Derek with a hand on his chest. Eyes narrowed, she reminded him to conduct himself properly while staying in their village.

When he asked for clarification, she explained, "Our village operates communally."

Derek furrowed his brow in confusion, but as they walked through the village, he began to understand. At the market stalls, fae and humans were trading goods instead of using money. The villagers had small gardens behind their homes and freely shared resources with their neighbors. It was truly remarkable how peaceful and balanced everything here seemed to be.

Derek's eyes landed on two fae and a human, all holding hands while walking. One's head on another's shoulder. The third gave a quick kiss to the one in the middle's forehead when they stopped to go into a shop.

Mia elbowed Derek when she noticed him staring for a bit too long.

Nidalle added, "Don't worry, it's a new concept for you. In Neutrale, we believe in being open and sharing things like goods, food, and even partners. This is rooted in our deep meditation practices that allow us to connect with magic on a profound level. Some of us even master a special form called 'Libra.' Through this connection, we have learned that material possessions and negative emotions like jealousy hold no value. What truly matters is our connections and community.

"Unfortunately, our openness has also attracted unwanted visitors who seek to exploit or take advantage of our kind residents. That's why we have the magical barrier around our town."

As they approached Nidalle's house, Derek considered her words. "If you're avoiding negative emotions, why do you have a barricade? Isn't fear a negative emotion?"

Mia jabbed him sharply in the ribs once more. Abhaya fixed him with an intense stare and began to speak, but was interrupted by Nidalle.

"No, Abhaya, he brings up a valid point. In my three thousand one hundred and eleven years of life, I've strived for perfect balance——after all, Libra is about balance. But I've come to realize that no matter how hard we try, there will always be flaws in our plans. You may think the barrier represents fear, and that may play a small part. Just remember, there is a staunch difference between fear and caution. We are not afraid of danger, we are discerning of what we let in."

The last line struck a chord with Derek. If he had been more discerning when he was around Sarika, rather than ignoring his instincts, he wouldn't have let her get so close to him.

Derek nodded. "Fear and caution *are* two very different things. I should know that better than anyone by now. You are just protecting your people, not sheltering them. I understand the difference now, and I apologize if my question came across as if I was passing judgment. I swear, I'm not going to take advantage of your people." He turned to Mia. "I already have everything I need right next to me, anyway."

Mia blushed at Derek's words.

Derek reached for Mia's hand as they entered Nidalle's home. He took in the surroundings, eyes scanning all the unusual objects scattered throughout. There were countless pieces of art crafted from various types of jewelry. Curious, Derek asked Nidalle about them, and she revealed that they were magical artifacts. She had accumulated them over her many years, some already imbued with powers, while others she had enchanted herself, alongside Abhaya.

"Thanks to the note you brought from Karrent, it looks like you'll be taking a few of these with you." She added.

Derek's excitement grew at the thought of possessing some cool magical items. But he quickly reminded himself that their mission was to secure aid against Malum. While powerful artifacts could certainly come in handy, they needed soldiers more than anything else. Derek gnawed on his lip. Did their commitment to balance mean they'd be pacifists? Or would they see the fight as a necessity to restore the dimension's balance of power?

The Chieftain continued, breaking Derek from his spiraling thoughts. "The note requested two items from me. One is a pair of bracelets that bond wearers together. They were crafted by a skilled fae from the Magia Forest during the war. The intention was for a husband to be able to return to his wife's side if he fell in battle, to say goodbye. Of course, there are plenty of other, and much more practical uses. The other item is a vial containing soil that was supposedly taken from the Start, the first dimension. I'm not sure why Karrent wants you to have it, but the letter instructs me to give it directly to you, and that only you will know when the right time to use it is."

Derek took the bracelets, slipping one onto his own wrist and then gently placing the other on Mia's outstretched arm. The moment the bracelets touched their skin, a soft glow emanated from both Mia's stigmata and Derek's arms. A sense of calm washed over them as the bracelets harmonized, releasing a soothing tone into the air. Nidalle explained that it seemed like the bracelets had connected, allowing either wearer to locate the other with ease by simply removing their bracelet.

After Nidalle handed Derek the vial, Abhaya warned, voiced tight,

"If that truly came from the Start, please handle it with caution."

Derek nodded in agreement and slipped the vial into his pocket. "Thank you for these gifts. They will definitely come in handy."

Nidalle's lips curled into a smile. "If you are really a semideus, there is something I would like to give you from my personal collection." She pulled a dusty tome off her bookshelf before gliding over to a tall cabinet made of an unfamiliar wood and retrieving a set of robes. As she did, a brilliant white light emanated from within the cabinet.

Derek's arms began to glow with the same light, making Nidalle and Abhaya exchange amused glances.

Nidalle chuckled. "If I didn't believe you before, I certainly do now."

She handed Derek a book, saying, "This contains detailed accounts of semideus from various dimensions, although many assumed that whatever created them had long disappeared."

Derek's face twisted with confusion. "Are you saying that one of my *parents* is from this Sacred Dimension?

"Well, not exactly." She replied, "On Earth, legends say that semideus are the children of gods and humans, but we're not entirely sure of their origins, or how far back their ancestry might be."

Nidalle handed Derek the set of robes. The moment he touched them, a powerful surge of energy ran through his body.

Abhaya chimed in, "These robes are believed to have been sewn in the Sacred Dimension. A rather taciturn figure that went by 'V' arrived one day with the cabinet. It came with a note that said Nadalle would know when the time was right. I guess this is us knowing."

Derek was bursting with questions, but he couldn't contain his excitement any longer. "Can I change somewhere?" he blurted out. Nidalle gestured towards a hallway, and Derek eagerly raced to try on the robes.

He quickly changed and came back out, smiling ridiculously. He was wearing flowing robes that fit him perfectly, made from a silky green fabric with intricate golden weaving and symbols. The sleeves cut off at the elbow, with a delicate tassel at the end of each.

Mia blushed as she looked at him; he had never seemed so mature to her, so self-assured. He looked like he belonged here, in this world.

Derek couldn't help but think to himself how he had always longed for a place where he belonged, and now he had found it. For a moment, he was filled with happiness, gratitude even. Guilt snuffed out those feelings as thoughts of Izzy crept into his mind. Yes, he had found a home, but at what cost? He had lost her. They all had. Because of him. His stomach twisted at the thought that he would have to face the one responsible in battle.

His chest tightened, and each breath felt more like a desperate gasp than a full inhale.

Mia watched the shift in Derek's expression, the way his eyes became haunted. Heart aching for him, she took his hand in hers, wanting to pull him back from wherever he'd gone. As their skin made contact, the bracelets on their wrists lit up, emitting a warm glow. The golden accents on Derek's robes transformed into a brilliant white, and Mia gasped at the immense amount of magic she could feel flowing within him.

It was slightly unsettling at first, frightening even, but then she could feel him reining it in. Gradually, the light faded as Mia held his gaze. She could see the emotional storm he was fighting through as his eyes flickered in and out of focus, but she could also see the strength and control etched into his features. He was able to reign in not only his thoughts, but his incredible power as well.

Mia's touch had a calming effect on Derek. Not like Sarika's magical influence. She grounded him, let him know he was seen, understood. The robes were also helping him focus his panic and magic. He could feel a strange cooling effect where the robes touched his skin. His mind was finally able to slow.

Derek looked at Nidalle, a bit sheepishly, "Sorry about that. Sometimes my brain likes to wander, and it makes me freeze up."

Abhaya's usually stern expression softened. "You have panic attacks?"

"They were getting better, but ever since I walked through the Anchor, I feel like they have been getting worse." Derek admitted. "Luckily, I have someone who seems to bring me back from the brink."

Mia's grip on his hand tightened as she laid her head against his arm.

"Let us get through whatever comes next and I will show you how Libra helped me overcome my own panic," Abhaya offered.

Mia asked, "Does that mean we can count on your support?"

Nidalle replied, "Neutrale will join you in the upcoming battle. We have many skilled fighters, and although Libra magic is centered around balance, it can also be a potent form of offense. Our most skilled healers will also accompany us, ready to offer assistance on the battlefield."

Derek was at a loss for words. He simply nodded, throat tight at her willingness to join them. Mia's joyful expression overflowed with gratitude.

"Thank you," she said softly, before turning to Derek. "It's late. Should we try to get some rest before we head back to Torvania?"

Derek nodded in agreement, "Nidalle, Abhaya, thank you both . . . for everything, would it be too much trouble for us to stay the night in town?"

"Not a problem at all. I will let the Tranquil Veil Inn know to prepare a room." Abhaya responded. Glancing at Mia's dirt covered outfit, she gently added, "I'll ask them to find you a change of clothes, as well."

Mia's eyes lit up at the prospect of fresh clothes. And a bath. Or several.

Derek and Mia made their way to the Tranquil Veil. Upon entering the room, they noticed there was only one bed. "I'll go see if they have another room, or maybe just a pillow for the floor." Derek suggested.

As he turned for the door, Mia grabbed his hand. "Don't be silly. After everything we've been through, I think we can share a bed. If we're going to be sleeping next to each other, though, I *definitely* need a bath first."

Derek's eyes widened. He hadn't even thought about it. She'd been held captive for however many weeks under that mountain. Derek admired how mission focused she was, but he wished he'd thought to give her a chance to recover in Oceanus.

"Of course! Uh, yeah, take your time. I'll be . . . here," he said awkwardly.

She grabbed the change of clothes the front desk had supplied her and slipped out to find the bathroom.

A smile grew on Derek's face as he settled in bed. He was going to get to spend a whole night next to Mia. His smile faded as he obsessed over what he should do when she got back. Was he supposed to cuddle her? Put pillows in between them? *Oh, God, my breath is probably awful.* What if he had another nightmare and kept Mia up all night?

He was still overthinking when she crawled into bed twenty minutes later. All of his anxieties melted away when Mia laid her head on his chest. Before he knew it, he was deep in sleep.

The next morning Derek and Mia shared a quick meal at the Inn before heading back to Nidalle's home. After they said their goodbyes, Derek asked, "Do you think, after all of this is over, would you be willing to help me . . . figure myself out?"

Nidalle walked over to him with a warm smile and replied, "Gladly, young one."

A weight lifted off Derek's shoulders. Ready to leave, Mia and Derek said their goodbyes, touched Torvania on Natalie's map, and were gone.

Nidalle turned to Abhaya, her expression grave. "This battle will be unlike any we've encountered before. If what Karrent wrote to me is true and the time of the prophecy has finally come, there won't be time to explain anything to that poor young man once it's over."

Chapter 29

Ignis

Unbridled joy pulsed through Barry's veins as he soared across the open sky, the wind rushing past his skin. He couldn't help but laugh at the exhilaration. Barry glanced back at Caldera, captivated by her beauty in that moment, her hair dancing behind her in the wind. The fact that they were getting closer to Ignis and the final battle that awaited them sat in the back of his mind, a constant anxiety. But for now, he wanted to savor every moment of peace left.

"You enjoying this as much as me?" He called back to Caldera.

She chuckled and slyly replied, "Probably not for the same reasons as you."

Butterflies assaulted Barry's stomach as she wrapped her arms around his waist and rested her head on his back.

Worry nagged at Caldera. She was aware that the upcoming battle would be challenging, despite all their preparation. Malum would not be an easy opponent to defeat. And if they did manage to defeat him, that victory would not come without a cost. Fear gripped her heart, but she just held Barry tighter, as if she could keep him safe with her will alone.

Eirene landed outside of the city Caldera warned, "The last time we were here, we were just passing through. This time, we're asking Talissa for a favor. And I know she will want something in return."

Barry said, "I am prepared. Buuut just to be safe, what kinda favor do you think she will want?"

"There is no way to know, but I am positive her asking price will be something I do not want to pay." Caldera admitted.

Barry instructed Eirene to stay just outside the walls and wait for them. They approached the city gates once again, the massive iron bars lifting as they braced themselves for what was to come. The fiery circle appeared around them, just like before. But this time, they were prepared for it.

They gazed towards the tower at the heart of the city and saw Talissa peering down at them from a window. Braving the flames that surrounded them, they made their way towards the tower.

Caldera turned to Barry just before they reached the door and quietly instructed him to let her lead the way inside. Barry nodded in agreement and held open the door for her.

Talissa stood in the center of the first room, waiting for them.

"Caldera, what brings you back here?" She approached, running her hand along Caldera's arm.

Fighting the urge to stiffen, Caldera explained Malum's return and their need for assistance in the upcoming battle. They requested warriors to join them in Torvania, as well as the Keeper of Ignis. Talissa gazed impassively at the two adventurers, seeming to take an eternity before responding.

To Barry's surprise, Talissa's face lit up with a wide smile.

"Caldera, it would be absurd if I didn't offer my assistance." Barry's shoulders had just begun to relax when she arched one perfectly manicured brow and added, "However, it would also be foolish of me not to ask for something in return."

Caldera let out an exasperated sigh. "I knew you wouldn't help me out of the goodness of your heart. What do you want, Talissa?"

The succubus gently ran her fingers through Caldera's hair. "I have two simple requests, darling," she purred.

"What are they?" Caldera nearly snapped.

"I want to expand Ignis' border," Talissa replied with a smile.

Caldera's jaw clenched so tightly that a muscle twitched in her cheek. "How far?" Caldera grit out.

"Double the size of our city," Talissa stated calmly. "And you won't even have to make offerings to the great flame. The land we acquire will serve as payment."

Caldera's expression twisted in conflict. She didn't want to destroy more of the forest for Ignis' expansion, but she also knew that the succubus possessed powerful magic that could potentially turn the tide in their upcoming battle.

Caldera winced. "It's done. What's next?"

Talissa shifted her focus to Barry, who was still standing by the door. She disappeared in a burst of flames before reappearing in front of him. She forcefully grabbed his chin and brought him uncomfortably close, their lips almost touching.

"Him." she said. "I want him."

Caldera's spear groaned under the force of her grip. "No."

Talissa shot a glance at her, reminding her that she had already agreed to *their* deal, and this one was Barry's decision. Turning back to face Barry, she continued,

"You need the Keeper of Ignis by your side? I can summon him for you. But only if you promise that if he falls in battle, you will take up the mantle as the new Keeper of Ignis."

Barry stammered, feeling uncomfortable with Talissa's lips so close to his, her predatory eyes holding him hostage.

"B-but, I'm not even attuned."

The succubus chuckled, low and seductive. "Oh, darling, I can take care of that for you. So, do we have a deal?"

Barry strained to turn his head and meet Caldera's gaze, but Talissa's grip was unyielding.

He knew this had to be a trap, but he didn't see much choice. They needed her help more than they needed him. "We have a deal."

Caldera's voice rose in panic, "Barry! You don't understand what you're doing!"

Talissa cut in calmly, "Please, Caldera. The deal has been settled. And if David makes it out alive, your precious puppet here will never have to join me."

She dug her talons into his cheek a little harder before letting go of his face. "It is decided then," she declared with a manic glint in her eyes. "Our army will set off for Torvania as soon as you depart."

With a sudden burst of intense heat, she smacked Barry on the backside, leaving behind tingling skin before vanishing in a fiery wake.

Caldera stormed over to Barry. He tensed, ready for her to berate him, even smack him with how stormy her eyes were. She just pulled him into a fierce hug, burying her face in his neck. "You have no idea what you've done," she whispered, her voice smaller than he'd ever heard it.

Barry tried to appear confident, but his breaths were shallow as the full weight of what he'd agreed to set in.

"We just need to make sure the current Keeper stays alive. And if he does fall, we will figure something out."

"But Talissa doesn't play by any rules or morals, Barry. She will find a way to manipulate the situation to her advantage." Her voice was harsh, but her touch was soft.

Barry placed his chin on top of her head. "We'll deal with that if it happens. Ok, gorgeous? For now, let's focus on getting back to Derek."

Caldera moved her head back to look at him, eyes searching. Whatever she found softened the tense lines of her face. She brushed her lips against his tenderly, feeling a surge of emotion for this foolish, reckless, brave man. He responded eagerly, and the rest of the world melted away. For that brief moment, nothing else mattered. In their embrace, time stood still, and Caldera wished it could last forever.

They broke apart reluctantly, resting their foreheads against each other as their heart rates slowly returned to normal. After a few minutes of basking in this quiet moment, Barry took her hand and headed towards the door. They stepped outside to an array of fierce succubi, fully armed and prepared for battle.

Standing at the forefront of the group was Talissa, her commanding presence radiating power. Next to her stood a muscular human male named David, his ferocity evident in the tight set of his jaw and the fire in his eyes. Barry only hoped that David's fervor wouldn't lead to his downfall in battle.

His gaze shifted from Caldera to the group gathered before them as she declared, "Alright, let's make our way to Torvania."

Barry called for Eirene, and a loud screech pierced the air as she descended from the clouds and landed gracefully on the streets. They mounted Eirene's back and together, they gazed up at the sky as Eirene took flight, carrying them on one final journey before their lives would be forever altered. It was their last ride before facing the ultimate battle. Their last ride before venturing into Oblivion.

Chapter 30

Creedence

Derek and Mia were finally standing in the heart of Torvania. Derek's eyes were fixated on Mia's. She chuckled and asked, "What are you looking for?"

Derek kept staring, a gentle smile ghosting his lips as he said, "I'm not looking for anything. I'm just enjoying what I have found."

Mia's heart just about stopped as she leaned in to press her lips against his. In the midst of their embrace, a familiar voice echoed from behind Derek.

"Diamond! 'Bout time you showed up!" They broke apart to see Johnathan approaching them, looking much better than when they all left in search of allies.

Derek sprinted over to Johnathan and yanked him into a tight hug. After the events of the past couple of days, his friends and Mia were the only things keeping him sane. Johnathan gestured towards Mia's outfit and Derek's robes.

"Why am I the only one not gettin' new clothes round here? Y'all gotta see Tah'quhal's new armor!"

Johnathan led the way towards the library. "So, Tah'quhal is already here, and there's a bunch of fighters from all over Luminfae setting up camp on the outskirts of town. So far, Terra, Oceanus, and the Magia Forest have arrived. We received a Torquewhirler messenger from Neutrale, saying they were on their way, and the letter Barry and Caldera sent Ortug said they should be arriving soon."

John walked backward through the library door, flashing them a proud grin.

"While y'all were touring Luminfae, I've been hittin' the books. Spent my time gathering all the Keepers, Chieftains, and members of the *Enchanted Ensemble* to meet here. I've really been putting my student manager experience to good use," he said with a wink.

Derek and Mia exchanged confused, somewhat amused glances, until Derek chuckled and raised an eyebrow. "Who exactly is part of this Enchanted Ensemble?"

Johnathan gave a dramatic eye roll. "We are, you big dummy! Every cool team needs a name." He leaned in real close. "At least the inner circle."

Mia and Derek both struggled to stifle their giggles. Teasingly, Mia suggested, "We could make our name——"

"Nope. Too late. The town blacksmith is already crafting rings for the team."

Derek laughed, knowing there was a very real chance Johnathan wasn't joking. "Okay bud, we'll go with Enchanted Ensemble."

They were still laughing when they entered the library's main hall. Around a large table in the center of the room stood a group of new and familiar faces. Tah'quhal was the first to greet them. He quickly updated Derek and Mia on how he had spoken with Torviid, chest puffing a bit with pride at their awed expressions.

Walking towards the table, Tah'quhal placed his hand on Derek's shoulder, whispering, "Torviid had a message for you."

As they fell back from the other two, Tah'quhal continued, "I know we have known each other but a short time. Even so, I need you to trust what I am about to say, Derek." He paused long enough for Derek to give a confirmative nod. "Torviid was unable to speak to me in his ethereal form for long, but he gave me some vital information. Someone from Earth has been aiding Malum. You must be vigilant about who you trust."

"Trey," Derek whispered, clearing his now too tight throat. "We found out while we were in Oceanus that Trey is Malum's descendant."

Tah'quhal looked at him understandingly. "I'm sorry. I know what it is to be betrayed by a friend. To feel like you have lost them to this darkness. Or that you never really knew them at all. I promise, there will be time to process everything, but for now, there is a battle plan that needs to be made."

Derek wanted to argue that it wasn't like that with Trey. That he was being forced. But the words wouldn't come. The truth was, Derek wasn't sure. He didn't know if he was just being naive, wanting to see something that wasn't there. Derek pushed back the tears that threatened to spill and made his way back over to Mia at the table, taking a seat next to her.

Mia asked, "What was that all about?"

"Oh, he just had a message for me." Derek responded, trying to mask his worry.

Now that everyone was settled, Derek looked around the table. He recognized Karrent and his friends, but there were a few new faces. Waving towards the raven-haired fae and the human next to her, Derek said, "Hi there, uh." He scratched at his head, not really sure what exactly he was supposed to say. "I'm Derek."

Serene and Stella stood from their seats, the former saying, "My, my, I never thought I'd meet a semideus in person! My name is Serene, and I proudly serve as the Chieftain of Terra." As she motioned to Stella, she continued, "This is our loyal Keeper, Stella. We will do everything we can to assist you."

"Hello there, mate!" Ortug burst out, unable to curb his enthusiasm. "I don't believe we've been introduced yet, but your friends have nothing but great things to say about ya. Me and Tae here," he nodded to the pixie next to him, "may not be Keepers or Chieftains, but we are Caldera's most trusted advisors." Ortug gestured towards a human sitting in the corner, "And that little bugger over there is

Codi. She's the Keeper of the Forest, but her mind was tampered with and she has been a mighty sourpuss ever since."

Derek scratched at his head, feeling a bit overwhelmed by so many introductions and conversation taking place. To add to his anxiety, the library doors swung open and Nidalle and Abhaya sauntered in. Thankfully, they spotted Karrent nearby and immediately joined him without bothering with introductions.

Johnathan turned his attention to the current group gathered in front of him.

"As we wait for the others to join us, I just wanted to take a moment to honor Chieftain Komipea." The room fell into a heavy silence. "While I didn't get the chance to get to know him as well as most of y'all, he was a truly remarkable fae."

"That he was." Serene thickly murmured, taking Stella's hand.

Johnathan gave her a sympathetic smile before continuing, "In my research, I came across the laws governing the selection of a new Chieftain for Torvania. In the absence of an heir, it is up to the other Chieftains of Luminfae to choose his successor. Once we defeat Malum, I would like all the Chieftains to meet back here as quickly as possible so y'all can make a decision."

The library doors were forcefully pushed open by an enthusiastic Barry, practically dragging Caldera in. Through the door, Eirene could be seen lingering outside.

"Barry!" Derek excitedly called out, running towards him for a tight embrace. "I'm so glad you're here!"

Barry winced at the pressure on his bad arm, but chuckled, wheezing out, "Me, too, Derek. Me, too."

Caldera scanned the room, looking at who had already arrived. "Where's Sarika?" she inquired.

Derek's smile quickly faded as he explained how Sarika had betrayed them all.

Turning to Caldera, he admitted, "You were right. She was working with Malum all this time, playing us for a bunch of jackasses. Her and her brother have been loyal to him for years."

Caldera wanted to shout at the heavens that she warned Derek, but she could tell the betrayal hurt him. Barry simply gave him a light nudge and told him it would be okay.

Caldera scanned the room again. "Are we just waiting for Talissa now?"

Right on cue, a ring of fire materialized near the table. Talissa and David emerged from the flames.

Talissa immediately set her eyes on Barry. She snapped her fingers and appeared right next to him, placing her arm around his shoulders.

"I sure hope this all goes smoothly," she said with a slight smile.

Barry, with a frown of disgust, said, "Derek, this is Tal——"

"Talissa, Queen of the succubus, Chieftain of Ignis." She cut Barry off as she ran her fingers along Derek's arm. "And that tall drink of water over there," she pointed to David, "Is David, Ignis' Keeper," she darted her eyes to Barry, "for now."

Mia rose from the table and Caldera took a step towards the succubus.

Jonathan quickly intervened to keep the tension from rising to a boiling point. "Okay y'all, everyone get around this table. We got a lot to talk about."

He took a deep, exaggerated breath as he looked out at everyone around the table. "We are all here to stop Malum, and I think I got a way to do just that. It involves every Keeper in this room." He paused for a moment, expecting someone to ask what his plan was, but the room was silent. He nervously laughed to himself and continued, "Every city, even Caldera's village in the Magia Forest, was strategically built on 'ley lines.'" He pointed out each city on the map, tracing where the ley lines ran, starting in Torvania, circling through each city, and ending back in Torvania.

"Ya see, I doubt the fae that originally built these cities realized it, but all the portals they was buildin' around can theoretically access other dimensions besides Earth." He began to talk with his hands, mimicking cars getting on and off the interstate. "Get this. These ley lines are like a highway system between dimensions. The portals act like the on and——"

"What does any of this have to do with us Keepers?" David called out.

Talissa gave him a sharp smack with her tail on the back of his head, urging him to pay attention as Johnathan carried on with his story.

Jonathan shot an annoyed look at David.

"If you'd just give me a dadgum minute," he snapped.

"Most of y'all here in Luminfae think that the Keepers were created by fae to protect against threats like Malum."

Stella interjected, "Well, yes. That is our duty, right?"

"It's our duty, but not what we were 'created' for. The first Keepers were not human. They were fae." Several of the keepers looked to their Chieftains or gave Johnathan doubtful glances.

Serene added, "I can sense everyone becoming uneasy. I would just like to say that I, too, have heard these stories."

"Thank you, Serene." Johnathan said before motioning towards his staff. "My Keeper staff dates back to when humans first began to roam the Earth, long before Malum. From what I can tell, magic used to be abundant on Earth."

"What happened to it, then?" Derek whispered.

Johnathan smiled at him. "Well buddy, the name 'Keeper' kinda implies knowing something that others can't. My best guess is that something happened that made them decide it was safer to keep magic a secret. Unfortunately, I don't think we have time to figure out what that something is that made the original Keepers hide magic from the third dimension, but I did find some information on the spell they used."

Nidalle spoke up, "I am not sure why we would want to know the spell they used? Are you insinuating we should use it again?"

Johnathan explained that Oblivion was a realm filled with dark and twisted magic, serving as the source of Malum's power. Every creature that draws on Odium magic makes the magic itself stronger.

If all the creatures that pull from it suddenly forget it exists, Malum would lose a substantial amount of his power. Plus, by making this entire dimension forget about magic, they could potentially prevent any future threats like Malum. If Malum gained the upper hand in battle, depriving him of his power source could significantly aid in defeating him.

Nidalle countered, "Odium magic is similar to Bonum or Libra——it is not limited to one place but can be found all around us. Each individual must learn how to utilize it. While most people are able to tap into Bonum easily, that is why many focus on it, erasing magic from a realm will not stop Malum from accessing Odium."

John's brows knitted together, and his lips pressed into a thin line as he tried not to glare at the Chieftain. He inhaled deeply before speaking.

"You ain't entirely wrong. Magic does exist everywhere, that much we know. But Oblivion and its inhabitants feed on dark and twisted magic, which then fuels Malum's powerful Odium magic. If we can eliminate this 'power source,' it will weaken Malum significantly. Think of it like a tractor. If ya don't put no fuel in it, it ain't gunna run."

Johnathan noticed the confused expressions on the faces of the fae in the room. It was clear they had no concept of what a tractor was. He chuckled and tried to explain. "Let's try that again. Imagine a river full of life and energy. But when you build a dam, it blocks up the flow. Parts of the river go dry and there is less life living in that area. That's what we want to do with Malum's magic."

Stella said, "Okay, let's say we all agree with this plan. How would that even work?"

"Let's have all Keepers place their magical items beside my staff," Johnathan instructed.

Stella was the first to comply, placing two daggers by his staff. Codi followed suit, setting her bow next to them. David hesitated, but Talissa gave him another light smack on the back of his head with her tail, and he reluctantly put down a pistol and combat knife on the table. Finally, Mia hovered her hand over the items.

Mia's tattoo glowed a brilliant blue, and she could sense the surge of magic flowing from the items and through her body. It was the strongest sensation she had ever experienced. But before she could fully grasp it, Johnathan seized her arm and pulled her back.

Still feeling the echoes of that magic in her blood, she asked, "What was that all about?"

"Every single Keeper here, well . . . except David, cause Ignis chooses their new Keepers, has a connection to the ancient ones. We all are direct descendants. And Derek . . . you are a semideus. Your bloodline runs deeper than any of ours."

Taking a step back from the table as all their eyes around landed on him, "Woah! Don't be looking at me now. I'm still learning exactly what I am and where I belong in all of this."

Johnathan gave him a reassuring nod. "Don't worry buddy, I'm just letting you know. Now look, I don't know all the specifics, but I do know the three things we need. To make it even better, we already got em . . . well, we got two of em, but the other shouldn't be a problem.

"The one we need to get is the essence of the Forgonium flower, and I already got some of the local fae working on that." His eyes met Derek's, and his voice grew somber.

"The Keeper's items are one of the other two . . . but the last one stumped me for quite a while. The *tears of loss*, that's what the scrolls said. I really didn't understand it, and then it dawned on me. The ancient Keepers must have shut off magic on Earth because of some great tragedy. Their tears literally fueled the spell."

Derek's chest tightened as he reached into his pocket, pulling out the vial of tears Mia had captured when Izzy died. "You mean we need these?"

"I think so buddy," Johnathan responded as he walked over and placed a hand on Derek's shoulder.

Derek's lip quivered as he asked a barrage of questions.

"How are we supposed to make this work? How will the Keepers even know the spell? Please, make it make sense."

Mia reached for Derek's hand in a comforting gesture.

"Correct me if I'm wrong, Johnathan," Tah'quhal said, "but by having all the Keepers gather together with their Keeper items, they will instinctively channel the power of the ancient Keepers."

As Mia recounted her experience to the group, she described feeling a powerful wave of energy flow through her hand when she placed it over the items. It was almost as if something inside of her had been stirred awake, but the sensation vanished as soon as John grabbed her away.

Johnathan's face lit up in a smile. "Y'all hit the nail on the head. My thinking is that the ancient Keepers purposefully sealed away the secrets of magic and scattered themselves throughout Earth, each safeguarding a different portal to Luminfae. And over time, they found human spouses to start families and carry on their legacy."

"But what's the damned incantation?" David stubbornly asked.

Turning back to face the rest of the group with an annoyed sigh, "I don't think there is one, or at least it wasn't mentioned in anything I found. That being said, y'all just heard what Mia felt when she put her arm over the items on the table. I think this may be more of a ritual. Mia is the catalyst. Her Keeper item is a part of her. Once we pour the mixture of the Forgonium and tears into the soil on Oblivion, we'd all need to get as close as we can to Mia with our items. Trying to channel our magic through her. My thought is that she can direct all of that magic to where we poured the mixture . . . and the reaction that happens should take care of the rest."

The group of fae and humans burst into undistinguishable chatter, all varying in opinions and taken by surprise of the drastic plan. Barry's voice rose above the commotion.

"How would David's items help us at all?"

Johnathan started to add, "Well, you se——"

Talissa cut in, "His knife and pistol are made from the very first Keeper item. When we select a *new* Keeper," she smiled seductively at Barry, "we toss the old one's item into the Everflame. What comes out is tailored to the new Keeper."

Abhaya stated, "Who cares where the items come from? Your theory may be correct, but that doesn't mean that it is the right course of action."

"We should not tamper with the balance of magic, regardless of what the ancient Keepers did," Nidalle added.

Codi, who had stayed silent so far, spoke out, "Helian and the Hellfire Brigade don't draw power from Oblivion. Their strength comes from an elixir given to them by power tripped assholes in the Sacred Dimension. How will stripping Oblivion of its magic prevent future threats from people like that?"

Her statement sparked a heated discussion on whether attempting this spell was the right decision. But before it could escalate into a full-blown argument, Serene intervened,

"None of this matters if we can't stop Malum. I know Helian well, and while he is a concern, he is not the current threat plaguing all of Luminfae . . . all of the dimensions. Malum is the reason we have all gathered here today. With Komipea gone, there are five Chieftains present in this room. Let us put it to a vote."

The group unanimously agreed to a vote, with Serene appointing Johnathan as the conductor.

Anxious, Johnathan scanned the room before speaking up, "Who here supports using the Keepers' abilities to erase all knowledge of magic from Oblivion? Vote by raising your hand."

The Chieftains were hesitant, looking to see who would vote first. After a few moments, Caldera raised her hand, swiftly followed by Serene. Nidalle tried one last plea.

"Karrent, we must consider the balance of magic in all of this. If Oblivion is cleansed of magic, it could set a dangerous precedent for eradicating magic elsewhere."

Karrent looked at her with a pained expression as he raised his hand. "Nidalle, we are not eradicating magic. We are just wiping Oblivion's memory, much like when we use the forgonium on a human."

"If you do not believe this will affect magic's natural balance, you are more foolish than I thought you to be. I vote no." Nidalle huffed, her arms crossed against her chest.

"Not that it would make a difference now, but I would have to agree with Nidalle on this matter," Talissa hissed.

With the votes tallied, Johnathan clapped his hands together. "It's settled then. Everyone rest up tonight. At dawn, we step into Oblivion."

As most of the Keepers and Chieftains made their way out of the library, Derek asked Mia, Johnathan, Tah'quhal, Barry, and Caldera to stay behind and help plan the upcoming fight.

Derek sat down in a chair, taking a moment to reflect on the chaos and turmoil that had consumed the past few days. After a few moments, he stood up, and looked to his friends.

"Okay, here is what I'm thinking. Johnathan, find us any maps of Oblivion. Tah'quhal, you and Caldera help me come up with a battle plan. Barry, give Mia a hand in finding anything useful for our fight, and can someone please find some food? I am starving!"

They worked tirelessly up until nightfall, fine-tuning their plan. As they discussed the final details, each sipping on a bowl of skrellux broth soup, Tah'quhal brought up a crucial point.

"Our main enemy is Malum. The army here will fight against whatever forces he's gathered, the Keepers will focus on their spell, and Derek will search for Malum. But there are two unknowns in this plan."

Derek nodded in agreement. He'd already been thinking the same thing. "Tarik and Sarika."

Tah'quhal hesitated before adding, "I wish I could confidently say that I can handle them both on my own. This armor may give me an advantage, but I can't be certain it will be enough to face them when they are together."

Barry placed his bowl down, face solemn. "You don't have to do it alone. I know I'm just a human with no magical abilities, but maybe I can distract one of them long enough for you to take on the other."

"Barry, no! It's too dangerous!" Caldera practically hissed.

"Babe, everything about this is dangerous. I don't think there is a cautious way to go about any of this," Barry spoke softly as he wrapped her tense body in a hug.

Caldera wasn't sure if she wanted to kiss him for his bravery or smack him for his foolishness.

Derek locked eyes with Barry, who was determined to move forward. Reluctantly, Derek agreed.

"If you're absolutely sure."

Barry stood his ground and Caldera bit her tongue hard enough to draw blood. She knew there was no changing his mind.

Derek addressed the group once more. "I'll go search for Malum. I might not be strong enough on my own, but maybe I can buy enough time for the spell to be finished. Tah'quhal and Barry, you guys find Tarik and Sarika. Johnathan and Mia, you two join the other Keepers in casting the ancient spell. Caldera, you'll lead our army alongside the other chieftains. And when this is all over, I'm going straight through that portal to sleep in my comfortable bed."

Now that everyone had their tasks, the group went their separate ways to catch some rest before dawn.

Time seemed to crawl by as the next few hours passed, the impending battle weighing heavily on everyone's minds. Derek couldn't shake the fear that had gripped him. His eyes trailed over Mia's sleeping form for reassurance. Slowly, his chest relaxed as he watched her even breaths.

Eventually, he untangled himself from the hammock they'd strung up outside, careful not to wake Mia. He settled onto the ground, gazing up at the sky as the sun slowly began to rise.

Derek watched the soft light spread across the horizon and let himself shed a single tear. Izzy loved sunrises. She always said it was her favorite part of the day. She would sit alone on her roof and watch it and say it felt like the sky was waking up just for her. So much had happened since her death. So much still lay ahead. But just for this moment, Derek let all of that fade away. It was just him, the memory of Izzy, and the sun that was still waking up for her.

Mia gently rested her hand on Derek's shoulder, causing him to turn and meet her gaze.

"Everything okay?" She asked, even though she knew the answer.

Derek stood up and cupped her jaw, his eyes never leaving Mia's.

"These next few hours could change everything. I need you to stay safe."

Mia's heart swelled at his words, the plea in his eyes. She gave him a watery smile. "No, I need you to be safe. You'll face Malum while I stay in the back with the other Keepers."

Derek's awkward grin spread across his face as he lifted his pinky finger in the air and promised, "I will do my absolute best."

Without hesitation, Mia intertwined her pinky with his and added, "Right back atcha', Lavender."

Mia thought there must be some kind of magic in their promise because, in that moment, their bond felt unbreakable. Whatever happens, he'd come back to her. Derek leaned down to kiss Mia, their lips meeting in a sweet exchange of emotions too powerful for words. As the sun rose higher in the sky, signaling the start of a new day, Mia pulled away and whispered, "It's time."

Chapter 31

Calm Before the Storm

Derek looked at Mia, his eyes glimmering in the new day's light. "Before we do this, I need to talk to the . . . I can't believe I'm about to say this . . . the Enchanted Ensemble." The sound of Mia's light giggle was a balm. He held onto that sound, that feeling, knowing he'd need it before the day was out.

Mia's perfect white teeth snuck out, biting her bottom lip in a little grin. "Well, let's go find them, Lavender. I'll see who is around the square if you want to search by the fire pit."

Derek shook his head with a half-cocked smile as they split up and searched the city for their friends. Derek quickly spotted Johnathan and Barry eating breakfast on something that closely resembled a picnic table.

Jonathan yelled out, "Come on now, get over here!"

Sitting down next to Johnathan, Derek watched his two friends as they joked and talked about all of their stories since arriving in Torvania.

A few minutes had passed when Derek's chest began to tighten ever so slightly. "*Not another panic attack. Not now.*" He closed his eyes and took a deep breath, trying to calm himself. His arms began to flicker with white light, but something was new. He could hear the faintest humming. A soothing melody ringing in his ears. With the tightness easing up, he opened his eyes to see his two friends staring at him.

"You okay there, buddy?" Johnathan asked.

Derek responded, "I will be. Sitting here, listening to you two, I'm just realizing how far we have come."

Johnathan looked out towards the horizon, a sad smile playing on his lips. "Ya know, Izzy would have loved it here."

"Dude, could you imagine Izzy running through this city? Non-stop asking every fae a million questions, just soaking in everything she could?" Barry asked, huffing out a laugh that kept him from crying.

Derek stood from the table. "It does feel like we are missing a piece of our puzzle, huh?"

"I dunno about y'all, but it'd be great if her and Trey were sitting here, arguing about whatever they always argued about," Johnathan said. "I mean, damn, there are even two empty seats here. It's like they was supposed to be here."

Barry got up and walked behind Derek and Johnathan. "Do you think we will see Trey again?"

Only silence was the answer. None of them knew exactly where Trey was, or why he kept showing up. Sure, they learned quite a bit about him through their journeys, but there still wasn't a real answer.

Quietly, Johnathan said, "If we see Trey again, I hope he isn't what everyone is saying he is."

"*When* we see Trey, after all this is over, we are going to get the band back together. We lost one friend already." Derek paused for a moment. "I can't lose another."

Johnathan gave Derek a tight hug, the kind brothers share when they are scared. Barry turned and wrapped his arms around the two of them, hoping this wouldn't be the last time they all got to share a real moment together.

Sliding away from the embrace, Derek asked, "We are going to win this thing, right?"

Before his friends could answer, Mia came walking up with Caldera and Tah'quhal. "Oh, good! You found the boys."

Their earlier conversation pushed aside, the Enchanted Ensemble talked for a bit, mainly ignoring the battle that was to come, Instead, they focused on tall tales and myths of Luminfae, everyone needing a distraction today..

As they talked, Derek's stomach knotted. He was about to go into battle, but he still felt like he was missing vital information. Blankly staring toward the ground, he repeatedly cracked his knuckles as he shifted from foot to foot.

"Caldera," Derek interrupted, "I know that there's been a lot going on, and I get that you promised to help me figure things out more after we face Malum, but I'm freaking out a little." He looked up at her concerned face, clearly having taken her, and the rest of the group, off guard.

Barreling on, he said, "I just can't shake the feeling that my nightmare is important. Ever since you recognized the lines from my dream, I've had this prickling sensation that *something* is about to happen. Something related to those words." Everyone had gone quiet, staring at him. "Can … can you *please* just tell me what's going on?" He looked at Caldera pleadingly.

Mia furrowed her brow, asking, "What dream, Derek?"

At the same time, Tah'quhal asked, "What words were in your vision?"

Derek had completely forgotten that he hadn't told them yet. Quickly, he explained to them about his nightmares. He could tell Mia was hurt that he kept it from her for so long, but she simply asked Caldera, "Does that sound like the prophecy to you?"

"The prophecy?" Derek questioned.

Caldera gravely confirmed, "I believe so."

"So y'all know what it means?" Derek asked.

Caldera recited, "To bridge the gap, unite the world's divide, with courage, he'll mend what's torn inside. The realms tremble as the battle nears. In his hands, the fate of all appears. To save Luminfae and realms beyond compare, he'll face the trials, his destiny to bear. With magic yet awakened and a brotherhood born, mend the pages from the tome once torn. The scales of fate demand a heavy cost. Balance is needed or all will be lost. Only love can stop the strife and bring in an everlasting light."

"Wait a second," Tah'quhal said in the silence that followed "Those are the same words I read in a book in Komipea's home. "

Mia said, "It is a prophecy discovered by scholars from Oceanus during the First Fae Wars. It was written on a scroll found in a cave on the border of Oceanus and the Wilds. The scholars argued about how old the scroll was, some saying it predated the fae, others swear it was just a prank a child was pulling. Either way, the people of Luminfae have long thought it to be a warning of the end times."

Caldera interjected, "It is largely considered a rumor but . . . the 'with magic yet awakened' could be speaking about you, especially if you have had this nightmare for so long. I wish I could give you more answers, but I promise I will help you find them after we defeat Malum."

Tah'quhal's face showed no emotion, but inside he was spinning. Everything Caldera had said, it all made too much sense. He was growing increasingly convinced this wasn't just a coincidence. Ever the warrior, he did his best to keep on a brave face as Derek began to lose his calm.

"You think this prophecy is about me?" Derek asked. "How am I supposed to use *love* to stop Malum? Do I need to give him a hug?" He questioned sarcastically. "Cause that sounds like a real bad idea."

Johnathan grabbed Derek by his shoulders. "Hey, buddy! Look at me. Listen to my words." Johnathan's eyes grew serious, his brow forming a straight line. "We don't have time to pick it all apart right now. The time to fight is here. A prophecy that might not even exist don't change nothing!"

"John's right, Derek," Barry added. "Only what we do matters. Just like on the football or baseball field, only our actions shape what's going to happen. If fate does want to intervene, there is nothing we could do to change it, anyway."

Derek's insides wanted to be on the outside, but he knew what his friends were saying was true. He wanted more answers, more time, but right now, it was time to fight. He squeezed Mia's hand tightly, looking to her for comfort.

Caldera approached the two of them. "Hear these words and may they bring you comfort. They are words we fae live by. Still I stand . . ."

Tah'quhal sounded off with pride, "Until I fall . . ."

Barry and John joined in, both placing a hand on Derek's shoulders. "I will head the lonesome call."

Derek was overwhelmed with gratitude for the people beside him. It was funny. For a "lonesome" call, he didn't feel alone in that moment. Not at all.

He could hear the rustling and faint conversations of their gathered army, and he knew it was time to take them into Oblivion.

Through a choked voice, he managed to say, "Thank you. All of you."

He turned to face the Anchor, knowing it was time to move forward. With each step he took, the "Enchanted Ensemble" was right behind him.

As they turned the corner, they were met with the full view of the army gathered together for the first time. The sight left them in awe. There were countless fae, orcs, succubi, pixies, humans, and other creatures gathered together for this fight. It was a powerful display of solidarity, courage, and selflessness. All were willing to put their lives on the line. All were prepared to charge into battle alongside someone who they had never laid eyes on before this day, this fight.

Serene emerged from the assembled warriors, and with unwavering conviction, said, "Derek, these brave souls are all here to follow you, the semideus. It would be wise for you to address them."

Before any of this, Derek would have sprinted away if he had to face a large crowd. But he had learned that being pushed out of his comfort zone kept him on his toes. He surveyed the audience once more before stepping forward to address the crowd.

"Hey everyone, you may not know me from Adam, but that don't matter now." He cleared his throat, focusing on not fidgeting. These soldiers needed a confident leader right now, not some green kid. "We stand here today, not as strangers, but as brothers and sisters in arms. We may be different folks from different walks of life, but we share one thing in common: the desire to stand up against darkness and fight for what's right." Derek's voice grew steady and strong the more he talked, the words pouring out of him as he looked at the sea of people that had gathered for their cause.

"Now, I ain't gonna stand here and pretend I got all the answers or that I'm some kinda' hero." Derek's lips tilted in a self-deprecating smile.

"Heck, I'm just a kid from a small town . . . But what I do know is this: when you step out on that battlefield, it won't be easy, but you won't be stepping out there alone. It doesn't matter that you don't know the warrior by your side, because each and every one of you is stepping out there today with the same fight. The same bravery. The same heart.

"We've all faced our fair share of trials and tribulations. We've all felt fear grip us like a vice and doubt creep into our minds. I'll be the first to admit, I have let my thoughts cloud my judgment more than once. I've felt like I was losing my mind, but today my mind is clear, and I hope yours is, too.

"So let's show 'em what we're made of! Let's fight with everything we got, not just for ourselves, but for the ones we love, for the ones who came before us, and for the ones who'll come after us. Let's make history today. Let what we do in Oblivion leave its mark across dimensions. Let it be known that we took a stand, and even if we fall, we will rise again to answer the call."

A quiet stillness descended upon the group, and Derek searched their anxious expressions, trying to decipher any sense of enthusiasm or motivation in them. He couldn't help but wonder how many were present simply because their leaders had ordered them to be. Cringing at the awkwardness that was sure to come, he made to turn around when the smooth, rich voice of an Oceanus warrior rose above the gathering, and began to sing.

"In realms beyond, where magic soars,
I sailed the skies in the First Fae Wars.
With a heart of courage and a sword of flame,
But oh, how I longed for my love's sweet name."
Other Oceanus warriors soon joined in.
"Hey oh, a fae's last ante.
Through realms unknown, where battles run plenty.
I'll brave the chaos, the mystical might,
But dreams of her keep me warm through the night."
Derek scanned the field of soldiers, their voices echoing within his heart. Mia hopped onto a nearby boulder and reached out to help him up beside her as she joined in singing along.
"In forests deep, and starlit glades,
I faced the shadows, and their dark crusades.
With the moon of the night, and stars as my guide,
Her memory, my beacon, in the darkest of tides."
Derek's arms began to glow their familiar white, the brightness almost blinding in its intensity. New, intricate blue patterns in the shape of lightning bolts appeared on his skin within the glowing aura. The crowd watched in awe as more and more voices joined in the song surrounding Derek's evolution.

Mia handed him a piece of the shattered amulet they got from Canter Mountain.

"Hey oh, a fae's last ante.

Through realms unknown, where battles run plenty.

I'll brave the chaos, the mystical might,

But dreams of her keep me warm through the night."

Derek could feel the power coursing through him. With the crowd singing in support and Mia beside him, his power surged ten-fold. Amid the singing, Tah'quhal shouted, "Semideus!" The crowd, those who weren't singing, chanted along with him. "Semideus! Semideus! Semideus!"

"Through portals wide, and sorcery's kiss,

I fought for our world, in a land of abyss.

With her face in my heart, and her love as my shield,

I'd conquer the chaos and darkness I'd wield."

As the army sang, Derek turned toward the portal, his powers still in full effect, and hurled a shard of the shattered amulet through the glowing archway. The portal shifted from a soothing blue to a foreboding dark red. Derek and Mia leaped down from the rock and approached the Anchor.

"Hey oh, a fae's last ante.

Through realms unknown, where battles run plenty,

I'll brave the chaos, the mystical might,

But dreams of her keep me warm through the night."

Derek glanced at his friends, his eyes landing on Tah'quhal. *"A true warrior, he came to find me and now he stands beside me,"* he thought to himself. Shifting his gaze to Caldera and Barry, he imagined them after all this was over. He wondered how the hell Barry would explain his new girlfriend to his parents. He knew Barry would figure it out. Barry always figured it out. Heck, he even figured out how to fit into a world where he didn't belong.

Looking at Johnathan, he thought, "*My best friend. He has been through everything with me. There is no Derek without John. I wouldn't be able to do what comes next without him here.*"

Finally, his eyes met Mia's. The one he never expected to need. A stranger to a crush. A crush to a friend. A friend to . . . a flame. Her touch could calm the raging seas in his mind. Her words kept him moving. He was unable to fathom doing this without any of them. Each one of these incredible people meant the world to him.

Steadying his nerves, he said, "Time to end this." As he stepped through the portal, he heard the final verse of the army's song behind him.

"Now the war has waned, and the battles have ceased.
I'll return to my love; my heart is released.
With the scars of a warrior, and a tale to be told,
I'll sail back to her arms, where my love takes hold."

Chapter 32

The Storm

The sun hung in the crimson sky, casting an eerie glow over the rocky terrain. The thick, putrid stench of the air stung their noses as they took in their surroundings. In the distance, revealed by flashes of red lightning, a solitary figure stood atop a looming tower. An ethereal cloud of red essence seemed to radiate from the figure. Beneath the tower, a massive army of dark magical creatures waited.

Derek and Mia stepped into the hellish landscape, hand in hand. Their friends, the Chieftains, Keepers, and army following behind them. Within minutes, the stage was set, and the battle was imminent. An almost tangible silence descended over Derek's army, not due to them being scared, but because they were buzzing with barely restrained energy.

Behind Derek stood a formidable army, unlike any other in Luminfae. Each line of warriors possessed their own unique abilities to aid the fight.

The fae commanded the elements with grace and precision——flames danced at their fingertips, water obeyed their every whim, and gusts of wind swirled around them. Alongside them were the orcs, powerful tanks of unmatched size and strength. Pixies, small yet nimble, flew through the air with bows and arrows. Succubi radiated charm and enchantment, their seduction as lethal as their talons. Interspersed throughout were the humans——tenacious and brave——skilled in a variety of combat, both of Earth and of Luminfae.

Each soldier wielded a unique weapon, from glowing swords infused with elemental abilities to staffs, crackling with energy, and bows etched with ancient runes.

On the other side of the desolate battleground stood a corrupt and dark horde, led by Malum. His side was a sea of towering minotaurs, harpies, elves bearing sharp teeth, and a variety of other fearsome creatures. The most frightening among them were the corrupted fae, once beautiful beings, now twisted by Malum's magic. They, too, possessed magic, but theirs focused on brutality and force with raging flames and spells that could warp the ground beneath.

A hush settled over the battlefield, the air thick with the weight of anticipation. "CHARGE!" A general from Malum's army shouted, sparking both forces to sprint towards each other, clashing like waves colliding in a tumultuous ocean. The impact was deafening, echoing through the landscape in a cacophony of sound.

The fae from Derek's army used their powers to conjure strong gusts of wind, lifting the pixies high into the air. From above, the tiny warriors unleashed a barrage of arrows, striking their enemies with deadly precision. The battlefield was engulfed in flames as fire magic erupted, reducing corrupted fae and other creatures to ashes. Others wielded water magic, forming protective barriers to send surges of healers out to those in need.

At the front lines, orcs charged fearlessly into battle, matching the brute strength of the opposing minotaurs. Succubi danced gracefully along the edges of the battlefield, using their charms to lure corrupted fae and elves into traps set by natare. Meanwhile, humans fought fiercely, supporting each unit with strength, wit, or supplies.

Malum's army fought back just as fiercely, fueled by pure hatred and aggression. The minotaurs mercilessly stomped orcs into the ground while elves pounced on anyone close by, devouring them like piranhas. Harpies swooped through the air, slicing through pixies with their razor-sharp talons. The fae who chose to join Malum sucked the air out from around soldiers to suffocate them.

From his dark tower in the distance, Malum watched as the battle raged on. He called upon fire and red lightning from the skies, using his connection to Oblivion and Odium to twist the flames into fiery tornadoes on the battlefield.

It was chaos. A frenzy of magic and hand-to-hand combat. Ortug led a battalion of orcs directly towards a small grouping of minotaurs that had been decimating their left flank. Never breaking his stride, he launched himself into the air and dug his ax into the skull of one of the nearest minotaurs. Running down the back of the slain creature, he shouted,

"Don't just stand there, ya wusses. Beat these beasts back to Mythos!"

A young female fae, unknown in name to many, watched as the minotaurs began to beat back the orcs, almost with ease. Their roars echoing across the battlefield. The young fae, frightened by their show of force, used her slight stature to slip further into the fight and sat on the ground. She pressed her palms together, fingers aimed in the air. With a deep breath, a primal growl poured from her throat on a suspended note.

The minotaurs from Malum's army stopped and stared at the lone fae, their heads and ears twitching in pain from the low tones. Those daring enough to approach fell to the ground, their bodies twitching and twisting until they stilled with a splattering pop. Ortug looked at the fae in awe of what she'd accomplished.

A corrupted fae witnessed the fall of the minotaur flank and quickly reacted. They pointed their fingers towards the young fae and the ground opened beneath them, swallowing her and her guttural tones whole. Ortug's admiration turned to horror, his stare directed where the unnamed warrior had been. He realized there was nothing left behind of the brave fae, not even a name for Ortug honor.

Protected at the back of the army, the Keepers huddled together in a tight circle near the portal. They pulled out their Keeper items and a brilliant light surrounded them. Mia's tattoo emitted a misty blue aura as she turned to Johnathan for guidance. She shouted to be heard above the clashing sounds,

"What now, John?"

Johnathan addressed the group.

"Everyone focus on what needs to happen. I will pour the forgonium and tear mixture in our circle."

Pouring the mixture into the soil, he felt a twinge from deep inside. It was like a memory trying to fight its way out of his soul. Slowly, he was able to shout something out. "*Magia oblita.*"

Stella, sensing the same thing building inside her, spoke the next phrase like it was rushing to escape her. "*Magia remota!*"

Abhaya experienced the same presence as she shouted, "*Magia occulta!*"

The mixture Johnathon had poured shot a beam of blue light into the sky, seemingly extending past the sun. It slowly began to spread across the horizon.

"Don't y'all stop now. Keep saying it!" Johnathan demanded.

The Keepers followed his lead, centering their focus inwards and pulling on the thread of magic that pooled in their core. As the vibrant blue mist from Mia's tattoo swirled around them, its power growing stronger with each passing second, a wave of magic flowed through their bodies. Gradually, the mist extended outward from their group, joining with the beam of light——it was working.

From atop his tower, Malum watched the unfolding events with a wicked glare. He fixed his eyes on Derek, whose arms crackled with bright white lightning. Derek stared from the ground, knowing his target stood hidden atop the tower. He watched as Malum turned around to address what looked like Sarika and Tarik. A burst of red essence shot from the tower, and only Malum remained.

Malum's dark sorcery continued to rain destruction upon the battlefield, consuming the majority of Ortug's battalion in flames. Derek's heart stopped at the devastation. The senseless death. Shaking with rage, he slowly raised his gaze towards the top of the tower and roared,

"I'm coming for you, Malum!"

Barry and Tah'quhal flanked Derek on both sides, ready to defend him until he could get to Malum. They ran forward into the middle of the battlefield, weapons drawn and magic readied, when a line of fire appeared directly before them.

"And where do you boys think you're headed?" Tarik taunted, appearing behind the fire with a sadistic grin.

Barry called out, "Go on, Derek. Taco and I got this."

Though his instincts fought against it, Derek had to trust them to handle this. He shot them one last concerned look and used his magic to propel himself off the ground. Beams of pure light pushed him forward, demolishing any corrupted fae in his path as he flew towards Malum's tower.

Barry stared down Tarik, cautiously advancing. He waited until he found an opening before striking, his sword slicing through the air with precision. But as it made contact with Tarik's arm, the blade passed through him like mist.

Tarik chuckled. "I do believe you already tried that, human."

Barry realized his mistake a little too late. Tarik's shadow arm reformed, shooting out as he cast a spell that engulfed Barry in red essence and lifted him high above the battleground. Caldera, fighting further back in the fray, saw Barry suspended in the air. She called for Eirene and they circled his essence engulfed body, trying to find a way to free him.

With a smirk, Tarik turned his attention to Tah'quhal, eyes lighting up at Tah'quhal's brandished swords.

"Oh my dear friend, would you like to dance?"

Tarik hummed a playful tune as his shadowy arm formed a sharp blade of his own.

"Please don't make me do this," Tah'quhal plead, unwilling to make the first move. His eyes were fixed on Tarik, whose shadowy arm pulsed with dark, malevolent energy. Red essence crackled and warped the air around him.

"Tarik, stop this madness! This is not you." Tah'quhal's voice was strained with grief and memories of friendship. "It's not too late to turn back."

Tarik's eyes glowed with an unnatural light. "You know nothing of who I am, what I have become. This is the only path I have."

Tah'quhal could have sworn he saw a flicker of remorse in his eyes, a moment of hesitation as he stared down the person he had spent more than a century calling a friend, a brother. With a roar, Tarik lunged, any trace of hesitation gone.

Tarik's shadowy blade meeting Tah'quhal's ethereal swords in a shower of essence. The ground beneath them trembled from the impact, and soldiers on both sides paused, momentarily awed by the sheer power of their clash.

Tah'quhal parried a series of rapid strikes, his movements a blur of blue tinged fire. He slashed his right sword with a sweeping arc of flames, forcing Tarik back. Tarik's dark magic absorbed the heat, the essence around him growing denser.

Tarik summoned a massive, dark wave that surged towards Tah'quhal. With a burst of flame, Tah'quhal cut through the wave, his swords glowing brighter as it channeled his magic. Tah'quhal pressed the attack, driving Tarik back step-by-step. He was relentless. Every blow as swift and powerful as the next.

Fatigue sapped Tarik's magic, each blow sending shockwaves down his already trembling arms. "Looks like all those years of me thinking I was better than you were correct," Tah'quhal taunted.

In a desperate final surge, Tarik swung his shadowy blade in a wide arc. Tah'quhal had his opening. He blocked Tarik's swing with one sword, using the other to slash at Tarik's exposed side. Tarik stumbled, and Tah'quhal used that falter to drive his blade through Tarik's stomach.

Tarik gasped, his shadowy arm falling limp as the red essence surrounding him dissipated. He collapsed to his knees, Tah'quhal still holding on to the hilt of the sword. Tarik looked into his old friend's eyes.

Tah'quhal swore he could see regret lingering in his stare. Tarik chuckled, spitting blood onto Tah'quhal's armor. Never breaking eye contact, Tarik spoke his final words. "You know not what has begun."

Tarik's eyes rolled back, his head falling slack. Tah'quhal's chest rose and sank slowly, his mouth slightly agape. He slid his sword out of his defeated foe, his friend. Blood dripping from the blade, he whispered to himself, "*What* had begun?"

With Tarik defeated, his dark magic faded, releasing Barry from his air prison. He plummeted towards the ground, eyes squeezed shut against the lethal impact that was sure to come. Tah'quhal, eyes wide, lunged forward, to do what, he was not sure.

Caldera, circling high above on Eirene, shouted,

"Catch hi—"

Eirene's sharp dive stole the air from her lungs. She raced beneath Barry, turned and flew back up towards him, giving Caldera a chance to reach out and grab him. Some would call it skill, others would say it was pure luck, but she managed to grab Barry and sling him onto the back of Eirene.

Barry looked up at her weakly and joked, "I was hoping I'd be the one saving you."

"Not this time, Bear." Caldera responded in a choked, serious tone.

Eirene landed next to Tah'quhal, and Barry grunted with pain. Although he didn't fall to his death, the force from Tarik's spell had left him quite sore.

The hard set lines of Tah'quhal's face seemed to have aged a century as he stared at the body of his former friend. He turned his stoic face to Barry, giving a nod to acknowledge he was glad he was okay.

Voice hollow, he asked Caldera, "Have you seen Sarika?"

His stomach sank as a blood-curdling scream emanated from the circle of Keepers. Something told him he had his answer.

They turned and squinted their eyes towards the center of the circle in time to see something dissipate into a crimson mist. Codi, the Keeper of the forest, lay motionless, a dagger of the same red essence protruding from her back.

Caldera cried out, "Codi . . . no."

Barry drew his sword and shouted, "Everflame!"

Eirene knelt down, and Barry, Caldera, and Tah'quhal quickly leapt onto her back. The griffin flew, full speed, towards the circle of Keepers.

Mia, her expression filled with desperation, turned to Johnathan for direction.

"No! No. no. no, what do we do now?" she pleaded.

Johnathan shook his head with a flicker of panic as he tried to come up with a plan. He gestured for the group to halt so he could gather his thoughts. Sarika didn't give him the opportunity. She briefly appeared behind David, plunging another dagger into his chest when he turned to face her.

"Shit." David murmured as he collapsed to the ground, struggling for breath.

Caldera leapt off of Eirene's back just before they had landed on the ground. She ran to Codi's side, Abhaya already speaking incantations in an attempt to save her. Barry raced towards David, dropping to one leg and sliding next to him. He shouted, "He's still breathing!"

Looking at her Keeper's eyes, Caldera knew the light was gone. No magic could bring her back. She let one tear fall from her face. Pushing down the emotions she wanted to let out, she placed a stilling hand on Abhaya's arm.

"Save David."

"But Caldera, Codi——"

"Abhaya, please. Codi is . . . gone. Barry made a deal with Talissa. If David dies, he is to become the next Keeper of Ignis . . . and I will *not* let that happen."

Seeing the fear buried in Caldera's eyes, Abhaya sprinted towards David, pushing Barry aside, and began focusing her magic on stabilizing him. Barry walked towards Caldera, hoping to provide comfort, but Stella was already holding her in an embrace. He overheard Caldera say,

"I saved Barry, only for Codi to die. I did what I am supposed to do, protect those that need it. Codi is who needed me, and I was not here."

Barry's head hung low. He knew she didn't mean it as an insult, but it still stung like one. He promised Komipea he would be brave. He promised to carry Everflame with honor, but his capture, his weakness, kept Caldera occupied. In his mind, Codi's death was just as much on his hands as it was on Sarika's. Caldera could have stayed with the Keepers if she had not been worried about saving him.

Atop Malum's tower, Derek finally stood face-to-face with the malevolent Fae. The stories he had heard did not do justice to the terror he invoked. Malum's slender frame was adorned with crimson stigmata, matching the streaks of red in his dark beard. The stigmata pulsed with a noxious energy that seemed to seep the life from his pale, sickly flesh. His eyes were a maze of red and black that sucked Derek in and sent chills down his spine.

Derek's arms glowed brighter than ever before, and his eyes burned with a fiery intensity. His magic felt hot, nearly boiling under his skin, wanting to explode. Lightning sparks danced from his fingertips, filling the tense air between them.

"So, it's come to this, semideus." Malum's voice was rough like sandpaper.

Derek remained silent, his expression unchanging."I have been trapped in this realm for longer than I care to remember. A fae, too weak to defeat me himself, ensnared me here with the help of the very beings I sought to eradicate. Can you not see the irony? Is it not wrong that any one being should possess such immense power? Perhaps I am the foolish one for thinking a semideus would betray their own bloodline."

Malum eyed Derek speculatively. "I assumed you would be angry about carrying their curse."

Derek's brow furrowed, puzzled. Sensing his uncertainty, Malum continued,

"You mean to tell me that you have no knowledge of the semideus curse?" He let out a dark chuckle. "Not one of your companions, Chieftains, or even the Keepers thought to warn you about this curse, not even Karrent, who should be *well-versed*?" He laughed openly now, his amusement as unsettling as his glower. "You are quite the fool! All this time, you have been using magic that is slowly consuming you, and you were completely oblivious." His voice was filled with mocking sympathy.

The air was sucked from Derek's lungs. His magic sputtered, arms fading and the crackling lightning stopping completely. With a voice almost too quiet to detect, he asked,

"What do you mean?"

Malum looked at him with sympathy, conjuring a red, misty dagger behind his back as he cautiously approached the bewildered Derek.

"The power you sought to unleash against me is consuming you from within." He placed his revealed hand on Derek's shoulder. "Look around, my boy," Malum goaded. "Your army is losing their will to fight."

Derek surveyed the battlefield, noticing that some of his troops had already retreated and those who remained were faltering.

"Your Keepers have failed in their spell." He hissed near Derek's ear. Derek's gaze shifted towards the far side of the field where he could see the spell had stopped. At that moment, he caught sight of a burst of red essence forming behind a glimpse of pink hair. Before he could react, Malum plunged his dagger deep into Derek's side.

Derek gasped, "Mi——"

His gasp turned to a cry of agony,

"AAAA!"

Derek's vision began to fade, his consciousness slipping away as the magic drained his life force. He strained to see what was happening at the other end of the battlefield, using all his strength to crawl towards the edge of the tower. The pain in his side was excruciating, but he clenched his teeth and dragged himself further.

Derek felt like his soul was spilling out with his blood, and he realized this could be his end. Blacking out from the pain, he watched the red essence and Mia disappear. He closed his eyes, feeling like he had failed, and prepared for the worst.

A voice rang out, familiar and comforting.

"Derek! Get up! Wake up, Derek!"

Chapter 33

Everything

He lay on the ground, grasping onto a thread of hope. His eyes were squeezed shut, hoping that this was the end for him. After all his efforts and struggles, he'd failed. He had disappointed himself, but most of all, he disappointed those who believed in him. The realization of his true purpose came too late as he now lay dying on the ground. All his efforts were in vain.

"Derek! Get your ass up!"

Derek pushed through the haze clouding his mind. He recognized that voice. He'd desperately prayed to hear that voice again. His eyelids fluttered open to reveal a figure kneeling before him, bathed in a bright pink glow. With effort, he focused on their features.

He was dead. Malum had killed him because he was staring at the familiar face of Izzy. He wanted to hug her, cry, laugh, but he couldn't move. He couldn't move, and she was pleading with him to get up.

"Ho . . . how are you here? I watched you die," Derek managed to choke out.

"I don't have time to explain everything, but I'm here to help you. You need to get up. This battle is far from over," she said urgently.

Derek dug down to whatever scraps of strength he had left and fought his way to his knees. His vision was still blurry, and his body was in excruciating pain, but he did it. Malum sneered at him as he attempted to stand.

"Humans never know when to give up. Always willpower this and willpower that. Learn to stay down like the bugs that you are," he taunted, snapping his fingers. Trey materialized beside him, emanating red essence from his hands. "My son, finish him. It's almost time for our departure."

With a cry, Derek dragged himself to his feet, clenching his left side as if he could force the blood to stay inside.

He stared at Izzy in disbelief, his back still turned to Malum and Trey, and desperately asked, "What do I have to do?"

Trey shot him a confused expression. "Who the hell are you talking to?" he demanded.

Izzy smiled wistfully, glancing back at Trey. "They can't see me. Only you can." Locking her eyes back on Derek, she waved her left hand in a counter-clockwise motion. "Do you trust me?"

Derek nodded, no hesitation on his face. Time had literally almost stopped. The only two moving were him and Isabella.

"I can't hold this for long. Fight Trey. Fight him with everything you have. Malum draws power from Oblivion and his offspring." Izzy begged.

"Offspring? I thought he was just a distant descendant?" Derek asked.

Izzy paused for a moment, throat bobbing. She swiped a tear from her cheek and took Derek's hand. His eyes widened, locking on her touch. He could actually *feel* her. He never thought he'd get that chance again, and his throat grew thick with emotion. Izzy's choked voice drew his eyes back to her face.

"I wish I had time to tell you everything. I wish we had forever. I wish none of this ever happened. But it did." Her voice broke. "Just trust me. Fight Trey . . . end this . . .and then find your answers."

Ignoring his stabbing pain, Derek pulled her ethereal form into a tight embrace.

"I'm sorry Izzy," his voice broke as tears streamed from his eyes. "I'm so sorry. I wish I had done something to save you."

"I don't blame you, Derek. You didn't know about any of this . . . *I* didn't know about any of this." Izzy squeezed him as tight as she could. "You always gave the best hugs, and . . . why do you smell like lavender?"

"Mia." Derek gasped, looking towards the field as his mind played back the sight of her being engulfed in red essence.

Izzy cupped his face, gently turning his head back to her. Her eyes were full of too many emotions for Derek to identify——love, grief, regret, pride. Her voice shook as she gave him her last message.

"I can save her, but once I do, I have to leave . . . forever." She steeled her voice. "Someone wants you to win this fight. That's why I'm here. But it also means that my time here is limited. I wish I was allowed to tell you more. Just please, trust me." She began to move her hand opposite the way she had earlier. "Strike 'em out, Diamond."

Time zipped back to normal, and Isabella faded away.

"Stay down, Derek," Trey demanded, his eyes begging Derek not to make him do this. "My father already warned you that your magic is destroying you."

Derek pulled the dagger out of his side with a cry and angrily threw it on the ground. Blood seeped faster from the wound, but he stood firm and channeled his magic once more.

"You were my friend!" Derek exclaimed. "This magic might kill me, but I'd rather my magic kill me than yours."

Trey flinched at the venom in his words. "I am trying to *still* be your friend! I am telling you, there is no winning this."

The vindictive rumble of Malum's amusement rose from behind him, twisting Derek's insides.

"You traveled all this way just to fail. My vision will not be stopped!" Malum jeered.

Derek yelled, "To hell with your vision! Even if I die here, there will be others to come that will stop you." He winced, his hand still pressed firmly over his wound.

Malum only laughed harder.

"So, they still preach the same falsehoods," Malum said mockingly. "Poor fool. You have no idea about the curse within you or what you're truly trying to prevent. Trey," Malum barked, "put an end to this."

Derek's expression turned to one of confusion, but he had no time to dwell on it as Trey launched a barrage of attacks. With a shout, Trey sent out tendrils of red essence towards Derek. Trey's earlier warning rang in his ears. They used to be friends. Part of Derek still believed they were, but now they were caught up in something much bigger——this was war.

A deafening clash of red and white sparks erupted between them. Derek's movements mirrored Trey's, countering each tendril that came his way with a beam of light or bolt of lightning. Every strike Derek gave or received, the pain from his side radiated through his body. A particularly hard blow made him gasp in agony.

Sympathy and regret flared in Trey's eyes. Derek knew that Trey didn't want to hurt him, but Malum was forcing him. Derek was done letting him. He tried to cast a lightning bolt around Trey, directing Trey with his head nods to get out of the way.

Trey actually listened. Moving to the side as the bolt zipped past him. The lighting seemed like it was going to hit its true target, but it only angered the ancient Fae more.

Raising his hand to deflect the bolt, Malum bellowed, "Foolish boy!"

Derek ground his teeth, clenching at his side as he rushed towards Trey. He saw something in Malum's eyes. Something he never wanted to see again. Just a few steps away, he saw a change in his friend's eyes——that all too familiar loss of light. Trey was gone. Derek looked down at Trey's chest and saw a tendril of crimson essence protruding through it.

As Trey's lifeless body fell towards him, Derek let go of his side, reaching out to catch him. The searing pain almost brought him to his knees. Before he was able to grab him, the tendril pulled Trey back towards Malum.

Derek was almost numb. The pain of his wound faded to the background as his mind tried to reject what it was seeing. Derek's eyes widened, but his vision was foggy, his body beginning to fail him. He could only look on in terror as Malum's crimson tendrils engulfed Trey. Their bodies merged into one sickening, twisted form.

Derek raised one arm as he fell to his knee, sending beams of light towards the abomination that had formed. His stomach sank as they bounced off Malum harmlessly. A deep and menacing voice echoed through the air, no longer belonging to Malum alone.

"I told you to stay down, semideus!" Malum had become a towering figure composed of shadows and oozing dark smoke. He was barely recognizable as a fae anymore. Long horns protruded from his head and massive wings hung from his back.

One of his hands held a whip of red lightning. In his other hand, flames blazed across his claws. A sinister smile stretched across his face that revealed his razor-sharp teeth.

"Let me show you real power," Malum hissed.

Black spots danced across Derek's vision as he forced himself back to his feet. He met Malum's eyes in a challenge. "You call that power?"

Derek opened his right hand as wide as possible, his arm blinding. The light from his arm coiled into his palm. Without breaking eye contact, he placed his hand over his wound, holding in a scream as the burning light cauterized his injury. Derek willed his voice to be steady. "Is that all you got?"

Derek thrust his arms forward, unleashing a beam of light towards Malum.

Malum summoned a red haze to swirl around him like a sinister cloak. With a swift motion of his right hand, the flames on his claws intercepted Derek's attack. The clash of elements caused a violent explosion, engulfing the top of the tower in smoke and debris.

Coughing up smoke, something deep inside of Derek stirred. Something tangible, something real. He tapped into a power he never knew existed and conjured blue flames in his hands that he formed into fiery orbs. He hurled them at Malum, who twisted away through the air with unnatural speed.

Malum struck back with a whip of dark red lightning. The tendrils of darkness lashed out at Derek. He leapt out of the way, the lightning nearly striking him. Derek retaliated with another barrage of blue fire. The flames surged forward with a blistering heat, pushing Malum back temporarily.

Derek's breathing was ragged, each inhale sharp and painful. The hastily cauterized stab wound throbbed with every movement. The deep, twisting pain was a stark reminder that his patch job did nothing to fix the internal damage. His strength was failing fast. Malum sensed this and smirked, circling Derek with a predator's gaze.

"You think those pathetic flames can save you?" Malum taunted, his voice dripping with malice.

Derek's jaw tightened. "We'll find out."

With a roar, Derek launched himself at Malum, his blue flames spiraling around his fists. He swung at Malum, who barely dodged the blow, the flames singeing the edges of his dark wings. Malum swiftly recovered, his clawed hand crackling with crimson essence as he landed a solid strike to Derek's injured side. Derek gasped, vision going white with pain. It took everything in him to avoid Malum's next attack, stumbling out of the way as he fought not to vomit.

Gripping his side, Derek countered with a swift, white light imbued kick, catching Malum off guard and sending him sprawling. He didn't wait for Malum to recover. Derek summoned a torrent of white flames that engulfed the ground around Malum, causing him to scream in fury. The red essence emanating from Malum's wings and horns intensified as he broke free from the inferno.

The two clashed again, a blur of white and red, light and shadow. Derek landed a hit, then Malum, each strike more vicious than the last. Derek swayed on his feet momentarily from the pain in his side, giving Malum an opening. He wrapped a tendril of dark energy around Derek's neck and lifted him off the ground.

"Is that all you've got?" Malum sneered, tightening his grip.

Derek clawed at the tendrils. He couldn't get any purchase——couldn't get any air. Derek's vision dimmed, but he focused on the white hot magic within him, summoning every last ounce of strength. He unleashed a powerful blast of fire and lightning, breaking Malum's hold and sending him flying backward.

Derek gulped in oxygen. His side ached, and warm blood seeped through where the fighting had reopened his wound. He was exhausted, but the fight was far from over.

The battle raged on, with neither side gaining a clear advantage for long. Derek's pure white magic, lightning, and blue flames seared through Malum's defenses, causing him to cry out in pain.

His blue flames wrapped around Malum's grotesque form, illuminating his twisted features. The brilliance of the white light forced Malum to shield his eyes, but he quickly countered with a ferocious sweep of his dark wings, sending a wave of red fire toward Derek.

The fire engulfed Derek, blowing over him and dissipating behind him. Heat singed his skin, the searing pain cutting through his body. He gritted his teeth and pushed through the agony. His own blood dripped onto the scorched earth, each drop sizzling upon contact. He retaliated with a burst of lightning that snapped through the air. Malum was momentarily stunned by the force, giving Derek a brief respite to recuperate his strength.

Malum threw himself back into the fight. Their powers clashed and spun in a deadly display of destruction. Blue and red fire intertwined, creating a vortex of magical energy that scorched the tower beneath them. Derek felt the weight of exhaustion creeping in, his muscles screaming for rest.

As Derek's strength waned, Malum gained the upper hand, his dark lightning getting increasingly close. Derek's muscles shook. He couldn't take much more.

A burst of bright pink light appeared at the top of the tower and surrounded Derek. He felt the flesh of his side knit back together, the burn blisters returning to unmarred skin. The energy filled him with power, making him stronger than ever before. He channeled this energy into one last powerful attack. The combination of his own lightning, white light, and the pink aura struck Malum with an incredible force. It sent him hurtling against the wall of the tower, leaving him disoriented and battered. But Derek stood strong, bolstered by his even more potent powers and unbreakable determination.

Malum's body slowly reverted back to its original form as he lay exhausted and beaten on the ground. The moment Malum was back to his former form, Trey's lifeless body reappeared next to him. Malum glanced up at Derek, pure hate in his eyes.

"Don't think I am so easily defeated."

With a spit of blood and a flick of his fingers, he summoned Sarika, Mia in tow. Derek looked in horror at the knife she held against Mia's throat. Rising to his feet, Malum cast a glare at Trey's body, muttering,

"I knew the trouble of seducing his mother wasn't worth it. The most useless of his siblings."

Taking a deep breath, the ancient fae's essence seeped from his eyes once again. He tilted his head in Sarika's direction and commanded, "Let her watch him die. Then kill her, as well."

Derek saw red, his jaw clenched so tightly that the muscles in his neck strained. Izzy's voice in his mind was the only thing that kept him from recklessly launching himself at Sarika.

"*When you see my signal, unleash all your strength.*"

Derek held himself still, muscles tensed, and watched as Malum began mumbling in an unfamiliar tongue. The wicked Fae's eyes glowed pure red, the sky turning a matching crimson. Both armies had exhausted themselves and were now just trying to hold their ground as they stared up at the scene unfolding above them.

Derek's perception of time again seemed to slow down. His eyes tracked Malum as he conjured a tendril of crimson mist, enveloping it in flames and red lightning. The attack was aimed straight at Derek. He knew he could dive out of the way. He knew he had the time to make it . . . but Sarika might kill Mia if he did. So he braced for the inevitable impact, eyes locking onto Mia's. He smiled.

If this was how he died, at least he was staring into her beautiful green eyes when he did.

Those eyes vanished, disappearing in a burst of pink light. Sarika was left with an empty knife, pointing at nothing but air. That *had* to be the signal.

He dodged the lethal tendril with a well-timed side step, narrowly avoiding its grasp. As Malum's blast blew right past him, Derek's eyes caught sight of Tah'quhal leaping from a ledge behind Sarika.

His sword struck true once more. The blade pierced through her back, emerging from her chest. Surprise washed across Sarika's face, mingled with fear and pain. Tah'quhal yanked the sword out of her chest as she slid to the ground. With Sarika defeated, Derek glanced back at Malum.

Derek summoned all his strength. As he did, his hair blew back as if caught in a gust of wind, and his eyes shone with blinding light. The energy Izzy gifted him raced through his veins. It felt like it could consume him. He *wanted* it to consume him. His arms crackled with lightning and radiant energy as he directed all of his magic into one concentrated blast towards Malum.

The impact was catastrophic. A sphere of pure white energy enveloped Malum, causing everyone around to shield their eyes from its blinding intensity.

Tah'quhal moved his hands away from his face, rapidly blinking to regain his vision. The only evidence of Malum's presence was the imprint of his shadow on the ground. It was over.

Derek collapsed to the ground, his knees slamming into the stone. The adrenaline left his body in a wave, his upright position wavering. He was exhausted. The pain he had endured and the immense amount of magic he had unleashed were too much. His eyes flickered, but he fought to stay conscious. He could no longer feel Izzy's presence, and his wounds slowly began to reappear.

Tah'quhal sprinted to his side as Mia appeared next to him, disoriented and looking around wildly. Mia shouted,

"Derek!"

She wrapped her arms around him, only to realize he was not hugging her back. She looked him over and realized how injured he really was. Her hands moved in swift circles over the wounds and she chanted a healing spell. Gradually, each wound began to close, but the stab wound proved to be more difficult. Between the quick and untrained cauterization and how Malum's Odium magic had tainted it, it required a more complex form of healing. She did her best to stabilize him, hoping one of their other allies could help.

Mia gripped Derek's hand while she gathered her thoughts. Grateful, she asked,

"What pulled me away from Sarika?"

Derek managed a watery smile through a fit of coughing. "Izzy. It was all thanks to Izzy."

Mia's eyebrow raised for a second, her eyes beginning to water. She leaned back into Derek's hug, this time feeling him place one arm around her.

Hearing the mention of Sarika's name, Tah'quhal's eyes frantically searched for her body, but it was nowhere in sight. His heart sank as he cried out,

"No! Where did she go?"

He looked around in a panic and then realized, "Trey, he's gone, too!"

Derek managed to stand up, still weak, even with Mia's healing efforts. Despite being worried about what them being missing could mean, he calmly stated,

"We can worry about that later."

Derek took a heavy step towards the edge of the tower, ready to face the chaos and carnage below. He paused and reached his hand out to Mia, needing to feel that she was safe.

Mia smiled at him, reaching her hand out to his, only to be met with air. In the span of a blink, he was gone, ripped from reality.

"No!" she screamed. Her panicked calls echoed through the air as she searched frantically for Derek, but he was nowhere to be found. Making her decision, she clutched at her bracelet, ready to find him, no matter where he'd gone. She called out Derek's name and yanked the bracelet from her wrist. And then, just like him, she too vanished.

Tah'quhal was left standing on the roof, alone.

Tah'quhal was frozen in shock.

"Derek? Mia?" he managed to sputter out.

He felt helpless. Here he stood, at the summit of the tower, adorned in his family's heirloom armor, and wielding enchanted swords, with full mastery over the magic surrounding him. Yet, he couldn't even comprehend what had just occurred, let alone stop them from vanishing. Tah'quhal scanned the surrounding area, searching for anything to tell him where they went.

Looking down at the battlefield, he saw that the Keepers were starting to panic near the portal. He couldn't do anything about Derek and Mia right now, but he could do something about this. He leapt from the tower, slammed one of his swords into its side, riding it to the ground.

The battle was over, and Luminfae's army had retreated back towards the portal. Only the Keepers and Chieftains remained on the field, engaged in a heated debate. In the center of it all stood a figure with a hood covering their face.

As Tah'quhal approached, he could make out snippets of the chaos.

Karrent was shouting at Johnathan for attempting such a risky spell that left them vulnerable.

Abhaya was still working her magic, trying to save David.

Tah'quhal tried to interject and explain what happened on top of the tower, but everyone was talking over each other in a frenzy.

As Caldera pleaded with Barry to flee, Stella draped a cloth over Codi. Talissa approached Barry seductively, caressing his face and whispering,

"You will be mine soon enough."

Caldera reached for her spear, eyes blazing, but Barry gave her a steady look to indicate that he would be alright. Deep down, he was panicking, but he had to maintain a calm facade for the others.

Tah'quhal again attempted to cut in, but his words were interrupted by the appearance of an older man through the portal. The man called out,

"Johnathan! John! Where are you?"

Johnathan turned to see his father running towards him. He froze, scared he was imagining it.

"Dad?" He asked in a choked voice, wet eyes taking him in. "Dad! I'm right here!"

Mr. Monton rushed to embrace his son, relieved to have found him unharmed.

"My boy," he said, voice laden with emotion, "I've been so worried. The rumors of 'Derek's Army' had reached Earth, but it took me and the others quite some time to escape. Where is Derek? I need to speak with him."

Panic shot through Johnathan at his father's words.

"Escape? Escape from what, exactly?"

Tah'quhal, having had enough of not being heard, shouted, "ENOUGH!"

All those around turning their attention to the warrior fae.

"After he defeated Malum, Derek vanished . . . followed by Mia."

Barry froze. "What do you mean, vanished?"

"They . . . they just disappeared. Just a flash and they were gone. No traces, no clues. Just gone. Before he vanished, he was able to end Malum and thwart his plans." Tah'quhal said with a hint of pride for Derek in his voice.

"Thwarted? He may have defeated Malum, but whatever he was planning has already begun." Mr. Monton's words hung heavy in the air.

A loud crack of lightning struck the ground just behind the group, causing them all to jump. The air was filled with dust and debris. As it settled, they could see Derek and Mia standing hand in hand.

Mia appeared unchanged, but Derek was now sporting intricate blue lightning bolt markings on his left arm. They resembled a more detailed adaptation of the stigmata often seen on fae. He even seemed taller, his muscles more defined.

The group rushed towards them, their expressions filled with concern. As they neared Derek and Mia, they could see the worry etched on their faces.

Barry had never seen Derek look so pale, the blood completely drained from his face. "What's wrong?"

Derek stared wide eyed at his friends, hands shaking uncontrollably. Mia squeezed his hand tighter, her own face tight with anxiety. He opened his mouth, closed it, then whispered,

"Everything."

Acknowledgements

Thank you for reading my book! I truly hope you had as much fun exploring Luminfae as I did writing this adventure. If so, please leave a wonderful review. Reviews are the lifeblood of indie authors like me. The more positive reviews we have, the more likely it is that others will pick up the book as well.

A lot went into this book, and I've had some great encouragement and love from folks along the way. But I would be remiss if I didn't thank a few very specific people for helping me on this journey.

First and foremost, I would like to thank God. He has given me strength and encouragement throughout all the challenging moments of completing this novel. I am truly grateful for his endless love, mercy, and grace.

I want to thank all my family and friends that encouraged me every step of the way. Even when this was just a "I bet I could write a book" you kept me motivated. I would love to name all of you, but I would need a whole chapter to do so.

Travis and Morgan, you two were the first people I told about my idea, and you never stopped supporting me.

Anita, you answered every question I had and the ones I didn't know to ask. You were a supporting voice from the very beginning, and I cannot thank you enough.

Sarah at StoryGarden Editorial, your suggestions were crucial to this becoming a reality. I believe this book is absolutely better because of your guidance and magic touch.

HulaLotus Design, a friend from TikTok that just happened to post about taking commissions again at the same time I started looking for a cover designer. It was just meant to be, and I cannot over state how happy I am with the artwork.

My parents, I know this book isn't necessarily your cup of tea but thank you for supporting me in this endeavor.

And finally, my amazing wife Kendell and my son Zeke. You encouraged me and inspired me to chase this crazy dream. You have sacrificed time on countless days to allow me to blaze trails in this crazy fantasy world. I love you both to the moon and back.

About the author

T.M. Ford is a husband, father, and author. His debut novel *Still I Stand* is the result of his love for the fantastical and a good story. His background is in telecommunications, having been in the industry for over 10 years, he has quite the love for technology. When he isn't spending time with his family, he is either rooting on the Tennessee Titans or playing a good RPG. He and his wife reside in Tennessee with their son where they enjoy playing disc golf and spending time with family.

Good reviews are vital for Indie Authors. The importance of reviews in helping others find and take a chance on an indie author's book is impossible to overstate.

If you enjoyed this book, would you help me get it in front of more people by taking a minute to give it a good review?

I can't tell you how thankful I'd be.

Check out this link. It will take you to T.M. Ford's website, where you can find the best places to review this book and help me get it to more readers who love good books just like you and me! You can also find all of T.M. Ford's social media and newsletter at the same link, just in case you want to stay in the know for what is next.